Praise for

THE DEAD-TOSSED WAVES

"*The Dead-Tossed Waves* was even more engrossing than *The Forest of Hands and Teeth*. Beautiful, romantic, horrifying, and heartbreaking."

—JENNIFER LYNN BARNES,
author of *Raised by Wolves* and *Tattoo*

"Fast-paced . . . it will be gobbled up by fans of the first volume."

—*Kirkus Reviews*

"The second book in Ryan's zombie series moves the story ahead in some surprising ways as it introduces compelling characters. Readers will be up late with this one, turning pages and biting their nails."

—*Romantic Times*

"Readers are sure to be hooked."

—*Publishers Weekly*

ALSO BY CARRIE RYAN

The Forest of Hands and Teeth

THE DEAD-TOSSED WAVES

▼ ▼ ▼

CARRIE RYAN

▲ DELACORTE PRESS ▲

This is a work of fiction. Names, characters, places, and incidents either are the product of the author's imagination or are used fictitiously. Any resemblance to actual persons, living or dead, events, or locales is entirely coincidental.

 Published in the United States by Delacorte Press, an imprint of Random House Children's Books, a division of Random House, Inc., New York. Originally published in hardcover in the United States by Delacorte Press, New York, in 2010.

Delacorte Press is a registered trademark and the colophon is a trademark of Random House, Inc.

Visit us on the Web! www.randomhouse.com/teens
Educators and librarians, for a variety of teaching tools, visit us at www.randomhouse.com/teachers

The Library of Congress has cataloged the hardcover edition of this work as follows:
Ryan, Carrie. The dead-tossed waves / Carrie Ryan.
p. cm.—1st ed.
Summary: Gabry lives a quiet life in a town trapped between a forest and the ocean, hemmed in by the dead w ho hunger for the living, but her mother Mary's secrets, a cult of religious zealots who worship the dead, and a stranger from the forest who seems to know Gabry threaten to destroy her world.
ISBN 978-0-385-73684-8 (hc) — ISBN 978-0-385-90632-6 (glb)
ISBN 978-0-375-89542-5 (ebook) [1. Horror stories. 2. Fantasy.] I. Title.
PZ7.R9478De 2010 [Fic]—dc22 2009030113

ISBN 978-0-385-73685-5 (trade)

Printed in the United States of America
10 9 8 7 6 5 4 3 2 1
First Trade Paperback Edition

Random House Children's Books supports the First Amendment and celebrates the right to read.

to Roberta Hatch
the light on the horizon that means home

to Douglas Keith Kidd
for loving her, and all of us, so much

and to love at first sight (and Chiquita bananas)

THE DEAD-TOSSED WAVES

▾ I ▾

The story goes that even after the Return they tried to keep the roller coasters going. They said it reminded them of the before time. When they didn't have to worry about people rising from the dead, when they didn't have to build fences and walls and barriers to protect themselves from the masses of Mudo constantly seeking human flesh. When the living weren't forever hunted.

They said it made them feel normal.

And so even while the Mudo—neighbors and friends who'd been infected, died and Returned—pulled at the fences surrounding the amusement park, they kept the rides moving.

Even after the Forest was shut off, one last gasp at sequestering the infection and containing the Mudo, the carousel kept turning, the coasters kept rumbling, the teacups kept spinning. Though my town of Vista was far away from the core of the Protectorate, they hoped people would come fly along the coasters. Would still want to forget.

But then travel became too difficult. People were concerned with trying to survive and little could make them forget the reality of the world they lived in. The coasters slowly crumbled outside the old city perched at the tip of a long treacherous road along the coast. Everyone simply forgot about them, one other aspect of pre-Return life that gradually dimmed in the memories and stories passed down from year to year.

I never really thought about them until tonight—when my best friend's older brother invites us to sneak past the Barriers and into the ruins of the amusement park with him and his friends.

"Come on, Gabry," Cira whines, dancing around me. I can almost feel the energy and excitement buzzing off her skin. We stand next to the Barrier that separates Vista from the ruins of the old city, the thick wooden wall keeping the dangers of the world out and us safely in. Already a few of the older kids have skimmed over the top, their feet a flash against the night sky. I rub my palms against my legs, my heart a thrum in my chest.

There are a thousand reasons why I don't want to go with them into the ruins, not the least of which is that it's forbidden. But there's one reason I do want to take the risk. I glance past Cira to her brother and his eyes catch mine. I can't stop the seep of heat crawling up my neck as I dart my gaze away, hoping he didn't notice me looking and at the same time desperately wishing he did.

"Gabry?" he asks, his head tilted to the side. From his lips my name curls around my ears. An invitation.

Afraid of the tangle of words twisting around my own tongue, I swallow and place my hand against the thick wood of the Barrier. I've never been past it before. It's against the

rules to leave the town without permission and it's also risky. While most of the ruins are bordered by old fences from after the Return, Mudo can still get through them.

They can still attack us.

"We shouldn't," I say, more to myself than to Cira or Catcher. Cira just rolls her eyes; she's already jumping with desire to join the others. She grabs my arm with a barely repressed squeal.

"This is our chance," she whispers to me. I don't tell her what I've been thinking—that it's our chance to get in trouble at best and I don't want to think about what could happen at worst.

But she knows me well enough to read my thoughts. "No one's been infected in years," she says, trying to convince me. "Catcher and them go out there all the time. It's totally safe."

Safe—a relative term. A word my mother always uses with a hard edge to her voice. "I don't know . . . ," I say, twisting my fingers together, wishing I could just say no and be done with it but hating to disappoint my best friend the way I've done too often before.

One day several years ago during the drought, Cira dared me to cross the wide river that separates our town from the Forest. We were gathering water at the spot in the river where there's a break in the fence when the Militiaman on duty suddenly got sick and left us alone. Cira teased me because I wouldn't try it. Because I was too afraid that the Militiaman would come back and see us and I refused to break the rule forbidding us from the Forest.

Finally she went on her own, standing in the middle of the rushing water, her skirt billowing around her knees and her hair blowing into her mouth as she laughed.

I could never explain to her how I felt about the

boundaries of our town. To me they were inviolate. They were what held me together, what kept me safe and protected and whole. To stray outside, even once, was too scary for me.

I couldn't explain how I was afraid of losing myself. I still can't explain it to her now. But somehow she knows.

"Here," she says, reaching to pull something from around her neck. "Take this." It's the necklace she always wears—just a simple black cord looped through the arm of a small plastic figurine of a superhero she once bought from a trader after he told her old stories about men who used to fly and save the world. She drops it over my head.

"He'll keep you safe," she adds as I feel the tiny weight of it settle against my chest under my shirt.

I'm about to protest when Catcher steps close to me and I swallow. Cira grins and fades into the darkness, knowing that her brother is my weakness. "You should come," he says. He places his hand against the Barrier, his fingers almost close enough to brush my own but not quite. He drops his voice just enough to be a rumble in the darkness, more vibration than words. "I want you to come with us."

I'm afraid to say anything, to break this moment. And so I nod. He smiles like a secret between us and I drop my head, embarrassed at every feeling crashing through me.

Cira, of course, has been watching our interaction and lets out a little shout and grabs my shoulders with excitement that I've finally caved in. Catcher's grin spreads a little wider and I wish I had the nerve to meet his eyes but I can't.

The moon's a bright cut in the sky as the rest of the group climbs, pulling themselves easily over the thick wall separating our town from the crumbling ruins of the old city beyond. Even Cira hesitates for a second, throwing a quick

glance back at me before finding crevices in which to slip her thin hands.

And then it's only Catcher and me left facing the towering wall.

I tug on the end of my braid, clenching my palm around the handle of my long-bladed knife strapped to my hip. I know I shouldn't be doing this. It's dangerous and stupid, and already sweat slicks along the sides of my neck. I glance at Catcher and have to tilt my head into the darkness to hide my dizzying smile.

I want to tell him that I've never crossed the Barrier before. I've never wanted to—I still don't. I've only stood at the top of the lighthouse where I live, and even then I feel overwhelmed staring out at the ocean and the Forest and the breadth of the world around us. Like it's too much to take in.

I think about my mother and her stories of growing up in the Forest and finding her way here to the ocean. And I realize in that moment, as I face the edge of everything I've known, that I don't have the same strength as my mother. I can't bring myself to leave Vista, even just for a few hours in the darkness beyond.

I force myself forward and trace my fingers along the Barrier. The wood is warm, still retaining the heat of the summer afternoon.

"I'm sorry," I whisper to him, turning away from the wall. "I can't do it." Before this moment I've never realized my own limitations. Before, I thought I'd be able to do anything, be anything.

Catcher slips his hand into mine, holding me in place.

His skin is warmer than the Barrier. "I'll help you," he says, his smile like the lighthouse beam, something to hang on to in an uncertain night. "Trust me." And he guides my fingers to the gaps in the wall, showing me how to climb.

I hesitate at the top, my legs straddling the thick wooden logs, and Catcher scrambles up to face me, his toes nudging my own. I look everywhere but at him. The night feels heavy, as if it can pin me here.

We've been alone together many times before, but something's shifted tonight. I'm suddenly so much more aware of how broad his shoulders are, how strong his hands. Of the way he looks at me and the sound of his breathing.

And I can't tell if something really is changing between us or if my own hesitation is causing my senses to spin. I dig my nails into the wood, the splinters pricking my skin. But the pain doesn't dull my fear, only scratches at the edges.

I open my mouth to tell him something. Anything. To explain why I can't go farther. To tell him again that I'm sorry. But he speaks first.

"I'm afraid of heights," he says. His confession is so unexpected that I catch a giggle in the back of my throat before I realize that I shouldn't be laughing. I cover my mouth with a hand, trying to smother my smile.

"This isn't that high," I tell him, trying to seem bold but not knowing whether I succeed at making him feel at ease.

He rolls his eyes, the corners of his lips tugged up a little. "I mean real heights," he says.

I notice again the roughness across his chin, the stubble of a beard. He's not the same boy who used to seek me out and chase me in games of tag or even the one with too-thin arms and a sharp Adam's apple.

"I remember one time Cira and I came to visit you at the lighthouse," he says. "Cira was just happy to be away from the chores at the orphan house, but I wanted to do something with our morning off. I wanted to climb. I wanted to see the view from the top."

He looks past me, his eyes unfocused. "Halfway up, I couldn't go any farther."

I swallow and put my hand back down to steady myself, suddenly too aware of the heat of him, of the wall, of the night consuming me.

"I don't remember," I tell him, because it's true. So much of my childhood is a blur, memories that tangle in my head and twist with stories so that I don't know what is mine and what I've been told is mine.

"You wouldn't," he says. "Nothing really happened. We came to explore the lighthouse and you and Cira played and I spent half the day sitting on the steps trying to convince my hands to let go of the railing and climb higher."

I close my eyes, trying to picture it, but I can't.

"Every now and then you two would run by. Cira would point at me and laugh—she was a brat even then. But you would just stand there and stare. Eventually, Cira got lost in some project and you came and sat next to me for a while."

"And then what?" I ask. I don't remember him ever wanting to see the view from the lighthouse. Ever wanting to climb the stairs to the gallery in all the years I've known him.

"And then nothing. We just sat there. You didn't say anything and neither did I. And then our morning was over and Cira started crying and I took her back for the afternoon chores."

"You never made it any higher?"

"Nope."

"You never tried again?"

He shakes his head.

I sit there, staring at the distance between our hands resting on the thick wall, at the way his fingers flex against the wood. I try to figure out what he's telling me. That it's okay to wallow in my fears? It's okay if we just sit here? And that he'll stay with me, even if I can't go any farther?

Suddenly I wish I were Cira. I wish I knew how to flirt, how to read guys, how to know what they're saying and what they want. I wish I could act with the sort of abandon that seems to infuse every movement she makes. Until this summer I'd never realized that it was a skill to have. That it was anything I'd ever need.

I was happy enough to let her be the one to toss her hair and tilt her head while I skipped rocks over the waves and kept watch on the horizon, making sure nothing interrupted our cocoon of safety.

Before I can stop myself I swing my leg over the Barrier and drop to the other side. A soft thud, and Catcher lands beside me. We're in the shadow of the wall, almost pitch-darkness. I feel his hand reaching for me, feel his fingers as they barely brush my skin.

In that moment I wonder if we can melt into each other in the blackness. There's nothing distinct about our bodies, nothing keeping us apart except the thick heat of summer rising from the ground below.

It feels boundless, the walls keeping my frame in place now gone, my world exploded, leaving me struggling to catch my breath, as if there's not enough air here beyond the town.

Suddenly my head feels too light. The world outside the Barrier too wrong. Too dangerous. My stomach feels hollow, the fear corroding me from the inside. I'm not supposed to be here, it's not safe. It's not allowed. I start to turn, feeling my body begin to shake apart as I reach for the wall. I have to go back.

And then Catcher's hand grasps mine and he pulls me close, reminding me of where I end and he begins. He pulls the knife from the scabbard on my hip and holds it out for me, the cut of the moon sliding over the sharp metal edge. I take it, my grip tight, hoping it will make me feel stronger.

"There's still the possibility of Mudo out here," he tells me, the word *Mudo* falling so easily from his lips but causing my own to quiver.

"The fences around the park always hold them," he adds. "But just in case . . ."

I try to swallow the fear, its taste hot and metallic like blood. He must feel me pulling away from him, ready to claw back over the Barrier to the safety of the town, because his grip remains firm as he tugs me closer.

"Don't worry," he says. "I've got you." His voice is like the night, deep and dark around me, and I try to relax against him. I try to trust him.

I've never been beyond the protection of the town and as we weave through the crumbled ruins at the edge of the amusement park, every shadow is the dead rising. Every scratch of concrete shifting is the moan of the Mudo craving our flesh. Every turn taking us farther away from our world and into the dead world.

I wonder how he can feel so comfortable out here. He was raised the same way I was, he learned the same lessons in class as I did: That the only safe places are those protected by walls and fences. That the dead will never stop once they scent human flesh. That an Infected who turns when there aren't Mudo around will become a Breaker.

And yet Catcher strolls through the ruins with confidence and ease. Every part of me envies him for this.

Something flickers past us, a hint of sound and wind. I jump. My heart seizes and I grasp at Catcher's shoulder. "Just a bat," he murmurs, and I can hear the smile in his voice.

There are rules for a reason, I want to tell him. *We're not supposed to be here.* But he pulls my arm tight in his and I can't help but fall into the feel of him.

▼ II ▼

One of the girls is talking about the Dark City as we catch up to them in the center of the amusement park. Her name is Mellie and she's two years older than I am—Catcher's age—and she twirls in the dark with her arms out by her sides, fingers brushing the still air. "At the first snow, I'm going," she says.

The brightness of the full moon reflects off the broken concrete of the ground. The light carves around the dips and curves of the old roller coaster, echoing Mellie's own graceful turns.

I crane my neck to look up at the coaster. I've only seen it from a distance, its humps rising from the decaying ruins like the back of some serpentine monster we once learned about in school.

I wonder what it would have been like to ride the coaster back then—perched at the edge of the fall and looking out at the world past the fences.

Which would be more terrifying, the sense of the ground falling from underneath you or the image of your best friend throwing herself at the fence, her mouth open, teeth flashing, fingers grabbing—the cacophony of moans?

I glance around me at the shadows thrown by the other rides, by the old buildings that have been stripped bare or crumbled in on themselves. In the darkness everything is frayed at the edges, making me scared of what could be hidden beyond my reach.

"Think of all the people in the Dark City," Mellie says, staring up at the stars. "So many possibilities, so many men." Her voice is like a song and one of the boys—a redhead named Griffin—steps toward her, wraps his hands around hers and joins her.

"We're not enough?" He smiles and laughs, pulling her around faster, and she tilts her head back farther so that the light of the moon trails along her neck.

I want to look away, feeling as if I'm watching some sort of intimate dance. But I can't. I've heard people talk about the Dark City my whole life. Even though it's over two weeks' journey by foot up the coast, it's the closest large city, one of the last fortified bastions from before the Return. It's where the Protectorate, the loose confederate government, sits. But it never occurred to me to want to go there. Never occurred to me I'd ever be able to pay the heavy rents to stay.

"Can you imagine living in those old buildings?" another girl says, walking toward where Mellie and Griffin are dancing. "I hear some of them are forty stories or more." She tilts her chin to her chest so that she's looking at Griffin through heavy-lidded eyes and he leaves Mellie to take this new girl in his arms, his grin wide. Their laughter's almost too loud in the darkness.

I'm so aware of Catcher standing next to me and I'm sure I must look as awkward as I feel. Mellie seems so graceful and free and beautiful and I wonder if Catcher wants to dance like the others are. If he wishes I were more like the other girls. I can't even imagine what it would feel like to spread my arms wide and twirl in the night, not worrying about the dark corners or the possibility of Mudo and death. I glance at where Cira leans her head close to one of Catcher's friends, as if they're oblivious to everything around us.

I cross my arms over my chest and grip my elbows. My skin is thick with goose bumps.

I can't stop thinking about what it must have been like here when the Return hit. The panic. The confusion. The bodies packed so close in one space. The inability to escape. The moans.

Always the moans.

The group migrates closer to the coaster, their voices buzzing with rumors of the Dark City and plans for leaving Vista. I wait for Catcher to go with them, for me to be left to follow behind. But he lets them go until it's just the two of us standing in their echoes.

He brushes his hand over my arm and I swallow down a million words. The air mingles with the scent from his body; it fills my head and replaces my fear of being beyond the Barrier. There's something about Mellie's abandon that makes me want to be free as well.

I want to be like her. I want to forget my constant worry and dance around the old amusement park rides, twirling with the faded animals on the carousel or spinning around in the chipped teacups.

But I don't. I just stand there and feel Catcher's fingertips against my skin. It's as if we're the first ones to find this old world. To slip past everything that used to hold us tight. The air outside the Barrier seems different, seems to hum with possibility. And every time I draw a breath of it I feel as though I'm leaving behind who I used to be and becoming something else.

I begin to think that maybe I've been wrong to fear the world outside the Barrier. That maybe I can be like the others my age and dream about making the trek to the Dark City. That maybe there's more to the world than hiding away in such a dead-end town as Vista.

Catcher opens his mouth to say something and I'm leaning toward him when we hear a shout.

"What about you, Catcher? You in for a race up the coaster?" Blane, one of Mellie's tagalong friends, says as she walks slowly toward us, one eyebrow raised high. Catcher's eyes flare a little in response and I try to study her grace. To memorize it. I feel the awkward hunch of my own shoulders and deflate a little. How could he like me when there are girls like her around?

"I'll leave the stunts to the twins," he says, nodding at the two brothers goofing around on the old wooden trellis, trying to show each other up.

"Aw, come on, Catch," she says, not letting up. He tenses next to me and I remember his confession—his fear of heights.

"It's me," I say. My voice is a squeak, the exact opposite of Blane's low purr. I try to clear my throat, try to stop my hands from sweating as every eye turns toward me. I'm not used to being the center of attention. I feel too keenly that I'm younger and not one of them, not part of their group.

"I . . . ah . . . I don't like . . . um . . . don't like heights," I say, utterly failing to hide my embarrassment.

Blane rests a hand on her hip, cocking it to the side, and is about to say more when Catcher slides his arm around me and I feel my body freeze. Afraid that if I move he'll somehow slip away.

"Gabry and I'll sit this one out," he says.

Blane narrows her eyes at me and then turns to the others. "Please tell me *someone* is willing to show us what they're made of," she says loudly, striding toward the base of the coaster, where the twins are already halfway to the top of the highest rise.

I wait for Catcher to let me go, as if he were only holding me as protection against Blane. But instead the pads of his fingers press against the skin of my shoulder, pulling me closer. I've never been so aware of my own body, so in awe that it could contain the quivering of excitement inside me.

I hear their shouts as they egg on the racing boys, shadows beneath the moonlight. Catcher tugs me away from them toward the carousel with the faded animals, the chipped red and green and purple and blue paint along its peaked roof.

I slide a leg over the unicorn, the tip of its horn long gone, and Catcher stands next to me. One hand on my thigh, the other on the pole by my head. His stomach slightly touches my hip and I squeeze my knees against the side of the ride.

I can feel the possibility between us. My sweaty fingers clench the pommel of the saddle, afraid I'll slip away, that somehow I'll take off and fly.

My mother once told me about her first kiss. I was feverish in bed—delirious, she told me later—but I remember her voice and how she told me about the boy she'd known growing up. He'd been from her village in the Forest and he'd been injured and feverish like me. She'd stayed by his bed, refusing to give up on him, and later when he was better she'd stood on a hill with him and dreamed of the ocean and kissed him then and there, with all the hopes of her future rolled out before her.

I think about that now, while Catcher's breath hovers around me. I can feel him, can feel the air pulse between us. His gaze flicks to my mouth and before I can stop myself I lick my lips, scared that maybe he isn't interested in me and nervous that maybe he is. More than anything I'm skittish about the silence. A pressure to say something gnaws inside me.

"I'm glad you decided to come with us," Catcher tells me.

I shift, relieved. The heat of the summer night causes my shirt to stick to my back. I don't know how to tell him that I've never wanted to test the Barrier before. That I'm not like Mellie and the others who want to go explore the world and I'm happy with the safety of home.

Instead I mumble, "I am too." And then there's silence between us again. I tap my foot against the unicorn's leg, wondering how to fill the awkward gap. A crazy thought circles my mind that I should admit how much I like him but I shake it away.

He reaches out and takes the tip of my braid in his hands, running his fingers along the fan of my hair, and I can't hold back my smile.

"It feels like things have changed," he says, and I don't know if he means in a good way or a bad way.

"How so?" I ask, my voice bordering on a squeak.

He focuses on his fingers in my hair, running the ends of it against the palm of his hand. I stare, mesmerized.

He clears his throat. "You know how you can know someone—or—think you know them—but maybe you only know them in one way?" He sneaks a glance up at me and I notice that his cheeks are red in the moonlight. I nod, my eyes wide, too afraid to hope he's talking about me and the possibility of us.

He takes a deep breath, letting go of my braid. As it slides down along my shoulder I realize that my lungs are burning, waiting for him to continue.

"Maybe you know someone as your little sister's friend," he says. "And then maybe something shifts. Maybe one day you hear them say something unexpected. Or hear the way they laugh and then suddenly you see them all over again. Like this time it's different."

He places a hand on my shoulder, his thumb on my collarbone. I have a hard time catching my breath, wanting so desperately to hear him tell me how he feels about me. That he thinks about me as much as I do about him.

"This time, maybe you see them as . . ." He pauses. Above us stars whirl and collide and eke out their light only for us. "Beautiful," he finishes, and my body explodes, my heart filling every part of me.

Catcher leans in closer. "Wonderful and funny and . . ." He leans in even closer.

My body tingles at being so near to him. I realize how right he is. How we still see people as who they were before and maybe not as they are now. I run my tongue over my lips and dive in, my voice shaking only a little. "And maybe you start to see your best friend's brother differently too."

I wonder what I'm supposed to do—if I should lean in to him as well—how this is all supposed to work and if I'm doing something wrong.

He smiles that secret smile, except this time I think that

maybe I understand what it is. Possibility sparks and skitters between us. He glances down at my mouth, his breath puffs against my lips.

Once, when I was a child, the ground trembled beneath my feet. They said that it was the earth shifting, settling. But in doing so it threw up a massive wave. I remember standing in the lighthouse and seeing it coming. I remember the compression of air before it hit, the way everything stilled and pulled back for just a breath, and held.

That's how it feels when Catcher moves toward me. The compression of air between us, the still pause, and then his lips brushing against mine.

I feel their heat first. Feel the way his mouth pauses over mine before pressing in again. I place a hand over his on the bar and he twines his fingers in mine.

It's as if everything in my life has led me to this moment. That this is what I've been waiting for. All the years growing up with Catcher, the times he chased me around the twisted streets of the town playing tag, the times he'd laugh as Cira and I would compose complex plays and act them out for him, the times he would linger just a little longer when I was around.

As if this entire summer we've been spinning around each other, coming closer and closer to some inevitable spark that's just ignited. As if this is everything that was meant to be. I press against him and he presses back.

I'm so wrapped up in my first kiss, in the excitement of being with Catcher, that initially I don't hear the tumbling moan through the night ripping us apart.

III

The moan echoes around us, slicing into the hum of our bodies pressing together, and is followed by a silence so complete that I feel empty inside. My heart skids in my chest, every fear from earlier in the night fizzing along my skin.

Catcher pulls away from me and I almost fall into the space his body just occupied. He stumbles from the carousel with his arms out, searching the night with his fingers. I'm still trying to focus, still trying to find my bearings when I see the Mudo girl careening toward us in the pale moonlight. Her moans echoing all around me.

Catcher understands everything before I do. It takes me more time to figure out that the Mudo girl is a Breaker. I've never seen one before because Infected become Breakers only when there aren't enough other Mudo around when they turn, and anyone infected in Vista is killed before Returning.

Tearing around the corner of one of the rides, the Breaker sprints into the middle of the park—a girl no older than us, looking almost normal except for the moaning. Her mouth open, teeth bared, hands clawing the night.

I react too slowly, my mind tripping over the fact that she's running. She pauses slightly, just enough to turn her head left toward Catcher and me and then right toward the rest of the group huddled around the coaster, still loudly cheering on the two brothers, who are almost near the top. Cira's in the middle of them, her arms raised, clapping.

They're all oblivious but if either Catcher or I shouts to warn them, it might lure the Breaker toward us.

I clamp my hands over my mouth, terrified to move. Terrified to draw her attention. My fingers dig into my cheeks and screams threaten to pour out, choking me. Only one thought blares in my mind: This can't be happening.

The Breaker veers toward the others—toward Cira standing at the base of the coaster—and then Catcher moves in a blur. The moonlight reaches only so far, leaving the edges around us soft and faded. He's a shadow, moving to another shadow. The flashes of his pale skin echo the gleam of the Breaker's teeth.

I jump from the carousel and am grabbing for my knife when I hear a high-pitched scream. I don't want to look up but I do. I don't want to see but I can't help it. The Breaker crashes into the group at the base of the coaster. They scatter but she grabs a girl, a tall skinny girl, and when she spins into the moonlight I recognize Mellie.

My throat stings, my eyes cloud with tears and my stomach twists in terror but still I see it. The Breaker grasping at Mellie's hair and yanking her to the ground, sinking her teeth into the flesh of Mellie's forearm and tearing. A spray of blood.

But that's all that matters. The bite will infect Mellie. The bites always infect. And the Infected always turn. Mellie is dead already.

Everyone else scatters and screams. The chaos of human flesh causes the Breaker to drop Mellie, the urge to infect more important than lingering over a fresh kill. Mellie's mouth moves in a whimper and she holds her hand to the wound. Blood spills through her fingers. She shakes and sobs and rocks.

The Breaker lunges for her next target. And all I can do is stand and watch. I try to make sense of it. To reconcile the dry lessons we're taught in school about the Breakers with the reality of the girl in front of me. And for the first time I fully grasp the stories from the decades after the Return, when the Recruiters would recapture cities only to find a small pocket of Mudo that would reignite the infection all over again.

I understand how the Breakers could keep the living from reclaiming the world.

But none of us had ever seen one. None of us had ever truly understood them. It's one thing to be told something in the safety of the classroom and another to see it in the flesh. We're too used to the Mudo that wash up on the shores—slow and sluggish and waterlogged—or the ones that find their way to the Barrier and press against it.

We were taught growing up how to defend against those. But this girl, she's too fast. A blink and she's already pulling down another boy. He swings an ax and it lodges in her arm but it doesn't slow her. Her teeth find his throat before he can dislodge his weapon and he falls, a stream of blood black in the night.

I take a step back, wanting to run away. Knowing the safest thing to do is run. But then I see Catcher. He's sprinting not toward the Barrier, but toward the Breaker. She veers from her next target, racing to meet him. He holds a knife in his hand, a blade that seems too small and useless against her impending onslaught.

Something inside me pulls tight and loud like a scream as she draws closer to him. It happens too fast. He steps aside at the last minute and she streaks past. He grabs her hair and yanks her head back, his hand against her throat. With a guttural cry he sinks the blade into the base of her skull, his arms jerking with the effort.

It's as if everything stops in the moment his wide eyes meet mine, her sagging body between us. She was already dead. Had been dead. She was nothing but want and need and infection. But still I can see something in his face and I know it's echoed in my own: regret and resignation.

She was once a girl. She used to be like us. Her body slips to the ground and he bends over her, pulling out his knife, placing his hands over her eyes.

And that's why he doesn't see it. Like heat lightning on the horizon, a flicker at the edge of my vision that's nothing but movement. It's Mellie crawling to her feet, teeth bared and hands grasping. She's already bled out, died and Returned.

I hear another scream that rips down my spine. Catcher twists toward the panicked group at the base of the coaster, where the Infected boy, the one bitten in the throat, jumps to his feet, moans frothing from his mouth.

Catcher pushes toward the group but Mellie's faster. I do the only thing I know that will save him, that will buy him time. I shout and yell, pumping my weapon in the night air.

It works. Mellie turns from Catcher and sprints toward me. I don't even look to see Catcher's reaction; I don't have time to think or give in to the terror pushing against my chest. I plant my feet the way I was taught. I tighten my grip around the handle of my weapon until I remember to loosen my muscles, to relax and wait for her to get within range of my blade.

I see every detail in the moonlight as Mellie moves closer. Her eyes are still clear, her long brown hair whipping freely around her face. Her skin bronzed and smooth, glistening with blood.

All I can think about as she runs toward me is the graceful way she danced earlier. All I can think about is how much I wanted to be like her. How maybe we could have been friends. How I could have tried harder to know her. How this isn't what's supposed to happen.

She was supposed to be safe. We were all supposed to be safe and happy and have futures to dream about.

I want to close my eyes; I want to remember her the way she was. To erase the sight of how she wants nothing more than to tear the flesh from my bones. To devour me. I want to give in to the terror that eats at me, claws me to the ground.

Run! my mind screams. *Swing!* it shouts. *Do something! Anything!*

The darkness of the night crowds around me, closes me into itself, blocks out everything but the sound of Mellie's feet beating against the earth, chewing up the distance between us.

My head roars: *Swing! Swing! She's too close! Swing!*

I clench my teeth, trying to keep my arm steady. The moment stretches thin, every strand of Mellie's hair floating behind her head, her mouth slowly opening, teeth glimmering. I focus on her neck. I think about my blade slicing through it. I try to wait. Try to remember the training.

I can't breathe. I'm choking. She's too close. I can't wait. I tighten my arm and slice the knife through the air with the force of my terror and panic.

My body twists. The blade slips easily through nothingness and I realize I've swung too early just as she crashes into me. If I'd waited a moment more I could have stopped her. Her arms tangle in mine, her head crashing against my chin as I tumble backward, my skull smacking the cracked concrete.

I hear the thud before I feel it. I see the movement before I understand it. Mellie's mouth, the one that earlier tonight spoke of dreams and the Dark City, lowers to me.

And then she's gone. The pressure of her body on my chest explodes. I roll to the side and see it:

Catcher. He tumbles across the ground, Mellie's teeth gnashing, her arms wrapped around him. She tears at him like a cat fighting drowning. I watch as her nails drag along his arm, drawing thin lines of blood. If anything, this drives her into a deeper frenzy.

I try to push myself to my feet but I stumble. I reach for my blade but I can barely tighten my fist around it. I pull my arm back, ready to swing again, but I can't tell where one body begins and the other ends. It's flesh and blood and teeth, grunts and moans.

Then there's a crunch. The sound of an old man cracking all his fingers at once. And there's nothing left but Catcher kneeling and panting. His hands still grip Mellie's head, her neck broken and body finally motionless.

He looks up at me, his arms slipping from her hair and dangling by his sides. Blood pools down his forearm and drips from his fingers. But that's not what I'm staring at. I'm staring at the crescent-shaped wound along the edge of his shoulder.

I'm staring at where he was bitten.

▾ IV ▾

I swallow. A puddle of blood forms in the dirt where it falls from Catcher's fingers. Around me all the screams fade to nothing—as if they've never existed.

"You . . ."

"Go home, Gabry," he tells me.

Behind us I hear the bells start to ring in the town, the signal for the highest alert. They must have heard our screaming back at the guardhouse next to the gate or someone must have run and told them. Now they know there's trouble out here and it won't be long until the Militia arrives to investigate.

"But . . ." *But what about you?* I want to say. What about the bite? What about the infection? I want to ask what will happen but I already know. Even though the bite's not severe, he's infected. The infection will eventually kill him. Icy ribbons of shock twine through me.

Infection means death. It always means death.

"Go home," he says again. His voice is breathy, as if he hears my thoughts. I can tell from his face that he knows as much as I do. He knows what will happen to him.

"The Militia'll be here soon. Don't let them find you," he adds. "You'll get into too much trouble."

I take a step toward him. What's left of our group huddles at the base of the roller coaster across the expanse of concrete. One boy holds a shirt to another girl's leg, tears streaming down both their faces. The twins are slowly climbing down the lattice of the coaster, Cira and Blane are hacking at the body of what was once a friend while another boy clutches his stomach and vomits.

The entire night is blood and sobs and infection and the glare of the moon on flashing blades. I retch at the squelching sound they make as they stab again and again and again. Hysteria tickles at the base of my skull. Everything's out of control. I want to cry, to collapse and close my eyes and cover my ears and pretend none of it's happening.

I need to get as far from here as possible.

But no one else has run away.

"I can't leave you," I tell him. Even though I want to escape. I want to forget what's happened and climb the stairs to my room and huddle under the covers, where it's safe. Where it's always been safe. But I can't leave everyone. "They know I was here, they'll—"

He shakes his head, cutting me off.

From deep inside I can feel the scream, I can feel it nudging out everything that was me before this moment. I can't stop staring at his shoulder. Can't stop imagining the echo of the Breaker teeth snapping.

"What'll happen to you?"

"Go home" is all he says. As if his lips never brushed mine. As if I were nothing and no one to him.

I want to drop to my knees and press my mouth to the wound. I want to take the infection into myself, to fill the void that seems to be taking over everything.

But I don't. I just stare at the bite and think about how I swung too early. If I'd just waited. If I hadn't been so afraid. I'd known to wait and I couldn't. It's my fault he's infected.

"What about Cira?" I ask. "I can't leave her." I feel around my neck for the necklace she'd given me. It was supposed to protect us and it didn't.

He shakes his head but desperation bubbles inside me. I call out to my friend, "Cira!" She looks at me and even from here I can see the splash of blood across her face. She stands over the mutilated body of the dead boy, a long knife clutched in her hand so tight that her knuckles glow white under the moon.

I wave for her to come. But it's as if she doesn't see me. "Cira!" I shout again. "Cira, over here!"

She screams and brings the blade down into the boy's body again and again. As if she can punish him for having been infected. For having turned Breaker.

My throat convulses and I press my hands to my mouth, my fingers digging into my cheeks as my eyes water. I whimper.

Catcher pulls my attention back. "Please, Gabry" is all he says. His voice is filled with such anguish that it slices into my heart. I glance at everyone else, their heads in their hands, their faces streaked with tears, their mouths open, wailing.

"For me," Catcher adds.

It's as though he's giving me permission to do the one thing I'm desperate for. So I turn and run, leaving everyone else behind. Back through the ruins, crossing in and out of shadows and hiding from the Militia until I hit the Barrier and pound at it with my fists. My knuckles rub raw and still I hammer at the old worn wood that's so thick it swallows up every sound.

As if it's the Barrier's fault for everything that happened. And maybe it is, I think, sinking down to the ground, my eyes shut tight. We never should have crossed it.

I keep seeing Catcher; I keep seeing the blood. Tears crowd my eyelids but they can't blur the memories that ache inside me with such a sharp fierceness.

I almost turn around. I almost go back. By leaving I'm abandoning them and it's not fair. In the distance I hear the Militiamen as they shout and run toward the amusement park. The bells in the town still ring their slow steady rhythm. My heart beats in time with each hit of the hammer to metal and I press my forehead to the Barrier, the dry wood smelling faintly of rot.

There could be other Mudo out here. I know I should climb back over the wall and run home. Even though I want nothing more than to hide in the night shadows here. To be absorbed into this nightmare and disappear.

The world's shrunk too fast. What was only hours before a new horizon of possibility opening in front of me has collapsed in on itself. I was right to fear the other side of the Barrier. I was stupid to allow myself to be lulled into believing it could be any better outside Vista. That there could be any place for me away from my mother and the lighthouse and the safety of town.

I climb the thick wall and don't pause at the top before dropping to the other side. Shadows move through the town, the dull moonlight swimming around them. I melt into the chaos of it all, keeping my head down to stay invisible to the panicking people scattering about.

Men flow from the houses with their weapons, shouting to one another. Women barricade windows and doors. But their sense of urgency doesn't touch me. I'm hollow and numb—nothing but a ghost.

A few times I stop and stand in the street, the town streaming past. I wonder if I should go back. I wonder how I was able to just leave Catcher like that. Leave Cira and the rest of them to face the wrath of the Militia and the Council. How I could think only of myself and abandon them.

But I don't go back. I just keep wandering, weaving through the houses in the narrow streets, my fingers loose around my weapon. Tears still burning my eyes.

Nothing tonight makes sense. The kiss after so much longing. My first time past the Barrier and the sense of freedom and desire.

But most of all the Breaker. Her speed. Her ferocity. They taught us about them by comparing them to certain animals, which can sense the gender balance of their environment: If the population in any given area has too many females, most of the next ones born will be males. It's the only way to ensure they survive.

Same with Mudo: If there aren't enough Mudo in the area, anyone infected will turn into a Breaker. Otherwise it would be too easy to kill them off. Mudo are only difficult to kill in large populations because one on one they're too slow. The Breakers, on the other hand, don't last as long but are much harder to kill in small numbers and can spread the infection rapidly.

Seeing it in person is different from hearing stories about it in school. Seeing someone you know die. Seeing her Return. Seeing her sprint and knowing you'll never outrun her.

I press my fingers against my eyes, wanting to push hard enough to erase the sight forever.

No one notices me in the chaos and I follow the path past the edge of town and through the trees to the lighthouse, my home with my mother. It sits on the edge of Vista, perched on the tip of the peninsula, away from the other houses and shops of the town. Its bowed wall is flush with the fence that follows the curve of the ocean. I stand and stare at the sweep of its light as it traces through the night, glinting in rhythm with my heartbeat.

Years ago—generations—Vista used to be a more important city, a port for trading. After the Return, as the roads became too dangerous for travel because of the Mudo, more and more people turned to boats and ships. With the lighthouse and small harbor, Vista was connected to the rest of the world. It was a center for news, goods, everything. It was a prize of the Protectorate. Until the pirates began raiding the ships. Until even the ocean became too dangerous.

And now we're nothing but a light on the shore, spinning for no one.

The windows are dark and hollow and I can feel the emptiness of the house from here. My mother must still be at the weekly Council meeting. I know I should go inside and close myself up in my room. She'd be worried thinking I'm outside while the alarm bells ring but there's no danger here. It's in the ruins, in the amusement park that feels so far away.

I skirt around the house and through the fence down to the ocean, not ready yet to go inside. The tide is creeping in, a dangerous time to be around the waves that may wash Mudo against the beach. But still I stand there and stare out into the blackness. I sense more than see the shudder of the light sweep high above me, illuminating nothingness.

Growing up, I used to stand here with my mother. She would stare at the horizon as if it were an impossible forever. As if it called to her, always needing her. But she would never go. She had a little sailboat she would tempt the waves with every now and again. I'd overheard whispers in the town about my mother—how they thought she was crazy for bothering to leave the shore.

Their words would cause my cheeks to burn. I was fiercely proud of her when I was a child, how she would do things no one else dared. Regardless of what people said, she'd bob out past the waves in her little boat, me on the bow and her at the rudder. There were times when I wondered if she would unfurl the sail and just keep going past the horizon. But she always turned back.

And as I got older and learned the risks she was taking, my face would heat with embarrassment that my mother was so different. That she didn't fit into the town. They didn't understand why she acted so recklessly. I refused to go with her anymore—it was stupid to tempt danger and leave the protection of shore.

Eventually she stopped sailing. She seemed to forget about the old boat on its shelf by the lighthouse, where it still sits. And just like everything else in our world, it's slowly and inevitably fallen apart: its sail tattered, its hull slightly warped. I wonder if I have the strength to drag it to the water. To hoist the mast, hold the sail and whip out into the night. Let the void swallow me.

Instead I let my feet sink into the sand, the waves tugging around my ankles. I think about the crescent wound on Catcher's shoulder and wonder at how everything can change so fast.

I imagine that's what it must have been like to ride the roller coaster back in the before time. One moment teetering at the top, the world laid out before you and the rush of life filling your lungs . . . and then the plummet. The lack of control. That's what I've started to learn about this world. It might give, but it always takes away.

▼ ▼ ▼

That night I lie in bed so aware of the sheets against my body. It's the first time I've thought about the feel of Catcher's skin skimming my own. The air is hot, close, heavy. It pushes me into the bed until I can't breathe and suddenly I panic. I throw off the covers, pressing my hand to my chest and gulping air. I can't believe I left them. I can't believe I ran away.

I stumble from my room and run up the stairs to the gallery, shoving my hips against the railing and waiting for the light to roll across the darkness and hit the curves of the coaster in the distance.

My body still vibrates. I'm safe, I remind myself. I'm safe. But it doesn't help. Because I don't know if anyone else is.

And I'm terrified that it won't last.

In the distance I see flickers of light where there should be none—the Militia at the amusement park. I wonder if Cira or one of the others is telling them about how I was there. About how I ran away. I'm just as guilty as any of them, only I ran before they found me. I stretch up on my toes and look down at the path that snakes from Vista to the lighthouse, waiting to see the light of torches. Waiting for them to come and take me away.

But they don't. Wind and light gather on the horizon and the lights in the amusement park fade to nothing and still I stand waiting.

I feel traitorous for being safe when my friends aren't. For being alive when they could be infected.

But most of all I feel traitorous because, even as I hate myself for it, I want more than anything to remember the feel of Catcher's lips against my own. Feel his fingers on my wrist. Just one memory from the night that isn't pain and fear and regret.

But I can't. I can only see the blood.

And I realize that I'll never see him again. I'll never feel him again. All the possibility and freedom I'd felt is gone forever.

V

The early-morning sun seeps around the edges of the window blind and highlights the creases in my mother's face as she sits on the side of my bed and pushes tangles of hair from my cheeks, even her lightest touch pulling me from the depth of my dreams.

Something tugs at my body, a memory that I'm supposed to be sad and upset, and it takes me too long to remember. Catcher's infected. The Breaker. Mellie and the others and me running away. Leaving Cira behind.

The emotions of the night before hit me, overwhelm me. I want to crumble in on myself but instead I hold my breath, swallowing back the sting of tears. I press the ridges of my nails into my palms, the sharp pain a focus.

"Mom," I whisper, letting her believe it's the weight of sleep that dulls my voice.

She tucks a strand of hair behind my ear. For most of my life this has been our morning ritual. Her coming into my room, sitting on my bed, gently waking me up to face the day.

Sometimes she sings a soft song; sometimes she tells me news of the village. Sometimes we just exist in silence.

More and more this summer I've shrugged her off, feeling acutely how very different she is from the others in Vista. I want to be more like the other teenagers, even like Catcher and Cira, who don't have any parents.

But this morning I let her twist my hair. I close my eyes and let her comfort me.

"I have to go meet with the Council, Gabrielle," she says before pausing. "Something happened last night. Something you need to know about."

I try to keep my breathing even, not wanting her to realize that I know what she's going to say. Even so I feel it catch, feel my chest tightening with the panic from the night before. I shouldn't have run. I should confess what happened.

But I don't.

I mumble a "What?" hoping she thinks my throat is tight from sleep rather than pain.

"Some of your friends were caught outside the Barrier," she says.

I feel the bed shift. "The Militia were notified. They found them in the amusement park by the ruins." I hear her swallow. "Apparently there were Unconsecrated nearby." I cringe as she uses the word *Unconsecrated,* a throwback to her old life and the way she was raised. Her refusal to call them Mudo like everyone else is just another reminder of how different she is.

"Some of them were infected and Returned," she says with a tight voice. She pauses again. "I'm so sorry," she whispers, clutching my hand.

I turn my head into the pillow, squeeze my eyes as tight as I can to keep the agony inside.

"They're voting on a punishment this morning," she

continues, "and then they're having a full town gathering to announce it."

I should ask her who was hurt. She would expect me to. I should ask her if Cira and Catcher were there, if they're okay, but I already know the answer and can't bring myself to pretend otherwise. She waits for me to say something and when I don't she walks to the window and opens the shutters so that she can stare out at the ocean.

The light's bright and harsh and I wince against it. I can only see the outline of her body as she turns back to face me but her shadow looks older than I've noticed before.

"I need to know if you were out there with them," she says. I want to see her face and read her expression but I can't. I push myself up on my elbows, the sweat-soaked sheets falling away. I open my mouth but nothing comes out.

"I need to know what to say if the Council asks me," she pushes. "I won't have a vote in what they do with the others. But I need to know about you."

I have never—not once—lied to my mother. And for a moment I think about telling her the truth. But I can't. I can't put her in the position of choosing me over her duty to the Council.

I can't bear her disappointment.

"No," I whisper, my voice cracking. "I was too afraid."

She drums her fingers against the windowsill and I hold my breath, waiting to see if she believes me. If the truth of my fear is enough to cover the lie that preceded it. And then, because I can't stand the silence any longer, I add, "I'll never cross the Barrier." I draw my knees up to my chest and wrap my arms around them. "I'll never leave Vista."

She looks back out the window and as the light slides along

her profile I think I see sadness. And I wonder if she's sad that I'm so weak and so afraid when she's always been so strong.

▼ ▼ ▼

I feel like everyone's watching me as I make my way alone through town to the square with the rest of the crowd gathering for the Council announcement. News of the night before is swift and I hear people murmuring. They must know I was there. They must know that I ran away and abandoned my friends.

Or they know that I wasn't there and they feel sorry for me. The only one not invited. The outcast. The one who was too afraid.

My hands shake as I walk past the old crumbling concrete boxes that house shops and homes. Rough-cut logs replace what time and age have dissolved, so that the buildings look like patched dolls with too many mismatched parts. Old women stare out the windows, kids' shouts echo up the narrow streets.

I don't want to be here. I don't want to face what happened. I want to run back home and crawl into bed. But I push myself forward anyway, swallowing back the acrid taste of regret. I have to see Cira. I have to make sure she's okay.

I finally make it to the center square of the town, the other residents of Vista pressing in around me. It feels too tight, the bodies near me slick with sweat and heat and a stench of hard work and long days. Even my own skin doesn't feel right and I try to stretch my arms and neck but can't move in the crush of people.

On a platform against the Council House are two large cages. In one are two boys and a girl. They sit limply on benches, their eyes cast down, staring at their feet. The girl has bandages wrapped around her arm, the boys both have bandages covering their legs. Blood dots the gray-white of the fabric and I shudder.

I remember seeing the girl get bitten. I remember the sound of her screams as the Breaker's teeth sunk into her flesh. I look away quickly, not wanting to see them, not wanting to see the blood and hopelessness.

In the other cage are five more from the night before and I'm relieved to see Cira among them. I stare at her, wanting to shout out but keeping silent. She stands with the rest, their eyes scanning the crowd, their shoulders held back, as if defiantly ready to face their punishment. But I know my best friend well enough to see that her fingers are shaking, her skin pale and lips thin as she presses them together.

I think back, trying to account for the whole group. Not everyone is in the cages and I wonder if maybe I wasn't the only one to run. At least four of us died last night or are missing: Catcher, Mellie and two others. My stomach cramps with the realization of it all—with the reality of what happened.

Dead. That means my friends—Catcher's friends and maybe even Catcher himself—are dead. Gone. Will never dance, run away to the Dark City, sing in the night, hold hands. The truth, the severity of it all, slams into me and I stagger back, catching my breath. A few hands push me forward, grunts sounding in my ears.

So much of me was hoping to see Catcher. Even if he was with the others who are infected. Hoping that maybe I'd have a chance to talk to him one last time. To hold his hand in mine so that I could remember it. Could remember him.

It's as if the spin of the world has stopped, thrown me off and away. I squeeze my eyes shut, seeing the bite on his shoulder in my mind. It didn't look severe—nothing he could have bled to death from—which means it would normally take days for him to turn. For the infection to spread, to shut down his organs. To kill him so that he can rise again.

But now, at this moment, Catcher should still be alive. The Militia should have found him last night, and that they didn't—the fact that he's not up in the cages with the others—means he's either turned or he ran away.

I force myself to breathe deeply as dizziness overwhelms me. I clench my fists and remind myself that I know nothing. Catcher could be okay. He has to be okay. I cling to this idea, this hope. I hold it as if it's the only thing keeping me from falling apart.

Never have I wished more that I were standing beside my mother. That I could slip my hand into hers and have her anchor me. But as the keeper of the lighthouse and the shore she's an advisor to the Council. She's with them, listening as they decide the fate of my friends. If I'd been up there in the cages, they'd have been deciding my fate as well.

A part of me feels lucky for having escaped the same punishment as my friends but my heart still skips beats and I wonder how long my luck will last. Wonder if it's only a matter of moments before someone in the cages spots me in the crowd and calls out that I was there last night and I'm hauled to the stage.

Around me I hear the whispers. I hear fear-laced voices murmur about the Breaker, speculating that she washed ashore and somehow made it past the dunes and seawall into the ruins. As they talk about the rumors of the night before, I see it all in my mind again and again: Mellie, kneeling on the ground with her hand over her arm, the blood seeping through her fingers. The look in her eyes as it was happening.

She didn't understand how everything could change. She was fighting against the inevitable. Against the reality.

And then she was nobody. She was nothing but a hungry shell.

I swallow and start backing my way through the crowd, tripping over feet and being rebuked for pushing against the flow. I'm at the edge, ready to run through the narrow streets and to the safety of my bed, when the people around me still and I realize that I can't go farther. I can't leave my friends. I can't hide from what happened.

Shaking and afraid, I wrap my arms around my chest and stand with the people of Vista. We watch as the Council takes the stage, watch as their advisors, including my mother, file onto benches behind them.

The Chairman steps forward and the world around me drops to nothing. Hundreds of people holding their breath at once.

"What are we if our barriers fail us?" he begins. "If our security fails us? If our safeguards fail us?" The Chairman's voice is deep, loud. It rolls over each one of us, filling the crevices between us. Everyone around me leans forward, all eyes on him.

"One bite," he continues. "One bite will wipe out a city. One bite is what wiped out our world so long ago. One bite is everything that stands between what we have built here and annihilation."

A few people shift; a child calls out and is hushed. "We have our rules for a reason. For the good of all. And we make those rules clear to all. Including the fact that sneaking past the Barrier is a serious offense. One of the worst offenses. Because once infection breaches our walls, we are all as good as dead."

My hair sticks to my neck in the heat as the Chairman's words drive into me. Everything he's saying is true and makes me wonder again and again why I didn't try to stop the group from going last night. The girl in the smaller cage is crying now, and even from here I can see the sunlight glisten off the tears trailing down her cheeks and dripping onto her knees. She doesn't bother to wipe them or hide her face. I watch as the boy next to her places an arm around her shoulders, and again it hits me—that could be me. And maybe it should be me.

"Last night several teens from Vista took it upon themselves to flout our rules, and some have confessed that this is not the first time such a breach has occurred." Heat creeps up my neck and claws at my face. I look around, expecting everyone's eyes to be on me. But they all stare at the stage. All paying rapt attention.

"I was young once, I understand the urge to test boundaries. But we have made it clear that some boundaries cannot be tested. And they have paid the price for their actions."

He sweeps his hands out to the cages on either side of him. "Two have already died, killed after turning. Three more are infected. The rest will be quarantined to ensure our safety. And two others . . ." He lets his head drop and then raises it slowly, his eyes scanning us all. I feel as though he pauses on me and I duck behind the person in front of me.

"Two others are missing. We're told that they were infected and that given the nature of the attack they also would have likely turned Breaker. Their souls forever gone, beyond the redemption of a quick and eternal death."

Whispers and murmurs swell around me at confirmation of the news. I just stand there limply, his words revolving in my head. Two died: Mellie and the boy I saw Cira killing. The three in the cage are infected. And two—Catcher and Griffin, the redhead who danced with Mellie—are still out there. Catcher wasn't caught by the Militia. My body begins to hum and buzz with the tiniest bit of hope—he could still be alive.

"But the real question is, what happens next?" The Chairman pauses, as if he's an entertainer and not the man appointed by the Protectorate to lead us. "The Council has been meeting this morning. We have heard a number of suggestions, advocates for and against those standing before you.

"You must understand that our lives are not about the individual. Our rules exist for the collective. They are about survival and safety. Millions of people have sacrificed their lives in this battle. It is our duty to honor those sacrifices. And you must know that we, as your leaders, do not take our duties lightly."

These are all words I've heard before, all warnings we're told over and over again. So often that they lose their power. But hearing them now makes me want to grab every person in this town and force them to see what I saw. Make them watch their friends bitten and turned. Make them see that beyond the Barrier is nothing but death and pain, no matter what dreams they might have.

He takes a deep breath, lowering his voice. Forcing us all to lean forward to hear him. "We did not come to our decision easily."

My entire body is numb with fear. I swallow. I don't want to hear what he's about to tell us but I know that not hearing won't change anything. The Chairman has never shown mercy in the past, even on lesser infractions than these. He will take any opportunity to set an example. To prove to the Protectorate that he can be a ruthless leader worthy of promotion.

"We have made our decision." He pauses again.

My eyes flick between the two cages. At the three Infected, their arms around each other, their knuckles white. At the quarantined, who stand defiantly even though their anxiety is obvious.

"The Infected will be taken by the Militia beyond the Barrier. There is nothing we can do for them anymore. They will be given their eternal rest."

A woman wails and tries to run through the crowd but people hold her back. I recognize her. She's one of the infected boys' mothers. Her screams become muffled as her neighbors pull her away. At least she has a chance to say good-bye, I think, wishing I hadn't run from Catcher so fast. At least her son had time to remember what it is to be alive before he's dead.

At least he won't become Mudo.

I cross my arms over my chest, trying to hold myself together. Everything feels cold. Even the heat of the sun burns like ice. I close my eyes, wondering why Cira didn't run away with me. Wondering what punishment she will face that I may not.

The Chairman raises his hand to his face, wipes at his eyes and for a moment I feel relief—that he'll show leniency, that maybe this decision was too hard on him and that he and the Council will be compassionate.

But then his voice hardens. "The others," he says, waving at Cira and the rest in her cage. "They will be sent to the Recruiters to serve for two years, though they will not be allowed to claim the honors that come from such service. They will not be granted full citizenship, nor will they be allowed to enter any of the Protected Zones, including the Dark City. Not after their service, and not ever."

VI

The crowd explodes around me. But I'm speechless. I can only stand there in shock. My legs wobble, my muscles refusing to hold me, and I sag against an older lady. She wraps an arm under my elbow.

"You poor dear," she says, clucking over me. "Are they friends of yours?"

I nod. Every city and town like ours that falls under the control of the Protectorate is required to provide a quota of goods and services, including young men and women to the Recruiters, the army of the Protectorate. In return we get protection, the benefits of a unified confederacy and the ability to trade goods with other members. We've never forced anyone to serve the Recruiters. We've never had to.

There have always been volunteers willing to risk their lives on the promised reward of guaranteed access to the Protected Zones and full citizenship to all who serve. While anyone with unique skills or enough goods to trade can pay the exorbitant rents to live in the Dark City, only those who serve the Recruiters are guaranteed a place to live, and those who distinguish themselves in service don't ever have to pay rents.

Except for the ones on the stage. Even after two years with the Recruiters they will not be allowed.

The punishment stuns me with its harshness. To be forced to serve, with no reward.

"Aren't you a smart one not to get caught up in that mess," the woman next to me says, patting me on the back.

But I was *with them,* I want to tell her. I should be up there with my best friend. I shouldn't be hiding. I shouldn't have run away but I don't know how to change it.

And even if I did, I can't find the strength or the words to step forward and turn myself in. I hear the Chairman speaking more but I can't make out what he's saying. I just stand there staring at the cages. Staring at Cira. They seem just as shocked as I am and it makes me ill how the Chairman has meted out his punishment in public like some sort of sick spectacle. Though I shouldn't be surprised, since the Protectorate has never really cared about our town; we're too far away from the Dark City and became useless after the pirates took over the seas.

Around me people begin to flow out of the square and I catch snippets of their conversations.

"Could have killed us all . . ."

"Can't believe the Council would do such a thing . . ."

"They brought it on themselves . . ."

"Those poor kids . . ."

I can't move. I can't bring myself to leave. So I just stand there, a rock in the middle of a river.

My best friend is being sent to the Recruiters. Everyone

there last night will be sent away, sent to the lines of the war to fight the Mudo, with no possibility to reap the traditional rewards of service.

Except me. And what scares me more than anything else is the thought that I won't get away with it.

And then questions begin slipping into my head: Why didn't the others tell on me? Why didn't they tell the Council that I was also there?

What happens if they tell on me now?

I glance back at where the Council is huddled around the Chairman to the left of the platform, surrounded by the parents of the Infected and quarantined. Some are resigned and some angry, shouting and crying and pleading. But no one is there to speak for Cira. As an orphan, all she had was Catcher and now he's gone.

I don't want to face her but I know I have to. No one stops me as I shove my way to Cira's cage. She doesn't see me at first but Blane does and she pushes toward me, fury creasing her face.

"Feeling guilty?" she yells. She slams her hands against the bar. "Come to taunt us?" She leans forward.

I jerk my head around, looking to see if anyone else heard her, and she just laughs. My cheeks flame. I'm embarrassed at having been called out on my cowardice and ashamed that we're on opposite sides of these bars. And then Cira steps forward, places her hand on Blane's arm, and Blane moves away. Leaves us alone.

I'm surprised to see my friend with so much sway over this older girl.

"Cira, I'm sorry," I murmur, because I don't know what else to say.

"It's okay," she says. "You were smart to run. To get away."

I shift, feeling only more uncomfortable. "I didn't want to," I tell her. "It was Catcher—he told me to go and I didn't think." I have to force my mouth to speak his name, my voice breaking at the sound of it.

Her fists clench around the bars. "Where is he?"

"I . . ." I shake my head, swallow. In my mind I see the bite on his shoulder, see the blood trailing down his arm. I thought Cira had seen it too. I thought she knew.

Her eyes bore into mine.

"I don't know," I finally say. I can't bring myself to even form the words of the truth.

I watch as her face dims, as if the last lights of hope are blinking out. Already resignation has settled in deep lines around her mouth. "But I thought he went with you."

I see my old friend in her eyes. I see the same hesitation that I feel—the vulnerability. But it's the last tendrils of hope I hear that hurts the most. I don't want to be the one to tell her about her brother, and yet I realize she deserves to know. I might have run from everything else but I can't run from this.

"Catcher was . . ." I swallow. "He was bitten. I thought you saw."

Her skin, already pale, becomes ghostly. As if she herself has Returned. She runs her tongue over her lips, wetting the cracks. "But he wasn't there when they came and got us. You're wrong, he must still be alive. He must be out there. Maybe he's hurt. You're wrong!" She raises her voice and the others in the cage step forward like a wall surrounding her.

I see the way they look at me. As if I'm the betrayer.

"I saw the bite marks," I whisper.

"But maybe that's not what it was," she counters. "It could

have been a scratch. He can't be infected. He can't!" She notices that people are watching us now and she lowers her voice. "You have to find him. There's something wrong. You have to go find him."

I step away, shocked. "You want me to go back there?" I ask, my eyes wide.

She nods, her mouth a tight white line in her face.

The thought of returning to the Barrier, of climbing over it again, makes my heart seize with panic. "But I can't," I tell her. "Not after . . ." I let my voice trail off. "What could I even do for him if I found him?" I protest.

"You can make sure he's okay," Cira hisses. "You can be there with him and help him if he's hurt. You can—"

I'm shaking my head, my hands trembling, and Blane steps forward and grabs my wrist through the bars, cutting Cira off.

"What?" Blane says. "You're willing to climb the fence for a good time but not for a friend?" The others grumble assent behind her. "Useless," she adds, throwing up a hand in my face, "we should've told them about you when we had the chance." She pauses, raising one eyebrow as the corner of her mouth tilts up. "I guess we still could," she adds.

I glance at Cira and see the hesitation on her face. As if she believes Blane. I start to feel sick. This can't be my only option. I grab at her hands. "I can't do it, Cira," I whisper. "I can't." Even to my own ears the desperation in my voice is clear, pitched high and cracking.

I feel the crushing press of panic again and I don't know what to do. I can barely breathe with it. Spots of color explode in front of my eyes.

Blane reaches through the bars and grabs my wrist again,

her nails digging into the tender white flesh as she pulls my grip from Cira. I focus on her, the edges of her hair blurring like a halo.

"You find her brother," she says through her teeth. "You find Catcher or else you're useless out there and there's no reason why you shouldn't be in here with the rest of us."

I think about them telling my mother I went beyond the Barrier. Telling the Chairman. For lying, for putting everyone around me at risk, my punishment would be worse than just being sent to the Recruiters for a couple of years.

My mother would know that I lied. She would never trust me again. I close my eyes, not wanting to imagine the repercussions and disappointments. I realize that I have no choice. I either go find Catcher or they'll turn me in.

"I'll go look for him," I whisper, ashamed that it takes such a threat to get me to take action.

Cira's shoulders relax a little and Blane drops my wrist. "You better find him," she growls.

I wait for Cira to defend me. For her to smile, even if just a little. For it to be like before, even though I know it never can be again. But instead the others in the cage pull her away from me, coddle her as one of their own. Leaving me standing alone, outside. I glance over my shoulder at the other cage, at the condemned. Overnight everything's changed. Twisted into complicated patterns that I can't unravel.

I open my mouth to say more but Blane turns Cira away from me. I stand there staring for a moment, wishing things could be like they were before. But they aren't and may never be. I shuffle down the platform, skirt the stragglers in the square and wander through the narrow streets until I reach the wide empty buffer zone between the town and the Barrier.

I stare at the wall, at the dark wood towering above the Militiamen, whose patrols have tripled. I think back to last night, how I promised myself to never tempt fate again, to stay safe within the confines of Vista. And yet here I am, trying to find a way outside once more. Only now it's hopeless to think that I'll be able to cross the Barrier with the Militia keeping out such a sharp eye. That I'll even be able to find Catcher if I could.

He was with the others when I ran away, and his bite didn't look severe enough to kill him so soon. There's still a chance he's alive and hasn't changed. And if the Militia didn't find him, it means he doesn't want to be found. It means he left just like I did but he didn't come back inside the Barrier. It means that something is wrong.

I press my fingers against my temples. It's stupid of me to think about climbing the Barrier. The Chairman made it clear what the punishment will be. Plus, what would happen if Catcher has already turned? Then I'm as good as dead if I find him.

I close my eyes against the sun, trying to block out the sounds of the town around me. But in the darkness of my mind I can't stop remembering last night. In my head everything happens slow and fast at once.

The Breaker, the panic, Catcher running, fighting her. Killing Mellie.

Seeing the Breaker's speed—facing it—I understand how it is that our world has never recovered from the Return. How even when we beat the Mudo back, infection can spark and rage again. All the stories we were taught about cities being cleared of Mudo only to discover one trapped in a closet or dredged from the ocean or lake during a storm make sense now after seeing it happen last night.

A hand falls on my shoulder and I jump, a scream catching in my throat. I open my eyes to find one of the Militiamen standing in front of me. I recognize him from school—his name is Daniel and he's older than I am. Most of his friends joined the Recruiters in the past few years but he was left behind because he was born with a crooked leg that causes him to walk with a long slow limp.

"Sorry, Gabrielle," he says. "Didn't mean to scare you."

I blink at him, surprised to hear him say my name, as we've rarely talked in the past. "No, I was . . . daydreaming. I should have been paying attention."

He smiles, shy. "A runner came from the Protectorate in the Dark City today and he had supplies for your mother. I saw you standing here and thought maybe you'd want to take them to her rather than have her wait for them to get sorted with the rest."

He holds out a small box, its lid already torn half open. He says nothing and to fill the silence I look through the assortment of gears and cogs, replacement and repair parts for the lighthouse. Daniel leans his head close to mine to see what's inside and for a moment I think of Catcher, of the way he would lean in to me while we spoke.

My hands begin to shake, rattling the box, and I take a step back to put distance between the memories.

I notice Daniel's face fall a little and I instantly regret it. He was always teased in school and I can see it in the way he holds his shoulders, as if he's steeling himself for blows.

"I'm sorry," I tell him. "I just can't stop thinking about my friends." I keep my eyes on the gears, on their sharp little teeth.

"Oh," he says. He hesitates. "The ones from last night were your friends?"

I nod. "Sort of, I guess."

"You were smart not to cross the Barrier with them."

I feel the heat spreading up my neck again. I can feel the way it sears my skin. The fear and anguish and shame rolling off me like a stink.

"Though if you ask me," he continues, "being sent to the Recruiters is more of an honor than a punishment."

"It's death," I tell him before I can stop myself. "It's stupid." My cheeks flush, startled at how vehement I sound.

Now he's the one to step back, a scowl darkening his face. "We're a city of the Protectorate. It's our duty. Besides, the chance at full citizenship and the ability to live in the Protected Zones are worth it."

"Vista is protected enough," I snap, tired of always keeping quiet. I grind my teeth and add, "I just don't see why you'd want to go anywhere else." I want to add that it's useless to fight the Mudo, to wage the never-ending war, but I know he'll never understand. Trying to change his mind is just as hopeless as trying to eradicate the Mudo.

He opens his mouth to respond, his skin reddening a little with anger. I might have pushed him too far.

I cut him off. "I'm sorry," I say, not having the strength to argue. I've uttered those words more today than I have in my entire life. "Thank you for bringing me this." I hold up the box. "It was very nice of you to go out of your way like that."

If I've learned anything from Cira in the last few months it's how to placate young men with compliments, and it works on Daniel. His shoulders relax and he smiles and tilts his head before slowly making his way back to the gate, finally leaving me alone.

▾ VII ▾

I spend most of the day wandering along the Barrier, watching the Militia pace and patrol. When I finally get back to the lighthouse my mother isn't there, though I know she'll be home soon, in time for the high tide. I lay the box on the table and then I pace around the small rooms. I want to run but I don't know where. I want to do something, anything, but I don't know what.

So I climb to the gallery and stare out around me, trying to figure out how I'm supposed to cross the Barrier and find Catcher. Trying to find the courage.

But there just aren't that many ways out of Vista. The town crouches on a peninsula, three sides protected by water and the fourth by a high thick wall that extends as a stone jetty out into the ocean.

There are old photographs in the Council House that show what Vista used to look like before the Return. A rambling sprawl along the coast of gleaming buildings and hotels and shops clinging to the ocean. A place where no one lived and everyone visited. A place for relaxation—as if in their world they could afford such time away from the duties and responsibilities that kept everyone alive.

Most of the stories about what Vista was like before the Return have been lost now. No one cares about the people who came before us. We're a dead end. We exist far from the core of the Protectorate, like a forgotten afterthought. Traders rarely come and visitors arrive because they are desperate or mistaken. Only the Recruiters are constant, returning every season to take their due: taxes for the Protectorate, soldiers to fight in the never-ending war against the Mudo and to ensure we're doing our duty to keep the lighthouse running.

The lighthouse perches on the very tip of the peninsula buffered from the rest of town by a span of woods. It's a relief to live on the outskirts, to be removed from the crush and bustle of the day-to-day life. Most people never even bother to walk the path through the trees and past the fence to the beach; they're too afraid of the ocean, where the dead can rise from the waves.

I once asked my mother if she was afraid to live out here along the boundary of the fence. She said that someone had to keep the lighthouse going and monitor the beaches to dispose of the Mudo that washed ashore during high tides.

We were standing on the gallery, the sun setting fire over the tops of the pre-Return buildings in Vista. She tented her hands over her eyes and looked past the town, past the river and into the Forest stretching out toward the mountains hulking in the barely visible distance.

"It's not always those out on the water who need an anchor," she said. "Sometimes there are others who need to know there's a world out here."

I didn't understand what she was saying then. But now, when I look past the Barrier and toward the ruins to the edge of the amusement park, I wonder about Catcher. I imagine being lost out there, seeing the stripe of light in the night and using it to find my way home.

Even though I know it's impossible, sometimes I like to imagine they can see our lighthouse in the Dark City way up the coast. I like to think that somewhere out there is a girl like me who stands in the night and wonders what else exists in the world but who is too terrified to find out. I wonder what her life is like, if she knows more about the world than I do.

From my perch I watch the Militia skitter along the Barrier like sand fleas on the dunes. There's no way I can climb the wall undetected, which leaves only one other way around: through the ocean.

When I think about leaving I can barely breathe. The panic that set in last night whispers around me. I press my fist to my chest, feeling each beat of my heart. Feeling the force of blood through every artery. I don't want to let Cira down—not more than I already have. And I don't want to let myself down either.

I realize that I'm terrified of going back to the ruins not just because I'm afraid of being caught, but because I'm terrified of finding Catcher. I don't want to see him infected. I don't want to see him turned and have to kill him. I don't want any of it. I just want to go back to the way life was before. I want to take back that night and pull it from the span of days.

But then I'd never have felt his lips against mine. And I'm not sure I'm willing to give that memory up.

From inside I can hear the dwindling echo of a bell ringing, the alarm that chimes every 745 minutes—when the tide is nearing its peak.

For as long as I can remember, my mother's life has revolved around the sound of that bell.

Mudo can't drown; they're already dead, and so the waves are often tossing them ashore. Most of the time they're downed in a quasi-hibernation from being in the water so long, but as soon as they sense people they rise and start after them. This means every day, every twelve hours and twenty-five minutes, my mother patrols the beach, ready to decapitate any Mudo that wash in on the high tide.

Many days nothing happens and my mother just stands there staring out at the horizon. Some days the tide will bring a few Mudo. And rarely, a storm will rage at sea, dredging up the dead to walk the shores.

When I was growing up my mother never allowed me on the beach during the highest tides. Whether to keep me safe or to shelter me from reality I've never figured out. I think she always liked the idea that somehow she could keep it all from me. That if I never saw the Mudo, if I never looked in their eyes, I wouldn't have to face the truth of them. I wouldn't have to face the truth of the world.

She once told me it was the only thing she could hope to give me—a life without the Mudo constantly pulsing in the background.

Now as I stand on the gallery and watch my mother walk onto the beach, the way she strolls back and forth just past the line of waves, tendrils of water reaching toward her, I realize that after last night there's nothing she needs to shelter me from anymore.

I know the reality of the world. I've seen the Mudo tear at human flesh. I've seen infection and I've seen them turn.

A hand tumbles in the waves, fingers skimming the white froth. My mother's back stiffens and she tightens her grip around the handle of the shovel.

The body is pushed to the shore and then pulled back again like a teasing dance.

The ocean finally deposits the Mudo on the sand and my mother walks over to it. I lean forward, watching.

It's a woman, wet tangled black hair spread across her face like a spider's web. Her skin, what I can see of it, is pale, gray and pocked. She's wearing what looks like a black skirt that's bunched up around her knees from the water. A dark shirt lies drenched against her body.

She rolls ever so slightly in the water and I hold my breath, waiting for my mother to deliver the final blow, to slice the blade through her neck, severing her head.

But it doesn't come. I stare down at my mother. She's just standing there, shovel held high above her head.

I watch as the Mudo starts to twitch. Her mouth opens and closes and she turns her head, sensing my mother.

Soon she'll push herself up, and my mother is doing nothing to stop her. She's just standing there staring and it doesn't make sense.

I lean my body over the railing. "Mother!" I scream. But the wind is off the ocean. She doesn't hear me. I scream again, but still nothing.

For a moment I want to jump. I think about tightening my fingers around the railing and tossing myself over, landing by her side. And then I turn and run. My body bangs against the walls as I fling myself down the stairs.

▼ ▼ ▼

As I run, I imagine all the worst possibilities. That I'll hit the beach just as I see the Mudo stand. That my mother will still be stuck there, as if touched by something that has taken her out of time and pinned her in place.

That I'll see the Mudo bite my mother.

My body goes cold and I sprint for the door as hard and fast as I can. I force myself to remember that my mother can defend herself. That she'll have killed the Mudo before I even get outside and how we'll both laugh at my panic.

"Mother!" I scream as I grab my blade from the entry and kick open the door. The salty wet heat slams into me and on the air I can hear a slip of a moan from the Mudo on the beach.

I turn the corner to the gate, my fingers fumbling. The Mudo is on her knees, pushing herself to her feet. She reaches one hand out to my mother and then another.

"Kill her!" I scream, rage and terror fueling my every breath. I don't understand what's going on, don't understand why my mother won't move, won't act. Flashes of last night explode in my mind: Me standing there in the face of the Breaker. Me failing and Catcher getting bitten.

The heavy sand pulls at my feet and makes it impossible to sprint. Stumbling across the stretch of beach, I've never felt so useless. Needing to be faster, needing to get there but my legs disobeying.

The Mudo's on her feet and lunges for my mother, who pulls the handle of the shovel from her shoulder and knocks the woman back. The Mudo stumbles a few feet, her wet black skirt wrapping around her legs and tripping her.

"What are you doing?" I scream. "Kill her!"

The Mudo reaches again for my mother and again she pushes her back. Like a cat toying with a mouse, she keeps pushing the woman away from her and the Mudo keeps lunging.

Finally I'm within striking distance. I'm about to pull the blade behind my head, to make right what I did wrong last night, when my mother grabs the handle. She wrenches it from my hand and tosses it onto the sand. With the back of her arm she pushes me away from the Mudo.

"I'm sorry," she says, and whether she's talking to me or the Mudo I don't know. My mother jabs her blade into the Mudo woman's knee, ripping through the tattered skirt and shredding the bones and ligaments underneath with a sickening crack.

I cringe as the Mudo stumbles. She reaches for my mother one last time, her hands waving in the air and fingers curling.

My mother stares at her for the tiniest moment and I'm about to shout again, about to scream at her to kill the woman, when she closes her eyes and lowers the blade, severing the Mudo's neck.

I press my hand to my chest, trying to gasp for air. I thought I'd lost my mother. And the enormity of that emotion washes through me, draining me of everything but anger that she could do something so stupid.

And fear that I could have gotten there too late.

My mother stares down at the Mudo's body. She reaches out her other hand and it hovers over the woman's face and then she pulls it back.

And I realize that this woman, this random Mudo on the beach, meant something to her. Suddenly my mother feels like a stranger to me. A woman I've lived with my entire life, that my very existence has revolved around, and there's still so much I don't know.

"Who was she?" I ask.

My mother doesn't look at me, just stares at the way the water licks at the Mudo's fingers, and I wonder what else I don't know about her.

I can tell that she's spinning the words around in her head, trying to figure out what to tell me, and this makes me feel like even more of a stranger to her.

"Nobody," she finally says, her voice barely audible over the crash of the waves. "She's no one. Just . . ." She clears her throat. "She reminded me of someone from where I grew up."

She speaks as if she's in some sort of trance, and I watch the way she stares at the woman and I think about Catcher. I wonder if this is what I'll be like when the time comes. I wonder if, like my mother, I'll have as hard a time making that final blow.

Just thinking about it causes everything to hurt and I realize that maybe I understand her hesitation now.

"How do you handle it?" I ask her. Desperately needing to know, needing my mother's help to ease the pain inside. "What do you do when someone you love or think you might love or could love turns?"

She looks at me, her glance still so far away, and slowly I watch as she focuses back on the world around us.

"It will be okay, Gabrielle. I'm safe. We're both safe. Nothing will happen to us."

But I shake my head. She doesn't get it and I can't find the way to tell her about Catcher. About what he's come to mean to me and what happened to him and that I snuck out past the Barrier with everyone else.

There's silence, there's the push of the waves to the shore, and my mother stares at where the water tugs at the dead Mudo. Then she says, "You'll learn how to let it go. You forget until everything is okay again."

For a while the waves roll between us, the last of the sun slowly fading away. I relive last night over and over again. Seeing Catcher's face move toward mine, feeling my stomach tingle with anticipation. I think about all the glances, all the times his hand slipped over mine. I close my eyes and try to remember his smell but the salt of the air corrodes the memory.

I try to forget all these details. To push them away into nothingness. But the more I try to let them go, the faster old memories surface, storming through my thoughts.

What use are experiences if we're not allowed to remember them? If we forget in order to avoid the pain of loss? What is the point of living if we have to always insulate ourselves?

"I don't know if I want to be okay," I say, shaking my head slowly. So many memories roll through me and I realize that this is who we are: memories and shared experiences. This is what ties us all together.

My mother bends down and sifts through the sand until she finds a shell, the inside gleaming pink like the sunset-washed sky. "It's what we have to do to survive," she finally says, running her finger along the sharp scalloped edges. "There's no point in holding on to memories that only bring us pain."

"Then what's the point of making any memories?" I ask her, my voice heated. My shoulders tense with agitation. "What's the point of any of it if all we're supposed to do is forget?" And then a thought begins to unwind in my head and I force myself to put words to it. “Would you forget me if something happened?”

Her eyes go wide. “No,” she says quickly with a gasp. “Of course not!”

“But what if I’d been up on the stage with the others this morning?” I think about Catcher and add, “What if I was one of those who didn’t come home last night?”

“I would go after you,” she says, grabbing my arms and turning me toward her. “I wouldn’t let you go like that. I would find you. Whatever it took.”

I measure my words and dole them out carefully. “So if you really cared for someone—maybe if you even loved them—you’d go after them?”

Her mouth opens and closes and for a moment she reminds me of a fish tossed onto the shore, unable to breathe. “I . . .” Her eyes mist over for the barest moment but she blinks it away.

She falls silent and I realize that I’ve struck something. That I’ve probed an area of my mother’s life that I never knew about before.

“It doesn’t matter anymore,” she says weakly.

I think about Catcher, alone and terrified beyond the Barrier. No one to talk to, to confide in. No one to pour his memories into so that he can be remembered. And I think about how I would feel if I were the one lost and alone and infected. It’s a terrifying thought that makes the edges of my vision burn dim.

I press my fingers to my lips, remembering how I felt around him. Right now I don’t know what to do or how to feel and I need my mother’s help. “Have you ever been in love before?” I ask, and then hesitate before adding, “Did you love my father?" She's never told me anything about my father, never talked about him or shared stories. I'd learned long ago not to ask about him. Not to wonder why my mother was so silent when I brought him up.

"It doesn't matter," she says.

"Who was he?"

She shakes her head, retreating.

"What happened to him?" I keep pushing.

She sinks down into the sand onto her knees, water rushing over her legs. Her skirt fans out around her, the fabric turning darker as it gets wet. "I loved two men when I was your age. One became infected and died. The other one I left in the Forest when I escaped." Her words are a whisper, barely loud enough to be held by the wind.

My mother rarely talks about her life before and this is the first time I've heard much about it. It's such a small glimpse of her life when she was my age and I grab on to it, hoping for more.

I kneel in front of her and hold her limp fingers. They're damp from the waves pooling around us, the skin already beginning to wrinkle and pucker as if tired with age. "Why didn't you go back for him?" I ask. "If you loved him, why didn't you go back?"

She looks at me, her eyes unfocused, as if she's not there, as if she's staring past me at someone else. "My brother once told me that you can't have truly loved someone if you're willing to let them go. If you aren't willing to fight for them," she says flatly, as if reciting a poem learned long ago.

"I always knew I loved him," she murmurs, almost talking only to herself. "But it wasn't the kind of love I thought I wanted. And I left him. I let him go." She stares at our hands.

"Maybe my brother was right and what I thought was love was just . . ." She doesn't finish. "Maybe I just loved myself more."

I don't know what to do or what to say. It's as if our roles are reversed and I'm the mother. I've never seen her like this, never seen her when she hasn't been strong and in control. It's terrifying to realize that even the strongest among us have such weakness.

She sighs. "I tried," she says. "I tried to go back. So many times I tried. The people in town didn't believe me when I told them I was from the Forest. They thought I was delusional. That I'd escaped from some pirate ship. They wouldn't send anyone back into the Forest, and when I could finally go myself . . ."

Her voice cracks and she swallows a few times. "I lived here for years helping Roger protect the beaches and then I left. I thought I could forget and move on. But I couldn't. The Forest kept calling back to me. And so I went back. I tried again. And that's when I found you and I thought the Forest was telling me something. I thought it was telling me to forget about the past and concentrate on the future."

As her words sink in her eyes snap into focus, widening so that the white surrounding the dark blue glows in the dusky light.

"When you *found* me?" My voice has no substance, as if it's less than air. I feel as if I've somehow woken up in the middle of the night in a strange place and can't orient myself, the shock pushing in like thick darkness.

VIII

My mother swallows and her fingers close around mine as I try to pull away. "Gabrielle, wait," she says, but I pull harder, wrenching my hand from hers.

"What do you mean, *when you found me*?" I ask, panic flooding through my veins, filling my lungs and choking me. I fall away from her, the damp sand soaking quickly through my skirt and chilling the skin at the back of my legs. Water splashes as she reaches for me but I keep backing away. Nothing makes sense and I shake my head, hoping to jostle the pieces back into place.

"Wait," she says again, and I stop. Waves push and pull around us, slicing between us. I stare at her and she stares back. She holds her hand out to me the way she would to a skittish dog, and I realize how terrified I am of what she's about to tell me. I want to tell her to stop, to forget this entire evening. But the demand won't press past my lips.

"You were born in the Forest of Hands and Teeth," she

says finally, her fingers trembling in the air, salt water dripping from them like tears. "I found you there. You were lost and alone and seemed to be in shock and so I brought you home."

"How?" I don't even voice the question, just form the word with my lips.

"You were on the path." The explanation pours out of her and I want to cover my ears and block what she's saying but it comes too fast, like a wall of water I can't run from. "I'd left Vista years before but I could not stop thinking about my village and so I decided to go back. I was going to look for them, look for the others I left behind. I found you and there wasn't anyone else. You were a child—almost catatonic. I didn't know what to do. I got scared and I ran.

"I didn't have anywhere else to go and you were so sick and needed help so I came back to Vista. Roger, the old lighthouse keeper, had died the year before and I told the Council you were mine and that Roger had taught me how to run everything and that I'd take it over. No one knew you were not mine originally. No one but me."

I stare at her dumbly and watch the drops falling from her chin, circles radiating where they hit the water.

"Why didn't you tell me?" It's all I can say, the only words I can pull from the whirl of my mind. Every memory, every moment in this town swims through my head and I can't make sense of it.

She looks down at her trembling hand still hovering between us. "Because I didn't want to remember," she whispers.

Rage tears through me. "Then why are you telling me now?"

She lets her arm fall. The waves break around us; the last gasp of light loses its battle with the evening. "Because you're right," she says. "We are nothing more than our stories and who we love. What we pass on, how we exist . . . it's having people remember who we are. We're terrible at that in this world. At remembering. At passing it on. And it is not fair that I'm the only one who knows your whole story."

I can feel every grain of sand pressing against my skin. I feel as though I used to be one giant whole and now I've been shattered to pieces and scattered into the night. There's nothing strong enough to pull me back together again.

She leans toward me in the darkness, the absence of stars and light. "You'll always be my daughter, Gabrielle. You're the daughter of my heart."

Her words strike like a fist against my chest, a brightness exploding inside me. I had another mother once. I belonged to someone else. Another woman used to comfort me. Another mother used to hold me when I cried and laughed.

I close my eyes. I try to remember her. I try to remember another life, another voice, another smell. But I see nothing.

I can't remember any of it now. Only one thought begins to grow inside me, edging past the confusion and rage. "Who am I?"

She puts her hands on my feet, my legs, crawling to wrap her arms around my shoulder. I want to tear the feel of her from my skin. "You're my daughter. You're Gabrielle."

"But I was somebody else once!" I scream the words, needing her to understand that she's taken everything from me.

"No. You've always been my little girl." I can hear her tears in the way her voice quavers. She draws in a shaking breath. "That's what my mother used to call me. Her little girl. That's what she said to me when she . . ." Her voice fades into the waves.

I press my palms to my eyes, disbelief and anger and confusion warring inside. "I was someone else's little girl first," I say, every muscle in my body pulling tight. I push away from her and stand up, the wet fabric of my skirt sticking to my legs. I stomp through the water in a tight circle, kicking against the salt spray, wanting to pull the world apart piece by piece.

"You were alone in the Forest," she says. "There was no one there. I looked. You were starving and barely even conscious. You were only four or five years old! You didn't even speak for a month after I brought you back and even then I wasn't sure you were going to live! You could barely even tell me your name!"

I stop pacing. I stare at her. "My name?" I ask, dazed. I have nothing from my life before, not even something as basic as my name? I take a deep breath but I feel as though my lungs can't hold the air.

"This . . . Gabrielle . . . it's not my name?"

The moon is barely crouching over the horizon but even so I can see the pale echoes of it against her face. She looks both old and young at once and I wonder how I could have ever thought I was her natural child. My hair is blond, bleached almost white by the summer sun and hers is black, now streaked gray with age. Her skin is pale and mine is tan, her eyes dark where mine are light.

But who grows up challenging their own mother's claim on them as a child? Why would I have ever thought I'm not who my mother told me I was?

She pushes herself up and comes to stand in front of me. "You kept saying something when I asked you but I couldn't understand," she whispers. "You wouldn't tell me anything. I didn't have a choice. I didn't know what else to do."

"Why Gabrielle?" I ask. It's the only thing I can focus on as I try to reorder every memory of my life. As I probe the truth of everything my mother has told me.

My mother steps back, her mouth slightly twisted, as if she's surprised at my question. "She was a girl I knew when I was your age," she says slowly and quietly as if she can rebuild this bridge between us. "She was from the Forest like you, but no one knew where. And I was the only one who knew she'd come from the Forest." Tears drip from her eyes. "She is the reason I escaped from my village. She is the reason I found the ocean.

"Listen, Gabrielle, I'm sorry." She reaches for me but I step out of her grasp. "Please," she says.

"No!" I shake my head. Too much is crumbling around me. Everything is too fast: Catcher's bite, Cira's sentence with the Recruiters and now this. Everything I've ever known has shifted underneath me and I don't know how to stand straight anymore. "You should have told me!" I shout at her. "I had a right to know!"

"I thought it was best. I thought . . ." She swallows. "I thought that I'd lost everything else in the world and that somehow God was giving me something to hold on to. I thought . . . I thought He was giving me another chance to love."

"You were being selfish!" I yell, the words raw against my sob-seared throat. "I didn't belong to you. I was someone else's daughter."

"You would have died," she pleads, holding her hand toward me. "I saved you."

I push my fists against my head, wanting to yell and scream and shout. I know she's right. I know that if I'd been left on that path something terrible would have happened. I could have been bitten and infected; I could have starved. But that doesn't matter to me now. What matters is that she never told me any of this before this moment. That she probably wouldn't have told me.

What matters is that she's been lying to me my entire life. Everything I've ever known and thought about myself is wrong—fake. And I don't know what I can trust right now, which makes me feel like I've been cast adrift. Shoved away from shore to battle the waves on my own.

I don't know how to make her understand. "How can you tell me to let it all go? As if the past doesn't matter?" I point at her, my finger shaking. "You want to just forget about what came before, but it doesn't work that way. I can't forget the people I loved and who loved me. Maybe you're fine with taking what you need and forgetting about the rest. With leaving the people you love out in the Forest to die. But that's not me. That's not what life is about." I'm left panting.

My mother's cheeks are crimson against the white of her face, as if I've slapped her.

I swallow. I've pushed too hard. Gone too far. Lost control and let myself fall into my emotions.

I shove my fingers through my hair, pulling against my scalp. I don't know how to make her realize how fundamentally this information changes everything about me and the way I've always known myself. I've always been Mary's daughter. And I can't stop thinking about who I am around Catcher—how he made me feel like I'm somehow important.

She's taken this away from me. The hope that I can be more like her. The idea that something of her is in me.

The fact that I belong to her.

I step back with my hands up, as if I can push the air and she'll be gone. "I'm not sure I can ever forgive you," I tell her.

"Gabrielle," she says, her voice low and even, her eyes narrowing slightly.

"No," I say, shaking my head. "That's not who I am. I'm not even sure that's who I want to be anymore."

"I'm sorry," she says. "I love you."

She waits for me to tell her I love her as well. She waits for me to forgive her. But all I can do is turn and run away down the beach. I've never hated my mother before and the feeling is like a pit of black nothingness collapsing me from the inside.

I keep going until I see the hulk of the Barrier looming in front of me. Lights bob along in the dark, the Militiamen on guard. My shoulders rise and fall as I stare at the wall and catch my breath. This is what it comes down to.

This is where it all began. If I hadn't crossed it I'd never have kissed Catcher. I wouldn't have known that he felt about me the same way I did about him. He never would have gotten bitten. I never would have talked to my mother about love and she'd have never told me the truth.

I wonder if she would have ever told me if not by accident.

I don't want to face this. I don't want to handle this. It's too much and I need for it all to stop. I need to catch my breath and figure out what to do.

But the earth keeps spinning, the waves keep crashing, the lamp in the lighthouse keeps turning. Nothing stops just because I feel as though it should. Just because I'm lost.

Frustration bubbles through me. If only I could just curl up here in the sand. Bury in like a clam and forget. Not have to worry about these responsibilities.

I think about my mother and how she said life was so much easier after forgetting. But even as I try to push him from my mind I think about Catcher. I think about the roughness of his chin against my neck. I think about my promise to Cira to find him.

I hear footsteps approaching and I look up. Daniel and two other Militiamen walk toward me, lanterns held high in front of them, casting shadows against their cheeks and eyes. I see the moment when Daniel recognizes me, the way his eyebrows rise and his steps falter. He reaches out a hand to me as the other Militiamen fade back.

"Gabry," he says, his tone concerned. But my name on his lips is a lie—my name is nothing anymore. It doesn't belong to me, and I push against the Barrier and run away down the beach.

"Gabry, wait!" Daniel calls after me, but I don't stop and his voice fades behind me. My name with it.

I push through the thick dry sand, my legs screaming with the effort, until I reach the base of the lighthouse. My lungs burn and muscles twitch but still my mind whirs. I look up. Light cuts across the sky, casting my mother's shadow against the glass. I watch as she stands and stares at the ocean.

This place has always been my home. And yet now I don't know what it is anymore. I don't know who I am.

Everything seems too far away, too hopeless, the weight of what I have to overcome too much. In the darkness I see the remnants of my mother's sailboat and remember days with her out on the water. Suddenly everything becomes clear: I have to find Catcher. And going out into the ocean is the only way.

IX

I watch my mother from the beach as she paces around the gallery, staring into the darkness.

I tap my fingers against my thighs, dig my toes into the sand with impatience, waiting for her to walk away so I can drag the boat to the water without her noticing.

I think about the universal law of gravitation—knowledge that's always seemed so useless. It was a short winter day when the Protectorate sent a new teacher to our town, a young man who arrived with a light in his eyes that slowly dulled as weeks went on, the cold pressing in tight and the snow falling deep and thick.

All the kids in town from six to sixteen were in one classroom together. The teacher tried to find a way to make the lessons interesting for everyone, and he had the younger children scouring for rocks to represent planets while he tried to walk the older ones through complicated math calculations.

No one believed him when he explained mass, when he

tried to teach us what held our feet to the ground. Some of the parents even pulled their kids out of the school—an extra pair of hands at home was more important than learning science that we'd never use.

But Cira stayed because she was an orphan and preferred lessons to chores and I stayed because my mother always thought education was important, especially science, which she'd never had a chance to learn growing up. I remember the desperation on the teacher's face as he tried to explain it all to us, to prove to us that the earth we knew was a giant mass spinning in space.

He had a small collection of books from before the Return which he shared with us, showing us pictures that looked like drawings, faded photos on yellowed paper of worlds within worlds within worlds.

Cira thought it was all a joke and preferred to look at the pictures rather than try to understand what it all meant. She held out her superhero necklace one day and asked him how superheroes were able to fly if gravity worked all the time. The teacher almost cried at her question, unable to determine if she was serious or playing a prank.

Midwinter he left without saying a word and the Protectorate didn't send another teacher until after the harvest the next year. Even after all this time I haven't made up my mind about gravity, about mass and rotation and force.

Until now. Until this moment standing by the ocean when I realize that my body is like the planets, the center holding every other part spinning around it. Remove the center and everything else collides and falls away.

My mother continues to stare toward the Forest and I continue to feel as though every part of me is expanding beyond my bounds. It will serve her right to worry about me,

I think. To understand what it must have been like for my other mother.

When she finally disappears from the gallery, I sneak to the side of the house and pull the boat from its rack. It scrapes against the sand as I tug and I cringe, hoping that my mother can't hear the noise over the crash of the waves. Every time the light cuts across the sky I tense, afraid of it giving me away.

It takes me five tries before I'm able to remember how to run the rotting lines through the mast and boom. The bow of the little boat rests against the edge of the surf and I stand staring at it, my hands on my hips and chest heaving with the effort of having dragged it across the beach.

I nudge the hull with my toe, noticing a few cracks where the wood is warped, but there don't seem to be any obvious breaches. The sail's almost useless, though, a giant tear down the middle and a few of the old patches practically threadbare.

I could go back. I could climb the stairs and slip into my bed. I could hold my breath, hoping that my mother will come and trail her fingers through my hair as if nothing's different. I could forget everything my mother told me earlier. I could try to forget everything that happened last night—bury it all down deep. I could forgive my mother for not telling me the truth.

But she's not my mother, I remember. I squeeze my eyes closed. She's everything I've ever known, a mother to me in every way. Except that somewhere, some other time, I had a different mother. I had another family I know nothing about.

What happened to her? Why was I left alone in the Forest? Why did she leave me? Why did she let me go? Could she have done it on purpose?

Light and dark swirl around me. Overhead the sky seems limitless, as if nothing's holding me to the ground. Too many questions. Too many possibilities. I grab a sickle and shove the boat into the water, wanting to escape them all. The hull scrapes across the sand and slaps against a wave, spraying me with water. I toss the weapon into the boat, where it rattles, its blade barely reflecting the moon overhead. And then I push until I'm thigh-deep before leaping into the boat and grabbing the sheet, hoping the old rope isn't too rotted to tug against the boom. I stare at the reflection of the moon striping across the water almost like a path and wonder what I'm doing. Wonder if I'm really able to do this. Break the rules again. Face the world outside the Barrier.

Heaving a deep breath, I tug on the rope until the sail snaps full of wind and the current against the rudder pulls me diagonal from the beach. I try to pretend that I'm just taking the boat out for fun. That I'm not running away and not about to cross out of Vista.

Drops of surf pelt my face as I gain speed, everything dark. Waves looming, crashing against the boat, making it wobble. Already water's seeping through the hull, collecting at my feet.

The last lights of Vista wink past, then the dark hulking rocks of the jetty as the boat skips over the water's surface. It was a mistake to try sailing around the Barrier, I realize. I can't do this. I can't break the rules again. I yank the tiller sharply, ducking as the boom snaps across the boat, and turn toward home. But then I see my mother standing on the gallery. Every time the light swings past it illuminates her shadow against the Forest. Where we're both from.

And I know I can't go back. Not right now. I can't forget Catcher the way my mother forgot the people she loved. I shove the tiller putting the lighthouse behind me and holding my breath as I drift past the Barrier. It seems so peaceful—so easy to forget the wall is the cause of so much misery.

I swallow, wipe the salty mist from my face and push back my hair. To my left, past the rows of whitecaps falling against the beach, loom the humps of the amusement park, the moon glinting off its rusted rails. Tightening the sheet, I steer toward land but the current's stronger than I anticipated, pushing me farther up the coast. The sagging sail can't battle the tide and my heartbeat pulses in my fingers as I urge the little boat to shore. Finally, well past the rise of the coaster and deep into the old ruins beyond the amusement park, the keel scrapes sand.

For a while I just bob, pushed ashore and then pulled back and pushed ashore again. The water in the hull covers my ankles, making the boat sluggish. But I can't bring myself to leave it. I'm too scared. I feel as though I could float here forever, just on the edge of where the tide meets the sand, this in-between place.

The beach is unprotected. There could be Mudo anywhere, everywhere. Downed in a quasi-hibernation until they sense a living person.

Before I can talk myself out of it, I jump from the boat and drag it as far away from the surf as I can. I crouch beside it, staring ahead at the thick stripe of dunes as I twist my fingers around the handle of my sickle. On the other side of the dunes are old seawalls from before the town shrank back to its present location. Past those walls hunker rows and rows of crumbling buildings that stretch all the way to the road that separates what's left of the ruined city and the Forest.

Each sweep of the lighthouse beam illuminates the humps of the coaster rising from the remains of the city down the beach to my left, and I realize just how far off course my boat drifted. I'm much farther past the amusement park than I want to be, but I don't have any choice but to keep pushing forward. Even though my mind screams at me to shove the boat back into the water and run home, I know I can't. Not just because Blane will turn me in and because I promised Cira, but also because I owe it to Catcher. He shouldn't have to face this alone.

Forcing myself to leave the boat behind, I will myself across the beach. I need to get to the other side of the seawall quickly. Out here I'm open and exposed—it's much more likely that if there are Mudo anywhere they'd have washed ashore and not made it off this beach. The sand is still warm, retaining the heat of the day, and thick with tangles of seaweed and driftwood. When I reach the dunes my feet sink and I stumble, dropping my weapon. I'm on my knees when I hear the moan.

To my left the sand begins to shift, a miniature landslide. A hand reaches free, claws at the air. A shock of terror so pure and deep runs through me that I feel as if I've been sliced by steel. I fall back, sliding down the dune. Every part of my body seizes, my mind flashing images of last night: Mudo, blood, bites, infection. I'm slow to react, too sluggish to comprehend what's going on. I scramble, my hands empty, and then I see my weapon lying out of reach.

Clambering against the soft ground, I drag myself toward my sickle as a fat Mudo man struggles to unbury himself. He's ungainly, even more uncoordinated than I am, but still too close.

I'm choking on screams, gasping for air. Finally my fingers brush the handle of my weapon. I try to find the calm I'll need to defend myself but all I can think about is last night. Doubts seep in around me, my mind telling me that I'll fail again.

I've forgotten how to stand, how to protect myself. All I see is the blood trailing down Catcher's arm.

Suddenly I know I'm not going to be able to defend myself. I realize I'm about to be bitten. Infected. Just like Catcher.

I begin to swing wildly, not waiting for the Mudo to be within range. My eyes beg to close, but I force them to stay open. Somehow the blade slices into the dead man's neck, but I didn't swing hard enough and it sticks before it can sever his spinal cord.

My hands are sweaty, the wooden handle slipping through my fingers as I try to tug it free. I start to scream, yelling for help even though I know there's no one else out here. I'm utterly alone.

The sand shifts and I lose my footing again but refuse to let go of my only weapon. I fall down the hill, pulling the Mudo man with me, my sickle still embedded in his neck.

Our legs tangle briefly and I scream again. I've never touched a Mudo before, never felt their flesh. It's like the skin of an apple left outside for weeks to shrivel and sweat. It's lifeless, pulled too tight and still somehow sagging. Bile rises to my throat and I gag—I can't believe how stupid I was to come out here. How lonely it will be to die alone.

We land with a thump at the base of the dune and I roll onto my back, pushing myself away from his grasping hands. I can hear other moans now, see other forms moving under the tall mounds of sand where they must have washed ashore downed and been covered.

The only thing I can think to do is to turn, run back to my boat, but the fat Mudo is pulling himself to his feet, my sickle still wedged in his neck. I'm not sure I can drag my boat to the water fast enough. Not sure I'll be able to escape.

I freeze. The world that seemed so still is now moving in the moonlight. Around me Mudo drag themselves from the dunes, all of them between me and the seawall. I'm trapped against the waves without a weapon.

My mind whirls, thoughts tearing through my head too fast to understand. I need to run. I need to escape. I need to defend myself. I'll never be able to fight them all.

I realize again that I'll die here. Be bitten. Infected. Return. No one will know what happened to me. This understanding flashes fast through my mind, flaying open every dark corner of my fears. My legs grow numb, my mind seizes and nothing works.

"Stop!" I shout at myself, driving the senseless foreboding away.

Against every instinct in my body I force myself toward my boat but I know I won't make it. There are too many of them now. I turn to the fence but they block that exit too. There's just a narrow gap in the cluster of dead around me and I dive for it and start running. To my right is the ocean, to my left are the dunes and behind me trails a wake of Mudo.

Air rips from my lungs. I only have to outpace the Mudo—that's what we've always been taught. Mudo can't run. I slow to a jog and suck in a breath. I can do this, I tell myself. I can survive. I repeat this over and over again with each footfall on the water-packed sand.

Until I remember the girl from last night—the Breaker. Which makes me remember Mellie and the sound her neck made as Catcher shattered it. Which makes me remember the timbre of her desperate moaning just before she died.

Mudo is supposed to mean "mute, speechless," a word

passed down from the traders and pirates who used to fill the harbor. But the creatures trailing me, the people-who-once-were, are anything but mute. They're nothing *but* noise—moans of hunger.

Sweat drips into my eyes, blurring everything around me except my memories of last night. I glance over my shoulder at the Mudo falling farther behind, and calculate the distance between us, then scan the darkness of beach ahead.

I only have to run far enough that I can cut through the dunes and make it over the seawall. My legs burn with the need to escape, with the desire to pound the sand and just keep running forever—to follow the coast until I find the Dark City. Lose myself in the crush of people there who won't know who I am, where I'm from, what I've done.

But I know I could never run that far. And even if I could I'd never have the courage to leave Vista for good. If there's anything I've learned after last night it's that all I want is to wrap myself even tighter inside the cocoon of my town, inside the safety.

I just have to survive tonight, find Catcher, placate Cira, and then I can put back together the pieces of my life.

For the first time since everything began falling apart I have hope that I can fix things. If I can survive maybe I can find a new kind of normal, a new kind of safe. And just as I'm beginning to think that maybe things can be okay I see a figure crest the dunes not too far up the beach from me. It's a young man with a shaved head, wearing a white tunic. He struggles down the sand and hits the beach at a sprint.

He runs straight toward me, his mouth open and teeth gleaming in the moonlight. And my heart freezes, my feet stumbling to a stop. It's another Breaker, just like last night.

X

I turn, but a wall of Mudo shuffles down the beach toward me. They're closing in on me too fast and I'm terrified to try the dunes, afraid that I'll lose my footing again, that the Breaker will get to me before I can escape.

I race toward the waves, hoping I can get deep enough that he flounders and falls beneath the surface before he can reach me—that no dead are hidden in the outgoing tide.

I'm knee-deep when the Breaker slams into me.

My heart stops. I wait for the bite, for the sting of his teeth sinking into my skin. I wonder what death will feel like as it burns its way into my body. Will I know the moment the infection takes hold?

I fall, my face slapping against a wave, my knee scraping the sand. I scream into the water. The salt scratches at my eyes as I lunge for the surface. He grabs my arm and pulls and I try to fight. I kick and claw and thrash against him. I scream again, choking as a wave crashes on my face. I swing wildly, my fists connecting with flesh.

The Breaker lets go and I flop back into the surf, my head slipping under for a moment. I come up sputtering, blinking furiously against the wet hair streaming over my face as I try to steady myself for his next attack.

But it doesn't come. He just stands there, panting in the shallow water. That's when I realize he isn't a Breaker.

My knees almost give way, my entire body going limp. I gasp for air, its salty taste relief to my lungs, as I push the hair from my face.

He stares at me, his eyes light in the darkness, and even though his teeth aren't bared it seems as if he'd devour me. He lunges toward me again and I stumble backward, falling under, my knuckles grinding against sand once more.

He pulls me up and I choke. He pauses, his hands on my shoulders, his eyes wide above sharp cheekbones as he takes in my face. It's as if he's waiting for me to say something, do something, but I'm mute as the moans around us begin to crest and crash.

He holds up a hand, water dripping from his fingers and skimming down his wrist. He reaches as if to trace the left side of my face but I jerk my head back, out of range of his touch. And as if I've broken some sort of trance he blinks rapidly and swallows, moving away from me.

"This way," he finally says. And then he grabs my hand and pulls me out of the ocean before I even have a chance to think about how strange the moment was.

The Mudo are closer now, their hunger a cacophony of inhuman pitches and tones.

We run up the beach away from them, the stranger and I. I fight for air but can't stop to catch my breath. He veers to the left and I see a narrow path through the dunes. I hesitate to follow him, afraid of getting trapped in the mounds of sand, but then the white of his wet tunic flashes in the moonlight and disappears. Suddenly I'm alone on the beach, nothing but Mudo stumbling after me.

A spike of terror shoots through me and I follow him into the dunes. Between the mounds of sand the night is silent except for my coughing and his breathing. I can't hear the moans, can't hear the ocean. The moon is hidden here, throwing us into shadows. I bend over and vomit.

And then he's pulling me again. Ahead of us is a locked chain-link gate stretched between the old seawall, and he barely pauses before scuttling over it. My fingers are shaking almost uncontrollably and the rusty metal bites into my skin. My arms and legs wobble as I try to heave myself up and the boy reaches down, pulling me to the top just as the first Mudo stumbles from the path behind us.

For an instant as the stranger and I hover at the top of the gate, I remember Catcher and me only last night, sitting on top of the Barrier facing each other. The memory is so sharp, so clear that it makes me ache with longing. For Catcher. For the night. For the ability to take it all back. For the chance to do it all differently.

But then the stranger drops to the ground and I let go of the fence, falling next to him. My legs buckle when I land and I collapse onto my hands and knees. The boy stands beside me and I cringe as the Mudo lunge against the fence, the metal rippling under their weight.

"Will it hold?" I ask, tilting my head and looking up at him. He nods, staring at them as they force their fingers through the links. I can hear their bones cracking. Their moans almost wails of anguish.

For a while we stay like that. The stranger staring at those who used to be and me on the ground, coughing, struggling to control my breathing and still not being able to shake the feel of the Mudo man's skin against my own.

I dig my fingers into the dirty sand, unable to convince myself that I'm safe. Slowly I sit back and run my hands over my arms and legs, needing to make sure that I'm okay and wasn't bitten.

While I do this I sneak glances at the stranger, wondering who he is and where he came from. He seems a year or two older than me. The white tunic he wears is soaked, plastered to his body. Two thick leather straps cross his chest and loop over his shoulders, holding scabbards against his back. I've never seen anyone dressed like him and I'm certain he's not from Vista.

Finally he turns to me, holding out a hand to help me stand. His skin is warm, his grip firm. His fingers linger against mine for a moment before slipping away. He looks as if he's about to say something but then he scowls and looks past me.

His head is shaved, making his cheekbones look sharp, his eyes light. Three parallel welts trace down the left side of his face and I realize that they're from me, from when I clawed at him in the ocean.

My heart begins to pound as I assess this new situation. Yes, I'm safe from the Mudo, but I'm alone with a complete stranger in the empty ruins of the old city. Even though he's wiry, he's larger than I am—certainly stronger—and I have no idea if he's alone or here with others. I have no weapon, my sickle still embedded in the Mudo's neck, and I suddenly feel naked without any kind of protection. As my mother taught me: It's not just the Mudo who can be deadly in our world.

He watches me as if expecting something. I take a step away from him, away from the fences and the Mudo. Water slowly drips down the back of my legs. "I'm sorry for earlier," I say to my feet. My voice feels weak, high. "I mean, for hitting you. Thank you, though." I glance up at him. "Thanks for saving me."

He says nothing and I look over my shoulder into the warren of shadows, the familiar panic whispering in my ear. The buildings out here past the amusement park are crumbled, the streets full of rubble and brush and debris. There's nothing I could use for a weapon except loose rock and stones; anything that could have been salvaged was taken years ago, leaving nothing worth anything behind.

The panic becomes more of a buzz, tracing along the hairs on the back of my neck. I'm not sure I could find my way out of here if I ran and I know that if I try to escape he'll be able to catch me before I get far at all.

I struggle to push my hair out of my face but it's wet and tangled so I fold my arms across my chest, clutching my elbows. My clothes are wet and stick to my skin, leaving me feeling exposed. Why did I take such a stupid risk?

"You're . . ." He pauses and clears his throat. His eyes are wide, the moon hovering over the horizon highlighting the shadows of his cheeks and lashes.

"I'm Gabrielle," I say, my voice a whisper. "Gabry," I add. I can only glance at him, afraid to look him in the eyes. Afraid that I'll see hunger or rage.

His eyebrows draw together and he just stands there staring at me, making me more uncomfortable. "I'm Elias," he finally says. But he doesn't move toward me, doesn't hold out a hand for me to shake. Behind him the Mudo pulse against the fence, writhe for us. Their moans filter through my head, mingling with the buzz of panic that tastes like old metal in the back of my throat.

I'm trapped on all sides by danger and I squeeze my elbows tighter. I finally glance into his eyes and see a flicker of confusion before he blinks it away. I look down, feeling strange and awkward. I don't know what to say to him or how to begin to speak to a stranger. I want to ask him not to hurt me but somehow I feel as though it would be the wrong thing to say. If he really wanted to hurt me he could have left me on the beach. He could have left me on the ground after I jumped from the fence.

I remember the way his hand hesitated over mine as he pulled me to my feet. He didn't feel dangerous.

He breaks the silence. "What are you doing here? Where did you come from?"

I'm taken aback. I'm the one who should be asking *him* these questions. I bite the inside of my cheek. "I'm from Vista." I glance over my shoulder into the darkness, trying to appear casual, trying not to let my voice quaver. "Are you alone?"

He doesn't answer my question. "If you're from the town, what are you doing out here?" He takes a small step toward me and the panic roars to life. I throw up my hands and try to walk backward but I stumble over the cracked concrete and start to lose my balance.

He lunges for me then and I swing at his hands, trying to push him away. But he's stronger than I am and his fingers circle my upper arms easily, his grip tight.

The only thought in my head is wonder at how we focus so much on the terrors of the Mudo that we don't think enough about the dangers of the normal world. Of the in-between places full of lawless and desperate scavengers.

For a moment we stand there with barely anything

separating us, his firm hold on my arms keeping me from falling onto the sharp edge of a broken wall. He could do anything he wanted to me right then. I could kick and scream and bite. But who would hear me? And if he's survived out here in the world between the protection of cities, he knows well enough how to defend himself against biting. I stifle a whimper, not wanting him to know how scared I am.

He must see everything in my eyes because his face goes pale. He steps quickly away wiping his fingers across his tunic as if brushing off the feel of me. I'm almost light-headed with relief.

"I'm not . . . ," he says, stumbling over his words, "I wouldn't . . ." He waves his hands at me as he continues to put distance between us. I see his throat tighten before he finally whispers, "I won't hurt you." He hesitates before adding, "Gabrielle."

There's something in the way he says my name. Maybe it's because I've grown up knowing every way that my name can sound, every way it falls from the lips of the people in my town. And he's someone new—a voice I've never heard before.

I nod. A sort of awkward silence stretches between us, my name the only thing floating on the air.

I try to bring us back to solid footing by answering his earlier question. "I'm looking for a friend of mine," I tell him. "We were out here last night and he never came back."

He lets out a long breath as if grateful for the change in topic. "Down at the amusement park."

I tilt my head. "How do you know?"

He looks past me into the darkness and for a moment I want to turn around, afraid that someone is watching me. "I could hear the bells and some of the shouting."

I stare at him and hesitate for only a moment before saying, "You're not from Vista," as if stating the obvious is important.

"No." He doesn't elaborate.

"I didn't think anyone lived out here," I press. I look around at the crumbled buildings, the fallen walls and caved roofs. So many dark shadows and crevices. This isn't a place where people live; people don't live in the in-between places.

After the Return the cities and towns were the most dangerous places, infection spreading and breaking too easily in larger, denser populations. But then as time wore on, people had to band back together. They had to build communities for goods, for food, for safety.

Cities and towns contracted, pulled in their borders, built walls. Which left a whole lot of space in between filled with nothing but Mudo. A few roads, like the long one from our town to the Dark City up the coast, are somewhat protected by the ocean and ruins on one side and the fence around the Forest on the other.

But still, travel is difficult at best, deadly at worst. It's as if cities and towns are like islands in a world where most everyone is afraid of water.

Which means that someone who lives beyond the protection of a town or city is suspect.

I've grown up knowing the reality of our world: The lucky among us live in cities and towns, within the protection of society.

But not everyone is so lucky. Some are cast out for infractions, for failing to follow the rules. Many are deserters from the Recruiters, whose names end up on lists with prices on their heads. Some see themselves as traders—scavenging the ruins and edges of the Forest. Almost all of them are desperate, and I want to know which category Elias falls into.

He rubs his chin and then grips the back of his neck. "I think I know where your friend is," he counters.

I narrow my eyes at him, not sure whether I can or should trust him. "How do you know? Why are you out here?" I ask, trying to figure out who he is.

He studies me and I see a brief flash of something cross over his face. Fear? Regret? Or maybe just the moon hiding behind a cloud before bursting through. "I'm looking for someone as well," he says. His voice is quiet and even.

"Who?" I ask, wondering if everyone in the world is lost, all of us searching.

He stares at me a little longer, and then finally shakes his head. "Never mind," he mumbles.

"Who?" I press.

He pauses before saying, "I just saved you from the Unconsecrated, which, I might add, are still after us. Who I'm looking for isn't important. I'd think just the fact that I *am* here would be something you might want to be thankful for."

I look at him closely, unsure if I heard him right. "You call them Unconsecrated." I pause. "Why?"

He's silent for a long moment. Waiting, I think, for me to say something. Then he shrugs. "Every town has its own word for them, passed down from the Return. It's the one I like best."

I've only heard my mother use that term. But then again, I've rarely met someone from outside Vista except the traders and Recruiters. "You said you'd seen my friend?" I ask.

"I think I know where he is."

His eyes are so intense that I have a hard time looking away. "Will you take me to him?"

Once again he looks past me and then rubs a hand over his head as if forgetting he has no hair to tug at. "Are you sure, Gabry?" He says my nickname carefully, as if testing it out.

I start to say yes but the word won't come. I have to force my lips to move, remind my chest to squeeze out air. "Yes," I finally manage. "Why wouldn't I be?"

He shifts his feet. "Your friend is infected," he says.

I close my eyes, feeling the pain come back. Seeing the bite wounds on Catcher's shoulder again.

"You have to trust me," he says, almost tenderly, when I'm silent. "I know what infection looks like." He seems to laugh a little then. Like a nervous sigh, just a puff of air. "He's infected. He's got a few days, maybe. But . . ." His voice trails off, slipping away to the sound of the moans behind him.

I nod. "I know." And it feels as if it takes everything I am to say those words. Of course, I suddenly realize everything I am doesn't exist anymore. For a brief moment under the shadows of the coaster with Catcher I thought I knew for the first time who I was and wanted to be. Since then all of that has been shaken.

The air around me seems too thick, too heavy. "I just have to see him," I tell Elias. "I just have to see him again."

When I open my eyes he's looking at me, pain etched in the lines around his mouth. I wonder, then, if he's lost someone to the Mudo. He said he knows infection, has seen it. I wonder if he's watched someone he loved get bitten. If he's watched the infection sear through the body, fester the wound, take control.

Elias turns and looks at the fence. The Mudo have multiplied, the moans echoing off the half-fallen walls around us. They pull at the metal links, which look too thin, too delicate to stop their onslaught. Elias reaches to the scabbard on his back and pulls out a long sharp dagger.

I see the flash of a pattern etched into the blade before he lunges at the gate, the tip of the knife slipping through the links and piercing the skull of one of the Mudo. The movement is so abrupt, so unexpected, I gasp. Elias grunts as he yanks the weapon free and lunges at another. I watch the Mudo man stay standing just a moment longer before slumping to the ground. The ones around him don't notice. Don't care. Don't stop. They don't move away, just keep thrashing against the fence, which bows under their weight.

My entire life I've watched my mother behead the Mudo that wash up on the beach after storms and during strong high tides. I've seen her turn them over, examine their faces, before pushing her shovel-shaped blade into their necks.

It always seemed as if she was looking for someone. As if she was waiting, fearing, that someone she knew would wash upon her beach. As if she regretted her job—regretted what the former people at her feet had become.

Elias takes no such care as he goes about his task. And I find myself looking into the faces of the Mudo, wondering who they used to be. The Mudo washed ashore always seemed so lifeless to me. So dead and distant. I never had to get near them. Not like those beyond the fences in front of us, who push and moan and are too close. Who in a dark night could be mistaken as human. They all had mothers somewhere, sometime in the past. Some of them had lovers. Children. Dreams.

All they ever had is gone. Nothing more than a senseless hunger that will never be satisfied.

I wonder, then, if one of the women could have been my real mother. One of the boys my brother. And soon one of them could be Catcher. The thought hits me hard, reminding me why I'm here beyond the Barrier.

XI

"Stop," I whisper. Elias doesn't hear me. His breath is ragged now with the effort of his kills as he shoves the blade through the fence again and again and again, grunting and almost screaming with a barely concealed rage every time another Mudo falls.

"Stop," I say louder. I lunge toward him, pulling his arm back before he can thrust his knife through the fence again. I'm almost sobbing, the tears clogging my throat. He looks at me and I notice the anger on his face. I see horror and terror before he lets a passive mask fall over everything.

He lowers his arm but I keep my fingers pressed against his skin. It's still damp, a combination of sweat and the ocean. Life flows from him, in the warmth of him.

He stares at where I touch him and then into my eyes.

I pull my hand away. His gaze is steady against mine and I step back.

"It's the only thing we can do," he says, and for a moment I think he means us. Think he means my touch. "We have to kill them. They'll cave the gate in otherwise. It's too dangerous." I realize then that he means the Mudo, he means killing them.

"I just . . ." I don't know how to explain to him how it all felt, suddenly wondering who the Mudo once were. Knowing there could be a connection between us. The thought makes me feel uneven, uncertain. "Never mind," I mumble.

"It's the only humane thing to do, Gabry." He waves his hands at the Mudo but I can't bear to look. Can't bear to imagine what it would be like to see the people I love on the other side of that fence—of what it *will* be like when Catcher is one of them.

It's disorienting—I'm not used to thinking of the Mudo as anything but monsters. They've never been anything else to me and I wonder now if this is how my mother has always felt. If this is why she treats them with such respect before killing them on the beach.

"This isn't fair to them," Elias adds. And I want to ask him what *is* fair about any of our lives. But instead I just nod as he tentatively raises his knife and I don't stop him as he resumes his task. I want to walk away but I don't. I want to cover my ears against the moans, against the blade scraping skulls and the sound of the chain-link fence, but I can't.

I stand by Elias's side as he kills them all and I continue to stand there as he pants after the last one slumps to the ground.

I remember my mother telling me earlier that we are nothing more than our stories. I look at the masses of dead flesh, at all the stories that are now forever silenced.

"I'm sorry," I murmur. For feeling weak.

"So am I," he says. He turns to me, his eyes bright and intense. "Are you sure you want to see your friend?" He holds his body frozen, waiting for my answer.

I want to tell him no. I want to beg him to carry me home. To erase my memories. I want to give up and not have to bear any of this.

But I promised Cira. And I promised myself. And it isn't fair for Catcher to go through this alone.

"I'm sure," I say, taking a step forward.

Elias shakes his head and then reaches his arm around to his back and pulls out another dagger identical to the first. He shrugs out of the scabbard and then hands it and the knife to me before he walks past into the darkness.

I buckle it to my side and then pause, looking at the corpses on the other side of the fence. They appear almost human in death, more human than they seemed just moments ago. And I wonder again what we lose when we die and if we retain anything of what we used to be when we Return.

▼ ▼ ▼

While the amusement park has stayed mostly as it was before the Return, the rest of what used to be Vista didn't. For generations, scavengers have picked it clean. Elias walks through the ruins with confidence, not questioning where he's going, and I stumble behind in the darkness, skirting the shadows cast by the fat moon.

"How do you know this place so well?" I gasp, trying to catch my breath.

"I've been looking for someone," he says again, but he doesn't elaborate.

He seems so confident out beyond the protection of the town and the Barrier, so sure of himself and his steps. I envy him for it. With every crumble of rock I jump, afraid it's more Mudo rising.

I jog until I'm closer to him, feeling safer when I can reach out and touch him. "Who are you looking for?" I prod. I try to see into the darkness, try to remember every turn and twist we make through the streets, but I'm already lost. It makes me feel even more uneasy.

He stops abruptly and I stumble a little before finding my footing.

The street here is wide. Gaping windows look down on either side of us from buildings nothing more than caves. In the far distance I can barely see the moon shining on the curve of the tall coaster and beyond that the cut of the lighthouse beam spinning through the night.

"Your friend's in there," he says, pointing down another street to a tall narrow building. "Third floor, left side," he adds.

I squint into the darkness. "How do you know?"

He raises a shoulder. "I keep track of these things. When you leave just keep the coaster to your right and go straight. You'll hit the beach and your boat."

I study him, trying to figure out who he is and where he's from. "You're not coming with me down there?" I ask. My throat suddenly feels dry, my palms sweaty.

He shakes his head. "None of my business," he says.

I hold out the knife he gave me but he pushes it back. "It's not smart to be without a weapon," he says.

I try to swallow. "Are there Mudo down there?" I ask.

"Not that I'm aware of," he says. "Other than your friend."

My stomach clenches and I grab at the sleeve of his tunic. "But I thought you said he hadn't turned, that he's just infected."

"I said he hadn't turned *yet*. He's still dangerous."

I look in the direction of Catcher's building and rub my palms on the hem of my shirt. I grit my teeth. "Fine, I'll just take care of myself," I tell him, knowing how stupid that sounds after his rescue on the beach.

He doesn't say anything, doesn't laugh. Just nods. "Good luck, Gabry." And then he turns and walks out into the darkness, leaving me standing alone on the empty street.

"Wait," I call after him, not ready to see him go. Not ready to be alone or to face Catcher.

He pauses and turns until I see his profile. His chest stills as if he's holding his breath, as if he's waiting for me to say something important. He takes a step toward me.

"Thank you," I finally say. He stares at me a moment and then shrugs before walking away. Every sound becomes amplified: the sound of his footsteps fading, the groan of buildings settling from the heat of the day. Cicadas buzzing, rising and falling. My mouth tastes bitter, my throat raw from screaming for help earlier on the beach. The ocean salt has dried, making my skin itch and clothes chafe under my arms.

I want to run, either after Elias or toward Catcher, but I know that running will only feed my panic and then I'll do something stupid. Mentally bracing myself, I take a deep breath and walk toward the building where Catcher might be.

I clench my fist around the handle of the knife, my shoulders tight and feet ready to sprint. There's nothing to indicate that Catcher's here, has ever been here. I glance behind me at the street, wondering if Elias is watching me walk into a trap.

But what else can I do? Run back to the beach where my boat is still surrounded by Mudo? Run toward the amusement park hoping that there aren't any Mudo out there, knowing that the Militia will find me and turn me over to the Council and ultimately the Recruiters?

I pause on the threshold to the building, its walls rising

above me to the stars. I place a shaking hand against the doorjamb and stare into the blackness. There's no way I can do it. No way I can force myself inside.

But a hand grabs me and pulls me inside anyway.

I choke and freeze as arms wrap around me. And then my body catches fire and I fight.

"Gabry." The voice is broken, ragged.

I stop struggling and fall against him. It's Catcher and he's here and he's alive and I'm finally safe.

▼ ▼ ▼

He seems comfortable in the darkness as he leads me up two flights of stairs and into an empty room flooded with moonlight. He walks to the gap of an old window and stands there, nothing more than a shadow.

I hesitate, watching him. Afraid that touching him would ruin this moment. Would make all of my fears and pain come rushing back. But still, I can't help it and I finally step forward and reach my arms around him, pressing my face into his back.

With each breath he draws, I can hear his heart. It sounds so strong, so full, and I press deeper against him. Hoping that if I hold him tight enough I can keep the infection from spreading.

He turns and faces me, puts a hand on my cheek, his thumb tracing the path of my tears. I reach up on my tiptoes, try to press my lips to his mouth, but he twists his head so that I kiss his jaw, his muscles tense and hard.

He steps away from me then, back to the window, and I stand in the darkness. A dull light flashes against the space between us and it takes me a moment to realize that it's the lighthouse in the distance. For a brief moment I wonder if my mother is still there staring at the Forest and if she misses me.

When the light hits again I see the stains on Catcher's shirt. The rips from where it was torn in his fight with Mellie.

"Come home, Catcher," I tell him.

"I can't," he says, his hands gripping the rotted frame of the window. "I'm infected."

I step forward. "How do you know? Maybe it was a scratch, maybe she didn't really bite you." I realize as I'm saying the words how hard I've been hoping they're true. That I've come all this way with the hope that what I saw last night was wrong. That Cira is right and that Catcher isn't infected.

But the longer the silence stretches between us, the more desperate my hope becomes. "Tell me you're okay," I say frantically. I want to beat my fists against his chest until he tells me what I want to hear but instead I just dig my nails into my palms.

"I'm infected, Gabrielle." His voice is scratchy and low, defeated.

"But how can you know?" I plead. I shake my head, words tumbling out. "You're not. You can't be. I can't—"

"I can feel it." He turns back toward me, his eyes hollow and lost in his face. I swallow, remembering the Mudo on the beach. How can the man in front of me turn into that? He's so strong. So warm. So alive.

And then I realize that the heat of his skin is fever due to the infection. That it's burning through him even as I stand here and stare at him. Eventually, just like everyone else who's infected, it will kill him.

I think about my mother telling me how she's seen people she loved turn Mudo. How she's been there at the end. To me it was just another story, another tale of her life in the Forest. I never truly understood what she was telling me. Never realized what it meant, what she must have endured.

I didn't think it would be this hard to face Catcher. But now I stand here and stare at him and understand why my mother made herself forget. I understand how much easier it would have been to stay in the town, forget about the Barrier and Catcher and how he makes me feel.

And then I remember again that she's not my mother, and the room starts to swirl around me. There are no sacred memories. Catcher steps forward, his hand out to me. "Are you okay?" he asks, and I grab on to him.

I don't want things to have changed so much. I want to go back to last night, when I only worried about how to kiss Catcher, when my mother was still my mother, when the world finally seemed to be opening up and when life hadn't spun so out of control.

"How's Cira?" he asks me. His shoulders are stiff as he waits for my response. I hesitate. "Please tell me she's all right. That she wasn't . . ." He doesn't finish the question but we both know what he's asking.

"No," I tell him, looking at my fingers, at the window, anywhere but in his eyes. "She wasn't hurt. She's back at the village." I swallow before saying, "She's okay."

Relief washes over him, his body sagging against the wall.

"Please come home," I beg him. A feeling wells inside me, pushing against my skin. If I can bring him home, if I can make him better, then we can figure out a way to erase the past day. We can figure out a way to go back to last night, to play it out differently.

This time as we faced each other on top of the Barrier we could choose differently. I could give in to my fear and take his hand and pull him back down toward Vista. We could both be safe. And then we'd never have ended up here, never have been confronted by this moment.

But of course, that wouldn't change the fact that my mother isn't my real mother. It wouldn't change that I'm not really her daughter. That I don't know who I am anymore. Even if last night had never happened, I'd still be lost.

"I can't come home," he says, almost like a moan, his mouth against my hair.

"Please," I whisper. Everything inside me screams, desperately wanting things to be different.

I can feel the way his body shudders under mine. The way his chest heaves. I can feel him sobbing in my arms.

"I'm scared, Gabry."

My chest aches. I think about him finding his way out here after last night. Stumbling through the darkness, terrified and bleeding. Of him spending the day here, tracking the sun across the sky through the empty window. Burning up with fever. Alone. Terrified. I wonder what I would do if it were me instead of him. How I would spend my last days, knowing what comes next.

"I'll stay here with you," I tell him. "I won't leave until . . ." I can't finish the sentence.

"You'll get in too much trouble." Every one of his tears scorches as it falls against me.

I think of Cira, of the others in the cage in the square, and I wonder if I should tell Catcher about them or if it will only add to his anguish. There's nothing he can do for her, nothing either of us can do.

"You have to go home," he says. "Your mother will worry otherwise and she might call out the Militia," he adds.

I feel the anger from before seeping through me. I still

don't know if I can face her. Too many questions swirl and crash inside me. Did my real mother wonder why I never came home as a child? Could she still be out there in the Forest, looking for me? Wondering about me?

He steps away from me, the lighthouse beam pulsing between us, ticking away the time he has left.

He's right—if I don't go home my mother will send them out after me. I'll be in as much or more trouble than Cira and the others. "I'll come tomorrow night," I tell him. "You'll still be here tomorrow." I mean for it to be a statement rather than a plea, but still I stand frozen, waiting for his answer.

He hesitates. "I should have a few days," he says cautiously. "It wasn't a bad bite."

I cringe at the word—the stark reminder of his infection. I look around at the empty room. I don't want to leave him. Don't want the night to be over. Don't want to face what the next days will bring.

"You should go," he says. "And you shouldn't come back. What if . . ." He swallows and his voice cracks as he continues. "What if I've already turned and I attack you?" He reaches out a hand, drawing his thumb down my throat. "I don't want . . . I can't hurt you."

"You won't," I murmur, placing my hand over his, holding it against my cheek.

"This isn't the way it was supposed to be," he says, his voice breaking. "I had plans. . . ." He squeezes his eyes shut, his entire face collapsing and body shuddering. "Last night, that was what my life was supposed to be. It's supposed to be you." He brushes his fingertips along my temple.

His words cut into me, his desires and dreams mingling with my own, throwing at me everything I've lost. Everything that will never be mine.

"Are you telling me I can't come back?" I ask him. As much as I desperately want him to say no, a part of me that's weak and scared wants him to tell me yes, to relieve me of my burden and terror of this place and what he'll become. What if I'm not strong enough? What if I fail him?

"It's not safe," he whispers.

"I don't care," I tell him. And suddenly I realize that it's true. Strength and purpose and desire bloom inside me, soaring through my veins.

We stare at each other, not knowing how to leave it. And then he reaches out and pulls me to him again, kissing my eyes, my cheeks, my jaw—everywhere but my lips. Then he drops my hands and goes back to the window.

"Be careful," he tells me. The muscles in his shoulders ripple as he digs his fingers into the wood of the sill.

I open my mouth. I want to tell him something, something he can hold on to when he's scared. I want to tell him that I think I might love him. I want to fill the room with the hope that maybe love can make it okay. But everything is so trapped inside.

Instead I turn and feel my way down the dark cramped stairs and out into the street, everything blurred with loss and pain falling on me, dragging me down.

When I look back at the building the gaping windows are silent and dark. I want to see Catcher standing and watching. I need a memory to hold on to other than the fading feel of his heat against my skin, the absence of his hand on my cheek.

I squeeze my fingers around the knife Elias gave me and start down the street, trying not to cry. I'm just heading toward the amusement park and the wink of the lighthouse beyond when a figure falls into step beside me.

XII

"He's going to turn, Gabry," Elias says. "There's nothing you can do about it."

I clench my teeth and keep walking. I want to tell him to shut up. I want to scream at him and tell him that he can't understand what he's saying and how much his words hurt me. I want to beat on his chest until he realizes that he's wrong, even though we both know he's not.

"What are you doing here?" I ask instead.

He puts a hand on my arm, stopping me, and I pull out of his reach, frowning. I want to remember the feel of Catcher's warmth, want to remember his scent. Not this boy's.

"If he turns I'm going to have to kill him." He says the words plainly, without malice, but they cut me nonetheless.

I slap him. Before I can stop myself I feel the sting of his skin under my fingers. He just stands there, half his face now red in the moonlight.

I clamp my hand over my mouth, my eyes wide, unable to believe what I've done. I swing around and keep walking, trying to control my anger and sorrow, trying hard to ignore the reality of our situation. After a moment he catches up with me. I start to climb over a tall pile of rubble when I hear him sigh behind me. "I'm sorry," he says, and I stop, my foot twisted between two rocks and my hands clenching the edge of a fallen wall.

Slowly I let go, sliding to the ground and kicking at the debris pile in frustration. I want to keep falling; I want to slip through the pavement and into the earth and sleep forever as if none of this has ever happened. I want the pain and fear to end.

But I don't want to accept this boy's apology. It's as if accepting his words means accepting the truth: that Catcher has little time before he's gone.

"You have to understand, it's not safe for him out there. For any of us. If he turns and there aren't enough other Unconsecrated around him in the ruins . . ." His words trail into the darkness.

"Then what?" I ask him, putting my hands on my hips, digging my fingers into the soft flesh until I feel bone.

He stares at me, his eyebrows drawn together, his lips tight. "You know what happens when an Infected turns and there aren't enough other Unconsecrated around," he says as if it hurts him to force me to remember.

I close my eyes, thinking of the Breaker last night and of Mellie. How they'd run so fast, been so out of control. Suddenly I see Catcher the same way and I shake my head to clear the image. I don't want to talk about Catcher, about his infection, anymore.

"Who are you?" I ask him. "Why are you out here alone in the ruins? You said you were looking for someone."

His fingers clench into fists and he starts to turn away

from me. He stares back into the city and then looks at me again and his shoulders seem to fall a little. "It doesn't matter," he says, his voice sounding old and worn. "I'm not sure I'll ever find her."

I rise to my feet and step closer. I want to comfort him. I want to find something to say that will give him some hope because I need to believe that hope can still exist. But I can't force the words from my mouth. Too much has happened in the past day to make me question the role of dreams in this world.

I turn away from him and watch the lighthouse blink in the night. I should be there, tucked in bed and safe. I should've never left. I start picking my way up the rubble pile toward home again.

"You don't want to go that way," he says. "The men from your town are still patrolling."

"I thought they'd given up," I say. Exhaustion eats through my bones. "Then I'll have to figure out a way to get to my boat."

He shakes his head and says, "There are still Unconsecrated on that stretch of the beach."

I slump onto the rocks at my feet and drop my head into my hands, my limbs heavy and worn out. I'm trapped. In the morning my mother will realize, if she hasn't yet, that I'm not coming home and eventually they'll start searching. If they find me out here I'll be sent to the Recruiters with the others.

When I raise my head Elias is still there. He takes a long breath and then holds out a hand. "If I get you home you can't come back," he says, pulling me to my feet.

"Fine," I tell him, not ready to think about tomorrow so soon. He holds my gaze a moment. "It's too dangerous,

Gabrielle," he says. His hand lingers along my wrist, so light and soft that I can't tell the difference between the hot night air and the warmth of his flesh.

"Promise me," he prods.

I feel myself leaning toward him as if he's the only light in the dark. I nod, unwilling to put my lie into words, and then he turns, his fingers dropping from mine, and starts walking toward the beach.

When we reach the seawall along the dunes I can see the footprints of the Mudo stretching along the waterline on the other side. We pause and listen but hear nothing, the crash of the waves drowning out most sounds. My boat rests where I left it, tilting to one side, the incoming tide reaching like fingers toward the hull.

Elias shakes his head. "This is stupid," he says. "We barely made it the first time. It's crazy to try again."

"I have to get back," I tell him.

He closes his eyes as if trying to come to a decision. And then his shoulders slump. "Fine." And he begins to climb the smooth boards of the seawall.

I follow him and drop to the other side, my landing soft and silent in the deep sand. I start forward but Elias holds out a hand, stopping me. I pull the knife he gave me from the loop at my hip, ready, and look around in the moonlight, wondering if there are more downed Mudo buried beneath us or if they all followed me on the beach earlier.

He leans in close, his breath hot against my ear. "You go ahead—I'll fight off any that follow."

I don't have time to be terrified. If I hesitate and give in to the fear then I might miss my chance to make it to the boat. So I nod and slide down the dune, hitting the beach at a run. I stumble a few times but finally find firm footing in the damp sand closer to the waves.

I look over my shoulder to see Elias still crouched by the seawall, ready. I make it to the boat and begin to push, trying to heave it out into the waves, but it's still full of water and deeply lodged in the sand. It barely budges. I drop my knife into the bottom and angle my body, trying to push harder, but my feet slip on the sand.

I glance back, seeing Elias's impatience. I try again and again and slowly the boat starts to move as I grunt and strain with the effort.

Behind me I hear footsteps and look up. It's Elias sprinting toward the boat waving his hands, his mouth open. I can hear the sound of his voice but not the words, which are too jumbled. I fumble in the boat for my knife but the water is dark and I can't see past the surface. I skid my hand across the bottom, feeling a sharp sting when the blade slices my palm.

Elias is almost on me. I finally understand what he's screaming: "Go! Get the boat in the water! Now!"

It's like last night when everything became slow and fast. Down the beach a Breaker runs toward us. And I realize in that instant that I recognize him. It's the redhead, Griffin, who was there at the amusement park with us. I barely spoke to him; he was the one dancing with Mellie.

My chest feels as though it's being crushed with the weight of this memory. I can't catch my breath and there's nothing to hold on to but the rails of the boat. Griffin is nothing anymore. He's no one and neither is Mellie. They're both dead, just like Catcher will be. I bend over and heave, spots flashing in front of my eyes. I almost want to give up, to slip into the waves and let them carry me away.

I'm jolted out of my thoughts when Elias slams against the hull. He screams "Push!" at me and suddenly the world snaps back into place. I can breathe again, the urgency of the moment infusing me with strength, and I dig my feet into the sand, throwing my weight against the boat.

It drags across the sand so slowly that it feels as though a hundred thousand waves have crashed onto the shore before we finally touch water. Elias pushes me into the stern as the bow slams against the surf. I look past his shoulder and see the thing that was Griffin racing closer, fingers tearing at the air and teeth bared.

"Faster," I pant. "He's getting too close!" I dig my hands into the water, using them like paddles trying to pull us deeper. The salt burns the cut on my palm as I thrash against the current but my efforts are useless, the waves too much of a force. Elias struggles against it all, the water cresting and crashing around his thighs as he tries to drive us farther from shore.

The sail hangs limp. The rudder and tiller jolt from side to side. A wave crashes into Elias, throwing him off balance. His hands wrench from the boat as his head dips below the water.

I reach for him, screaming, but the current pushes us apart. Another whitecap crashes on top of him, sending him tumbling. I look down the beach where Griffin sprints toward us, about to reach the waterline.

Leaning out over the boat, I shout for Elias to grab my arm, but our fingers are too slick and he slides away. He kicks in the water. His body slides through the waves until he can grasp the side of the boat. But when he tries to pull himself in, it tilts and almost capsizes.

We're frozen in that instant. Him floating. Me leaning

away from him, trying to balance the little boat. The boom jerking back and forth between us.

And then the Breaker hits the water at a full sprint, his moans seeping into the night as he stumbles and trips and claws his way forward. He's like an animal, a crazed beast bent on destruction.

I scream again for Elias but he just looks at me. The drag of his body through the surf is keeping us in the shallow water. Keeping us in reach of the Breaker. The boat tries to slice through the waves but Elias's body pulls us back toward shore.

I know what his plan is a heartbeat before he does it. I watch as his fingers go slack as his hand slides down the hull. As he lets go. The boat lurches deeper and I lunge for him.

"No!" I yell. His slick skin slips through mine and I grapple, trying desperately to hold on, to get a firmer grip on him. His head bobs above the surface and then sinks. I reach as far as I can and feel my fingers connect with his tunic. Once, twice I try to grab it but the fabric floats past my fingertips. I reach out one last time and finally I catch him. I pull with all my strength, the boat tipping underneath me. The lines snap and rattle against the boom, the empty sail ripping.

Griffin fights his way through the waves behind us, getting closer, but I refuse to leave Elias, refuse to let another person become infected because of me. "I'm not letting you go!" I shout to him. And finally he begins to kick and struggle again, pushing to try to get into the boat.

I heave him against the hull, leaning back to balance his weight as he clambers over the side, collapsing into the bottom as Griffin's moans crest around us. With Elias safe I grab the line and pull the boom in tight, twisting the tiller. Elias kneels in the middle of the boat, his chest heaving and head bent over his knees.

Behind us Griffin reaches out his hands, and his fingers are just about to close over the rudder when the wind snaps the sail, jerking the boat forward to cut through the waves away from the shore.

We stare at each other, Elias and I, both drawing in ragged breaths as Griffin flounders in the surf, his moans silenced by the salty water. I pull at the tiller and the boat sluggishly cuts parallel to the shore and we sail toward Vista and the lighthouse blinking in the distance. Elias leans back against the bow, water seeping through the cracks around him.

My hands are shaking, my body buzzing. Flashes of what just happened spark in my mind but it doesn't feel real. "I don't . . ." I stop and try to breathe. "I knew him," I finally say. Griffin will either be dragged to the depths or washed back onto the shore. I wonder if the current will drag him down to our beach. If it will be my mother who has to cut off his head. I still can't comprehend it all, that last night he was alive just like me and now he's gone—all of who he was disappeared. He's nothing more than a monster now.

Elias says nothing. He leans forward and reaches for my hand, prying the rope from it so that he can study the gash across my palm.

I close my hand into a fist and he tries to pry my fingers open but I don't let him. "I knew him," I say again. I'm so angry at the world that everything inside me boils and I have to press my lips together to keep it from escaping. "Just like Catcher and Mellie and everyone else. It's not fair."

I yank my arm away but he doesn't let me go. Instead he crawls closer until he cups my palm in his hands.

Beneath us the boat bobs and rocks, the water slowly leaking through the cracks. I bite my lips. I know the world isn't fair but that doesn't make it any easier.

He prods at the raw flesh of my hand and I stare at the top of his head, at the way the moon gleams off it. "If your friend really cared about you he wouldn't let you take such risks," he says.

I squeeze my fingers around the cut and pull away, feeling the sting inside and out. I don't need him telling me what Catcher feels about me. I'm already confused enough about it.

"It's selfish of him to ask you to come back, to have to see him like that," he adds.

I clench my jaw. "He didn't ask," I tell him, gripping the line and jerking the boom in tight against the wind. But it's too late. Elias has planted the seed of doubt and its roots have already taken hold.

"I'm not letting him go through that alone," I say. He leans back against the hull and stares at me. The shreds of the sail cast a shadow over his face so that I can barely see his expression. But I can make out his mouth, the whites of his eyes.

"Wouldn't you want someone there?" I ask.

He closes his eyes and winces ever so slightly. If I weren't staring at him so closely I would think it was just the boat rocking underneath him and not something roiling inside. I wonder for the first time if he even has anyone in his life or if he's totally alone.

As we glide past I see the amusement park and the Barrier huddled along the shore, lights like fireflies where the Militia patrols.

"Why'd you go out there tonight, Gabry? Why risk your life?" he asks in the darkness. He trails a hand in the water over the side of the boat and I watch the wake created by his fingers.

A thousand reasons crowd my mind. Because of Catcher's smile, the way his hand feels in mine, the crinkle of his eyes when he looks into the sun, his fear of heights, his laugh, his smell. The way he makes me feel—the way he's always made me feel—as though I'm the most important thing. Because my mother told me to forget and I wanted desperately to remember.

"Because I promised his sister I'd find him," I finally say, wanting him to know that this isn't just about me.

"Why didn't she go herself?"

My hand twists the tiller and the boat turns into the wind, its sail falling limp. We sit there, small waves lapping against the hull. My stomach feels sick with guilt. "She couldn't," I say. "She can't." I swallow. "She was caught outside the Barrier last night and is in quarantine before they send her and the others to the Recruiters." Once again the enormity of how fast and far everything is changing pummels into me.

I feel him move forward and he reaches a hand out and touches my knee. "It'll be okay," he says. It's as though I can feel every ridge on his fingertips. I shift, suddenly uncomfortable.

The little bit of kindness makes me want to believe him but I can't. "No it won't," I tell him. "The Recruiters are a death sentence."

I push the tiller until the sails fill again with a rustle and a snap.

"Not for everyone," he says. He crouches in front of me and lifts my chin. His face is still lost in shadow, only his eyes barely visible. He looks as if he's about to say something but then a wave rocks the little boat and he grips the sides with his hands. My first thought is that I wish he were still touching me, as if the feel of him could keep everything around me from lurching. I shake my head, quickly scattering the idea.

"Not everyone who joins the Recruiters dies," he says softly. "Some come home. I did." He reaches under his tunic and flips out a silver disk attached to a leather cord around his neck. In the sweep of the lighthouse beam I recognize the seal of the Recruiters on it.

I try to fit this new piece of information into the small amount I know of Elias. "You were in the Recruiters?" I ask, my voice a whisper. It doesn't make sense. I thought he was an outcast living beyond the safety of towns and cities. The disk proves he served with the Recruiters and is a full citizen with the opportunity to live in the Protected Zones. He should be there, not here cast aside in the barren stretches between civilization. "What happened?"

He stares at the black horizon. I watch his throat tighten, his jaw clench. He reaches a hand up to his head, his fingers brushing against his shaved scalp.

"It doesn't matter," he says absently, tucking the disk back under his tunic and staring into a distance or a time that I can't see. He settles back against the hull, crossing his arms over his chest and closing his eyes.

I want to tell him that it does matter, that I want to understand him. Understand what my friends will be going through. But I don't know how to ask such questions and he's still a stranger.

No part of us touches in the small boat and suddenly I miss the comfort of it. I imagine reaching for him, taking his hand or brushing my foot against his knee, but he's pulled into himself. My cheeks burn as I swallow down these thoughts.

"Elias," I say. He opens his eyes and in the darkness they seem colorless. I want to tell him that there's something familiar about him, about how I feel around him. That something about him makes me feel safe, as if it really will be okay. But his gaze is so intense that I lose the words and all I can say is "Thank you."

Once we hit land he helps me pull down the mast and drag the hull back up to the storage rack. I hesitate by the door to the lighthouse, everything I thought I knew about my life waiting past those walls. "I'm going back tomorrow night," I tell him.

He shows no surprise. "Please change your mind," he says. "Please don't go back."

We're standing so close, the hypnotic rhythm of the waves wrapping us together. With every breath I take I feel as though I rock toward him.

But then the beam of the lighthouse sweeps over us and I take a step back, the moment broken.

"If you can't promise me you won't risk it, I'll watch you and stop you from going," he says, his hand grasping my wrist. "Please."

I look down at his fingers against my skin. "I have to see Catcher again. I promised," I tell him, shaking my head before pulling away and slipping inside.

XIII

On the edge of sleep I think of Catcher. He's bending over me, lips close to mine, his heat all around me. I close my eyes and press against him. I sink into him, into a perfect world of nothing else. No death. No infection. No worries.

But in my dream Catcher morphs and changes. The world around me turns to water and then suddenly it's Elias I'm holding in my arms and his lips brushing against my own and I don't pull away.

I wake up gasping, my fingers clutching at the sheets and blood roaring in my ears. It takes me a moment to calm the pounding of my heart and even longer to realize that my mother's in the room, standing by the window and staring down at the beach.

"Mom?" I ask, pushing up to my elbows. The wisps of my dream still crowd around my head, a tangle of confusing desires. I squeeze my eyes shut, trying to force the images away.

My mother says nothing, doesn't even look at me, and so I say again, "Mom?" kicking back the covers and throwing my legs over the side of my bed.

She lets the blinds fall back and comes to sit down next to me. In her hands she holds a small thin book and she traces her fingers over the edges of it as if she's nervous.

Other than yesterday I've never seen my mother hesitate, never seen her unsure of herself. It unsettles me watching her that way now.

I feel so distant from her even though our shoulders touch, and our hips and knees, as we sit side by side. I want to tell her about last night, to apologize for running and ask her to forgive me. But I don't.

Finally she breaks the silence and tension. "I'm sorry, Gabry," she says. Her voice is defeated, without the current of strength that I'm so used to hearing. "I probably should have told you before about where you came from."

She stares down at her hands pressed against the cover of the book and I can just make out the title between her slim fingers: *Shakespeare's Sonnets*. I always thought our hands were so similar, always thought it was a trait we shared.

But even that thought was built on a lie and this realization makes it all so fresh, so clear how deep the betrayal is.

"I just thought it would be easier," she says. "The Forest—it's so cruel." She almost spits the last word and I watch as emotions crowd her face: anger, fear, grief, resignation.

"I guess I thought it would be easier for both of us if we forgot about the Forest—if we could just let it go."

Her face has so many more lines on it than I remember, and her hair is shot through with more white. I should tell her it's okay; I should tell her I forgive her, but I can't. If there's anyone in this world who I should be able to trust it's my mother, and that makes it all so much more painful.

She thumbs through the pages of the book, fanning out the corners. I know she's waiting for me to say something but I don't know what and so I stay silent.

She heaves a deep breath and holds it. "I'm going back into the Forest, Gabrielle."

"What?" I say before the word even forms in my mind, a thousand protests behind it. "Why? How? I don't—" I can't even find the way to ask the questions and I shake my head. Suddenly the idea of losing her starts to seep through me and I swallow bitter uneasiness.

She places a hand on my leg, curling her fingers over my knee. "It's what I have to do, Gabry," she says. "Last night I thought about you and everything you said and you're right. I should not have let them go that easily—should not have let the past go."

I can't even process what she's saying because I'm too wrapped up in trying to figure out what this means for me, for the lighthouse and Catcher and my future.

"What about me?" I ask, my voice sounding small and hollow.

She turns and looks at me, her eyes bright against the pale of her cheeks. "I want you to come with me."

I can't help it—I leap up, pushing from the bed and backing toward the window. "No," I tell her, shaking my head. "No," I say again, sure of my answer.

"Gabry—" I know she's going to try to convince me and so I cut her off.

"I can't, not into the Forest. No." I wipe my fingers over my sweat-slicked upper lip, fear burning through me. "It's too dangerous. It's off-limits. It's full of Mudo!" My voice escalates as I pace the room.

My mother just sits on the bed, her face and body not betraying her emotions, which infuriates me even more. I've lost too much recently; everything's changed too fast and I can't take this—not now. I need my mother, her support and love and help and protection.

"You can't go," I tell her.

"Gabry—" This time her voice holds a hint of a warning but I don't heed it.

"No, the Council—they'll find out. They'll punish you, and what will happen to the lighthouse? What will happen to me?"

She stands up and walks over to me, placing her hands on my shoulders. I want to pull away but I don't because her touch feels too much like when I was little and needed her reassurance. "The Forest is safe enough, Gabrielle. I've been through it twice and I can do it again. The trick is just the first part—running from the gate over the waterfall to the path a few hundred yards in. I know you, Gabry, and I know you're strong enough to do this."

I want to tell her yes, I want to give in and follow her orders. To let her lead me and just blindly follow. But I think about Catcher and Cira and I can't do it.

"Why?" I ask her, the pain I'm feeling lacing around the word, infusing it.

"I have to know what happened to them," she says simply.

"But it's been years," I tell her.

She shrugs. "I shouldn't have given up on them. I shouldn't have stopped hoping. I should have done something." She pauses and looks past me. "I just have to know, one way or another."

“And so you’ll leave me—abandon me—to find out? To risk your life? What about me?”

“This is why you should come with me—we can find out about your past too,” she urges.

I shake my head. “No, not into the Forest. I can’t.”

“But the Forest doesn’t have to be dangerous—”

“You’re the one who taught me to be afraid of the Forest!” I shout at her, letting go of any restraint or reserve. “All my life that’s what you told me—beware of the Forest of Hands and Teeth! You told me that it’s nothing but death and desperation!”

“I wanted you to grow up safe, Gabrielle,” she responds pointedly, “not scared.”

I stare at her. I couldn’t have been more shocked if she’d slapped me. And my words are designed to cut her just as deep: “Whose fault is that?” I ask, crossing my arms over my chest and raising one eyebrow.

We stare at each other, both of us breathing hard as if we’ve been physically fighting.

From the main room downstairs I hear the little bells chiming that high tide is near, the signal for my mother to start her patrol. She walks to the door and looks back at me.

She tries again to convince me to go with her into the Forest but I don’t give in. I tell myself that I can’t leave Catcher or Cira but I know the reality is that I’m too scared. And I know I can’t tell her this because I don’t know if she’s ever felt fear like mine.

“Please think about it, Gabry,” she says. “After I clean the beach I’ll come back and we can talk about it more.” She touches the doorjamb as she leaves, automatically rubbing her fingers over the words etched there—a line from one of

Shakespeare's sonnets. I turn away from the familiar, screaming inside. Then I hear the echo of her steps as they disappear down the stairs.

"I can't," I tell the empty room. I wish I were strong enough, as strong as my mother. But I'm nothing like her. When she was my age she had her entire life wrenched away; she spent years trying to find safety. All I've ever known is security and I'm too terrified to give it up.

▼ ▼ ▼

Pounding wakes me up and for a minute I think it's just my head throbbing from sleeping too long in the heat. I stare groggily at the walls of the lantern room, at the fresh etchings of another Shakespearean sonnet my mother carved into the low walls last night while I was gone. I think about her asking me again to come with her into the Forest and how I refused again. I'm still shocked and amazed at my own ability to say no.

With bright eyes she told me that all I had to do to find her was follow the light and then she walked away and I watched her go through the binoculars before falling asleep outside on the gallery.

I hear more pounding and realize belatedly that it's coming from downstairs. In an instant I wonder if it's my mother, if she's given up on going into the Forest and come home. Hope blooms in me hot and fierce and I sprint down the steps to the main door.

When I throw it open, though, it's Elias. The sun glares behind him and my sleep-slowed mind struggles to figure out what's going on. "Elias, what are you do—"

"On the beach," he cuts me off, pointing over his shoulder

and gasping for air. I look past him and see them: the bloated bodies of the Mudo washed ashore, a few of them already sensing us and struggling to stand.

From inside the house I hear the insistent chime of the bells signaling the tide change. I've been so used to hearing them, so used to my mother being the one to answer their call, that I didn't even recognize the sound. I wipe my hand over my face as the enormity of my mother's abandonment settles in. Even though she told me she'd return in a few weeks I feel her absence like a permanent ache.

Her duties have fallen to me and I've already failed.

"Here," I say, grabbing a sharp-bladed shovel from a rack by the door and thrusting it into his hands. He turns and runs back to the water, his motions practiced and sure as he begins to decapitate the Mudo. He kills two in quick succession, leaving two more, who stumble toward him. He thrusts the blade against the knees of one of them and I hear the snap of bones breaking. He swings the shovel at the other, smashing its head, then stands over it to sever the neck.

I grab another shovel and stride out onto the beach next to Elias. He doesn't say anything as I approach a Mudo lying twisted where the waves abandoned her.

I don't take the same care my mother did when I decapitate the Mudo. I don't want to think about them as anything other than monsters. I refuse to wonder about where they're from and how they ended up here. I can't let myself imagine families missing them, how they died, who they once were.

I'm just content to end their misery. End their infinite hunger. The same thing I'll have to do for Catcher when the time comes—something else I refuse to think about now.

My arms shake when I'm done with the last Mudo and the

waves tuck the decapitated bodies back into their depths. The late-afternoon sun makes everything harsh, the heat over the water breaking the light into a million colors.

Elias drives his shovel into the sand, propping his arms on the handle. Sweat gleams on his skin, traces the lines of the muscles along his shoulders where the short sleeves of his tunic are tucked up.

I should thank him for waking me up. For helping me clear the beach, because I'm not sure I could have done it alone. "What're you doing here?" I ask instead, trying not to wince at the confrontational tone of my voice.

XIV

Elias rubs a hand over the back of his neck. "You're welcome," he says, sighing, and I narrow my eyes at him.

It's somehow different to be here with him in the daylight, as if it was easier to talk when the darkness masked more of our faces and emotions. I dig my foot into the beach, spiraling sand over my toes. I feel prickly and defensive, my skin tight with sunburn and my head pounding from dehydration.

"Thank you," I finally say.

"I was worried," he adds. I look up into his eyes, at the earnest kindness I see there. And it's that small bit of tenderness that's my undoing. It makes me realize how alone I am here. How Elias might be the only person who was thinking about me—worrying about me.

Suddenly I'm overwhelmed thinking about the empty lighthouse. All the empty nights that stretch ahead of me: alone. The only person between the ocean and Vista. My eyes tear up.

"What's going on, Gabrielle?" he asks. "Is everything okay?"

I stare down at my feet, at the way the water pools around my toes, and nod. But the word that leaves my lips is "No."

He shifts, as if suddenly uncomfortable. "The tide should carry away the Unconsecrated," he says. "The beach should be safe for a while."

"My mother always called them Unconsecrated too," I tell him, watching a wave slip over the chest of a dead Mudo. "She grew up in the Forest. She . . ." Memories flood me, choke me. Her stories crowding around my mind, blurring together. I want to tell him that I'm from the Forest also but I can't find the words. "She . . ." I start again, but nothing comes.

Finally I let my shoulders drop. "She's gone," I say. "She went back into the Forest and I let her go without me." My voice feels hollow.

He doesn't move, just stands there staring out at the horizon.

"She's gone. My best friend and everyone else my age I knew are all being held and are about to be handed over to the Recruiters. And Catcher . . ." I almost choke on his name. "He'll be gone too. Everyone will be gone and I'll be alone," I tell him. Admitting it makes the fear seem real and it squeezes at me.

Sand shifts under my feet as he closes the distance between us. I feel his hands in my hair and then he pulls me to him. I resist at first but then I realize that Elias is the only one I have left right now. He's my only ally. I'm not sure if I should trust him, if I can trust him, but I feel as though I have no other choice unless I want to be utterly alone and I'm not sure I can handle that right now. If I can stand losing everything so quickly.

He holds me tight, his hand pushing my cheek against his shoulder as if he can keep my shattering pieces together. As if he understands what's happening to me. I don't want the feeling to go away.

"Please don't go back," I beg him. I think of the darkness, of being alone in the lighthouse with the night closing in. "Please don't leave me alone here. What if more wash ashore? Please stay."

His voice cracks when he answers. "I can't, Gabry, I'm sorry."

"Please," I whisper. I don't want to be alone, am not sure I *can* be alone. I never have been before—the thought of it terrifies me.

"You're the only one I have left," I say, looking up at him. I let him see my pain and vulnerability, hoping that he'll realize how much I need him. How much I'm begging to trust him. I feel naked in this moment and I almost think he'll say yes, his face betraying his emotions. But then he turns his gaze back to the ocean.

"I'm sorry," he croaks.

I take a deep breath, wondering why I ever allowed myself to trust anyone in this world. How much easier it would be if I didn't care.

For a heartbeat I wonder if this was my fate when I was left in the Forest as a child, after I was lost and before my mother found me. If this helplessness and solitude has been so ingrained into my life that it's all I can aspire to, all I should expect.

I survived then, I must be able to survive it now. I have no other option.

I stare into the side of Elias's face and can sense his hesitation in the way he holds his body so tight. I feel his conflicted emotions heavy in the air between us but also his resolution.

There's nothing I can say or do to keep him here. He'll leave just like everyone else. I feel stupid for even having asked him to stay. He's a stranger—someone I barely know. Someone who clearly has as little reason to care about me as I do about him.

And so I push softly away from him, letting go of his comfort and warmth, and walk back into the lighthouse, leaving him behind to stare at the waves.

It's cooler inside the lighthouse, the darker air a refreshing change as I climb the stairs. The door to my mother's room is cracked, slants of light soaking the scarred boards of the landing. There's a single bed pushed against the far wall under the window; it's neatly made up, an old faded quilt stretched taut across it.

The sun glares through the window, the stretch of water the only thing beyond. Leaning against the pillow is a photograph of my mother and me. We're standing in the ocean; she's behind me with her arms wrapped around me. I'm just a child, laughing as the waves crest around us.

I remember when it was taken. An old man with an even older photobox had come to Vista willing to trade housing and food for a photograph. The town wanted to turn him away but my mother took him in.

He stayed with us a week, snapping two photos on the last day. I remember the water was cold, the tide quick and waves tall. But I was safe and warm in my mother's arms. If I look closely I can see the shadows that haunt her face. As if she is lost in that picture, lost in the blur of water and sky and I am the only thing holding her firm.

Beside the photo is the book my mother was holding this

morning when she asked me to go with her into the Forest. I pick it up, run my fingers along the edges, wondering if I can still feel the heat of her touch.

I sit on the bed, the mattress sinking under my weight, and flip through the book, the words on the page as familiar as walking.

When I was a little girl my mother took a knife and carved bits of the poems into the doorjambs of the lighthouse, spots she always touched with her fingers when she entered or left rooms. I asked her once why she did this but she's never been able to explain it to me. I think about the one she carved into the lantern room last night, of her reminding me that the light will always take me home.

And I wonder if she's out there now, waiting for that light to appear on the horizon, showing her that I'm strong enough to move forward without her even though I'm not sure I am.

▾ ▾ ▾

Though I've been dreading it, I go to visit Cira at the end of the day. The Council moved everyone into the jail in the basement of the Central Hall, and the Militiaman standing guard says nothing to me as I walk down a short flight of stairs into a closed dank room divided in half by thick vertical bars.

A few families press against the bars, their fingers twined around the hands of their jailed children, eking out every moment together they can before being sent away. I have to stop when I see it. I swallow, the scene so similar to the Mudo pressed against the fence on the beach last night.

I want to run back aboveground but I force myself forward. Cira rushes to me, laces her fingers through the bars. "Catcher?" she asks, breathless with anticipation. Her eyes are bright, her cheeks pink. So hopeful and alive. "Did you find him? Is he okay?"

How did I not prepare myself for this? How did I not think of a lie, think of some way to break this to her? But in my silence she understands, her face slipping into despair. "No," she whispers. "No."

"I found him." I lean in close so that those around us can't hear. "He's in the ruins past the amusement park."

Hope flashes through her and I shake my head. "He's infected, Cira."

She stumbles back. A few of the others crowd around her. Blane takes her hand and Cira leans in to her. They glare at me.

I realize then that she's not mine anymore. That we've taken two separate paths and they'll never join again. She's with them, she's with the others bound for the Recruiters. And I'm left behind. The one who ran away.

Just two days ago she was the one I would have told about my mother's revelation about where I came from. The one I'd have gone to after my mother left for the Forest. Together we would have figured out what to do, how to move on. Two days ago she was my best friend and not a stranger.

I want the feeling back again. That feeling that there's someone in the world who knows me as well as I know myself. Someone who won't let me go through all this alone.

"I'm going back to see him," I tell her, stepping forward, needing her to hope. "I promised him I'd be there."

Her eyes are red-rimmed. Everything about her is limp, as if she's already given up and those around her have to keep her standing.

She looks thinner than before, even in only two days, and

her skin is gray from being locked inside. "Cira, are you eating? Are they bringing you food and water?"

She doesn't respond. Just stares through me as if I've disappeared. I wait for her to say something. I look toward Blane, pleading with my eyes. "Is she okay?" I ask her.

Her hatred is palpable. "What do you care? You're the one who left Cira behind," she says. "You're the one who doesn't know what it is to be a friend."

I press my lips together and focus on the floor where cracks spider-web through the concrete. I try to take a deep breath but I'm too shaky. I want to tell Blane that I tried to get Cira to come with me, I tried to get her to run away as well. But the words taste bitter in my mouth because I know I could have tried harder.

I blink rapidly, praying that I don't cry in front of this girl. "Please make sure she's okay," I finally say. She nods before turning away, leading Cira toward a bench against the far wall.

I stand there a little longer, a small part of me hoping that Cira will look up at me. That she'll see my pain and come and take my hand and tell me what's wrong. But she just folds in on herself, taking a cup of water from Blane with shaking fingers but not drinking.

Finally I slink back through the door and up the stairs, leaving my best friend behind.

XV

Everything seems muffled as I walk back home to the lighthouse. The sounds of the town, of people constructing platforms and erecting decorations for the arrival of the Recruiters. Even the feel of the late setting sun is dull against my skin.

At the beach the waves are sluggish, unable to budge the carcass of a large decapitated Mudo on the sand. But when I step into the house it's as though everything sharpens into focus and the air is alive with the sound of emptiness.

And then it hits me with full force: My mother is gone. She's left me. Our conversations from last night and this morning spin around me in the silence, piercing against my skin and boring into my skull. I'm the one who convinced her to remember. I'm the one who told her that forgetting is useless.

I'm the reason she's gone. She could be hurt out in the Forest. She could be Infected and it would all be my fault. Because I made her go alone, too scared to go with her.

I press the palms of my hands into my eyes and bend over, a wave of nausea rising in my throat. I'm so tired of feeling useless and weak and alone. I'm tired of messing up and putting the people I love in danger.

I'm tired of being afraid, of allowing fear to hold me back. I clench my fingers into fists. I have to find Catcher. I have to talk to him, explain what's happened and ask for his help.

Elias's face flashes in my mind, the memory of him holding me this morning prickling along my arms and legs. But I force those feelings away and try to remind myself that he's a stranger. That he turned me down when I needed him. He doesn't know anything about me and never will.

Strapping the knife Elias gave me around my hip and slamming the door to the lighthouse behind me, I stride to the beach. I don't care what the risks are: I promised Catcher I would be there, and I need him as much as he needs me.

But when I look at the rack where we stored the boat last night, I realize that it's empty.

Elias must have taken it when he left, and with it the only way for me to get back to the ruins safely. I want to scream out my frustration at how everything seems to be falling apart so quickly and there's nothing I can do to keep up.

I kick at the sand but the wind throws it back against me, biting at my skin. I race to the waves and am up to my thighs in the water, my heart pounding, when I realize where I am and what I'm doing. There's still a whiff of daylight, sunset blinking on the horizon.

I gasp when I think about it. Can I really do this? Can I really swim my way to the ruins, to Catcher?

The idea tantalizes me, makes me believe I can be strong and invincible. But I know that if I spend any time thinking about it or reasoning through I'll never do it. I'll find a thousand reasons why this is stupid, why I should turn back.

I push deeper into the ocean. I promised Catcher I'd come back. I promised him I'd be there. He wouldn't be infected if I'd been able to kill Mellie. If somehow we'd been able to stop the Breaker earlier none of this would have happened.

I slice my arms through the water, my feet lifting away from the bottom. I try not to think about the darkness creeping in, about the dead that could be in the depths. I try not to think about what I'm doing.

One thought pushes me forward: Catcher. I must get to him before he turns. I can't let him die alone and turn into a Mudo. I can't stand the idea of him becoming a monster. With the world spinning and unraveling around me, being there with him is the only thing I can control, the only thought that can ground me. I have to prove to myself I have the strength to follow through on this one thing.

What's the worst that can happen? I ask myself. There could be Mudo in the water that aren't downed. I could get bitten, infected and pulled into the deepest parts of the ocean, turning Breaker almost instantly. I sputter and press myself forward, tamping down fear that crawls up my throat, squeezing my lungs harder the farther away from shore I get. With my eyes closed the sea feels like an endless pit.

I pull back above the surface and start to swim, angling out to where I know the tip of the jetty should be, at the line of boulders that separates the town from the amusement park and ruins. I'm almost there when I feel something brush against my foot and I scream, choking on water.

Something like hair tangles in my hands and I rear above the surface. I try to rip my fingers free as I kick out at everything I can't see. My mind shrieks with thoughts of arms grabbing me, teeth sinking into my flesh.

I flail, beating at the water and pulling myself to the jetty, slipping on the slick rocks. I crawl over the jetty as fast as possible, gulping air. I look down at my hands, my arms shaking and heart screaming. Wrapped around my fingers are lengths of seaweed, glistening under the moon.

I glance down the jetty to where it meets the Barrier wall, tiny lights of the Militiamen flickering in the night. It won't be long until the patrol moves closer, until they'll be able to see my shadow hulking among the boulders.

Before I jump back into the water on the other side of the jetty I look behind me at the lighthouse etched in the darkness. I feel as if I'm leaving something behind. Something that I'll never be able to come back to. And then I realize that I've forgotten to light the lantern. I curse my stupidity and for a moment I consider going back. I think about my mother in the Forest; what if she looks to the horizon for the light? What if it's all she has to hold on to?

But Catcher's waiting. I promised him. And if I go back I know I'll never leave again and he'll be left to face his fate alone.

My chest tightens and I stop to take a calming breath. Then I slip back into the water, pushing myself toward the shore stretching in front of the ruins.

The beach is empty when I pull myself slowly from the waves, water trailing down my bare legs. A strong wind gusts behind me. I hover at the edge of the surf, waiting for the moon to shift from behind the cloud cover for better light and cocking my ear to try to hear any moans over the rush of water.

The Mudo from last night are gone, the beach quiet, and I

slowly make my way toward the dunes, my feet sinking into the warm sand as I pull Elias's knife from my belt. Still no Mudo.

I reach the seawall and climb the boards, which are worn smooth from the highest tides crashing against them. Once I'm on the other side the streets of the ruins stretch ahead of me like a labyrinth and suddenly the confidence and drive I felt earlier disappear entirely.

The night air glides over my arms, brushing against the water droplets and causing my skin to prickle. Doubts crowd around me and I can't force my feet forward. I stand unmoving and stare down the cracked road, a fine coating of sand brushed over it.

"You can do this," I say aloud, my voice sounding hollow and out of place among the decayed buildings. I think about Catcher. I think about what Cira would do if she were here and I reach under my shirt and grasp the plastic superhero figurine she gave me. She'd never be afraid—she'd charge ahead in search of her brother.

And so that's what I do.

▾ ▾ ▾

I take a few wrong turns searching for Catcher's building, the streets and rubble beginning to blur together. In my head the route through the ruins is so clear that I felt certain I'd remember how to get back to him.

And yet at every intersection and every turn I find myself second-guessing and I'm fairly sure I've gone in more than one circle. My damp clothes feel heavy on my body, the drying salt causing me to itch and my skin to feel tight.

I'm standing in the hollow between two crumbled buildings, trying to figure out which way to go next and wanting to kick the nearest wall in anger, when I hear a soft sound on the breeze, a hint of something mingling with the crickets and my own heartbeat.

I hold my breath, straining to hear, wondering if maybe it's Catcher, as the sound resolves into a song, the voice bright and clear and definitely a woman's.

Tilting my head, I try to figure out the words of the song and even start walking toward it before I stop myself. By then I make out an underlying beat to the music and at first I think it's a drum, that maybe it's the Recruiters making their way down the long road to Vista. Then I realize that it's not a drum, it's feet walking, and it's not coming from the main road but from much much closer.

My body tenses in worry, wondering who else could be out in the ruins. A part of me wants to run to them, seeking safety in numbers, but a larger part urges caution.

The thrum of people walking grows louder and I realize that they're very nearby. Quickly I cast my gaze around, looking for a place to hide. There's a small cave created by a half-fallen wall and I scramble toward it.

I pause at the entrance. The moon is high tonight, its light almost as bright as that cast by the lighthouse, but the little nook is dark and I have no idea what else could be hiding inside.

Then I sense movement and I whip my head around to see someone turning the corner up the street. I slip into the darkness, clutching my knife tight, and squeeze back as far as I can, trying not to scream as I feel something small scuttle over my ankle.

The singing grows louder, bouncing between the walls of the old street, the pounding of footsteps closer and closer and closer. Sweat and salt water drip down my neck. And then I see the feet passing by, the hems of white tunics falling to their knees over dark pants.

Just like what Elias wears. Absently I wipe at my lips with my hand as I try to figure out what's going on—who these people are and what they're doing out here. Wondering if Elias is with them. I hold my breath, hoping they won't notice the dark puddle of water where I was standing earlier or the trail of damp ground leading to my hiding place.

They shuffle past, the song still twining among them, and growing muffled with distance. The concrete digs into my knees; my legs are sore from being so scrunched up in this little hole. Carefully I ease my head out into the moonlight and gaze down the street. They're gone, the ruins now empty of everything but echoes.

I look the other way, the calm neglect of the ruins settling back over everything. I wonder if Catcher heard them, if he's standing at his window watching the strange group weave through the streets.

Slowly I crawl out of my hiding place, keeping to the shadows. I sneak around the next corner, the sound of the singing always ahead of me. I look around, trying to find something familiar to lead me to Catcher's, but I know I'm lost.

It would be easy to find the ocean again—just retrace my route through the streets with the rise of the coaster to my right. But I'm not ready to face the waves again. I took a risk coming here to see Catcher and I'm not willing to give up so fast.

I stop in the hollow of a broken doorway. In front of me is a huge empty expanse of concrete dotted with bushes and small trees growing from cracks. At the far end of the expanse is a large wall carved with thick stacked-stone arches. In the glare of the moonlight I can make out a large rusty sign hanging at an angle. Letters have worn out, leaving the words CHARLESBURG AMPHITHEATER barely readable.

Disappearing under the center arch is the trailing line of the singers, all in white tunics with shaved heads, just like Elias. I squint, straining to pick out details, but it's difficult to tell any of them apart at this distance with so little light. I'm surprised to see this many people out here in the ruins, surprised they could be so close to Vista and I wouldn't know anything about them.

But I realize that if I can find Elias among them, he can lead me to Catcher.

I wait several moments after they disappear into the amphitheater, until the night settles back into normalcy: cicadas buzzing and tree frogs humming. I clench and relax my grip on the knife, nervous. A few drops of water slide from my wet hair down my back and along my legs.

All I have to do is make it across the concrete expanse and into one of the arches, I tell myself. Just take the next step and then another. I force one foot forward, trying to crouch against the branches of trees and hulking mass of bushes.

I feel keenly every heartbeat, every thundering throb of warning, but I keep going. Slowly, as I get closer, I can hear the singing again. Hear the chant of deep voices.

I touch my fingers to the stones of the arch—not the one they walked through but another one off to the side. I slide underneath it, pressing into its shadows.

Beyond the arch is something I've never seen before: a long sloping depression, as if someone scooped out the ground a long time ago. Cut into the slope are terraces scattered with broken benches tangled in weeds. In the center of the bowl is a stage capped by a dome with no walls.

I shrink against the side of the arch, feeling the warmth of the stones through my shirt. The tunic-wearers still sing but then another noise reverberates around the grassy edges of the bowl: moans.

XVI

I jump to my feet, knife clutched tightly in my hand, and am ready to run when I realize that no one else is reacting. The people continue to chant and sing as they make their way down a crumbling set of steps.

Fear twists my stomach. Why aren't they running? Why aren't they grabbing weapons?

The line of people splits as it hits the bottom of the hill, climbing onto the stage, and that's when I see the Mudo swarming in the shadow of the dome.

I jerk my head back, slamming it into the wall of the arch with a thick thud. I grunt at the pain and then slap a hand over my mouth. My breathing is ragged but I'm terrified to move. Afraid someone will see me, that someone might already have noticed me. I shrink as deep into the shadows as I can, keeping myself frozen.

My eyes bounce around the scene. None of the people seem to care about the Mudo as they walk toward them. And then I realize that the Mudo aren't moving—they're reaching into the night, their fingers swiping at the air, but they're all stuck in place.

There's something terribly different about them. About the way they look and the pitch of their moans.

My stomach drops when I realize what it is. The Mudo aren't moving because they all have collars around their throats, chains and leashes keeping them stationary. And the people in the white tunics aren't worried about them because the Mudo are missing their teeth and the bottom of their jaws: They can't bite.

Which means they can't infect. Their faces are twisted, looking less human and more animal, but despite my disgust I find myself leaning forward to see them closer. The living walk among them as if they aren't even there, as if they're harmless—not the definition of death.

Suddenly the singing stops and silence pervades everything, tempered only by the hollow moans. I'm afraid that any movement will give me away and so I stand stuck in the curve of the arch, staring. I scan their faces, trying to find Elias, wondering if the man who saved me could be here—be a part of this.

Last night in my dream his face was so vivid, so unique. But now with so many men and women and boys and girls wearing white tunics with their heads shaved, they start to blend together. They all blur in the light of the moon.

The Mudo squirm against their restraints, pushing to get closer to the living flesh. There must be more than a dozen of them, their moans raspy and reedy. And yet the people leading them look unconcerned at the way death lunges for them.

Suddenly it's clear who these people are. We learned in school about cults, about the crazy religious group called Soulers who worship the Mudo. Who lead them around like pets. I imagined them as crazed loons with long stringy hair, running around half naked. Not like this: not ordered and sedate and almost normal.

Not like Elias. He killed the Mudo last night—I watched him drive his knife into the skulls of every one of them. He wouldn't have done that if he worshiped them, would he?

But why else would he be dressed like them? Why would he be in the ruins at the same time they are? What if he believes in what they do? Questions bombard me until one thought hammers into my mind: Elias knows where Catcher is. What if he's just waiting for Catcher to become Mudo? What if he's then going to turn Catcher into one of the jawless?

Panic sears my throat. I have to get away from them. I have to find Catcher and warn him.

But just then I hear someone speaking, her voice bright and sharp as she walks up the pathway leading directly toward my hiding spot. I close my eyes, hold my breath. My body screams to run but I'm terrified they'll see me. I peek through my eyelids. She stops about twenty feet in front of me and turns back to the stage, every eye on her.

It would just take one person to glance up above her, to squint into the shadows of the arch and see me. I barely breathe—even try to will my heart to stop pumping, afraid that the pulse on my neck will give me away.

The woman speaks of God and the promise of resurrection, her words cutting through the air. A young boy who looks to be twelve or thirteen steps out of the crowd, his body lean and lanky. His tunic is whiter than the others, a little tight along his shoulders. His fingers flutter over red ribbons wrapped around each wrist, clenching and unclenching and twisting as though he can't control them.

Two men separate themselves from the group of Soulers and walk to the back of the stage. When they reappear they each hold a pole attached to a collar around a Mudo woman's throat. Her mouth opens and closes; her intact jaw snaps at the air, her teeth bright in the moonlight. I swallow. This one isn't harmless like the others. This one can bite and infect. Tears blur my vision and I press my cheek to the stone wall.

They hold the Mudo woman tight, chains digging into her neck and sinking into her dead skin as she struggles against her restraints.

The other Soulers in the circle kneel and bow their heads, their faces now hidden from me. All except the boy with the red ribbons around his wrists, who stands and faces the Mudo biting at the air.

It's my chance to run, to tear away into the night, but I can't force my legs to move. Only to slowly allow myself to slip down the wall until I'm pressed against the ground, the horror of what's happening trapping me here.

The Souler woman still stands in front of me calling out orders. Someone hands the boy a sharp knife and I wonder if this is a kind of archaic sacrifice we weren't told about in school, a symbol of defeating death by killing it in an elaborate ceremony.

The boy stands and stares at the Mudo so long that a few of the Soulers shift and raise their heads. But then he lifts the blade and the moonlight flashes off the design etched into the metal before he draws it along his own skin.

I shudder and gasp. Blood streaks down the boy's arm, the Mudo surrounding him writhing at the scent of it. He clenches his fist, red drops falling from his knuckles. He lets the knife slide from his hand and fall to the stage.

And then he steps forward into the Mudo's waiting arms.

I feel the scream building inside me, tearing along my veins. Pain radiates from my bottom lip as I bite into it to keep silent, my chest heaving as I try to swallow.

The Mudo lunges, grabs the boy and pulls him toward her. He willingly obliges, stepping closer to her snapping mouth. The Mudo's teeth rip into the boy's flesh along his neck but he doesn't pull back. I watch as he tries to keep his mouth locked shut but he can't and a tear glides down his face as his body crumples in pain.

The Soulers around him vibrate with excitement, some rising to their feet as the Mudo bites and bites and bites until the boy finally stumbles back.

The two men force the Mudo to the ground and someone slips a mallet into the boy's hands as he drops to his knees next to her. Even from here I can see that he's in shock. His chest rises and falls rapidly, his arms shaking. He struggles to lift the mallet and bring it down against the Mudo's jaw. He can't put much force behind the swing but the weight of the mallet head does its job and I hear the crack of teeth and bone.

Even that doesn't stop her moaning, but now bits of teeth fly from her mouth as she works her jaw and the boy wipes his face on the sleeve of his now blood-drenched tunic. He sways back, placing his hands out to brace himself, but his arms have no strength and he collapses.

The woman who'd been standing in front of me runs down the hill and jumps onto the stage, falling onto her knees next to him. She pulls the boy into her lap, his blood seeping around them both.

She takes a collar and slips it around the boy's neck. Then she folds him in her arms, squeezing him in a desperate embrace. Her voice is soft but I can still hear it on the wind up the hill. "You'll live forever now," she says, her face wet with tears.

I can't believe what I've just watched, even as the sounds and images cycle through me. My body and mind revolt and I scramble away from the shadow of the arch. I'm not careful enough with my movement and just as the boy's head snaps up, his jaw working and a moan rumbling from his lips, I drop my knife and it clatters to the ground.

My heart seizing with fear, I glance at the Soulers—wondering what they'd do if they found me here spying on them, if I'd also be sacrificed. But no one runs toward me or calls out. All their attention is focused on the boy who's just turned. They struggle to attach a leash to his collar as he reaches and stumbles for the living around him.

I'm letting out a breath of relief and am picking up my knife when I notice that one of the Soulers isn't facing the boy. Instead his eyes are trained directly on my hiding place. It's Elias, and for a split second I think maybe he hasn't seen me or that even if he has, he'll let me go. But he breaks away from the others and walks quickly through the tall grasses in the overgrown aisles.

I turn and run, bolting from my hiding place and plunging into the ruins. I don't bother looking back but I can already hear the footfalls of him coming after me.

I have a head start but Elias is stronger than I am. I race through the ruins, not paying attention to which way I'm going, just keeping the rise of the amusement park to my right so that I know I'm headed to the ocean. Sometimes I hear his footsteps behind me, slamming against the ground as he chases after me. "Gabry, wait!" he calls, and hearing his voice makes me run faster, harder.

All I can see is the boy, the way he let the Mudo bite and infect him. It's unforgivable that they let him make such an awful choice. That Elias just stood there and watched. He was a child!

Elias catches me as I reach the seawall, his hand grabbing my foot as I launch myself over. I kick out and feel my heel connect. I need to run, I need to get away. I need to get back to the lighthouse and crawl into my bed and figure out what I saw tonight.

I struggle over the wall and fall to the sand, stumbling when I hit the ground. I hear the thump of him landing next to me and before I can stand he rolls on top of me.

His body presses mine into one of the dunes and we both wheeze, our chests competing for space as we gasp for air. I'm nothing but blind panic. Then my body explodes. As if this is the end, as if I'm drowning and this is my last chance to break free to the surface. I thrash against him, kicking my legs and beating at him with my arms.

I try to scream and this time Elias clamps his hand over my mouth. I try to bite him, feel my teeth sinking into his fingers, but he only winces and tightens his grip until I relax my jaw.

His body's heavy on mine, crushing me. I feel his lips against my ear. "It's okay," he says.

"It's all right, Gabrielle," he repeats, as if I'll believe him if only he keeps saying it.

The scent of him so close invades my body, his skin slick against my own. I pause, holding my breath.

"You're safe," he adds.

I want to believe him. I want to trust him as I did last night. I want to let him keep me safe and make it better. But I can't. Not anymore. Not now that I know who he is. Not after what I just saw.

I turn under him until his face hovers over mine. The moon reflects off the edge of the dune nearby, casting shadows under his cheeks and curving along his jaw.

I stop struggling for just a moment and he eases his hand from my mouth. I lick my lips and can taste the remnants of his sweat. "You're a Souler," I say. "You're one of them. You let them—" I can't even finish the sentence because bile rises in my throat at what they did to that little boy.

I can't believe that the hands holding me now, the body that stood by as that boy willingly infected himself, belong to the same person who comforted me so easily this afternoon. Who was able to make me feel so safe.

"It's not that simple," he says, his eyes exploring my own as if he's hurt by my accusation.

"It is," I tell him. "You killed that boy. That little boy. You just stood there and let it happen." I shake my head, still unable to believe it.

I think about Catcher alone in a ruined building, waiting for infection to overtake him. I think about how Elias knew where he was. As if he was waiting for him to turn. Wanting him to turn.

"They're monsters," I say, barely giving voice to my words. I don't know if I mean the Mudo, the Soulers or both. And then I stare him directly in the eyes. "You're a monster."

"Let me explain," Elias says.

"No." His face is so close that I can feel the heat of his breath. "You made your choice," I add.

He opens his mouth to say something more but I don't give him the chance. I raise my knee as hard and fast as possible, catching him unaware. His eyes go wide as he sucks in his breath. He tries to grip my arm but I twist away from him easily, rolling past his grasp. I pull my knife from my hip, wrapping it tight in my fist.

"Gabry," he rasps but I don't turn back. I sprint down the

beach, cutting toward the water as fast as I can, careening into the waves. I glance back and see the flash of white, Elias struggling to his feet and stumbling after me.

I dive through the surf, paddling through the water as hard as possible. My breaths are ragged, my skin stinging with salt, but I push through the pain of it. When I finally reach the stone jetty my hands slip on the rocks as I try to haul myself out of the water. The pale dome of Elias's shaved head bobs as he swims after me.

For just a moment I hesitate. I'm surrounded by darkness, the fathomless water, the infinite sky, the lightless land. Nothing exists here; nothing is real. I think about falling back to the water, letting myself sink deep, letting the air seep from my body.

And then I jump from rock to rock until I'm on the other side of the jetty and dive back into the water, pulling myself toward the lighthouse.

Elias is a stronger swimmer, his strokes more even than mine. As I drag myself from the surf, letting the waves help shove me to shore, I know that he isn't that far behind. I push my hair out of my eyes and stagger up the beach to the lighthouse.

I pause at the door, leaning my head against it, trying to control my breathing. Water stings my eyes, the salt of tears and the ocean dripping from my chin. I feel more than hear the movement behind me and I pivot with my knife raised, expecting to find Elias.

But it's not him. It's another figure that limps from the shadows, dragging his bad leg through the sand.

"Didn't mean to sneak up on you," Daniel says, stepping closer.

XVII

I can't stop myself from glancing past Daniel to the edge of the waves where I see Elias creeping from the water. I can't face Elias, can't stand the idea of being near him. But I'm afraid that if Daniel sees him he'll find out I was outside the Barrier and I'll get into terrible trouble.

"I'm sorry," I tell Daniel, trying to smile and fumbling to put my knife back in the sheath at my hip. "I wasn't expecting anyone."

His grin is wide but his eyes narrow as he pulls himself closer, moving slowly. "Seems like an odd time for a swim," he says.

From the corner of my eye I watch Elias sneak up the beach. "It's an outgoing tide," I say, flustered, and step toward the door of the lighthouse. Daniel trails after me. "It's the safest time to see the stars." I swallow as Elias draws closer, so clearly visible.

I have to get Daniel away. "What brings you all the way out here at such an hour?" I ask, trying to distract him.

Daniel tilts his head. "I just thought I'd check on you," he says. "You seemed upset when I saw you at the Barrier last night."

Behind Daniel, Elias stops moving, drawing himself up a little straighter. He'd be stupid to let Daniel see him and yet he's not doing a good job of hiding. He just stands there, his hands hanging limp by his sides, staring at me. If Daniel turns around at all, even glances at the ocean, he'll see him.

I put a hand on Daniel's arm to keep his attention on me but he seems to take it the wrong way. He raises an eyebrow and I find myself fumbling for words.

"I'm rude to keep you standing out here in the dark," I finally say, pushing open the door behind me. "Please come in."

He looks at me for a moment and I feel the water trailing down my back and thighs. He smiles again as I step aside and walks into the lighthouse. I glance back at Elias. He's still standing there, the moon lighting his profile. His brow furrowed as if he's asking me a question I don't understand and don't know how to answer. I close the door, cutting us off, and lean my head back against it.

I want this night to be over. I want to be alone. I close my eyes and take a deep breath, trying to find some sort of peace and calm within myself. I'll keep Daniel occupied long enough that Elias will leave and then once Daniel is gone I'll finally be by myself. I just have to make it through the next few moments.

I paste on a smile and step forward.

Daniel walks around picking up items from the various shelves and examining them while I light a few lanterns. By the time the room is lit he's circled back to face me.

He stares at me as if waiting for something. It's like he knows something I don't and it unnerves me. I walk into the kitchen to find a cloth to dry my face and arms, then stoke the fire in the stove and place a kettle on top. Daniel walks up behind me and I try not to flinch at his nearness.

He reaches out and his fingers brush the side of my waist and then he's tugging Elias's knife from the scabbard at my hip. The muscles along my neck jump and I have to grab the edges of the counter to keep my hands from shaking. I don't like the feel of him being so close.

"This is interesting," he says, twisting the blade in the air, light sliding off the patterns. I can't tell if he's just casually noticing or prying for information. I let the air tighten with silence before I feel compelled to respond.

"Thank you." I squeeze past him and pull down two mugs, setting them by the stove. As casually as I can I unwrap half a loaf of bread and set it out as well, trying not to think about my mother kneading the dough, her essence everywhere.

He walks closer to me, angling the knife between us so the light bounces from the blade and into my eyes. I squint back at him.

"You know, I've only ever seen work like this once before," he says. "Very unique." He sets it on the counter next to me, his fingers brushing my own. "Of course, the one I saw was part of a pair. The pattern was such that when you held the two blades together there was an inscription: *Blessed and holy is he that hath part in the first resurrection: on such the second death hath no power*."

I try not to blink; I try not to show any reaction at all even though my fingers begin to tingle and my blood seems to hum. It never occurred to me that the patterns on the blade could mean something, could be the top half of letters.

"Ever heard it before?" he asks, raising an eyebrow.

I shake my head no, afraid that my voice will quaver if I try to speak, because I *have*. It was part of the song the Soulers were singing—they chanted it over and over again as the Mudo woman sunk her teeth into the boy. I shove a piece of bread into my mouth as an excuse to stay silent a moment longer.

Luckily the kettle begins to wail and I turn back to the stove, hiding my expression.

From the corner of my eye I can see Daniel shrug, then place a finger under the blade, testing its balance. "I wouldn't think so," he says. "It's a Souler expression. You remember learning about them, right?"

The bread is suddenly dry in my mouth, sticking to my cheeks and tongue. I shake my head.

"Crazy cult that sacrifices people to become Mudo. Believes it's the path to resurrection and eternal life." I turn to get a better look at what he's doing and catch him as he runs a finger along the sharp edge of the knife. "They go city to city trying to convert people. And if they ever came here . . ." He glances at me, drawing the weapon along an imaginary throat. "Odd that one just like it would end up with you," he says.

I'm pouring water from the kettle and my hands jerk, sloshing scalding water along my thumb and down my wrist. Before I can react he grabs a towel and takes my arm in his, drying it. His fingers linger over the puffy cut on my palm.

"I found it on the beach," I sputter. "The knife," I clarify. "Washed ashore."

"That doesn't look good," he says, his head bent over my hand ignoring my explanation.

"It's fine," I say, trying to pull away. I don't want to be

touched, don't want anyone to even be near me. I just want to crawl into myself and forget.

He glances up at me. "Your mother's pretty good with plant medicines. Doesn't she have something for this?"

He steps even closer, I can feel his breath; I can feel his skin and his smell and his want.

I drop the kettle on the counter, some of the hot water spilling out and dripping onto the floor by Daniel's foot. He steps back, reluctantly letting me go. "It's fine," I say again. Even I can hear the way my voice shakes.

He tilts his head a bit, a sharp look to his eyes. "Where *is* your mother?" he asks. He sticks the knife into the counter next to me, its tip barely digging into the wood. I take a step back from him, reaching for a clean towel from a drawer as an excuse to put distance between us.

"I noticed the lighthouse isn't lit," he says, moving closer. His voice is deeper and there's something about it that raises the little hairs along my neck.

I close my eyes, cursing myself again for leaving without lighting the lantern. Of course such an oversight would draw the Militia here. The Protectorate demands we keep the house lit even though traders haven't tempted the pirates in years.

"She's sick," I tell him. "I'll do it now," I add as I hurry out of the kitchen and up the stairs to the lantern room. I open the lamp and adjust the wick, my hand still shaking as I listen to the thump of Daniel following me, his bad leg slowing him down. My shoulders sag; I'm relieved to be alone even for just a small moment.

But being alone means my thoughts stray back to Elias and the Soulers. I scramble over to the windows and scan the beach below, making sure Daniel won't be able to see Elias if he happens to glance outside. Nothing moves in the darkness and I wonder if Elias is still out there, if he's looking up at me even now.

I shiver and glance past the Barrier into the ruins. Are the Soulers still out there? Is their sick ceremony still going on? I squint, trying to find the amphitheater, and I think I see a spark of light, a soft glow where they should be, and then nothing.

Daniel's steps grow louder and I turn back to the lamp and light it quickly, then busy myself with winding the gears.

He steps into the room and immediately the space feels too small. Too tight and too high. There's only one exit and his bulk blocks it. He holds the knife, the blade gleaming in the light.

I set the lamp spinning but Daniel's presence unnerves me and I'm distracted. The tip of my finger catches between the teeth of two cogs and I cry out at the sharp pain. The glare of the light sweeps over us, the brightness almost a physical force.

Daniel steps farther into the room and I skirt the lantern, pretending to examine another set of gears while my finger throbs.

He notices my mother's recent carvings on the low walls. Stoops to run his fingers over the first few words of the sonnet. "What's this supposed to be?" he asks. He's still gasping from the effort of climbing the stairs.

"My mother likes poetry," I tell him, refusing to look up. The gears click under my hands, teeth fitting against each other and then gliding away.

He glares up at me, straightening. "This is Protectorate property." The light slides over him and he's silent until I meet his eyes. I watch as beads of sweat trail from his forehead down his temples and along his cheeks to his jaw. My mother has carved pieces of sonnets into almost every doorway of the lighthouse; it never occurred to me she might get in trouble for it.

Before I can figure out how to respond he brushes a hand through the air. "The Recruiters are arriving the day after tomorrow. Hopefully your mother won't be too sick—or too busy defacing property—to show up with the other advisors. The Chairman's expecting her. He sent me to deliver the message personally. And to reprimand her for shirking her duty as the lighthouse keeper."

The light makes another sweep around the tiny room and slaps me in the face, piercing my vision. I close my eyes, the darkness an explosion of bright spots. Cira will be gone in two days. The Recruiters will be taking her and the others away. I should have been going with her. "Of course my mother will be there," I tell him. Hoping I sound convincing.

With my eyes closed I don't realize he's crept nearer until he wraps his hand around the railing next to me, his arm almost circling me. He's too close, there's not enough space. I can't breathe, can't even think. His chest presses against my shoulder, his mouth almost to my ear.

"Is your mother asleep?" he asks. And I can hear it all in his voice as my skin breaks out in goose bumps. Suddenly I feel helpless and trapped. I almost call out, hoping that Elias is still outside, that he can come to my rescue.

But then I remember how he left me alone to go back to the ruins. How he chose the Soulers over me. And thinking about the Soulers makes my stomach twist.

I need to get Daniel out of the house. I need to find a way to get him away from me.

His breath is hot on my neck, his body crowding me

against the glass. I turn my head away, cringing, but his hand grabs mine, his fingers digging into my palm. "Come on, Gabry," he says.

And so I do the only thing I can think of to get him to leave me alone. "I saw the Soulers," I tell him, my heart pounding.

He stops moving, stops pressing against me and I slip past him, stepping out onto the gallery. The air out here is so much cooler, not infused with the smell of Daniel and my fear. He comes after me quickly, his leg dragging over the grating of the floor and sending vibrations up through the metal railings.

"What are you talking about?" he asks, clearly suspicious. The light continues to spin, hitting us and then trailing away into the darkness. The wind whistles slightly as it shifts around the vent over the lantern room.

"Out there in the ruins," I tell him, gesturing past the Barrier. I try to step away as he moves closer but he pins me to the railing again, his chest pressed to my side, pushing his cheek into the crook of my neck so that he can follow where I'm pointing.

"I saw lights out there earlier." My voice is shaking and his flesh feels slick with sweat. "And during the day I think I saw movement through the binoculars—a group of people wearing white. It just occurred to me that it could have been the Soulers."

As he squints his body presses against me even more, the railing digging into my hips. The only way to move away from him is to lean out over the emptiness. If I tip a little bit farther, or if Daniel pushes slightly harder against my back, I could flip over the railing and fall into the nothing. I glance down at the beach so far below, wondering if Elias sees me. If he's worried about me or if he hears me telling Daniel about the Soulers.

My muscles tense, waiting to see if Daniel believes me. Waiting to see if he'll leave me alone. The one thing I know about Daniel is that he's always had more loyalty to the Militia than to anything else. He would do anything to make himself shine in the eyes of the Council.

He turns his head toward me, sweat from his cheek dripping onto my shoulder. "Excellent work," he says. "*If* you're telling the truth."

He pauses for a moment, his breath moist in my face. And then he just smiles, the light playing along his teeth. "Good night, Gabrielle," he says, before limping back into the lantern room and down the stairs. I hear the thump and drag of his bad leg, the thud of every step down the lighthouse, until the door closes below and he struggles back across the beach to the path through the woods toward town.

I allow myself to collapse onto the gallery floor, the wind licking cool along the back of my neck. Swallowing, I twist my fingers together in front of me until my knuckles glow white, trying to figure out what game Daniel's playing and what I should do next. Everything's happening too quickly. I just want to sit here and pretend that nothing has changed. But I know it's useless. Everything is changed. My best friend will be taken away. The Council will find out my mother's gone. And Catcher will die.

The only question is, what will be left of me in the end?

▼ ▼ ▼

When enough time has passed that I'm sure Daniel is gone I slip downstairs and outside into the darkness. The moon is disappearing beyond the town into the Forest and I feel the need to wrap my arms around myself even though the night is hot. I peer into the shadows looking for Elias and even try calling his name a few times, but he's gone.

I feel waterlogged and heavy as I climb back up to the lantern room and stand there for a moment, staring at the words of the sonnet my mother carved on the walls. I wonder where she is. If she's safe. If she's thinking of me.

Completely devoid of energy, I step outside onto the gallery and watch the beam of light cut through the night, illuminating the world around me. In the distance I look again for the pinpricks of the Souler lanterns but they're well hidden. I brush my hand over my face, weariness pulling heavy on every part of me, exhaustion from the day creeping in.

I wonder what Daniel will do with what I told him. If he's told the Militia and even now they're preparing to storm out the gate after the Soulers. I feel a slight twinge of responsibility, as if maybe I should have thought longer before saying something. But then I remember what that boy looked like, bloody and broken. I remember the sound of his moans.

Pushing the thought away, not wanting to deal with it now, I let my head fall back, close my eyes and feel the rush of wind from the ocean.

I finally understand what my mother meant about forgetting. About how much easier it is to let the pain slip away and fade into nothing. If I could forget today I would. If I could erase every moment I would do so happily and without hesitation.

XVIII

In my dream I'm sitting in my mother's boat. My back is cupped by the bow and the sail hangs limp, barely rustling in the soft summer air. All around me is nothing but waves marching endlessly away. I can't see land and I know I should be terrified but there's something about the rocking of the boat that keeps me comfortable and safe.

Sitting at the stern, his hand resting gently on the tiller, is a large man I've never seen before. But somehow I know that it's Roger, the man who cared for the lighthouse before my mother took over, the man who found my mother on the beach when she escaped from the Forest. He doesn't seem bothered by the lack of wind and just sits there, his other hand holding the limp damp line. A rusty-edged shovel sits in the hull of the boat between us.

"I'll pass it to you then, I guess," he says.

I blink at him, wondering how I can know what he looks like, how he sounds. "What do you mean?" I ask him.

"The light. The beach. They're yours now. If you'll have 'em."

My chest squeezes a little at the responsibility. I shake my head. "They're my mother's," I tell him.

When he smiles it's wistful, lines crinkling at his eyes from years squinting into the sun. "Nah, it was never hers. She wanted this." He spreads his hands out wide, wider than they should be, and skims them over the waves. "She just wasn't ready to let go of the rest. Wasn't willing to stop waiting."

I shake my head, trying to figure out what he means. "Waiting for what?" I ask him.

He looks at me as if expecting me to answer my own question. As if I should somehow already know what he means. "For everyone," he finally says. "For them." He points at the waves with his chin.

I look down into the water and that's when I see them dancing under the surface. The people. They stretch and glide and twist, just as Mellie did before she was infected. I pull back into the boat but it's not enough—I can't get away.

Their hands flutter under the water. I open my mouth to scream but it's laughter that comes out. I try to scream louder but I keep laughing and laughing. Roger leans his head back and laughs with me and I want to grab for him, beg for help, but nothing happens except the laughter.

The bodies in the water rise higher and higher, bubbles pouring from their mouths. When they pop to the surface it's not moans that I hear but whispers. Then their hands are reaching over the rails, are trailing along my skin. They pull me out of the boat and into the water and I wait for the teeth.

They slide their lips over my skin, whispering whispering whispering. They tell me their names, they tell me their lives, they tell me their pain. Roger stands in the boat and looks down at me, his face a shadow against the bright blue sky. I can't struggle, I can't stop laughing, I can't resist these people-who-once-were.

I wake up fighting to breathe and I realize that I'm still on the gallery and rain is crashing down around me. I pull myself into the lantern room, the memory of fingers grabbing me in the dream causing me to rub my hands over my body to erase the sensation.

Lightning streaks across the horizon, a spark in the heavy gray morning. I glance down at the beach, where the waves are already starting to churn. A storm usually means Mudo dredged from the ocean; it means more Mudo than I can take care of alone.

I just want it all to go away. I'm too tired. I don't want to deal with any of it anymore. Thunder reverberates under my feet and I sigh deeply. Pushing strands of dripping hair out of my face, I start making my way downstairs, not bothering to change into dry clothes before draping an oilskin poncho over my shoulders and trudging through town to ask the Militiamen for help clearing the beach.

In the center square, decorations hang limp in the rain—lanterns dripping and water pooling under brightly woven banners. The stage is draped with swaths of cloth in the colors of the Protectorate. The Recruiters' visit is always a cause for celebration for those who aren't leaving with them. It's Vista's chance to shine, to prove it still deserves its place in the Protectorate. But today it all looks muddy and soggy.

I skirt the activity, avoiding eye contact as I tug my hood low over my face and walk to the guardhouse by the gate. Daniel sees me before I get too close and he limps out to meet me, his mouth pulling into a slow smile. In the damp gray it's easy to forget last night, how dark his face looked as shadows crept about it when he leaned over me, Elias's knife gleaming between us.

"How's your mother, Gabrielle?" he asks.

I try to smile as well but I know it doesn't reach my eyes. "Better," I tell him. "Though with the storm coming in I think we'll need Militia help on the beach."

He nods and I think about my dream, about the whispers of all the dead. I tap my fingers against my leg with agitation. I wonder now if I shouldn't have told him about the Soulers. If I should have waited, given Elias a chance to explain it all to me.

"Listen—" I have to clear my throat before I can continue. "About the Soulers and what I said last night—"

Before I can go on he cuts in, his eyes gleaming. "You were right," he says, almost bouncing with excitement. "About what you saw from the lighthouse. It was the Soulers."

"Oh" is all I can say. He waits for my enthusiasm but I can't muster it. His eyes narrow.

He steps closer to me; only a few drops of rain are able to penetrate the space between us. "The Protectorate values loyalty," he says, his tone a little sharper. He feels too near and I drop my hand to my hip out of habit, a defensive stance.

He glances down and sees my fingers resting on the hilt of the knife. I know he recognizes it from last night: the Souler knife. He cocks his head to the side. "And to be honest, the Chairman's always questioned your mother's, since she's an outsider. Claiming to be from the Forest, no less."

His hand closes over mine, over the knife, and I try to pull away but he tightens his grip. I wonder if the other Militiamen are watching us, if they have any idea what Daniel's saying. I wonder what would happen if I called out to them, if I shouted for help. But I don't trust that they wouldn't just ignore me, leave me to Daniel's whim.

"There's no reason for the Chairman—or me—to doubt *your* loyalty too, right?"

I stare at his narrowed eyes. I never knew him that well growing up. He's older and was friends with boys who all left in the past few years to join the Recruiters. I've always wondered if being left behind because of his leg made Daniel angry, bitter against the Protectorate. I can't tell if his warning is because he's unquestionably loyal to the Chairman or because he cares about me.

A part of me wonders if I could tell him the truth. I want so badly to be able to trust someone and have them say that everything's going to be okay. I wonder if maybe I'm too suspicious of Daniel. But his fingers bite into my wrist and nothing in his expression betrays his emotions.

Just then there's a shout from the head Militiaman, Wesson, who's standing on a platform with a view over the Barrier. Daniel eases away, the tension between us popped like a bubble.

Militiamen begin to crowd around the gate as it grinds open, and Daniel steps in front of me, shielding me from the world beyond.

"What's going on?" I ask, but he's no longer focused on me.

"Stand back just in case," he says, placing a hand against my stomach to push me farther behind him.

More Militia begin to crowd around and I feel their agitation—it vibrates in the air. They clench weapons tight in their fists and stand poised on the balls of their feet.

The gap in the gate widens enough that over Daniel's shoulder I can see down the old road. I recognize them instantly: the Soulers. They're being led by a group of Militiamen from Vista, their black shirts soaked and the blades of their scythes and axes gleaming in the rain.

The Soulers walk slowly, purposefully. Each wears a white tunic. The hems of their pants and skirts are thick with red mud, and most of them are so thin that they seem almost emaciated, with gaunt cheekbones and sunken eyes. Even in the dull light it's easy to see how worn they look, how brittle their bodies appear.

They look nothing like they did last night, menacing in the dark shadows of the moon. Now they appear harmless and weak. Except for the Mudo they tug along behind them on rigid leashes.

I swallow against the tension buzzing along my arms as I scan the faces of the Soulers, wondering if Elias is among them. I feel stupid. I know I should want him to be captured, I should want him to pay for being part of a cult that could do what I saw last night. But I can't forget how gentle he was with me—how he saved me on the beach.

More Militiamen rush through the opening, crowding around the group and creating a chaos of shouts and moans.

Daniel spits on the muddy ground, still holding his arm across me, his flesh heavy against my body.

They're too far away for me to see if Elias is there, and my irritation is hard to hide.

"What'll happen to them?" I ask.

Daniel shakes his head. "They'll be quarantined," he says simply. "The Protectorate may allow the Soulers to go settlement to settlement preaching their filthy lies wherever they want, but it's *our* right to quarantine anyone seeking entrance to Vista."

As the Soulers draw closer even more Militia pour out of the gates, their weapons held ready. The sky vibrates with thunder and lightning. I stare at first the Soulers and then the Militiamen, the strain and tension of the moment filling the air.

One of the Soulers steps forward, an older man, slightly stooped, his eyebrows shot through with gray. Attached to his wrist is a rigid leash leading to a jawless and toothless Mudo.

"The Third Order of the Soulers begs entrance to your city, that we may spread the word of God and the truth of his salvation through resurrection." He spreads his arms wide as he talks, his tunic plastered to his skin. The movement jostles the leash and the Mudo he's holding stumbles slightly, reaching toward a Militiaman.

Daniel tenses in front of me and I cringe as everything seems to happen at once. The Militiaman swings his blade at the Mudo. A young Souler woman jumps forward to stop him. The Mudo moans, reaches, his jawless face dripping rain.

And the ax slices across the Souler's chest.

Blood seeps through her tunic, a spray of red. Everything's still for that moment. The woman wobbles. In her hand she holds her own leash, attached to a Mudo next to her. Her fingers go limp and the chain slips from her grasp.

I recognize her—she's the woman from last night, the one who held the boy as he turned. She's the one I wanted to rip to shreds for what she allowed to happen to him. But now, seeing her standing there with the blood, the disbelief in her eyes, everything changes.

She looks so different now. Frail where she was strong, round where she was sharp. She looks older, more hunched over, as if the weight of everything has finally grown too much. She collapses to the ground.

The scent of her blood hits the air and saturates the space around her. I know the instant it reaches the Mudo. They erupt, their moans high-pitched and fevered. They all stumble toward her and the Soulers try to yank at their chains to keep them at bay. They tug at their collars as if they might tear through the air, pull themselves to the woman.

The Militiamen explode, screaming and shouting. They swing at the Mudo, the Soulers begging and pleading for mercy, afraid that another one of them will be hit. The rain intensifies and people slip in the mud.

The Mudo the woman was leading is the boy who sacrificed himself. His teeth are gone, as is his lower jaw. And now that he's free, now that the chain is loose, he reaches for the woman.

If he had teeth he would devour her. But instead he just pushes himself against her, eternally hungry.

The Militiaman with his ax dripping blood swipes again, embedding the blade in the Mudo boy's neck, and he falls over the woman. She screams and clutches at him, the vision so similar to that of last night—but so horribly different.

Bile rises in my throat as I watch the woman reach for the Mudo boy's face. She shoves her fingers into what used to be his mouth, frantic, as if she might somehow infect herself before her injury takes her. I step back, wanting to run, wanting to get as far away as possible from what's happening. From the screams and shouts and moans and blood.

The Militia decimate the Mudo, decapitating them even as

the Soulers plead for them. The Militiamen push the Soulers away, forcing them to kneel on the ground. Everything's out of control and wrong.

"We're members of the Protectorate!" one of the Soulers shouts. His voice shakes as he cries out. "You're required to offer us protection! We've done nothing wrong! We're here for peace; we're here for God!"

No one listens. I should want the Soulers to pay for what they did last night but seeing them like this, weeping in the mud, I don't know what to think or how to feel. The woman who was hit with the ax falls slowly back until she's lying prone, staring at the sky with blood everywhere. The dead Mudo boy lies across her lap, his spinal cord severed at the neck.

In the chaos I look for Elias, terrified that he's in danger, unable to reconcile this feeling. I don't see him, though the Soulers have begun to look alike, covered in mud and streaked in red, rain dripping down their faces like tears.

"I don't understand," I say to no one.

Daniel finally steps away from me and joins the rest of the Militia massacring the Mudo. I know it's best; I know the Mudo are monsters and should be killed. But something about it feels wrong. The joyful savagery in the Militiamen's eyes . . .

This is my fault. I caused this. I told the Militia about the Soulers. Unable to watch anymore I turn and run back to the lighthouse, leaving everything behind.

XIX

By the time I get back to the lighthouse, rain is coursing in from the ocean, the waves rolling hard against the sand bringing more and more Mudo to the beach. It doesn't take long for the Militia to arrive, and I can feel the energy radiating off them from the recent confrontation. I try to avoid speaking with them, though when a few ask about my mother I tell them she's ill and in bed.

All seem to take me at my word except for Daniel, who just stares at me, the corner of his mouth turned up, his eyes narrowed. As the day wears on and patrols rotate off the beach to come inside and dry off, Daniel lingers the longest. But thankfully we're never alone together.

As Catcher's third night of infection nears, I refuse to even consider that he's turned. I can't stop thinking about him. I should be there—I promised him I'd be there—and I feel as though I've failed him again. The fear and worry roll through me like the thunder through the sky, until I have to get away from the Militia and from Daniel's curious stares.

I steal away for a moment, pretending a need to check the lantern, and I climb to the top of the lighthouse and lean out over the railings toward the ruins.

The wind whips my hair around my head, strands plastered to my face by the rain, and I'm instantly soaked. Of course I can see nothing—the encroaching night is only darkness and water. Out there somewhere Catcher is dying. And he's alone.

Unless Elias is there waiting. Planning to turn him into one of their jawless Mudo.

Guilt and anguish crush me, making me feel physically weak and ill. My heart is breaking. I should be there; I promised him I'd be back and I wonder if he knows it's the storm keeping me from him or if he thinks I've abandoned him. I want to sprint down the stairs and race to the Barrier. I want to dare the Militiamen here to follow me. To stop me.

But I don't. I can't help but think about Elias's words the other night—that if Catcher truly cared he'd forbid me to take the risk to see him again. I kick at the railing, pain thrumming up my toe, furious at Elias for making me question Catcher's feelings.

I press my hands to my face, not wanting to admit some small sense of relief about the storm. Glad that I have an excuse not to muster the courage to cross into the ruins again. Happy that I don't have to face those fears tonight.

I remind myself that some infected people make it longer than others. It's the end of his third day and the bite was small—Catcher has to have a fourth day. It's what I have to believe so that I don't crumble here to be washed away by the rain.

As the storm rages through the night I keep boiling water over the stove for the Militia; I make hot tea and fresh bread and I try to pretend that somewhere out there a man I might have loved isn't dying.

The Militiamen laugh. They slap one another's hands and talk about their kills, sometimes whispering rude things that I wonder if they intend for me to overhear. Daniel is the worst. It's like a holiday for them—rarely do they get to dispose of so many undead. Only the biggest storms dredge so many bodies up and toss them ashore.

I try to smile as the wind screams outside. I try to pretend that I'm like them, that I believe in what they do. That the Mudo are only monsters. But then I think about Catcher and all my beliefs haze at the edges. I can't think of him like that; I refuse to accept that he could be like the other Mudo and that some part of him won't remember me.

▾ ▾ ▾

The storm doesn't break the next day. If anything it intensifies. The Militiamen are even starting to look a little haggard. I pretend to make trays for my mother, brushing off any offers to help and polite inquiries into her health.

I carry the trays up the winding stairs into her room and I sit on the edge of her bed and I stare out the window into the storm-buffeted ocean, eating the food I prepared for her.

There's no way Catcher will make it through the night. I know this as well as I know that there will never be a world without the Mudo. I feel hollow when I think of him. More than hollow.

Catcher will die alone. In an empty room and in an empty city. He's the first and only boy I thought I could love, the first one who saw something in me worthy of attention. And I'm not sure I'll be able to find anyone like him again—someone I've known for so long that trusting him feels like breathing.

A knock sounds at the door and I drop the tea I've been cradling. The scalding liquid splashes down my leg, the mug shattering on the floor.

I can already see the knob turning, can hear my name on their lips. I jump to the door, press my body against it and then ease my way through a small crack, closing it behind me. I try not to show that my leg stings from the burning water. My upper lip is already sweating with the effort of appearing relaxed and casual.

It's Daniel, and I try to force out a smile that probably looks more like a grimace. He doesn't step back to allow me to pass and so I'm crushed against the door. I can't open it to give us space or he'll see my mother's empty bed and will know she's not here.

"How's your mother?" he asks, pretending he's just being polite.

"She's resting," I tell him, willing him to believe my lie. I feel off center up here alone with him, and unable to figure out why he's so intent on where my mother is. "All this noise, it hasn't been good for her."

He looks over my shoulder as if he's hoping to be able to see through the wood. He nods. "I'm sure," he says unconvincingly.

He doesn't move and I'm afraid to leave him here alone. Afraid of his obvious suspicion. "The others," I say, trying to appear calm and as though I'm not afraid of him. "They'll be wondering where we are. The coffee must be low, I should go tend to it."

Daniel smiles at me then, as if he's indulging my whims. "Okay, Gabrielle," he says. He stands there a moment longer, the air too heavy around us both. I can smell the beach on him, smell the Mudo. The scent tears at my throat, sinks into my stomach, and I feel sick. I want to shove him away, to tell him to leave me alone. But instead I just clench my hands by my sides.

Finally he turns and walks slowly down the stairs, leaving me gasping on the landing as if I'd never breathed before, my fists shaking and my fingers numb.

▼ ▼ ▼

Even though the sky clears that evening, the swollen waves still toss the Mudo against the shore, their bloated bodies like lost mounds on the beach. And so the Militiamen continue in their shifts, their pace less frantic but still as intense.

The lighthouse feels too close, too warm with all the men staying there. With Daniel and his glances and glares. I try to escape outside but they're there as well. Walking the length of the shore, their axes and sickles ready for the next body. As the light hazes they gather wood and try to light fires that struggle to ignite and then pop and crackle, throwing weak halos onto the sand.

I escape upstairs, excusing myself to tend to the lamp. I coax it to life, wind the gears but don't set it spinning just yet. I stare at the light wondering if Catcher will be alive to see it. Wondering if my mother will look for it on the horizon. Does anyone still care anymore about me and this light?

I drop the sliver of wood I used to light the lamp, its small flame fluttering through the air until it falls as a burning red ember. I've taken over my mother's life, I realize. And suddenly I imagine my entire existence unfolding in front of me, ruled by the chimes announcing the tides, measured by spins of the lamp.

I see it all: waves crashing and stretching, the sun swapping with the moon, blazing the horizon orange over and over again. The Forest tangles over the fences that are too old and too endless to maintain. The ruins crumble to nothing more than rubble, the coaster finally giving way to gravity as Vista gasps and chokes and tries to hold on until one day the lighthouse gears grind to a halt, no supplies from before the Return left to repair them. The Protectorate abandons the useless town that fades, forgotten, into the future.

And during all of it, at every tide, I'm here: standing alone on the gallery and waiting. For my mother, for the hope of Catcher and Cira. Every dusk I light the lamp that no one follows. Every high tide I decapitate the people-who-used-to-be—people like Catcher and Mellie—and I am safe and alone and old.

And there's no one waiting for me, no one who knows me. No one to share my life and experiences with. It's me and the ocean, the tides and the lighthouse and wave after wave folding time to the shore. Unlike Roger, there is no Mary to wash upon the beach. Unlike my mother, there's no child to rescue from the Forest.

And now I understand what drove my mother back into the Forest, only to find me. What made her keep me to stave off the endless empty horizon. What made her want to forget and ultimately what caused her to remember.

I'm suddenly aware of how little I know about my mother's time before me. I know she's from the Forest. I know she left her village, fought her way to the ocean. I know she's stronger than I could ever hope to be. That she created this life to raise me in the safety that she never felt growing up.

I know my mother loved but I don't know what it felt like, other than that it caused her to want to forget. I know she left Vista at some point—traveled to the Dark City and beyond—and yet something drew her back. But what about her dreams? What have I ever known about those?

It's as though my blood has reversed its flow and runs backward through my body, I feel so keenly the loss of my mother in that instant. I want to crawl to her and have her tell me that it will be okay. That I'll always be safe.

I want her to tell me that even though the world can change course in a week, it will always keep spinning and turning.

I trace my fingers over the gears of the lantern, the greasy teeth sliding sharp under my touch. I think about all the times my mother's hands rested here as she looked out into the world.

I realize now that I have my own decision to make: I can accept what I see. I can set the lamp to spinning tonight and every night after, safe within the barriers I've constructed around myself.

Or I can risk everything: run for Catcher and take of his last moments what I can. Open myself up to the possibility of failure and pain.

I stare at the rain gasping against the windows of the lantern room. I think about how different my life would be if I never crossed the Barrier that night. If when I sat on top of that wall with Catcher I'd pulled him back.

I wish I were stronger. I wish I were my mother. But I'm not. I set the light spinning, the harsh light blinding me with every turn, my heartbeat thumping with it.

▼ ▼ ▼

The Militiamen leave early the next morning. The beach is pristine, the sand smooth and clear. The waves are like ripples in a bowl of water. As if the world has not raged for the past two days.

It's always the strangest after a storm; how the world can be so dark and wind-whipped one moment, tossing Mudo endlessly ashore, and the next it's as if the Mudo never existed. As if the world spun backward in time to the pre-Return days.

I go and stand at the water's edge, let the saltiness lick at my toes. I think of walking into the tide, of just putting one foot in front of the other until it consumes me. I can see flutters against the surface at the surf line and I know the calm is just a mirage, that Mudo still tumble out in the depths.

The enormity of my decision last night crashes over me, the length and breadth of my life alone. I realize that I just want something to take into that solitude to hang on to: one last kiss from Catcher. One last embrace from Cira. Something to remind me that I could be loved, I could be a friend if I were willing to take the risk.

And then I start running. Away from the shore, through the fence and over the dunes. I sprint up the path through the woods, the air under the trees thick and humid. Once I reach the town I cut around the edge, everything a blur as I weave toward where Cira's being kept.

But I'm fighting against streams of people pouring from their houses and thronging toward the Barrier. They swell around me, the current too strong to resist and I'm carried along with them toward the main gate.

The Militia, some of whom were up all night at the lighthouse working on the beach, stand along the Barrier, tall and proud in their black uniforms. Their expressions are so sedate, so rigid and unblinking as they stand at attention, that it's hard to remember how they were over the past few days: dripping with rain, raucous as they shared bawdy jokes, telling tales of their kills. I pull strands of hair from my braid and let it fall into my face, hoping to avoid making eye contact with any of them. Hoping to somehow stay beyond their reach.

Everyone's there, the entire town shuffling and mumbling. And when the bell rings three times everyone hushes. The gate groans open. And the crowd cheers. I walk forward slowly and it's as though no one can see me. As if I'm nothing to them. I hear the thump of a drum, the blare of a horn.

The familiar sound hits deep in my stomach. The march of the Protectorate, the tune we're taught as children and sing every morning before classes. My lips move automatically, the words rote. And I find myself singing along as the Recruiters march into town.

XX

While everyone else celebrates the arrival of the Recruiters, I slip away from the crowd and into the basement of the Council House to visit Cira before they take her away. She sits on a bench tucked into a corner with her knees pulled up to her chest, her cheek resting on them. She's thin and drained and I can already tell she's given up. Seeing her so small and scared, I can't believe she could be the same girl from the river. The girl who was willing to do anything. Who was so brave and bold in the face of everything in our world.

I want to grab her hands and drag her to the river and throw her in. I want her to remember her own strength. I want to ask her how I'm supposed to believe in superheroes if she won't believe in herself.

I clutch the figurine she gave me under my shirt. Most of all I want her to promise me that she'll stay alive and fight.

Finally she sees me and her eyes light up. When she gets closer she slips her hands around the bars and I wrap my hands over hers. "Catcher?" she whispers.

I drop my gaze to the ground, wishing I could somehow avoid this conversation. Not wanting to heap any more pain on her. I don't know how to tell her I've failed them both.

I shake my head and I can see everything crumble inside her. I squeeze her wrist tightly but it's a useless gesture. She's not the same. Her eyes are dim and dull.

"Cira," I hiss through my teeth. "Cira, look at me!" I'm desperate to find some way to help her, to give her something to hold on to.

She barely focuses on me. It's as if she's underwater, being dragged down into the depths by the Mudo, but she's not even struggling.

"You can't give up," I tell her. I think back on all we've been through together, all the times she's been the strong one. The person I wanted to be. I don't know how to bring that back in her and it makes me feel useless.

When she talks she barely moves her lips, as if even that isn't worth the effort. "Why not?" she asks. "Why bother with it anymore?"

I open my mouth to protest but I see a small spark ignite in her eye, an ember of who I know she can be.

"No, really, Gabry. Tell me what's worth it. Tell me what we're doing just barely clinging on here. Why? Tell me what's the difference between you or me and the Mudo?"

"The Recruiters isn't a death sentence," I tell her, echoing the words that Elias said to me only a few days ago.

"He really liked you, you know?" she says, and for a moment I'm confused, Elias still flooding my mind and heat straining up my neck. "He used to talk about you all the time. Ever since we first met you that day at the lighthouse." She pauses. "We would have been sisters."

Pain sears at my chest, thoughts of Catcher and what could have been flashing through my mind.

"I wish I could take it back," I tell her. "I wish I could go back to that night and stop us from climbing the Barrier."

She shrugs one shoulder and lets it fall. "I used to think that," she says. "When they first caught us I thought that. But now I don't know." She looks around at the others pressed against the bars. At the families being torn apart. "Sometimes I think it's just inevitable."

A thousand protests come to my lips but she presses a finger against them before I can say anything. "I'm sorry," I whisper.

She smiles. "You know, I like to think of you out there, standing in the lighthouse. I like to think that I'll be able to see it from wherever they send us. That I'll see that flash of light on the horizon and I'll think about you and Catcher and that maybe it will make fighting that stupid war worth it."

I can feel my cheeks flush. "It's not fair that I'm out here," I tell her, my heart thudding at the words but knowing I have to say this. "I should be in there with you; I should go with you—"

She cuts me off. "Someone has to stay behind," she says.

I pull the superhero figurine from around my neck and pass it to her. "Please don't give up," I tell her again.

She looks at it dangling from my fingers. "There's no such thing as heroes," she says, pushing the necklace back at me. "Not anymore."

A familiar anger starts to prickle up my spine. "Why didn't you come back with me that night? I called to you. We both could have run. You'd be safe now."

She looks at me. "I'm not you, Gabrielle." Her voice is soft, as if she senses my anguish. She touches the little figurine, causing it to sway back and forth. "You've always been your own person. And me . . ." She smiles a little bit but it doesn't reach her eyes. "I'm only as good as those around me."

I try to understand but I don't. "Cira—" I begin to protest, but she pulls me into a hug the best she can through the bars and I think about all the things we've shared in our lives. All the ways we've taken care of each other. I never thought I would have to face anything without her; I never thought we'd be apart.

Holding her, I realize again just how much I'm going to miss her and how much strength she's given me. I'm terrified that I won't be able to find that strength on my own.

The Militiaman announces that it's time for us to leave. As I walk out I glance back over my shoulder and see my best friend standing there with the others, ready for the river to whisk her away.

▼ ▼ ▼

I don't bother with the Council ceremony honoring the Recruiters. My mind is too full for me to be able to go along with the show and pretend I respect them, so I slink around the edge of the cheering crowd as the Recruiters parade into the town square. Their black uniforms shimmer in the light, their eyes hidden by hats pulled low against the sun.

Their show of force over, the Militiamen have left their posts along the Barrier to join the festivities, only a few remaining behind to guard the gate. I realize that they've inadvertently given me a chance to get to Catcher and I breathe a little easier.

I'm trying to calm my jitters, to remind myself that I can do this—I can make it over the Barrier and through the ruins to Catcher this one last time. Just to tell him good-bye. Just to make sure that if he's turned there's someone to end it so that he isn't forced to exist as a monster.

As I walk through the empty streets I hear the weaving echo of my footsteps bouncing off the walls around me and my heart forcing the blood through my body. There's a spot near where the Barrier curves away from the town, a part almost hidden from the constant Militia presence at the gate. It's the same place we crossed that night almost a week ago. I stand for a moment tucked into the shadow of the wall, gathering my courage, and creep my way around the turn.

The sun is bright and hot, the cicadas a loud buzz that seems to build inside my chest. I take a deep breath and press my fingers into the gaps of the sturdy logs, not caring that it's daylight. Not caring what happens if I'm caught. Just needing to take one last gasp of the person I could be if I didn't fear so much.

All I can think is that if I climb fast enough I can save him. That maybe Catcher is still alive.

I don't even hear the footsteps, don't hear the breathing until too late. A body slams me face-first against the Barrier with such force that I lose my breath. My world explodes with terror and shock. I gasp at nothing, willing my body to inhale, when I'm turned around, my back thrust against the wall.

"And to think there was a moment when I was going to trust you," Daniel says, gripping my throat. I try to swallow but can't. His hand smells like sweat and mildew. "I've been following you, Gabrielle. Wondering when you'd mess up." He pushes hard against me, his breath hot in my face. I squirm and struggle but he only holds me tighter, splinters from the Barrier digging through my shirt and into my skin.

Panic explodes in my head and I swallow again and again, trying to tamp it down.

"I always figured you'd been out there with the others that night," he says. Squeezing me for emphasis. "You and your friends, thinking the rules don't apply to you. Thinking you can get away with whatever you want."

I shake my head. I want to tell him that I always follow the rules but he doesn't let me speak.

He leans in close, his body almost crushing mine, pressing me hard into the wall. "I watched you, you know," he says. "I watched the way you threw yourself at Catcher this summer. The way you'd pretend that you were scared just so he'd put his hands on you." I close my eyes against his breath and try to turn my head away but I can't escape him.

"Where is he now, huh?" He shakes me and I try to think of what to say, how to get him to leave me alone and let me breathe. But sparks are firing in front of my eyes and my chest aches for freedom. I need space. I need air. I need him to let me go. I need to get away.

I tense my arm, wanting to shove him off, but he's faster. His fingers twist around my wrist, his thumb digging into the bones until my hand goes numb.

Suddenly I'm not sure I'm going to be able to escape him and the panic rises high in my chest. He's in complete control of me and in this shadowy nook there's no one who will see us, no one who can come to my rescue. We're alone out here in the shadow of the Barrier. Dread begins to buzz along my skin, terror at what he could be planning for me.

As if he can read my mind he cracks a smile. "Where's your little boy now? Not here to rescue you, huh?" He laughs and I gag, my chest convulsing, my vision blurring. "I'm guessing he's still out there. Too afraid to come back. Too much of a coward to face service with the Recruiters." My body flares hot, my muscles rigid and weak at the same time. I can't get enough air. I can't focus on what he's saying. I'm about to pass out but I cling to the scraps of awareness, afraid of what would happen if I were totally defenseless.

His grip tightens around my wrist, his bad leg pressed against the outside of my thigh. Everything in me revolts against his touch. "You should hear Cira and the others cry. Sometimes when I'm on duty guarding them, I like to go and listen to them pity themselves. You ask me, they got better than they deserve for putting us all in danger like that."

I can only move my mouth, no sound will come out. "Stop," I try to say. "Stop." All I can think is that I have to breathe or I'll pass out.

His mouth hovers over mine as his fingers loosen on my neck so that I'm forced to suck in huge lungfuls of air. I choke and cough as my body tries to adjust to the sudden release of pressure and he just smiles.

My nose runs and tears clog my eyes. My vision wavers, my throat burning sore with each sucking inhale. "Here's the thing," he says, drumming his fingers against my neck. "With all of them going, that doesn't leave many of us here. Just you and me, really. And I figure pretty soon you'll be wanting a husband. Someone who's a true citizen of the town so that no one can cast doubt on your loyalty. No one will wonder at the rumors that you used to sneak past the Barrier."

He presses his nose against the crook of my collarbone and inhales deeply. I gag again. It's too much—him so close, his body so tight against mine.

"And trust me, there are rumors," he adds with a leer. "At least, there will be soon."

My mind spins uncontrollably. Trying to take in the

situation. Trying to figure out what I can say to protect myself. I have to get away from him. I have to escape and he's too close and too strong and I feel totally helpless.

"There will definitely be rumors about why your mother isn't at the ceremony today. Or why she wasn't doing her job the night of the storm," he says, his lips within a whisper of my jaw. "Someone's bound to start asking questions, don't you think? They're already suspicious with her being an outsider. Of course, if you're mine, no one's going to look too deeply."

He pulls back and examines me, his face an ugly jumble of anger and glee.

"Sometimes things just work out the way they're supposed to, Gabrielle," he says in my ear. "Sometimes you've got to learn to give in to the inevitable."

The word sparks in my mind: *inevitable*. It was the same thing Cira said, the same excuse she used for giving up. Fire begins to storm inside me, seeping through my muscles, causing me to clench my jaw until I feel as though my teeth will break.

It's the need to do something—anything—to regain control of myself, of my situation, of this world and this man in front of me.

I turn my head toward him until our lips are barely touching. I lean in ever so slightly, feeling his hips press against mine. I can sense his smug satisfaction. He thinks he's won. He thinks I'm his. The taste of it is sour and acrid in my mouth.

And then I let my body go limp, forcing his arms to hold me still. It throws him off balance on his bad leg and for just a moment his hand loosens around my wrist.

I don't think. I don't hesitate. I just reach for Elias's knife on my hip and flick my arm until the blade is pressed against Daniel's flesh.

Time stops. I'm sure the waves on the beach pause before crashing, the trees stop their tussle with the wind and every bird turns our way. Daniel's eyes open wide, the realization closing in fast.

It's so much easier than I ever thought it would be to slide the knife into his body, to do it without thinking. And at the same time it's so much harder to force the blade to slice the skin, cut through muscle and glide along bone.

His body tenses, his lips purse. And then my muscles contract, driving Elias's blade deeper.

We stand together for a moment, he and I. I feel the heat seeping from him, the damp spilling onto my chest and stomach. We're suspended just that one heartbeat: him and me and nothing else. His life everywhere around us.

I remember then all the times I'd seen this boy made fun of. All the times I watched as the other kids taunted him. Spat insults at him. All the times I turned my head, pretending not to notice him watching me. All the times I never defended him.

I remember when he stepped forward to join the Recruiters and they rejected him in front of the entire town because of his bad leg. I remember the humiliation of it as if I can taste it.

I want to tell him I'm sorry. For this and for everything. But I can't find the words. He starts to slump and I help him to the ground. He doesn't grab for me or try to stop me as I pull the blade free. He says nothing as I turn away and climb the Barrier.

When I'm at the top, just about to jump over to the other side, I look down at him. Hands clutched over a blooming red on his chest. His bad leg tucked underneath him. His eyes on me.

I know in that instant we'll forever be connected. It's as if we're the same person sharing the same blood. I want to tell him I'm sorry, to beg forgiveness, but he just stares at me.

And then I jump over the wall and am careening through the amusement park to find Catcher. I don't care that I'm covered in blood, that the scent of it will draw the Mudo even more. I only care about Catcher and running from the terror of what I've just done.

I race through the cracked streets of the ruins, trying to find my way back to Catcher's. This time it's daylight and I see the distinctions I missed when I was here the other night. I weave through the streets until I find Catcher's building and then I take the steps two at a time, not caring about the darkness or my reeling heart.

At the landing outside the closed door to his room I force myself to stop and wipe my sweating hands along the edge of my shirt. My fingers tremble slightly as I grip Elias's knife in front of me.

After coming all this way, after everything I've risked, I'm terrified to open the door. What if he's died and Returned and I have to kill him? I don't know if I could. What if I fail the way I did with Mellie? The way I did on the beach?

I press my ear to the door, the air in the hallway musty and still. Sweat drips along my spine. I can't hear anything. I take a shaky breath and push it open.

XXI

I stand in the doorway and stare, dropping the bloody knife in despair. The room is empty. For a moment I wonder if I'm in the wrong place. If in my terror and fear I ran to the wrong building, got turned around in the ruins the way I had before. But I can still smell a hint of him in the air. I can still see fragments of his presence around me. The dust on the windowsill is scattered where he stood, his hands pressed against the opening as he stared out toward the lighthouse and the town.

He's gone. The room is silent. I collapse onto the floor, overwhelmed.

He wouldn't have left. He wouldn't have gone anywhere—he knew I was coming back. Which means that Elias must have been here. I squeeze my eyes closed. I don't want to imagine Catcher as one of the Souler Mudo; I don't want to think of his mangled face. Of the pleading moan. Of him being tugged around on a leash.

I don't want to think that Elias could have done that to him. I've been hoping that Elias was somehow different.

I let my head fall back against the wall, banging it to get the image of Catcher as Mudo out of my mind. But it doesn't work. I failed him. Just as I failed Cira by leaving her behind. And my mother by letting her go into the Forest alone. And everyone else.

I have to find him. I promised him I wouldn't let him be Mudo. I have to at least follow through with that.

Pulling myself to my feet, I stumble back into the dark hallway, down the stairs and into the blazing midday. I retrace my steps through the streets toward where I saw the Soulers last, my feet dragging and the sun scorching my head.

Heat hovers along the stretch of concrete, rising and brushing my legs as I walk toward the three arches of the amphitheater. As before, I tuck myself in the shadow of one of the arches, creeping forward on my hands and knees, my knuckles scraping the ground where I clutch my knife. I hear the moans before I see anything. The remains of the Souler Mudo, the ones they left behind when they came to Vista, are all tied in a pack in the shade of the stage's large dome.

Holding my breath, I scan their sagging faces. From this distance it's hard to see details, their appearances blurring. My body buzzes with the hope that Catcher won't be there. That I'm wrong about Elias.

But then I see the flash of his hair, the white-blond of it shimmering in the shadows. I see the familiar curve of his cheek, the line of his shoulder.

Catcher shuffles through the herd of Mudo, stopping to stand among them, his lips parted as if he's moaning. I press my palm to my mouth, biting it to keep from screaming.

I didn't realize until now just what it would mean to see him like this. The pain and the horror are unbearable. I shove my fists into my eyes, wanting to claw out the vision of Catcher as Mudo.

My hands start to shake and I can't force them to stop. I try not to stare at my fingers, at the blood that's dried in the cracks of my skin. Not my blood but someone else's. The enormity of the last few days slams into me—the walls between the compartments where I've stashed each bit dissolve. I toss the knife aside, scarlet red still blurring the blade.

I've just stabbed someone and his blood coats my skin and clothes. I wipe my hands on the ground until they sting but still they're stained crimson. Catcher's gone. Returned. Mudo. I never got to tell him good-bye.

Everything is wrong. Everything has changed. I've lied and broken rules and killed someone. I've broken my promises and failed. I don't know who I am anymore.

And then the sobs break over me. Painful, they flatten me to the ground. I don't have the energy to fight anymore.

I startle when arms wrap around me but I don't bother protesting. I'm too ready to give up on everything, willing to let whatever happens to me happen. But then I can tell by the way he pulls me to himself, by the way he holds me as if he could push the pieces of me back together again, that it's Elias. I can tell by his smell and his strength and the way he leans his cheek against my hair.

I don't know how he found me—how he knew I was here—and I don't care. I want to hate him; I should hate him for who he is and what he's done to Catcher. But for just a moment I allow myself to soak in his comfort because I need his strength. To fall into the feeling of him against me, another heartbeat with mine. And then I take a deep breath and lash out. Pushing him away.

"You monster!" I sound feral, my voice a tear-fueled growl. I take everything and channel it into rage as if he's the reason for all my pain. Wanting someone else to blame other than myself.

He stares at me without answering and I lunge at him. "You horrible monster!" I pound on his chest. "I hate you I hate you I hate you!" It feels so good to scream. To feel as though I could tear apart the world.

He takes my wrists in his hands and pushes me away. He sees the blood along my arms, across my chest. His eyes flare wide, his breath a gasp. He throws me to the ground.

"Where are you hurt?" he demands. He pulls at my shirt, his fingers searching the skin along my stomach and sides. I writhe against him but he straddles me, keeping me on the ground.

Fury boils over inside me and I scream. He grabs my face, holding my head steady. His fingers dig into my cheeks, forcing my gaze on him. "Gabry, where are you hurt?" I'm surprised to feel the way he trembles and I realize that he's scared, that he's panting with fear. I feel the fight drain out of me.

"I'm not," I whisper. But I want to tell him that I hurt everywhere, that I hurt so deeply I don't know how to fix it.

He sits back on his heels, still straddling me, looking down at me. I take advantage of his hesitation and gather all my strength and buck my hips up, throwing him to the side. I roll and grab the knife. I pounce on him, holding the blade against his throat.

"You're disgusting." I have a hard time finding the words I want to say. "What did you do to Catcher?" I shake him and his eyes bulge a little as the blade nicks the corner of his jaw. "What did you do?" I shout into his face.

Our breathing is like a storm, my heart the thunder.

"Nothing," a voice behind me says.

Everything stops. My throat hitches. I don't want to turn around. I don't want it to be a trick or a joke. I don't want confirmation that the hope charging through me is a lie.

I stare down at Elias. He smiles, just barely—a painful sort of smile.

I swallow and turn slowly. Catcher stands there, half in the shadow of the arch, hesitating before he runs toward me. The air compresses in its familiar way before our bodies collide and he grabs at me and I grab at him, not understanding what's going on—how he's still alive and for the moment not caring. He's here in my arms now and that's all that matters.

His skin is almost unbearably hot against my own but he feels strong and his heartbeat reverberates through me. He's nothing like the weak, dying person I left a few days ago.

I push away from him and stand back, glancing between him and Elias, who still lies prone on the ground. It's hard to find the right words. "What's going on?" I ask. "I don't understand. You're supposed to be . . ." I can't say it.

"Dead." Catcher says it for me.

"Mudo," I whisper.

He smiles. "Same thing."

I can't help but let my eyes trail down his neck to the spot on his shoulder where the bite mark is. It's still an angry red welt, scabs stretching over where each of Mellie's teeth punctured the skin.

"It's been almost a week since you were bitten," I say, shaking my head. None of this makes sense; he's supposed to be dead. The Infected aren't supposed to last that long. A bare sort of singing feeling starts to weave through me: hope. Catcher's still here. He's still alive.

"I was there, I saw it. You told me." My voice rises, all the pain and fear and regret that built up in me ever since that night breaking free. "You told me you were infected."

"I was," he says.

"He still is," Elias says from the ground. I look over at him. He's sitting, one arm draped around a knee. Remnants of three scratches trail down his face from the first night I met him in the ocean and a bruise blossoms around his eye from the other time I attacked him on the beach. Now he presses a hand to his side where I just hit him and a small red cut from my knife edges along his jaw. There are traces of blood on his white tunic from where he held me, where Daniel's blood seeped from me to him.

I clench and unclench my hands, frustrated at not understanding. "People don't last this long infected," I say. "It's been too much time. I don't understand." They glance at each other and then Elias slowly stands. He picks up the knife I'd dropped by his head and holds it out to me, handle first.

"He's immune," Elias says.

XXII

I stare at him, everything around us still and somber except for my heartbeat, which can't contain itself. And then I stare at Catcher, waiting for him to explain. Because there's no such thing as immunity. They'd have told us growing up if there were. "That doesn't exist," I finally say. "No one is immune. They've always made sure we understood that: *No one is immune.*"

I look back and forth between Elias and Catcher. It's what they tell us from when we're old enough to listen. It's what we've always known: There's no cure, there's no immunity, there's no escape. Once you're bitten, you're infected and dead.

"You said it yourself. It's been six days, Gabrielle," Catcher says. "There's no other explanation."

But I'm looking at Elias. I'm trying to decide if I trust him. If I can trust a Souler. He seems to understand what's going on here, to know more than he's saying.

I want to believe him. I want to think that Catcher will be

okay. That I haven't failed him. That something in this world can be good. Even though it goes against everything I've known and believed.

I have so many questions but only one thing matters to me now. I stare at Catcher, barely able to breathe. "You're okay?" I ask him. "You're . . . you're better now?"

I watch as he clenches his hands by his sides. As the muscle along his jaw tightens and jumps. "I'm still infected," he says.

"What does that mean?" I ask him.

Elias answers before Catcher can. "It means the Mudo don't sense it when he's around them. It means they don't attack him. It means the infection won't kill him—he won't turn—"

Catcher cuts him off. "It means we can go home." He walks over to me and takes my hand, presses it against his chest. His skin is so hot I can feel the heat of him through his clothes. "Go back to the way things were," he adds. "Pretend none of this ever happened."

Elias crosses his arms over his chest, his lips pursed tight. But I don't care about him anymore. All I can feel is my heart singing. He's okay. Catcher's going to live! Just moments before, I thought he was already dead, already Mudo. I thought I'd never have the chance to talk to him again, to hold him and have him understand me. And suddenly all that fear is washing away and hope is budding inside me.

"We can go back to Vista, Gabry. We can go back to the way it was before. You and me and Cira . . ."

I lean my forehead against his shoulder so that he can't see my expression. The air in my throat chokes me but whether it's sobs or hysterical laughter I don't know.

The reality of our situation strikes deep. He still thinks things can go back to how they were. That his infection is the only thing that's happened in the past week.

But now I've killed someone. Even if I wanted to, I can't ever go back to Vista. The Militia will find out it was me. They'll execute me for killing one of their own.

It's impossible for me to go home.

I can't believe how out of control everything's suddenly become. My deepest wish—that Catcher would be okay—has come true but at the expense of everything else. If I'd only known. If I'd even dreamed it was a possibility.

"Why didn't they tell us about immunity?" I ask, my voice on the edge of a wail. It's not fair, none of this is fair. My mind scrambles, trying to figure out a way to make it work, to get back to my old life but everything leads back to the reality of Daniel's death and Cira's punishment.

"It doesn't matter now," Catcher says, his hand wrapping around mine. "I'm okay, that's what matters. I can't wait to tell Cira."

I'm already shaking my head and backing away. "You can't," I tell him. He steps closer but I hold up my hands, waving him away. "We can't go back," I say, almost choking on the words.

Elias says nothing, just tilts his head as he watches me, his expression unreadable.

"We'll find a way to make it work," Catcher says, but I'm shaking my head.

"It won't work," I tell him. I twist my fingers, running the pad of my thumb along the cut on my hand, feeling the pain radiate up my arm, grounding me. "I lied about Cira," I whisper.

I stare at the heat wavering on the concrete, at the clouds building in the sky above, anywhere but at Catcher. "They came after us that night, the Militia. I got away but the others didn't. The Council voted to send them all to the Recruiters." My voice is limp as I finish, afraid of what he'll say.

Catcher's head falls back. I watch as he clenches and unclenches his jaw. "You didn't tell me," he says, his voice even. "I asked about her and you said she was okay."

"I know." My words carry hardly any sound at all. I'm overwhelmed by how everything's shifted and changed underneath me again. "I'm sorry," I add uselessly.

He turns away from me, pushes his hands into his hair and yanks. "Where is she now?" he asks. His frustration and anger cut through me, slicing at my happiness that he's still alive.

"They have her in the Council House." I swallow. I want to explain, to tell him that I thought he was dying. That I didn't want to add to his pain. But I don't. "The Recruiters arrived today. They'd started the swearing-in ceremony when I came here."

He bangs a fist against the stone arch and I jump at the sudden violence. I want to go to him, to pull away his pain and anger. But I don't. I'm afraid he'll push me away.

He places both hands on the wall and breathes deeply.

I look over at Elias. Embarrassed that he's watching this, that he knows what I've done.

"We have to go get Cira," Catcher says, his voice muffled. He turns to face us. "I'm not letting them take her. I told her I'd protect her and I will."

"How?" I ask. "They're not going to give her up."

When he looks at me his eyes are cold and hard. "I don't care," he says. "I'll find a way." He stalks into the amphitheater, down toward the stage, and I start after him.

"Catcher, wait!" I call out. Without even turning around he throws up a hand, waving me off. I stand there watching him go, Elias behind me. I'm afraid to face him, mortified at being dismissed by Catcher in front of him.

Just when I thought I was putting all the pieces back together they've cracked and fallen into different patterns, this time with sharper edges. I don't know how to make it work, how to make it right.

A familiar feeling of uselessness tingles inside me. "I've messed it all up again," I say.

On the stage below, Catcher stands facing the tethered Mudo, staring at them. They don't even notice his existence, don't reach for him and it makes me feel cold. It looks so wrong to see him so close to them.

Elias shifts and comes to stand next to me. His hands are by his sides and I know that I'd just have to twitch my fingers to touch him, to feel his comfort.

"Why didn't they tell us about the immunity?" I ask him weakly.

He sighs and raises a shoulder. "It's rare, Gabry. Really rare. I guess they didn't want people getting their hopes up, letting people turn just to see and causing the infection to rage again. Most people don't know about it."

What he says makes sense but I don't care. I cross my arms over my chest, to avoid the temptation of touching him as much as to hold myself in. "How do you know it's immunity? That he won't turn in a few days? That it's not just taking longer?" I hold my breath waiting for his answer, hoping that I'm wrong.

"Only the Immunes can do that," he says, nodding toward Catcher. "I learned about it when I was in the Recruiters. Immunes are the only ones the Unconsecrated don't sense."

My stomach twinges at the word *Unconsecrated*. Thinking of my mother. Remembering that she's gone. I shake the thought out of my head.

"It's how I knew it about him," Elias continues. "When the storm came in I thought you might not make it back. I went and brought Catcher here to the camp, figuring he'd need food and water while he waited . . ." He swallows, not wanting to finish the statement, and I look at him, examining his profile. A soft sheen of dark fuzz has begun to grow on his head and his skin is tan from so many days outside in the sun.

I have to ask him the question that's been hammering in my mind. I take a deep breath, pushing my nails into the soft flesh of my arm to force the courage. "Would you have . . . I mean, if he'd turned, would you have done that to him? Made him into one of those?"

We're both looking at the Souler Mudo, at their disfigured faces. The moans swirl around us like a breeze.

Elias scowls, his shoulders tense. "No," he says simply. But I still don't know if I can trust him.

"Why do you worship them?" I ask.

He takes a deep breath, blowing it out through pursed lips as he turns toward me. I notice again how his eyes are almost colorless, the sharpness of his cheekbones. "I don't worship them," he says.

I don't understand. "But you're a Souler," I tell him, as if it's obvious.

He studies my face and I want to look away from him but I force myself to keep his gaze. I squirm a little under his scrutiny. "I'm not a Souler, Gabry," he says. "That's what I was trying to tell you on the beach. I'm not one of them."

My eyes widen and I shake my head, feeling as though he's

playing some sort of trick on me. "But you're here with them. You were there the other night. You watched them sacrifice that boy. And you're dressed like them and look like them." I could keep going but he holds up a hand for me to stop and I fall into silence.

He presses his fingers to his forehead, pushing at the skin as if trying to gather the words he needs. I bristle, waiting to hear what he has to say.

"I told you I was looking for someone," he says, and I nod. "It's my sister. I'm looking for my sister." He swallows. "I lost her." I can hear the desperation in his voice and it makes me feel physically weak. I want to close my hand around his but a part of me is still suspicious of him.

"She was all I had left and I promised I'd take care of her and she's gone. We'd been living in the Dark City but neither of us were citizens. I was only allowed in to trade and sometimes even then I could barely make the rents. I joined the Recruiters so that I'd get citizenship—so that I'd be allowed as a permanent resident of the Protected Zones and I could take her with me without having to pay anymore. But when I came home after serving she wasn't there." He pauses, wiping a hand over his face.

"I couldn't find her anywhere and I thought maybe she'd been forced to leave. I had to find her." His words come out in a rush, his voice cracked. "A single man can't travel through the Protectorate. The roads are too dangerous, with Unconsecrated and bandits. Half the towns and cities won't even let you in the gates if you're alone."

He leans toward me, speaking fast now, his breath weaving hot around us. "The Soulers are recognized by the Protectorate. They're nomads—they can go anywhere and be granted access. Joining them was the only way for me to search for her."

It's so much to take in at once that I feel stunned, having to retrace everything we've ever said to each other. To rethink every thought about him in the softer light of this new information.

His eyes are so earnest, so full of pain, that I want to believe him. I can see in his gaze that he needs me to believe him. "But you were there when they let that boy die. How could you even watch that? How could you be a part of it? How can you stand to be around them?"

He opens his mouth and then shuts it again, pressing his lips together into a thin line. "They're not monsters, Gabry. Everything in this world isn't black-and-white. They have their reasons for what they do, for what they believe, the same way we do." He shrugs. "My sister means everything to me. I'll do anything it takes to find her."

I shake my head, not wanting to hear more. "I don't know," I tell him. "I don't know what to think." My heart aches for him and his loss but I can't reconcile it all in my head, can't make sense of it.

I walk away from him, out of the shadow of the arch and down the bowl of the amphitheater toward Catcher. He still stands staring at the Mudo. I don't get too close, a dread of their moans too deeply ingrained in me.

He turns to face me and I realize how terrifying it is, seeing him there so close to those monsters.

"I want to go back, Gabry," he says. "I want it all to be normal again."

Behind him the Mudo sense me, their arms reaching past Catcher for me. My breath catches as I try to swallow the unease. I close my eyes against them, against him. More than anything in the world I wish I could give this to him: normalcy. But too much has changed. Because of me we can't go back.

"I can't go back to Vista," I tell him. "I've done something. I'm in trouble. And you can't either. They know you were there that night. You'll get sent away with the others."

"I'm not leaving Cira," he says. His voice thrums around me and then I feel his hands grabbing mine. I open my eyes. His face is so close that I can't help but flash back to the night we first kissed. "And I'm not leaving you either," he adds, his voice softer.

I exhale slowly, relief mixing with fear and guilt.

"We'll go get Cira and we'll run away," he says urgently. "The three of us, we'll go somewhere to disappear."

"They'll follow you," Elias says and I jerk my head around. He's walking past us toward the back of the stage where bags are stacked in the corner. "If you take something or someone from the Recruiters they'll do anything to get it back. And you," he says, pointing at Catcher. "If they find out you're immune they'll never let you go. You're too valuable to them."

My mind races, trying to think up options, and then I almost jump when it comes to me. "My mother's boat," I say, the chance of joy beginning to tingle through me. "Elias took it. Do you still have it?" I ask him. When he nods I continue. "We could take her boat. We can try and find somewhere else. We haven't heard reports of pirates in years. We could make it and the Recruiters couldn't follow us."

"But what about your mother?" Catcher asks. "Will she let you go?"

I glance away from him, bring my fingers to my mouth and bite at the nail on my thumb. I want to tell him that she's already let me go but the words won't come. "She'll be okay," I finally say.

Elias raises his eyebrows at me as if he expects me to say more but I don't.

"Now we just have to figure out how to get Cira," Catcher says.

Elias still looks at me, making me feel uncomfortable. "That's the easy part," he says.

XXIII

My hands shake as Elias and I pull the boat up the beach toward the lighthouse. We left Catcher back in the ruins—at dusk he'll bring the Souler Mudo to the Barrier and push them over. They'll spread through Vista, their moans signaling a breach—enough of a distraction that Elias and I will be able to break into the Council House and rescue Cira.

It's just turning high tide but the beach is still clear. Elias sits in the shade of the lighthouse, watching to make sure no Mudo are washed ashore, and I head inside. I stand in the emptiness and quiet for a while, remembering the stories my mother used to tell me when I was growing up.

I can't stop imagining her coming back here and wondering where I've gone. I think about leaving her a note so that she won't worry but dismiss the thought—what if someone else found it? I climb the steps to her room, the book of Shakespeare's sonnets still lying open on her bed. I flip through it before shoving it into a small pack along with an extra shirt and skirt. I dig around in the closet until I find some of Roger's old clothes, which smell musty and feel well worn.

On my way out the door I grab another bag for Elias and toss in food and a few canteens. As I pack the boat with extra supplies Elias changes. He looks different now that he no longer wears the white tunic. He looks almost normal.

I realize that I'm staring at him and I go back to sifting sand through my fingers. He joins me and we sit side by side, waiting for the sun to sink into the water and for Vista to erupt with the breach. My heart thuds with anticipation as my mind races. I think of all the ways this can go wrong; it seems impossible that our plan will work.

But what other choice do we have? Except that there's one variable that doesn't make sense to me.

"Why are you still here?" I ask Elias, digging my toes into the cooler layers of sand.

Out of the corner of my eye I watch a muscle along his jaw twitch.

"I said I'd help and I am," he says, not looking over at me. He pushes himself to his feet and walks closer to the water. The horizon is a mix of orange and red and purple. "Besides, the other Soulers are still in your quarantine. So long as they're being held I'm not finding my sister."

I look at his back, Roger's old shirt a little big on Elias's frame. "What's her name?" I ask, wanting to understand him.

He's quiet for a while and I stand, brushing the sand from my knees and walk toward him. There's something that seems so strong, so safe and familiar except that I don't know anything about him.

Together we stare at where the sun is about to collide with

the earth. I hold my breath, whether waiting for him to answer me or for the fire to spread on the horizon, I don't know.

"Annah," he says softly. "Her name is Annah." He looks at me and I look at him and I realize that I'm still holding my breath.

"What's she like?" I ask him. His face twists just a little but he never stops looking at me.

"She's strong," he says. "Beautiful and sweet." I see the memories swimming behind his eyes. It feels as though I'm intruding too far in his life and I've already turned away when he says, so softly, "She's a lot like you."

I stop. I look over my shoulder at him, wondering if I heard him right. Wishing that I could believe him.

"That's not what I'm like at all," I tell him, the words painful to admit. "I'd love more than anything to be strong. But I know I'm not. I'm weak and afraid and useless." I swallow and he steps closer to me. I think about what Daniel looked like after I'd stabbed him. I think about the Souler woman who was killed at the gate to Vista. I think about Catcher the night he was infected.

I'm the cause of all of it. I'm the one who's a monster. "Everything I do, I just mess things up."

"You crossed the Barrier on your own to help Catcher," he says, and I shake my head.

"I had to do that. The other ones who were caught that night were going to turn me in otherwise," I say, needing him to stop believing that I'm something I'm not.

"You went back for him," he says. "Why won't you believe the best of yourself?"

"Because that's not who I am," I tell him adamantly. My heart trips for a moment as I wonder if I could ever believe him. If I could see myself through his eyes. If someone other than Catcher could make me feel worth something. But instead I shake my head.

"Then tell me who you are." He eases closer. I can feel the edges of him in the space between us.

I can't think with him so close. With his words encircling us, pulling us tighter together. I think about opening my mouth and pouring everything out—how scared I am, how terrifying it is to have lost my mother and wonder if she's still okay. To have had everything in my life shift so fast that I still reel from it every morning and every night.

And how I'm worried that I'll never really know who I am and what I want. That I'll always be the girl messing everything up. The awkward one on the fringes wanting something more but too afraid to do anything about it.

"I don't know who I am anymore," I whisper.

He erases the distance between us until my head buzzes. "Yes you do," he says, his voice hovering over me and around me as if we can occupy one space together. I close my eyes and wait for him.

My skin tingles with want but he doesn't kiss me. Not the way Catcher did. He leans against me until our lips barely press together, our mouths open, every part of us twining through our breaths.

I want to press harder. I want him to pull me tighter. But he doesn't. We just stand there barely touching.

And then the bells from town begin to clang. My eyes go wide and I stumble backward. I clasp a hand over my mouth as memories of Catcher slam into me: his smell, the sound of his voice, the feel of his skin under mine. I'd forgotten all of it—I'd let Elias erase it all.

Shame and anger roar in my head. And as if he can see it all tumbling through me, as if he can smell my regret, his face hardens. He turns and strides back up the beach. "I'm sorry," I call after him, but he doesn't respond and I chase him and try to grab him but he pushes off my touch.

"Where's the Council House?" he asks, his voice cold and sharp.

"I'm sorry," I tell him again but he shrugs it off.

"We don't have time to worry about something that doesn't matter," he says. "They'll realize the Mudo can't infect, and we need to get your friend before that." He picks up the pack I'd brought out for him and slings it over his shoulders.

My cheeks flame with embarrassment and I raise a finger and point up the path toward town. He takes off at a jog and I follow, the small bag carrying clothes, food and my mother's book slapping against my back. I feel stupid. But what hurts most of all is that his almost-kiss *did* matter to me, and it clearly didn't matter to him.

▼ ▼ ▼

Vista is screams and moans and the glint of weapons. People pour from the center square through the streets, panicked and running for the safety of home. We're lost in the cacophony of it all, everyone else so wrapped up in their own terror that no one bothers Elias and me as we sprint to the Council House.

I push everything else from my head and focus on the moment and the task at hand. No one guards the doors; everyone's been called by the ringing bell to defend the town. "We don't have much time," Elias says. "It won't take them long to figure out it's not a true breach."

I shove my way inside and down the stairs where Cira and

the others are held with the Soulers. It's a disconcerting sight, the Soulers in their white tunics on one side and the new Recruiters in their black uniforms on the other. "What's going on?" one of them shouts. "Get us out," screams another one. The air is thick with fear.

Elias kneels in front of the barred door and pokes at the lock with the tip of his knife. I search through the thin faces for Cira. She sits limply against the back wall, barely bothering to look up at the commotion.

"Cira." I slip my hand through the bars, reaching for her. Her head rolls on her neck, her hands slack in her lap. "Cira," I say again.

She looks up at me, her eyes hollow and unfocused. She raises a hand slackly as if to wave at me and that's when I see the blood trailing down her wrist and dripping from her fingers.

XXIV

"Cira!" I scream, but it's as if she sees right through me, as if I'm not there. "Someone help her!" I yell to the others crowded against the bars but no one does anything. No one moves, they just hover around Elias as he works on the lock. I try to push at them, I try to grab them and make them see Cira on the floor in the corner but they pull away from me.

These are her friends, the people whose fate she shared. She's spent the last days with them, has lived with them here in this tiny cage. And yet no one seems to care. No one bothers to help.

The lock clicks and the heavy gate swings open with a groan. Everyone inside begins to spill against the opening and I shove through them, fighting the current of bodies to get inside. I run to Cira, sliding to a stop beside her.

I grab her cheeks, force her to look at me. Her lips waver a bit before turning into a smile, trembling around the edges. "Gabry," she says, her voice soft, weak.

“Cira.” I choke on her name. I pull at her clothes, yanking back the sleeves of her black Recruiter jacket. The material is damp, her blood seeping onto my skin, staining it a deep red once again. The cuts on her forearms are jagged and wide and raw. They’ve begun to clot, the blood thick, but when I clamp my hand over them it begins to well again.

I don’t know what to do. “Help me!” I call out. I look over my shoulder at the now-empty cage, at Elias talking to one of the Soulers. “Elias, help!”

He looks up and in an instant takes in the situation. He rushes over, dropping his pack and kneeling on the other side of Cira. “Keep pressure on them,” he says as he tugs an old skirt from my bag and tears it into strips. He pulls Cira’s jacket from her. She tries to help but her movements are slow, uncoordinated.

“’S okay, Gabry,” she murmurs, her lips barely moving. “It’ll be me and Catcher now. You go.”

I squeeze her wrists tighter in my fingers and she doesn’t wince.

“No,” I tell her. I gulp back tears and terror. “No, Catcher’s here. He’s okay, I was wrong.”

Her eyes open wide before drooping shut. “But you said . . .” Her breathing’s shallow.

“Hold her arms above her head,” Elias says. “Keep the pressure on.”

“Where’s Catcher?” Cira asks. I can see her struggling to understand, fighting the energy leaking from her body.

“He’s here,” I tell her but her eyes slip shut and I’m not sure she heard.

A shadow falls across me and I look up. Blane stands in the opening to the cell, hesitating before following the others out.

It reminds me of the night in the amusement park, the moment I chose to leave them all and run. She looks afraid; she looks ashamed. As if she's waiting for my permission to abandon her friend. "How did you let this happen?" I ask her.

She looks at me a long moment, her eyes bright and her mouth opening and closing on a hundred excuses. "I couldn't stop her," she finally says. "I tried." Her voice is thin and hitches with regret. "I'm sorry," she whispers. She stands in front of me, as if I could tell her anything to make it okay. She reaches out her fingers and brushes them against my own and then she turns and runs up the stairs.

I look across Cira at Elias. I want him to say that she'll be okay. That she's going to be fine. But I can tell in the way he glances at the door that he's worried. That he's more than worried.

"What do we do?" I ask. I think about the little sailboat, about dragging her through town.

"We should leave her," he says, his voice barely a whisper. "She needs rest, she needs someone who knows what they're doing. She shouldn't be moved."

I look at her. At her pale cheeks and white lips. All the blood. He's right. I know he's right. Any chance we would have of escaping is at risk with her. She'll slow us down.

I press my forehead against hers. "Cira," I whisper. I can hear the tears in my voice. I want to ask her why but I already know. *Inevitable*, she would tell me.

For the space between heartbeats it feels as though it's all my fault. If I hadn't run that night but stayed with her. If I'd allowed myself to be caught, to be caged with her and sent to the Recruiters. I could have been there with her. I could have given her someone to lean on. Someone to hold on to.

I could have stopped her. We could have made it together.

"I'm not leaving her," I say.

I lean back and look at Elias. He searches my face with his eyes but he doesn't question me. He just nods and takes her arms and wraps them tight with the strips of cloth.

"There's not a lot of time left," he says. "They'll realize the breach is by the Souler Mudo—that they pose no threat but terror." He looks across the room to the dark stairway where everyone else ran. And I realize that he could have run with them. That he should be with them, out looking for his sister.

"You can go," I tell him. "She's not your responsibility." The words are harder to say than I thought they would be and I realize that I've grown to trust him. "Neither am I," I add.

He turns to look at me, his body still, and he squints. "I'm going with you, Gabry."

I stare at him too long. I should tell him to leave. I should tell him that I have nothing to give him and that he's better off with the Soulers looking for his sister. But before I can say any of that he slings his pack onto his back and puts his arm under Cira's shoulder, helping her to her feet. My throat feels raw and tight when I see him so tender and gentle.

He turns toward the stairs and I slip under Cira's other arm. "Thank you," I tell him, though those words will never be enough to express my gratitude. He grunts under Cira's weight as she slumps against him trying to walk.

Together we get her out of the Council House and into the confused streets beyond. The buildings around us are shuttered and reinforced, most families tucked inside. And yet people, mostly boys and men, still stream through the streets shouting and waving weapons. They race to the Barrier to help defend the town.

A few people run to us, offer to help, but Elias just murmurs "Infected," and they eye the blood-soaked bandages before stumbling away and leaving us alone. As we near the edge of the buildings and start on the path leading to the beach a figure bursts out of the darkness.

I almost drop Cira in my fright and before I can even reach for my weapon Elias has his knife brandished in his free hand.

"Cira," the person gasps, and I realize with relief that it's Catcher. He steps toward us, then races to his sister hanging limp between us. "What's going on? What happened to her?" He grabs her face. "Cira," he calls to her, "Cira, look at me!"

Her eyes droop open and a small smile barely touches her lips. "Catcher," she says, her voice exhausted and dry.

He looks at us. "What happened?" he asks again.

I don't want to tell him what she did and so I brush aside the question. "She'll be okay," I say. "What are you doing here? Why aren't you at the boat?"

He shakes his head. "Militiamen are all over the lighthouse and beach," he says. His eyes cut to me in the darkness. "They're looking for you, Gabry. I overheard them talking about Daniel." He pauses a moment. "He wasn't dead when you left him, Gabry. They found him before he died. He told them it was you."

I feel like I've been punched, all the air sucking from my lungs at once. I stumble under Cira's weight and Catcher takes her arm from me. Behind me I hear Catcher and Elias talking rapidly, trying to figure out what to do. Where to go. But all I can think about is Daniel.

I knew I killed him and yet hearing it from someone else—knowing it for sure—makes it somehow different. I realize then that there's a difference between the possibility of hope—the idea of things that we can never know—and the starkness of reality. The weight of knowledge.

Elias and Catcher debate whether to go back to the ruins, to try to make a run for the boat. Around me I can still hear the echoes of town, the ringing of bells and shouts of men. I realize again that there is no escape. That everything is catching up to me, the end.

Gravity pulls me and I think about giving in. I think about my mother and how horrified she would be if she knew what was going on.

And she's what makes me realize where we can go. Where we can run that they might not follow us. "The Forest," I say flatly. I feel a crazy urge to laugh at my own words. Just a few days ago I was too terrified to even think about going into the Forest with my mother and now I'm suggesting that we follow in her footsteps.

Catcher and Elias don't hear me and I turn around to face them. "The Forest," I say louder. They both stare at me, their mouths open in midsentence.

"That's crazy," Catcher says. "There's nothing in there—we'd be killed as soon as we crossed the fence." And then his face blanches. "I mean, you would all . . ." His voice trails off and it hits me again just how much his immunity has changed him.

Elias stands there quietly and then he says, "She's right." He starts to nod his head. "She's right, it's the best place for us to go."

Catcher pulls Cira away from us. "This is absurd," he says.

"No," I tell him, wanting to stop the words from coming. "My mother's from the Forest. There are paths—a village." Even as I'm explaining I want them to talk me out of it.

“There aren’t paths,” Catcher scoffs. His cheeks burn red, his eyes narrow. “We’d know about them if there were any. There’s a bridge across the waterfall and then a gate to nothing.”

“But if there are paths,” Elias says, looking straight at Catcher, “you’d be able to find them. You can go into the Forest and look.”

I nod my head. Catcher opens his mouth to protest but Elias cuts him off. “Look, we need to go somewhere else,” he says, his voice low. “We’re not safe standing here.”

Catcher glances between Elias and me and then at his sister. He purses his lips and then he wraps his hand around her waist. “You promise there are paths? That we’ll be able to escape?” he asks. “That we’ll be safe?”

I want to tell him no, that the Forest terrifies me. But at this point I think it’s our only hope and so I nod and we start running.

XXV

As we wind through town toward the bridge over the waterfall we begin to hear murmurs that the breach was a hoax, a drill of some sort. People begin to throw open the shutters on their houses and we hear shouts from the direction of the Barrier to our right. We work our way to the left, weaving through the streets northward until we reach a band of woods separating the town from the river.

The sound of rushing water begins to drown out everything, even our breathing. We stop at the near side of the bridge and lower Cira to the ground. She stares up at us with deep eyes but says nothing. Elias continues to sweep the area with his gaze, constantly looking over his shoulder. Everything's dark, shadows hiding shadows, the trees overhead blocking out any hint of the moon or stars. The sound of the waterfall pounds around us.

Every outline of a tree or flash of leaves makes my heart leap. My eyes play tricks on me, conjuring figures in the shadows that never materialize.

Catcher crosses the bridge over the waterfall and hesitates only a moment at the gate on the other side before pushing through into the Forest. I stand on the near side of the river, my fingers laced through the fence that borders the water before it plummets over the falls.

When I can no longer see Catcher moving through the trees anymore I turn and face Elias, the sharp metal links of the fence cool against my back. I feel uncomfortable around him after this evening, after we almost kissed. Just thinking about it causes my skin to burn.

The silence between us, touched only by the pounding of the waterfall, seems full, like a cloud about to burst. Part of me wants to apologize again but part of me is still angry at the way he seemed to brush it off so easily. Finally I decide upon the safest thing to say. "Thank you," I tell him, gesturing toward Cira leaning against the tree with her eyes closed. He slices a hand through the air, cutting me off.

I wish I could pull the words back into myself, pull back every instant I'd ever trusted Elias or thought about him. I start to walk away from him but he grabs me, holding me still. I open my mouth but he puts his hand over it.

"Shhh," he whispers into my ear. And even though the night is hot I shiver at the touch of his breath.

He cocks his head to the side, listening. I think I hear something, the barest hint of a noise I can't quite put my finger on, but he stiffens. I feel him move, his hand ever so slowly lowering to his knife.

I do the same as I become instantly aware of everything in the night around us. Before it was just darkness, the pounding of the waterfall and Elias's touch but now I find the subtleties underneath: the shallow rise and fall of Cira's breath, the slight tang of her blood in the air. The feel of a soft breeze over my cheeks, the weight of the knife in my hand.

A bush rustles down the path and I tense. Elias steps forward and I pace behind him so that I'm guarding Cira. There's a hint of movement and then a long low moan. I drop to a crouch, my heart thudding and erasing every other thought or feeling. I grab for Cira's arm, trying to pull her around my shoulder, trying to help her stand.

Just then a Mudo stumbles into view, her steps jerky, one foot crooked and a gleam of white bone jutting from her ankle. Her hair is long and blond, lanky in her face, and her shoulders are bare. In the moonlight I can just see a spray of freckles over her chest, see that the nails of her right hand have been torn free and that her pinky is hanging by nothing but tendons and strips of skin.

She moans again, reaching for us as she shambles closer. Panic rings through my veins. I have to get Cira, I have to get across the bridge. But she's dead weight; I can't rouse her. I want to call for help, to scream but I choke back the urge.

"Cira, honey, come on, we have to go," I plead, grabbing her face in my hands, trying to wake her.

"No," she mumbles, "sleep."

"Cira!" I can hear the panic in my voice, the tone rising shrilly.

"It's okay," Elias says calmly. He's walking toward the Mudo, his steps slow and careful. "She's one of ours."

I swallow back bile as he gets closer to the woman. "Just kill it, Elias," I tell him, but he circles her. She turns and reaches for him, stumbling and tripping and then pushing herself back to her feet, her ankle crunching as it ratchets at an even more severe angle.

I step away from Cira, holding my knife in front of me. "What are you doing?" I yell at Elias. "Kill it!"

But he doesn't. He lets the thing touch him, pull at him. Just like the others her lower jaw is missing, her teeth gone as well. Her moan is pitiful and hollow.

"Her name was Kyra," he says. "She thought this would be eternal life." He pushes her away from him, his touch almost gentle. I want to throw up.

"What are you doing, Elias, just kill it," I tell him again. Seeing him like this terrifies me. "You said you're not a Souler. I thought you didn't believe what they did." I inch closer, preparing myself to kill the thing if he won't.

He moves so fast that it's a blur. He grabs her, presses his fingers into her cheeks and pulls her around until she faces me. I stumble back and tighten my grip on the knife. My heart thrums, pounding hard in my head, and it's difficult to catch my breath. Even though these Mudo aren't supposed to infect I don't trust it.

I don't trust Elias.

The Mudo girl's moans sweep through the air around us, her anguish something I can almost touch. "This is who we all really are," he tells me. "This is all we'll ever be. Shells. Meat. Existing."

I stare at the girl. I think about my own blond hair, so similar to hers. I think of how plain I always felt it made me look. Of all the ways I tried to dress it up for Catcher. I wrap my arms over my chest and cup my sharp elbows. "I'm nothing like her," I whisper.

I wait for him to tell me I'm right. That he could never think of me the way he thinks of the Mudo. But he says nothing, just draws the blade sharp and deep across the Mudo's throat, severing the spine. He lays her gently on the ground and kneels next to her.

The night goes back to what it was before and I glance over my shoulder across the bridge, wondering where Catcher is. Wondering if we've made the right decision to come this way. The trees on the other side of the river shiver and groan and I have to bite my lips to keep my teeth from chattering with fear.

Seeing Elias like that, everything about the past few moments, makes me anxious. I thought I was beginning to understand this boy. "You don't really believe in all that Souler stuff, do you?" I ask him evenly. I want him to tell me no. I *need* him to tell me no.

He looks at me from the corner of his eye and sighs, sitting back on his heels. "I don't know what to believe," he says. His voice is so heavy, so sad, that I take a step closer to him.

"They're dead," I whisper. "They're monsters. They only want to kill us and eat us and infect us."

He shakes his head, reaches out a hand to touch the Mudo's face but then pulls back. I cringe, horrified at anyone wanting to touch one of them, even one that's dead. "Then what happens to who they were?" he asks.

"It's gone. They're just like anyone else who dies," I tell him. I don't want to think about the Mudo being anything but monsters. What would that mean? That there's something left of who they are trapped in a body that wants only to consume us? That every time we kill a Mudo we're killing a soul? I refuse to believe it.

"How can you know?" he asks simply.

"Because that's the way it is," I say, louder than I mean to. My shoulders tense. I don't want to hear his argument, don't want to think that there's any way I could be wrong. If there's anything in this world that's clear—that is black-and-white—it's that the Mudo are dead. There's nothing left of who they used to be.

Elias stands and walks over to me. "I just don't know if it can be that easy," he says.

Frustration blooms and spreads like a rash up my chest and neck. "They're dead," I say more firmly. "They get infected, they die and something causes them to stumble around. Something causes them to chase us. But it's not them. When they die everything that used to be them is gone. It just . . ." I search for the right word. "It just disappears."

"What about the Breakers?" he asks. "Why are they different just because there aren't other Unconsecrated around when they turn? How do they know?"

"I don't know—it's just what happens," I say, aggravated by his ability to twist my words. Around us the night hushes, holding its breath, and I purse my lips. I'm tired of this conversation, tired of Elias making me second-guess something I've known my entire life in the same way I've known that the tides would never fail.

"It's the way it's always been," I tell him. "They die. That means they stop being who they were."

"But what about people who die and come back to life who aren't infected?" he asks. "People who drown and their heart stops and then it starts again. It happens—they die and come back. But they're still the same person. They don't lose anything from having died."

I tug on my braid with exasperation, not understanding why he won't let the discussion go. "That's different. Those people who drown aren't infected. If they were they'd come back Mudo. Probably Breakers if they turn underwater."

"You really think it's that simple?" he asks.

"Yes, it is," I tell him, trying to squelch my own hesitation. "Infection leads to death. Death leads to Mudo. Mudo leads to hunger. It's been that way since the Return and it's the way it always will be."

I turn to walk away from him, to go check on Cira, hoping he understands that I'm done talking to him. But I still hear his next question.

"Then what about Catcher?"

I stop, my back ramrod straight and my hand clutching my knife. I let my head fall back on my shoulders as I stare up at the night sky.

He walks closer to me, until I can almost feel him in the darkness. "He's infected," he says softly. "Are you saying he's not the same person?"

My heart pounds in my chest, my mind circling over and over our conversation. I want to tell him he's wrong, that nothing's changed with Catcher. I want to be furious with Elias for twisting my words but I can't. Because there's no logic to the Return, to the Mudo. There's never been a way to understand it.

"I hate you," I tell him simply. Because right now that's the only way to describe the way I'm being eaten inside, the pain that rips through me.

Elias reacts as if I've slapped him. I know I should take it back. I know I've gone too far and I'm just opening my mouth to apologize when another voice cuts in. Catcher steps off the edge of the bridge toward Cira and I wonder how long he's been there. How much he's seen and heard.

"I've found the path," he says, his chest rising and falling as he struggles to catch his breath. "It's not too far but we're going to have to run as fast as we can." He kneels in front of Cira and pulls her into his arms.

I'm just walking over to him to help when I hear a new noise. This one is a deeper hum than the moan of the Mudo woman earlier. It takes me a moment to realize what it is: the braying of a dog. And then a man's shout laces through it. It's behind us, coming from the path that leads down to Vista. Through the trees I see a spark or two of light and I know they're after us.

XXVI

Catcher doesn't hesitate but jumps to his feet with Cira in his arms.

I can hear the rustling of leaves, of the men on the path closer and closer. I grip my knife tighter and stare across the bridge at the Forest. In my mind I know it's our best hope but my body won't move. It's against everything I've ever been taught, everything I've ever known.

"She has fresh blood all over her. It won't take long for the Unconsecrated to track us," Elias says, nodding toward Catcher and Cira.

Catcher doesn't stop, just walks across the bridge, the glow of the water underneath him highlighting his bare arms that grip his sister. "We'll make it," he says, and I wish I felt his confidence.

I look back over my shoulder. Maybe we could go downriver a bit, climb down the edge of the falls and cut back to the beach by the estuary. Maybe there's another way we can hide from the Militia and Recruiters. And that's when the first dog bolts from the path, running toward us with teeth bared, and I know we're out of choices.

The simmer of panic explodes. "Go!" I shout. "Run!" The old bridge sways under our weight and pounding feet as we sprint across it. In the gaps between the wooden planks the waterfall churns and roars, racing into the black emptiness below. I can almost feel the flames of the torches behind us as we reach the other side of the bridge, as Elias slams against the gate and struggles with the latch.

The old boards beneath us buck as more feet pound on it. Their shouts for us to stop sear up my spine and finally Elias shoves through the gate, swinging it open until it snaps wide against the fence. We pile through, slamming it shut behind us, and then we're in the Forest.

We don't stop. Catcher holds Cira tight as he races through the trees and brush. Elias and I follow, tripping over roots and fallen limbs. I glance back over my shoulder and see the men pausing at the fence. I see their mouths moving but I can't hear their shouts.

Because all I can hear now are the moans. The Mudo have scented us. They know we're here. And they're coming for us. Closing in slowly around us, stumbling from the darkness.

At first I'm convinced we won't make it. That we've just made the biggest mistake possible. Anything—being sent to the Recruiters, facing execution, being jailed—all of it would be better than this.

Anything would be better than being ripped apart by Mudo.

I hold my knife tight. At every leaf that turns in the blackness, at every twig that pops, I swing. Cold terror seeps through my bones, tightens my muscles. In my head I'm just screaming pure panic, trying to swallow it back and focus on what needs doing. Trying to put one foot in front of the other. Not lose sight of Catcher since he's the only one who knows where the path is.

As the ground rises sharply beneath me I stumble and trip, my hands skidding out in front of me. Elias calls out my name. Then he's there by my side, hauling me to my feet. He pulls me behind him, twisting us through trees and brush. Thorns and vines tug at my face and hair and scratch my skin as I push forward.

Ahead of us Catcher is like a dim ghost, a figure barely perceptible in the darkness. I'm terrified to take my eyes off him again. Terrified I'll lose sight of him and our only hope. I feel the Mudo around me, feel their moans against my ears. So far we've been able to outrun them but we can only sprint for so long.

The Mudo will catch up eventually. They always do.

And then something wrenches me back, causes my skirt to tangle and tighten around my legs. I go down hard, pivoting as I fall so that my hip slams the ground. Undead fingers pull at my hem. A Mudo without legs tries to haul himself closer. I kick at him. My heel rams into his arms and head again and again.

His fingers crumple but still hold tight to the folds of my skirt. I drag myself across the ground, trying to get away. Elias runs toward me and doesn't even hesitate before driving his foot into the Mudo's skull with a sickening crunch. At last the fingers relax. Elias hauls me to my feet. More arms and fingers grab for me in the darkness as I hold what's left of the skirt close to my body.

Catcher shifts Cira in his arms and slows. I worry that maybe he's gotten turned around, that maybe he's lost and we'll run in circles in this dark Forest until we can't run anymore. Elias grips my arm and I pant as we stumble behind Catcher.

And then I see it: the gate hulking in the darkness, the bare edge of it gleaming in the rising moon. Hope shivers inside me but I'm afraid to reach for it, afraid that by hoping I'll lose focus. Stretching away from the gate are fences bordering a narrow path. Vines twine through the links, absurd flowers blooming in the night.

Catcher tugs, the gate swings open and we race inside. The first Mudo hits the fence just as Catcher throws the latch behind us. I stumble backward from the force of the Mudo, from the sound of it wrenching itself against the metal. More and more join the first, tugging and pulling.

I turn in a circle, afraid that we might have just trapped ourselves in an even worse position. I stagger down the path a bit, holding my torn skirt close to my side so that I'm nowhere near the fences that line the trail. The grass is high and thick here but I see no signs of Mudo inside the path.

Outside, though, they twist and writhe against the old chain links. I make my way back to where Catcher and Elias stare through the gate, back the way we came. We all gasp for air.

"Will it hold?" I whisper.

No one answers me. We just stand there staring at the Mudo slowly piling against the other side of the thin metal, which groans and shifts under their weight.

Catcher sets Cira on her feet and she sways but is able to stand while sagging against him. He presses his palm to her cheek and she leans in to him.

"You're alive," she says, her pale lips bright in the moonlight. "I thought you were dead."

He smiles and presses a kiss to her forehead. I have to turn away from it, the burning joy of seeing them finally together. I can't stand that I'm the one who told Cira her brother was lost and the reason she almost died.

"I'm alive," he murmurs. "Everything's going to be okay now. I promise."

My throat tightens as if he's talking to me. As if he's promising me that we'll be okay. I want to believe it. I want to hold on to his words but they dissipate in the darkness.

Elias is the one to break the moment. "We should keep going," he says. He glances at the fence straining under the onslaught of the Mudo and I know what he's thinking: that even though we're on the fenced-in path we're still at risk. That as long as we're in the Forest we're always at risk.

Back the way we came I can still hear shouts. I close my eyes, begging that just this once we'll have some luck and they won't choose to come after us. That we're not worth the risk.

Catcher hands Cira a canteen and she drinks hungrily. "Where are we going?" she asks between gulps.

I look at Elias and he back at me. I think about my mother, about her village somewhere on this path. Is it still there? Is she somewhere out there ahead of us? I'm afraid of hoping for either one, afraid to want something that might not be true.

"First we get away from Vista," Elias says before I have a chance to respond. "And then we figure out what's next."

The path in front of the gate is wide enough for us to stand in a small group but it narrows quickly so that it's almost impossible to walk side by side. Cira's still a little woozy on her feet but the water has fortified her some and she's able to take a few steps with Catcher's help.

I try to stay back and help them but I quickly get in the way. I try to walk nearby to hear what they're saying but they tilt their heads close, their voices a low murmur. A few times I hear them giggle and I ask them what about, hoping to join in the conversation. But soon I realize that they're so wrapped up in their own reunion that I'm getting in the way.

I'm left to walk behind Elias, helping to cut back thorny vines and tamp down the taller grass. I don't say anything to him as night falls even deeper around us. I'm still stinging from our earlier conversation. Instead I think about my mother.

Did she make it this far? Are my feet falling where hers recently tread? Did she stop and stare into the Forest and think about turning around? Think about coming back for me? I shake my head, positive that she wouldn't have. In my mind I picture her striding down the path, her steps long and sure and her chin held high.

She wouldn't tremble the way I am. She wouldn't wince at every branch that cracks the way I do. She wouldn't want to claw her ears off at the incessant moaning from the Mudo that always pull at the fence on either side of us.

My eyes water and I swipe at them with the palms of my hands, feeling even weaker for the tears. I take a deep breath, trying to calm myself. Trying to find some sort of strength.

That's the real problem, I think as I slide my thumb along the flat side of my knife, feeling the ridges of the pattern. It's not that my mother lied to me about who I am and where I'm from. It's that I always thought I could be like her. That something in her—what made her so sure and strong—could be in me as well. I just had to find it.

But the fact that I'm not hers means that I really am nothing like her. And that I have no hope of ever being like her.

I almost run into Elias's back before I realize that he's stopped. His head's thrown back and he's looking up. "What's wrong?" I ask, my body tensing for some unseen enemy.

He doesn't say anything, just points up into the sky. I stare at him. "Look," he says.

I take a deep breath, suspicion clouding around me. And then I slowly tilt my head back. The evening sky let go its last grasp a while ago and the darkness has settled in deep. The night smells like flowers and dirt. Like death and blood. The heat of the day rises from the soggy ground and wraps around my ankles.

"What is it?" I ask, feeling impatient and dirty and exhausted and scared.

Elias moves closer, standing behind me, and leans forward until his cheek is almost against my own. I have to catch my breath from the feel of him so near. Anger toward him still simmers inside me but I also can't help flashing back to that moment on the beach and I can't help but realize that if he turned his head and I turned mine, our lips would touch.

I don't want to like him. I don't want to care about him. It's so much easier to hate, to dismiss what he says so that I don't have to think and question the world and everything I've been taught.

Before I can shift away he takes my hand in his, the feeling jolting down my arm, and raises it with his to point into the sky. I turn my head, looking back down the path behind us, wondering just how far back Catcher and Cira are. Wondering if they can see us standing here.

And then Elias whispers in my ear, "Look in the stars." My breaths shudder slightly and I swallow; my vision pulses the same beat as my heart. I follow to where both of our fingers now point. It's hard to concentrate on anything but him, but finally I see it—a tiny bit of light moving steady through the stars. "What is it?" I ask.

"A satellite," he tells me.

I have a hard time focusing on what he's saying and I scan back through everything I learned in school, trying to place the word. He drops our arms from the air but keeps our fingers twined. I want to push him away and pull him closer at the same time. Instead I just concentrate on breathing, watching the trace of light through the sky.

"It's from before the Return," he says. And I remember it now. I remember the teacher telling us about them when he taught us about gravity and the solar system. Elias's thumb skids over my knuckles and my thoughts scatter. Was it just a tic or did he do it on purpose? My heart is racing and I'm sure he can feel my pulse pounding just under every inch of my skin.

"I've never looked for them before," I tell him. "I guess I thought they were gone by now. Like everything else." My voice feels scratchy, my tongue thick. It's hard for me to think about anything other than how close he is. How nice it feels to be holding hands, to have someone to lean on.

"Anything that flies fascinates me," he says softly. I hold my breath, wanting him to say more. Wanting more of this glimpse into who he is. "It's just strange to think about them still up there, still going round and round when everything down here has collapsed and they've become useless. They just . . ." He searches for the word as the wind slides over us. "They just keep going. As if nothing's changed."

I think about how much our entire lives are like that. We're set in motion and then we spend our lives maintaining that motion, but to what end? For what purpose? It never bothered me before. I was happy.

A twig snaps behind us and I jump away from Elias. Catcher and Cira's voices unravel up the path in the darkness and I turn my head, my entire face burning, hoping they didn't see Elias and me together. I cough in the darkness and glance at Elias. He still stands where I left him but he's no longer looking up at the sky.

He's staring at me and the expression on his face causes my breath to hitch. It's like regret and pain and desire. I have to look away, afraid of what my own face shows in return. I'm too confused; I don't know how to feel or what to want.

He steps closer to me and I tense. "I wish I knew how to make it right for you," he says. His voice is so quiet that I can almost believe it's the wind speaking and that he's not saying anything at all. "I wish I knew what you wanted." He turns and continues up the path into the darkness.

I look back where Catcher and Cira draw nearer and close my eyes. So do I, I think.

XXVII

We keep walking, Elias pulling food and water from his pack to pass around. The moon rises and sets and just before dawn we find a small clearing in the path where we try to rest. Catcher and Cira continue to murmur until their voices fade into sleep and Elias snores lightly. That leaves me, staring up at the sky, trying to find a glimmer of a shooting star or a satellite. I keep trying to remember: Have I walked this path? Do I remember these trees? This smell? Those sounds? Memories dance just out of reach until dreams lead me under to twirl away the thoughts.

The next morning is muddy and gray, the air hot and still. Cira has bruises under her eyes but she's able to stand on her own. She eats and drinks some water, a little color returning to her cheeks. She's able to walk a bit without leaning on Catcher, but still, our progress is slow and the Mudo continue to press against the fence on either side of us, pounding and pulling and moaning.

It's impossible to mark the passage of time, impossible to tell how far we've walked. We just continue, one foot in front of the other, the pack on my back chafing at my shoulders.

I don't even notice when Elias stops walking and again I trip into him, stumbling and catching myself by grabbing on to the fence. I'm not used to the fences, to being so near the Mudo. I'm not used to having them press against me until it's almost impossible to breathe. I feel Mudo fingers tug at my own and I scream and fall, clutching my hand to my chest. My heart pounds and I close my eyes to calm my breathing.

When I open them Elias has dropped his pack and is standing over me holding out a hand to help me up. "You okay?" he asks and I nod as I get up, pulling my hand away quickly as Catcher and Cira round the bend behind us.

I step back and focus on adjusting the straps of my pack.

"What's going on?" Catcher asks, and my cheeks flame red, thinking he's talking about me and Elias. That he sees something that isn't there. I glance sharply up at Elias but he's not looking at me.

"There's a gate in the path," Elias says, pointing.

If possible my face burns even hotter. I feel stupid that my first thought jumped to Elias. I twist my fingers tighter in the straps of my pack and step toward the gate, hoping to hide my expression from everyone else. Why should I even feel guilty that Elias helped me stand up? Why should I think that Catcher would mind?

I clear my throat, pretending to examine the gate that spans the width of the path. An object gleams under the handle and I brush at it with my fingers. "I think there's something here," I say. The others have been passing around water and they pause as I squat to get a better look.

There's a small bar attached to the fence and etched onto

it are the letters *IV*. "I think it's like the numbers my mother taught me when I was younger," I say, glancing back at them. "It says *IV*, which means four."

"Does the path keep going past it?" Cira asks.

I squint through the links into the distance. "Seems to." I wrinkle my forehead, studying the letters. Something tugs at me, pulls at the edge of my mind. But trying to catch it is like trying to capture snow and I'm left with nothing solid.

"Our options are to go forward or turn back," Catcher says. "So long as the path's clear I say we take it."

They walk through the gate and I'm left squatting on the ground, still trying to figure out what feels so familiar. If I came through the Forest with my mother I must have passed through this gate. I'm startled when Elias reaches down for me again and this time I ignore his hand and stand up on my own.

The contents of my pack shift a bit and I press my hands into the small of my back to ease the ache.

Elias tilts his head. "Everything okay?" he asks, and the expression on his face seems to show genuine concern.

I turn and follow the others down the path. "Fine," I tell him as I keep walking away and he closes the gate behind us.

▾ ▾ ▾

Our day is cut short when Cira can't walk any more, her legs trembling and face pale with sweat. Catcher helps her to the ground and Elias lights a small fire and we spend the early dusk swatting at mosquitoes and saying little. None of us knows what to talk about.

It feels as if we're strangers, too terrified to discuss our current situation yet also too scared to talk about anything else. Finally the moan of the Mudo and the buzz of the cicadas become too much for me to handle and my legs begin to tighten with the need to move. I'm not used to being constantly surrounded by people, my every gesture and sound and movement scrutinized.

"I'm going to walk a bit, see what's ahead," I tell them, and then I pull out my knife and start up the path before anyone responds. I'm not too far away when I hear a familiar footstep crunching through the dry grass and Catcher calls out my name. I stop and wait for him to catch up.

"It's stupid for you to be walking alone, Gabry," he says. My shoulders tense. I want to tell him that that was my point, that I want some time away from everyone to think. To figure out what's going on. But I don't say any of that because it's been so long since we've talked, since I've been near him, and it feels good to have it be just the two of us in the dusk.

I reach out and take his fingers in mine. "How are you doing?" I ask him.

He looks at the ground, at our hands, at the fence—everywhere but into my eyes. He shrugs, a wash of emotions blurring over his face. "I don't know," he finally says.

It's not the answer I'm expecting. I want him to confide in me; I want to feel as close to him now as I did the moment we kissed. I know that everything else has changed since then but he's alive, he's survived being bitten. His immunity shouldn't change anything between us and yet somehow I feel it has. I wish I could find some way to make him talk to me but instead I just hold his hand tighter.

"Did you tell Cira about everything?" I ask him. "The immunity?"

He nods. "I'm not sure she really understands it. But she was so happy she cried." He smiles a little at this and I'm reminded how much I love to see him smile. How much we used to tease each other. I try to smile back but it's strained and feels wrong. He stares at our hands, at the way our fingers are interlaced. "I'm not sure I really understand it either," he says softly.

"What's it like?" I ask him, hoping to understand what he's feeling.

He breathes deep against me, his chest almost brushing my arm. "Physically, it's like . . ." He pauses. "It's like fire. It's like being in a room with no windows and no door and the heat just builds and builds and builds until you can't breathe."

"Does it hurt?"

He's silent. And then he says, "I think the worst part is not understanding. Not knowing if I'll suddenly turn. What would happen if I died . . ." He trails off and the silence stretches between us again.

I'm afraid of breaking the quiet but I have to know. "It'll be okay, won't it?" I ask, tilting my head up to his, trying to recapture that closeness we had before it all changed. That hope and future. He pulls his fingers from mine and starts to walk down the path. The evening air pools around me where his body had been and I feel desperate and alone.

I don't understand what I've done wrong and I chase after him but the path is too narrow for us to walk side by side. He crushes through the tall grass, his hands swiping out in front of him.

"Catcher, wait!" I call.

He stops in front of me and I see his shoulders rising and falling rapidly as if he's trying to catch his breath. He doesn't turn around and I go and place my hands on his back, tracing his spine. "Don't do that, Gabrielle," he says, glancing over his shoulder for just a moment, his eyes bright, before he turns and stomps on.

"Don't do what?" I ask him, not understanding what he's talking about.

He turns abruptly and my hands press against his chest. He grabs my wrists and holds them away from his body. "Don't remind me of how everything's different. Of us."

My eyes go wide, my jaw dropping, but I don't know what to say. He's so severe and angry and I have no idea what's going on.

He shakes me slightly. He opens his mouth but it's as though he can't find the words. And then before I know it he lowers his head to mine but stops just as his lips are hovering over my own. His skin is almost painfully hot, the heat scorching up my arms.

I have a hard time catching my breath. I ache to twitch my head forward, to press my mouth over his. I lean forward just barely and he backs away, keeping the distance between us.

"I want this—you—so badly," he says, his teeth clenched. "I want to forget everything. To just pretend that nothing's changed and you can be mine and I can dream about us together one day."

His fingers are tight around my wrists, squeezing me. My chest feels bound as all the air is pushed from my body. He's saying all the words I've always wanted to hear from him—that we could be together—but somehow it's all wrong now and the pain of it is almost physical.

"I *can* be yours," I tell him. "I *am* yours."

His grip on me tightens and he closes his eyes, his breath shuddering as he brushes his mouth across my cheek and then along my jaw and across my forehead. His heat marks me and I'm shaking because I want so much more of him.

I try to reach for him, to pull him closer but he pushes me away. He stands there staring at me, both of us gulping air. A line of sweat weaves down my back. I wait for him to say something—anything to explain what's going on. But he's totally silent.

"Catcher," I say, moving closer. My voice is a whisper, a plea, a question. He just holds up a hand to keep me away. And then he turns back and runs down the path to the others. I don't even bother to chase him. I'm too stunned to even move. I can only bend over at the waist and grasp my knees with my hands, trying to breathe. Trying to figure out what just happened and what I've done wrong.

I feel bruised and sore and dazed. The Mudo are still moaning, only now it's impossible to see them clearly in the darkness. It sounds as if they're all around me, as if I'm trapped by them. I hear snaps and rustles from the Forest, each sound scraping across my nerves.

I start down the path to the safety of the others and by the time I make it back I'm almost sprinting, positive that the fences have been breached, that the Mudo are chasing me. I burst into the small clearing where Elias and Cira sit next to a fire. He jumps to his feet, catching me in his arms.

"What's wrong?" he asks. He looks past me up the path, reaching for his knife.

My words are choked with panic. "Mudo," I gasp. "The moans . . ."

Elias pushes me behind him and takes a few steps down the path. Cira reaches for me.

"Did they breach?" Elias asks. He looks ready to fight.

"I—I don't know," I stammer. "They seemed so close. Like they were right there on the path."

He waits a while longer, the moans wafting over and

around us. Finally my heartbeat calms, my mind clears. No bodies stumble into our little band of light.

"I think I just let it get to me," I finally say, embarrassed at having panicked. "It was just dark and . . ."

Cira holds my hand in hers. "It's okay," she says softly. "It's okay to be afraid."

I turn to her, not realizing until now how much I needed to hear that. She pulls me into a hug and I want to sag against her but I'm careful, knowing that she's still weak from dehydration and blood loss. I should be the one holding her, not the other way around. But right now I just need someone to reassure me.

"Where's Catcher?" I ask her, wondering if I've driven him away completely.

She studies my face. Did Catcher tell her about me? Did he tell her about our almost-kiss? About him running away when I tried to press against him? Does *she* understand at all what's going on with him?

"He said he wanted to retrace our steps, make sure no one followed us into the Forest," she says, yawning.

I narrow my eyes and glance at Elias, who shrugs. I didn't even think about that possibility—the chance that the Militia or Recruiters might be after us. It seems like it would be such a stupid risk—one that none of us is worth. I lie down beside Cira, wondering with each twig cracking if it's the Mudo coming after us or if it's some other threat we don't know about yet.

▾ ▾ ▾

"They've followed us," Catcher says abruptly the next morning. We've been passing what little food we have around and trying to ignore the shuffling of the Mudo along the fence on either side of us. I stop mid-bite at Catcher's words and wait for his eyes to flicker toward me, to see something that shows me how he feels about what happened between us last night. But he's been avoiding my gaze ever since he got back.

"What?" I ask. Cira and Elias echo the same question.

"I cut through the Forest last night—these paths curve a lot," Catcher says. Cira stiffens as her brother talks about roaming through the Forest with the Mudo but she doesn't say anything. "I made it almost all the way back to the river and to Vista." He glances at Elias and then down at the strap of the canteen that he twists in his fingers. "They're making the Soulers extend the fences on the path to the bridge over the waterfall so that they can follow us without risking running through the Forest."

Elias blanches and then clenches his hands into fists, the muscles tight along his jaw.

"What are you talking about, Catcher?" Cira asks, and I nod my head, still not understanding what's going on.

"I don't know who it is—whether it's the Militia or the Recruiters or both. But they're preparing to enter the Forest. To come after us on the path."

Suddenly everything I'd eaten that morning feels sour in my stomach.

"Why would they come after us?" Cira asks. "They can't care about me that much. I know I was supposed to join the Recruiters but why would they risk it?"

I push myself to my feet and take a few steps away from them. In my mind I see Daniel. I see the stain of red on his shirt. I see the way he looked at me. They're after me, not Cira. They're not going to let me get away with what I did. It's all catching up to me except this time I've put my friends in danger too.

The realization dazes me and I start chewing on my thumbnail, turning everything over in my head. Everyone else talking falls to a buzz that fades into the background with the moans. "I'll turn myself in." I don't even realize that I've spoken, don't even remember forming the thought.

Catcher and Elias and Cira stare up at me, all of them surprised. "It's me they're after. For what I did to Daniel. I'll go back down the path. You keep going. You'll be safe." I say the words in a monotone but it feels good to own up to what I've done. As if retribution for my running away that night at the amusement park has finally come full circle.

"I don't understand. What does Daniel have to do with this?" Cira asks, her eyebrows drawn tight.

I turn to her but I can't make myself say it. Catcher reaches out and takes her hand, shaking his head as if telling her not to ask. She presses her lips tight.

"That doesn't make sense," Catcher says.

"No," I tell him. My heart is light, fluttery, like a hummingbird beating in my throat. "I killed him. I have to own up to it."

▾ XXVIII ▾

Cira gasps, raising a hand to her mouth. Her eyes are wide and I look away from her.

"I've made up my mind," I tell them. And I have. I'm terrified but this feels right.

Elias stares down the path, tapping his fingers against his hip. "Did you see them? See the Soulers?" he asks. His forehead is furrowed, as if he's lost in thought.

Catcher nods.

"Who else was there? Were there Recruiters?"

I look back and forth between the two, trying to understand what point Elias is trying to make.

Catcher nods again. "Yeah, I think they were the ones shouting to the Soulers how to put the fences up."

Elias presses his lips together and then runs a hand over his head, rubbing the hair growing in. "It doesn't make sense," he tells Catcher. "The Recruiters wouldn't care about Daniel. Wouldn't get involved in what they thought was Vista's business to handle." He laces his hands together and pulls on the back of his neck, his shoulders tensing. "And you're sure you saw the Recruiters involved?"

"I'm pretty sure," Catcher says, but his voice is hesitant. "I can go back and check, though. Tonight."

Cira grabs his hand. "It's too dangerous," she murmurs to him.

"Gabry can't go back there," he says to her under his breath. "They'll kill her."

Hearing it put so starkly hits me like the crush of a wave. "Why else would they be after us?" I ask them. My voice barely carries any volume.

"Did anyone see you?" Elias asks Catcher, cutting into our conversation. "When you took the Mudo to the town did anyone see you with them?"

Catcher's eyes open wide. "I . . ." He hesitates, thinking. "I don't know. I don't think so." He looks up at the sky as if trying to relive that stretch of time. Everything around us seems to go quiet, the birds ceasing their morning chirps, even the moans receding just a little, as if all the Mudo waver at once. And then Catcher's face goes pale and he drops his gaze back down to face us.

"There was someone," he says. "When I got over the Barrier. I didn't think about it because they ran when they saw the Mudo."

"But you think they saw you with the Mudo?" Elias asks.

Catcher nods slowly. Cira and I stare at each other, both of us clearly lost about what's going on.

Elias presses two fingers against the space between his closed eyes. "They're not after Gabry," he says. "They're after Catcher. If they saw him with the Mudo they've figured out he's immune."

"So what?" Cira asks. "So what if he's immune? Why would they care enough to risk the Forest?"

I hug my arms around my chest. The relief makes me feel weak, makes it hard to stand. They're not after me; I don't have to turn myself in. But these thoughts make me feel traitorous. How can I be relieved when Catcher is now the one who could be in trouble? When we've merely switched places?

"You don't understand," Elias says. "Immunity is rare—rarer than rare. Practically nonexistent. The Recruiters are desperate for Immunes."

Cira opens her mouth to protest but he cuts her off. I can see the agitation prickling at Elias's body as he talks. "An Immune can go anywhere. Do anything." He begins to pace, tight little circles that make me dizzy to watch.

"Do you know how many towns and cities are out there that are so overrun with Unconsecrated that it's impossible for any living person to get to them?" he asks. "Everything in the safe areas has been picked over. All the cities that survived—we've taken what we can from them. Think about all the places out there where an Immune could go and get supplies. And not just that: an Immune is the perfect weapon. They can walk into the middle of one of the hordes and kill every last Unconsecrated. They can rescue trapped men." He puts his hands to his head. "The Recruiters, they'd do anything to get their hands on an Immune."

Cira's face is as pale as mine feels. I never considered this about Catcher, never thought about what the immunity really meant on a larger scale. All I cared about was that he hadn't died—wasn't going to die. That we could still be together. My legs feel shaky and I let myself crumple until I'm sitting on the ground. We're all silent, considering this new information, each of us figuring out how it changes us and our relationship with Catcher.

"Then I'll go back," he says softly.

Cira yelps, "No!" She grabs his arm. "Not when I thought I'd lost you before. Not now—I need you. No, Catcher."

He places a hand against her cheek but she just shakes her head. "No," she says again. "No."

"It's like Gabry said." He glances at me, holds my eyes. "It's the only way to keep us safe. To keep the people I love safe."

I can't help but hold my breath when he says this. To feel the sizzle of the words along my skin. The people he loves, I think. "You can't go," I tell him softly. "Please."

In just that second it feels as if we're alone here. That everything else that's going on drops away. There's no Mudo, there's no infection or path or Recruiters. It's just us, looking at each other the way we did that night in the amusement park before our first kiss. I want to take this moment and wrap it up tightly and hold on to it forever.

But then Elias clears his throat and I'm snapped away. "That won't stop them from coming after us," he says. "That's the problem. The Recruiters can't control the Immunes—they just walk away into a horde or something if they want to escape. So the Recruiters capture and keep anyone close to the Immune. That's the only way to make sure they come back—hold someone they love and the Immune will do their duty and always come back."

I draw in a sharp gasp, looking at Cira.

"Me?" she says, her eyes wide and frightened.

Elias nods, glancing at me. "All of us," he says. "We all escaped with him. Therefore they'll think we all mean something to him. I've heard about it happening before."

Catcher spits on the ground and walks away from us down the path, his hands laced tightly behind his head, knuckles white. I want to go take his arm in mine, soothe him, but the implications of what Elias is saying reverberate in my head. We're all targets now. None of us can go back.

"We have time," Cira says to her brother. "You said they weren't even in the Forest yet. That the Soulers were still connecting the path to the bridge."

Catcher shakes his head, pacing back to us. "I can't, Cira," he says. "I can't let them use the Soulers like that. If any of them die it's my fault."

I'm about to tell him that if they die from being infected it's probably what they'd want but Elias speaks up first.

"They're not forcing the Soulers to do the work," he says. "They're doing it voluntarily. That's the thing. To the Recruiters you're a tool. But to the Soulers you're like a prophet—you've survived the infection. They'll do anything to get to you, just as much as the Recruiters will."

Catcher drops his face into his hands. I just stand there staring at everyone. A part of me wants to release the pressure and fear inside me, to laugh at how everything's changed so quickly again. At how crazy this world can be. Last week Catcher was just a normal guy with a normal future ahead of him. And now he's gone from facing his own death to facing a cult that wants to worship him and an army that wants to use him.

"What do we do?" I voice the words I'm sure everyone else is thinking.

"We keep going," Elias says simply.

We sit in silence, everyone lost in their own thoughts, trying to make sense of what's happening. And then Catcher sighs and offers a hand to Cira and then one to me. His skin is still hot when I grasp him but it's now a familiar heat and I wonder if I'll ever think of Catcher again as he was before.

I stare down the path as we start moving again. Somewhere ahead of us is my mother. All I can hope is that if we can only find her everything will be okay. The way it was when I was a child and I'd scrape my knees and elbows and she'd kiss them to make them better. All my life she's been able to make it all right. It's the hope that I hold on to as we walk and walk and walk on this endless path.

▼ ▼ ▼

Because Cira is still weak and slower and Catcher and Elias have stayed back to walk with her I'm the first to come to the branch in the path and I drop my pack to the ground.

The fences on either side of the path seem different here, more fragile. The metal twisted and fatigued. I bend my fingers around it and tug, wondering if it can hold off the Mudo. When I pull my hand back my palm is coated in black like ash and I wipe it against my shirt.

The Forest here is thick and lush, but still fairly young growth. In the distance I can see a large tree with old burns and I close my eyes, trying to think back. Do I remember a fire? Do I remember the blackened tree trunks?

I kick at the fence in frustration and I hear the clank of something shifting. I bend down to look and that's when I find a bar identical to the one on the gate, this one crusted with ash and dirt. Surprised, I smudge away the grime until I see the letters: *VI*.

This is the second number I've found, the second marker on the paths. I sink back on my heels, realizing what it means: The Forest has a code. Whispers of something skirt around the edges of my mind, tugging and then dancing away. Nothing I can grasp or examine.

"It looks like the paths are marked," I tell the others when they catch up. I point to the bar. "This one is number six and the other is eight. The last one at the gate was four."

"We must be getting deeper into the Forest," Catcher says. "Maybe they're like depth markers or something. A way to tell the distance."

I scrunch my face. "Maybe," I say, but I'm not convinced. I glance at Elias but he's silent as he helps Cira to the ground, where she drapes her bandaged arms over her legs and takes deep breaths.

We should rest here. We shouldn't push her as hard. And yet every time we try to make her take a break she refuses. We're all aware of the Recruiters at our backs.

"Which way?" I ask.

Catcher considers the two paths. "We could scout," he says, but Cira's already shaking her head.

"We need to keep going," she says. "It looks like that one goes back to where we came from." She points a finger toward the path that branches out to the right. "I say we take the other one so we make sure not to double back."

Her eyes are still bruised and sunken but her skin looks healthier. I haven't talked to her about what happened, about what she did to herself. I resist the urge to reach up and clutch the superhero I still wear around my neck. I wonder for a moment if she would have cut herself if I hadn't taken it from her. If I hadn't left her alone or if I'd been able to give her some sort of hope.

I want to tell her I'm sorry, but I'm too scared to talk to her. I let Catcher be the one to walk with her, Elias the one to check in on her. Even now I start to walk ahead down the path, hoping to avoid her, but she calls out my name and I stop, my nerves bristling.

She doesn't say anything more and I slowly turn toward her. She holds out a hand to me and I help her up. Catcher and Elias go forward and when I try to join them Cira pulls me back, tucks her arm in mine. I don't miss the grimace as her bandaged forearm brushes against me.

"You'll have to stop avoiding me at some point," she says. I try to smile, try to brush off her words, but she just pulls me tighter to her side as we start following the others, winding through the moans drifting in the humid afternoon.

I struggle to think of something to say, something to talk about that isn't Catcher and immunity and death and the path and her arms. But the more I search for a safe topic, the more my mind screams at me to ask her why, why, why.

"Just ask," she says, and I have to laugh, remembering how it is we've always been best friends. Even now, with everything else around us falling apart, we can still be the same.

I squeeze my eyes shut. I think of the blood dripping from her fingers. "Why?" I whisper.

She watches our feet as we walk, the blur of step after step after step and for a moment I think she's not going to answer. "Do you ever wonder about the Mudo?" she asks.

I shake my head but I'm lying. I'd never thought anything of them before I met Elias. Before I learned about the Soulers. Before Catcher became infected.

She laughs a little, just a puff of air against the side of my neck. "Me neither. They were just these things out there beyond the Barrier. They were what kept me from trying to go to the Dark City, what kept us all locked in and isolated. I never really cared about how they came to be. Who they once were. And then that night with Mellie and Catcher and everything at the coaster. When that girl came at her like that. I don't know. . . ."

I hear her draw a deep breath, as if to steady herself. "I fell apart," she says. "That Breaker came running at us and I panicked. If I'd been able to do something . . . anything but just sit there and scream . . . maybe none of this would have happened. I didn't want to have to go to the Recruiters and face the Mudo again. I didn't want to fail again."

I stop and turn her to face me. "You didn't fail, Cira," I tell her, shocked to hear her saying the same words I've felt. "We were all afraid. I still am. You can't blame yourself for what happened."

She puts a hand on my arm. "Neither can you," she whispers. I suck in my breath and she smiles. "I know you, Gabry. I know how your mind works. I'll stop blaming myself when you stop blaming yourself." She cocks an eyebrow at me. It's such a Cira expression that I laugh, feeling how easy it is to slide back into our friendship.

She turns back to the path, swinging our arms between us. "Now let's stop talking about the sad stuff and get back to the good stuff. I see the way Catcher watches you. Especially the way he looks when you and Elias are talking. So let's hear the whole story."

I blush, embarrassed that Cira's noticed but also flushing warm inside. I didn't realize that Catcher still looked at me the way he used to; I thought he'd given up on me. I want to spill everything and ask her to help me sort through the confusion but I'm not ready to talk to her about it.

"I won't kiss and tell," I say to her in a singsong voice and she throws her head back laughing. This is what life is about, I think. And I can almost forget where we are as we continue down the path together giggling and sharing stories.

XXIX

It's dusk when we come to the next break in the path. Storm clouds are creeping in overhead, the sky rumbling. This time there's a large square with paths leading off in each direction, a gate at each intersection. Cira and I have trailed behind the other two and when we catch up, Catcher has already scouted down each path a little ways.

"They're marked," he says when we join him in the center. There's space here for us to spread out a bit and I help Cira to the ground. Her breathing is shallow and her cheeks a vivid red but she refuses to rest whenever I ask her.

I walk around to each gate and squat, looking at the markers: *IX, XXX,* and *XIV*. I turn the numbers over in my head, trying to find some sort of meaning.

"It doesn't make sense," I tell no one in particular. "I thought the numbers were going up, that they were just increasing, but . . . I don't see the pattern." Sweat drips down my back and chest and along my cheeks. The air is unbelievably close and heavy with the impending storm.

"It wouldn't help anyway. Not unless we know what we're looking for," Cira says, still trying to catch her breath. I worry she's pushing herself too hard.

"Maybe we should stop here where there's space to spread out," I suggest. Catcher frowns but I tilt my chin toward where Cira can barely hold her head up. I know we want to put as much distance between us and Vista as we can, but we can't do so at the risk of pushing her over the edge.

"Fine, I'll gather wood for a fire," Elias says, starting down one of the paths with Catcher trailing along to help.

Cira's fallen asleep and I sit with her for a while, staring at my hands, tracing the edge of the cut across my palm from the night I first took the boat past the Barrier. Thunder ripples overhead, the concussion of it whispering around me.

I wonder where my mother is out there. And that makes me think about my other mother—my first mother. I close my eyes and breathe in the sweet scent of almost-rain. I try to remember. The sound of the wind through the trees so similar to the crash of waves. So that for just a moment, just this one minute, I can believe I'm back at the beach. That my mother will come to me soon.

Why didn't I go with her? Why did I let her go back into the Forest alone? It seems so stupid now, so silly for me to have stayed behind. Especially now that I ended up following her after all.

I reach into my little pack and pull out her book of Shakespeare's sonnets. Rubbing my hand over the cover, I think of all the times she read it to me. I think of the hours she spent carving lines of the poems into the doorjambs of our house, something I never understood and that she promised to explain to me at some point when I was older but never did.

There are too many things I don't understand about her, I realize. So much that I missed.

Flipping it open, I turn to the first page and begin to read Sonnet I. At the line "Thyself thy foe, to thy sweet self too cruel," I think of the way my mother would press her fingers against these words every time she left the front door to the lighthouse, the engravings softening over time at her constant touch.

I read Sonnets II and III, not recognizing any of the lines from the doors of our house. But I do remember the line from Sonnet IV—"Thou of thyself thy sweet self dost deceive"—from the door to a sparsely used closet on the lowest floor, and from Sonnet VI—"Then what could death do, if thou shouldst depart"—from the curve in the wall at the bottom of the stairs.

My head starts to swim a bit, my stomach rumbling, and I glance down the paths wondering where Catcher and Elias are. Lightning shatters the sky, illuminating the world around me in stark brightness. I tense, waiting for the thunder. Cira doesn't even move, her breathing steady and deep.

But something has caught my eye and I find myself staring at the little bars with the Roman numerals on the gates. As a game I flip to the corresponding poems to read. Sonnet XXX, "I summon up remembrance of things past, / I sigh the lack of many a thing I sought," was carved into the landing at the top of the first flight of stairs. Sonnet XI's lines were gouged into the back hallway.

And then I start to wonder—what if there's a pattern to the way my mother chose what to carve where? My heart starts to beat faster and I close my eyes, mentally walking through the lighthouse and reading the words on the doors.

I gasp as everything starts to fall into place. The first gate, with the Roman numeral *I*, matches up with the line carved into our front door. The next gate we walked through, number six, has the words from the base of the stairs. At this crossroads there are three gates for us to choose from. Two of them have lines from the poems carved into closet doors but one of them is on the stairs. It's as though the words are leading me somewhere.

With shaking hands I flip back through the book. At the top of the stairs in the house there's another quote and I scan the pages, searching. I want to shout with excitement as I trace my fingers over the lines of Sonnet XV. I flip through the book for the words carved into the door of my mother's bedroom.

Everything around me fades away: the moans, the feel of the wind tugging on the pages. All I care about is piecing together this puzzle, figuring out what clues my mother left. Did she do this for me? Or was it her own way of remembering? Her own way to find her way back through the Forest?

And then I remember what she told me the day she left—that to find her I just had to follow the light. I'd always thought she meant that the lighthouse would always be my home, that so long as it stood it would be her home as well. But now I remember the words she'd carved into the lantern room before leaving.

It's as if my heart doesn't beat as I flutter through the pages, the lines playing through my mind again and again: "Nor shall Death brag thou wander'st in his shade, / When in eternal lines to time thou grow'st: / So long as men can breathe, or eyes can see, / So long lives this, and this gives life to thee."

And then I find it: Sonnet XVIII. My eyes blur, not even

reading the letters. My mother wasn't telling me to follow the light to go home, she was telling me how to find her in the Forest. There's no other reason she'd have left this book behind for me. No other reason she'd have carved the words and told me to follow them.

I smile, feeling so close to my mother in this moment, as if she's been playing this little game with me my whole life and I've finally figured out the pieces.

When Catcher and Elias get back from gathering wood I'm about to burst from excitement. I can barely contain myself as I tell them about what I've figured out—the tie between the book and the paths and the words carved into the lighthouse. While I'm not sure I've totally convinced them that I'm right, at least we know what to look for and that there's really no other reason for us to choose which path to follow.

After we eat some of the food that's left, Catcher doubles back through the woods again trying to see if the Recruiters have entered the Forest and how far behind us they are. Elias builds a small fire and Cira continues to sleep through it all, her body still recovering.

I sit next to her, staring into the flames as the storm still threatening in the darkness and the silence between Elias and me stretches around us. He has the sleeves of Roger's shirt rolled up over his elbows, and the light from the fire flickers over his skin. In the way he sits with his back straight and muscles tight it's clear that he's always aware of everything around him.

Even though I try not to I think about the moment on the beach when he almost kissed me, my face flushes and my body thrums from the memory. I want to ask him why he did that but I'm too embarrassed.

Sap pops in the fire, the logs shifting and tossing sparks into the sky, and Elias looks over and catches me watching him. I'm sitting with my knees pulled up to my chest, my arms crossed and my chin resting on my hands. I want to bury my head in my arms but I don't. I hold his gaze, in that moment feeling more bold and confident than I have since the night I first skimmed over the Barrier with Catcher.

I'm so energized from figuring out my mother's clues that I can't sleep. Wind brushes through the tops of the trees, reminding me of the sound of waves, and I close my eyes pretending I'm back on the beach with Elias.

"Tell me something about you I don't know," I say. It's easier to find the words in the darkness, easier to forget he's a stranger.

XXX

Elias smiles just a little and the heat creeps into my face even more. "What don't you know?" he asks, and I can't keep myself from grinning.

I raise an eyebrow. "Everything," I tell him, my voice breathier than usual.

He laughs then, a small and quiet laugh that lifts his shoulders and causes his eyes to crinkle. It reverberates in the night and I realize that I haven't heard him laugh before. I also realize that I like it, especially how warm it makes me feel.

He glances down at the empty space next to him on the other side of the fire and I hesitate. I'm still stung by his earlier rebuff, still angry at him. But it's tiring to stay so mad, especially when we're the only two awake. I scoot around next to him. We're close enough that the light plays gently over our skin but distant enough that I can't read every expression.

He thinks for a moment. "Do you know what a Skinner is?" he asks. I shake my head. He leans back and his shoulder brushes mine. My first instinct is to pull away but I feel daring tonight so I leave it be, the hairs on his arm whispering against my skin.

"It's a name for people who go into the Forest looking for things," he explains. "Sometimes they're looking for something specific—maybe someone has put a price on some kind of gear needed for a machine. But usually it's just for anything that can sell or be traded."

I knew that people scavenged the ruins but not that people would actually risk going into the Forest to search. I feel bumps break out on my skin just thinking about what it would take to push someone past the fences. I've never realized that people could become that desperate and it makes me understand more and more how much I don't know about the world outside Vista.

"Why are they called Skinners?" I ask.

He looks up into the sky as if gathering his thoughts. "After the Return, for a while, when people thought things would go back to normal eventually, some people would hunt the Unconsecrated just for whatever valuables they might have on them. Usually it was things like jewelry, money. Anything they might have died with. But then, when supplies started running out, they would take whatever they could." He shrugs. "A lot of times that meant taking everything, including clothes and shoes. Everything but the skin."

I shudder. "That's awful."

Elias shrugs again. "It's not a job that anyone would really want. But if you're smart and fast you can find enough skinning to survive."

He leans forward and rests his elbows on his knees. His shoulders are hunched and he rubs the back of one hand against the palm of the other slowly. "See, my sister . . ." He hesitates just a little but presses on. "We were orphans at an early age. We didn't have anything—no one to really look out for us."

My chest constricts at his words, an ache for the little boy he'd once been. I lean forward and watch the side of his face as he keeps talking.

"The thing is, I'm not that scared of the Forest. I knew there were some safe spots. I knew how to get to places no one else could go. I was actually a pretty good Skinner for a while. Enough that we were allowed into the Dark City to trade and even had a place to live there."

The fire catches a piece of dry wood and the flames jump a bit, illuminating his expression. He keeps rubbing one hand over the other and staring at them but I'm pretty sure his mind is in the past, in some moment I can't touch. I almost hold my breath, afraid that breathing too deeply will pull him out of where he is, and I'm eager to know more of this memory.

"There was this one winter," he continues. "It was worse than any of the others. Cold enough that most of the Unconsecrated were downed and enough snow that they were covered—the Forest was nothing but pure white.

"Most Skinners would give up. Too dangerous to go into the Forest when you could accidentally step on Unconsecrated. But I didn't have a choice. Not with my little sister and needing to trade to stay in the city. It was a bright blue day when I went into the Forest and I could smell the snow coming but I kept pressing deeper."

He stops and glances at me, his eyes bright. "Have you ever heard silence?" he finally asks. "Like real silence. Not the ocean, not the Unconsecrated. Not even the humming of insects or chirping of birds."

I'm mesmerized by him. By the feel of him so close and the way his voice trails along the curves of my ear. I shake my head.

"It's the most beautiful thing in the world," he says. "I just . . ." He pauses and looks back into the fire. "I just kept walking. Wrapped in this white nothingness. I ended up in this town. Not a town like the others in the Forest, fenced off and protected. But a real town that had been hit by the Return and just left to die. It was so still, nothing moved. I could walk down the streets and imagine what it might have been like to live in the before time.

"The thing is . . . there was this monument in the town. It had a plaque attached to it that talked about some great world war that the town had sent soldiers to fight in." He smiles. "It was an airplane," he says. "An actual airplane that they'd mounted on this rock in the middle of town."

I close my eyes and try to imagine it but I can't. I've only ever seen old pictures in books and even then it's hard to fathom machines spinning people through the air.

"I got to run my hand along the edge of its wing," he says, his voice full of energy. "I even got to climb inside it. Think about it. Being able to fly. To just float above everything."

"What was it like?" I ask him, wanting to be there with him.

"Big," he says. "Impossible that it could ever stay in the air. I spent the whole afternoon in that plane. Wishing with everything I had that it would just take off. Take me away from there."

He's silent for a moment and when I open my eyes he's

staring at me. Except that now his gaze is serious, intense. The laugh lines are gone from his face and his forehead scrunches up a little. I swallow. It feels as if with this one gaze he's dismissed everything but me and him and the memory of a frozen plane.

"There was a part of me that really believed that if I truly wanted it enough . . ." His voice is almost hoarse, threaded with sadness.

"What happened?" I whisper. Suddenly I'm not sure if he's talking about the airplane or about us.

He looks at me for a while, for so long that I want to glance away. I don't know what to think or how to respond. I don't even know if I want to hear his answer.

"Nothing," he finally says. His voice cracks, just barely. "Nothing happened. I just sat there, the plane never moved. It began to snow and I was trapped in the town. I ran into the closest building, which turned out to be full of books—a library. The storm lasted for almost a week and then I left. I probably read everything in that library that had any mention of flying."

My heart is pounding so hard that I'm sure he can feel it crushing the air between us. Though we're not even touching I feel as though his body has been all over mine.

I press my lips together and draw a deep shaky breath. "Do you still believe that if you truly want something enough it can happen?" I ask. I think of all the times I wanted to stop the world from spinning, all the times I wanted to go back and start over again. All the things I've wanted to undo or take back. Did I not want them enough?

Elias shifts until he's so close to me that I can feel the warmth of his lips hovering over mine. I can smell the sweetness of his skin, the tang of grapes we've both been eating. "Yes," he says, barely making a sound.

I feel dazed and dizzy, afraid to move and his mouth almost touching mine but not quite. It's impossible to breathe anything but him, to feel anything but him.

"How else would I be here now?" he murmurs, the vibration of his words tingling along my lips.

Cira coughs and shuffles on the other side of the fire, snapping me out of the moment. I push myself away from Elias, scrambling back until I'm standing in the darkness, the air suddenly cold so far from the flames. It's like jumping into the ocean on a scorching afternoon, jarring me from the bubble of heat with him. Behind me the Mudo moan and the fence clanks.

"I'm sorry," I say, and immediately I know that I've said the wrong thing again. That by apologizing I've made him think what we were doing—how close we were—was a mistake. That I regret it. And I don't know if I do or not.

His face, so vulnerable before, shuts down into a scowl just as it did on the beach when I apologized for almost kissing him. "I don't mean—" I start to say, reaching toward him.

He brushes a hand in the air, waving my words away. "It was stupid of me," he says.

I'm surprised how much his words hurt. "Elias—" I say, trying to get him to understand that I'm not pushing him away, I just don't know what I want anymore.

But he cuts me off again with the shake of his head. "Drop it," he says.

My stomach lurches with embarrassment at how I can suddenly feel like nothing in his eyes when just a few moments before it seemed that I was everything. I still stand there, but he turns his back and lies down in front of the fire, closing his eyes.

I don't understand what just happened. I don't understand how I feel anymore. All I can think about is Catcher the night he was infected—but rather than the feel of his lips I remember him telling me that sometimes you can think you know someone and then they say something or do something and suddenly everything changes. You don't think of them the same way. That's how I feel about Elias except that I'm still so unsure of him. I don't know where he fits in my life or where I want him to fit.

▼ ▼ ▼

The skull sits surrounded by a mound of dying flowers. Elias, Catcher and Cira press against the gate at the end of the path, staring beyond it to where the fences stretch out in huge arcs, creating a wide open space. But I'm focused on the flowers. The tips of most are brown and dry around the edges, the petals limp and almost colorless, the stems peeling where they've been plucked from the ground.

It's the end of another thick and humid day, the air heavy with unspent rain and heat. I swipe at the sweat on my forehead, my palm coming away slick and wet. I stare at the skull, tracing the fissures that crest its dome.

"What number is it?" I ask them.

Catcher reads the letters off to me. "Fourteen," he says.

I think of the words carved on the door to my mother's room: "Thy end is truth's and beauty's doom and date." I always thought it a depressing line, never understood why she would want it in her room. Why she'd want to be reminded of death when it's so constant on the beaches outside. But one thing is clear: We're supposed to pass through this gate.

Because he's immune Catcher is the first one to go, doing a sweep of what's beyond to make sure it's safe. I stare at the skull and the flowers. While the bones are faded and old, the flowers have to be recent. Someone else has been down this path not too long ago. And a feeling swells inside me, a recognition that it could have been my mother.

I reach down and trace my finger over the curve of the skull. It's separated from the rest of the body, which usually indicates decapitation—which would mean that whoever this used to be was Mudo or infected. I shiver and stand back up but my eyes are still drawn to it. I wonder if in the past, before the Return, when the dead stayed dead, the world was littered with bones like this. What it must have been like to live back then.

"It's all clear," Catcher says, opening the gate and startling me. "But it's a little strange," he adds. "It's not really a path. I mean, the path continues on the other side but there's a huge open space in between that's fenced off. I think"—he looks back over his shoulder into the emptiness behind him—"I think it might have been a village at some point but now there's nothing left."

XXXI

He steps back and we file past him. The fences stretch out to either side of us, arcing around almost out of sight in the distance. In front of us is nothing: scrub trees, tangles of vines and bushes heaped over mounds of something that used to be.

"We should camp here," Catcher says behind me. "There's enough space and I want to try to circle back through the Forest—see if the Recruiters have started after us and how much time we have. Maybe throw them off at some of the gates and splits."

Cira tries to talk him out of it but I know she won't be able to. I want to tell him to be careful but he brushes my concerns off as well. He and Elias clear a spot for a fire while I wander around and explore.

I feel exposed here. The sky above is too wide after days under the canopy of the Forest. I'm used to keeping my arms tucked in, my steps even, because of the fences so close. Here I can fling myself about—run if I want to.

But I don't. It's just too open. It's unsettling.

I stumble over a pile of rocks and pull aside the weeds and vines to find what looks like remnants of an old stone wall. Shadows of scorch marks still smudge along the edges of it. Except for the ruins beyond the amusement park, I've never seen another village or city and I wander through it, trying to figure out how it was laid out. I find random objects: a few knives, a pot, the heel of a leather shoe.

I stroll down what I think must have been a wide street. Thick tangles of vegetation choke walls and spill out of collapsed doorways, making it almost impossible to pass.

Something crunches under my foot and I yelp, jumping aside. It's an old bone, now shattered and jaggedly sharp. I take a step back but there's another crunch. I twist around and realize that there are bones—skeletons of every size—everywhere. Some of them have holes in their heads with steel arrowheads that rattle inside. I take another step back but my ankle turns when my foot slips on a skull.

My breath comes in pants now. I reach out to try to grab something to hold on to, to keep me standing, but there's nothing there and I collapse in the sea of bones. They're everywhere: skulls, ribs, femurs. My stomach lurches as my hands scatter them, trying to push myself to my feet.

I scramble over them all, horror choking me. How many people were there? How many bodies are scattered throughout this place? I think about my mother, about her living in a village in the Forest. Is this where she grew up? Is this where I was born? I can't help but wonder what happened to this village and the people who used to live here. Are there ruins like this all over the world? Villages that were? Is this what Vista will be someday?

It makes me think of a picture that the teacher who taught

us about gravity once showed me. It was a photograph taken from space, probably from one of the satellites that Elias pointed out to me. The teacher told us it was the pre-Return world at night and all I remember is a sea of darkness with more lights than stars in the sky. All of them cities and towns and villages and houses.

I wonder what would happen if you took that picture now, how the darkness would have grown. And I think about what all those satellites have seen: villages like this one winking out one by one until there's nothing left.

I wrap my arms around my chest as the sunlight leaches from the sky. Is that all we have left? Is that all we are? Lights on a map that are slowly dying, hanging on for nothing?

▼ ▼ ▼

That night I'm left alone with Cira by a bare ember fire. I feel full of all the things I haven't told her, of all the secrets between us.

"Something's different with you and Catcher," she says. She's pulling the bands of cloth off her arms and using the hem of her shirt to clean the edges of her wounds. I look into the blackness of the Forest, into the sweep of stars across the sky, anything but at her and her cuts.

"I can't figure out what's changed about him," she continues. "I thought he'd be happier to've survived the bite, but . . ." Her voice trails off and I know she expects me to say something to fill the gap but I don't have anything except questions. Once I thought I understood Catcher, or at least was starting to. Now I feel as if he's more of a stranger to me than Elias.

I stare at the ground watching a beetle navigate a blade of grass. The air tonight is still and hums with mosquitoes and cicadas. And moans. Always the moans of the Mudo. They writhe against the fence, even more animated than usual with the scent of Cira's dried blood in the air.

"Remember that time when we saw Mellie kissing Daniel behind the Council House on a dare?" she asks. She's still wiping gently at her arms. I nod, staring into what's left of the fire. I try not to think of Mellie as I last saw her. Or of Daniel and the blood.

"I used to think that the worst thing back then would be to get caught doing something like that. That the worst problems we'd face were who we'd end up with. Not stuff like this. Not death and infection." She cringes as she pulls a bandage stuck to the wounds on her right arm. "I just can't believe they're gone now. I don't know how to handle any of it. Don't know what to do to help Catcher. Or you. Or anyone."

I pull my braid over my shoulder and tug on it. "We always knew it was a possibility," I say. "We were always told what happened outside the Barriers. We've known about the Mudo." I sigh. "We shouldn't have gone that night," I add softly.

She pauses, her fingers hovering over a pile of fresh cloth strips to use as bandages. I glance at her and that's when I see the puffiness of the wounds. The streaks of angry red radiating out from the cuts. She sees me staring and tries to hide them but I grab her wrists and pull them toward the light. Her skin is hot, almost as hot as Catcher's.

"Cira," I say sharply. I try to keep from panicking, try to keep my tone even. But I know what the streaks and heat mean; I know she's got a blood infection and she's had it for a while. "Why didn't you say something?" I rack my brain, trying to remember what plants and herbs to use to bring down the swelling. My mother used to make it and the recipe is just on the edge of my mind.

She pulls away from me. "There's nothing we can do out here, I didn't want anyone to worry," she says, rewrapping the wounds.

I shake my head. "We could have done something," I say. "Does Catcher know?"

"No."

"Cira, you can't keep this from him," I tell her, my voice low. We both know he'll be insane with worry but he should be aware of what's going on.

She purses her lips, her way of telling me to stop arguing. But she's my best friend and she's hurt and I'm angry that she hasn't told me about this, that she hasn't allowed me to help her. This isn't like us, keeping secrets.

She edges closer and leans against me. "It's going to be okay, Gabry," she says. She's still the same girl who waded into the river while I stayed on the bank and cried. She's still the one to hold my hand and tell me it will be okay.

"Maybe we should go back to Vista," I tell her, my voice thick with memories and longing for that time before everything changed. "We can find something for your arms."

She shakes her head and raises a hand to smooth my hair off my face, pulling it loose from my braid and then combing the tangles with her fingers. How many times did she do this when we were growing up? How often did we sit around gossiping and sharing dreams?

But what is there to gossip about now? The people we knew—Mellie and Daniel and Blane—are dead or joining the Recruiters. The dreams we used to have seem so far away now, like the faded satellites circling in the night with no purpose, no way to call them back.

▼ ▼ ▼

In my dream I'm running down the path through the Forest. It's lined with intricately woven metal fences and I'm chasing a girl but I don't know who she is. She's young and lithe, her long blond hair blowing behind her in the wind. The fence is crowded with Mudo, all of them wearing the white tunics of the Soulers, and they pull and yank at the delicate metal, causing it to sway and rattle.

My lungs sear with the icy cold pain of having run beyond my limits, but I'm afraid that if I stop my legs will no longer hold me and I'll collapse. I'm not fast enough, I can't reach the girl, and somehow I sense that she knows this but she won't slow down.

And then I see her reach for something and she grabs the photograph of Mary and me in the ocean—the picture of us laughing in the waves—and she tosses it high over her shoulder. I try to catch it but it floats through the air, morphing and twisting until it's a bloodred bird that flies off into the night, scarlet feathers from its wings drifting around me.

The girl turns to face me then, and instantly I recognize her. It's me—I've been chasing myself.

I stop and fall on the ground and while the Mudo tear down the fences and crush around me, I stare at the bird as it drifts higher and higher, letting its feathers float around me and bury me. I watch satellites whirl through the sky, blinking a message I'll never understand, as the girl who was me runs away into the the dark Forest.

And then I feel a hand around my wrist, a familiar hand, and it pulls me out of my dream. I wake up gasping and find Catcher kneeling next to me in the darkness. The fire's nothing but shifting embers and I can hear the even breaths of Elias and Cira sleeping.

"It's okay," Catcher says. "It was a dream." But I'm still struggling to breathe, my heart beating so hard it shakes me. He pulls me against him and I curl into his heat. I feel the pound of his pulse echo through my body. It's so strong that it's hard to believe it carries infection. It's easy to pretend that nothing's changed. To imagine we're back in the darkness of the amusement park, the summer stretching out endless and full of possibilities around us.

I look up at his face, reach up with a finger and map out his jaw in the night. I can feel his muscles move under my touch. I let my hand drift to the back of his neck and I push my fingers into his hair. I lean my head toward him, tugging him to me.

In the darkness it's easy to believe that tonight's like any other night in our town, just the two of us in the amusement park flirting with our futures.

But this time he doesn't allow his lips to brush mine—he tilts his head away.

"Why won't you kiss me?" I ask.

XXXII

Catcher's voice is like a hiss of raindrops hitting a smoldering fire. "Because I'm infected."

"But you're still alive. The infection means nothing," I tell him, feeling desperate to believe that nothing *is* different. I push the image of him standing among the Mudo at the amphitheater from my mind. I concentrate on how solid he feels under my fingers. On how infinitely human he is.

"It means everything, Gabrielle," he says.

"How?" I sound petulant but I don't care.

He squeezes his eyes shut. "Because what if it means I can infect you?" he whispers.

I suck in a quick breath. It's something I haven't considered, and sitting here now in his lap I feel instantly vulnerable. I swallow, my throat straining as I push down the sudden fear that leaps around me. What if he's right? There's no way to find out without taking too big a risk.

I don't know what to tell him. I don't know how to

challenge what he's saying. And my silence tells him everything. He sets me from his lap and stands and starts to walk away from the fire.

I scramble after him. "Catcher," I call out softly, trying not to wake the others.

He starts to jog but I refuse to let him go. I'm tired of not knowing what's going on with him, what's going on between us. I stumble over rocks and debris that he seems to skim right over and it's not until he's reached the fence that I catch him. He pushes his fingers through the links as if grabbing hold, as if preparing to climb.

"Wait," I tell him, desperate to make him stop. I come up behind him. I press myself against him and wrap my arms around his chest. "Wait," I say again, needing to have him listen to me even though I'm not sure yet what I want to say. His heat wavers over me, always that incessant reminder of his infection.

I press my lips to the base of his neck and I wonder if he can feel me trembling. I kiss the contours of his shoulder. Can he sense my fear? Does he know how miserable I've been? He sags slightly as his breath shudders through him.

"I can't, Gabry," he says, but he doesn't stop me. I twine my fingers around his, gripping the fence with him, the barrier between our world and his world.

"You're just like me," I tell him. "We're the same," I add, but I'm not even sure I believe it. I don't know what to do with him now. I don't know how to talk to him. To this boy constantly on the edge of death. Everything I've ever known, everything I've ever learned tells me that he should be dead. Should have died days ago.

What do you say to someone who faces that?

I try not to think again about Elias and the Soulers and their beliefs about the Mudo and humans, how we're intertwined. Instead I pull back the folds of his shirt and I press my lips against the edge of the red welt on his shoulder. The only visible remnant of the wound that infected him.

Just then a Mudo lunges against the other side of the fence and I pull back, Catcher's heat leaping through the air between us. He turns and leans on the metal links. Behind him I can see the moon glinting off the cloudy Mudo eyes; I can see the outlines and edges of their broken teeth and hungry mouths.

I try to hide my horror but I know that Catcher can see it. "You're not like them," I tell him again, trying to convince us both, but I know he doesn't believe me.

"I can't take the risk, Gabry," he says. "I'll never know if I'd infect you." And then he turns and climbs the fence and before I can reach for him he's on the other side. He pauses and slides a finger through the links. I reach out and grab it. "This is part of me now," he says. The Mudo around him push as if he's not there, as if he's one of them, and his grasp falls from mine.

I want to shout for him to come back but I press my lips together to keep silent. I want to tilt my head back and scream at the world for doing this. For making everything so complicated and unfair. I want to pound at the fences and kill all the Mudo, end their moaning that won't ever stop.

But I don't. I just stand there and stare at them. They were always nothing but monsters, nothing but animated death to me before; a scourge to be dealt with. Yet Elias's questions still circle through me, making me wonder if anything of who these people were could be left behind, trapped inside.

Because if I'm alive and the Mudo are dead—what does that make Catcher?

▼ ▼ ▼

I wake up the next morning to the sounds of screaming. I'm lost, struggling from the depths of sleep, cresting to the surface to find chaos. It takes me a moment to realize that it's Catcher shouting and he's yelling for his sister.

He sprints toward the fence, his hand raised. "Cira, wait!" he calls out. There's panic in his voice, threading through the words.

My heart jumps and I'm instantly alert. I look to the ground next to me where Cira slept and find the spot empty. My mouth goes dry, a thousand possibilities spinning through my mind. I surge to my feet, my toes and fingers numb with sleep.

I catch movement out of the corner of my eye and see Cira at the fence line. She's already climbed halfway to the top and for a moment I can't make sense of it. Can't figure out why she would be trying to get into the Forest. What she could be running from or to.

But she keeps pulling herself higher and I realize that she's about to reach the top. Already the Mudo are shifting through the trees, shambling toward the promise of her with their arms outstretched.

Sweat coats my body. Elias is already chasing after her by the time I stumble up behind him.

"Cira!" I cry out in surprise and alarm at the same time Elias yells for her to stop. She pauses and looks over her shoulder at us. At her brother.

For a moment I think she'll stop. I think she must be delirious or asleep. That she'll hear us and slip back down to the ground and the safety inside the fences. But she just turns and keeps climbing.

"Stop! What are you doing?" I yell. She doesn't listen. Doesn't look at me again. It's as if I'm not even here, as if none of us is. I push harder, trying to make it to her before it's too late.

Elias is almost to the fence. He reaches for her but she swings her legs over and jumps to the other side. We're both too late.

"Cira!" My throat is almost raw. "Come back!" Too many thoughts hit me and tangle at once: that she's in the Forest, that it's not safe, that she doesn't have a weapon, that if I only scream louder she'll hear me and understand.

Horrified, I watch as Mudo shuffle toward her. She runs past them into the trees, stumbling through the thick underbrush.

I reach the fence and beat it with my fists. "Cira!" I shout. I twist my fingers around the rusty links and scream louder. I don't understand what she's doing, what she can be thinking. The metal of the links digs into my fingers but I don't care—I just pound harder.

Catcher hits the fence next to me and doesn't hesitate before launching himself over it. He lands on the other side and sprints after his sister. The Mudo don't even turn toward him. Don't even notice he's there.

I feel the sobs beginning to build. Beginning to suffocate me. "Please come back, Cira," I try to scream, but my voice catches and breaks.

I can only watch as Catcher cuts toward his sister and the Mudo close in on her, block her from view. They choke off the distance between her and the fence and they begin to stumble in from either side as well. The blood dotting the bandages on her arms intensifies their need, their craving, and they lurch closer.

"We have to help her." I start trying to climb. "We have weapons, we can keep them from her," I say, desperate to do something other than stand here and watch.

But Elias pulls me back, wraps his arms around my body. "We can't," he says. "There are too many. They'd get to all of us."

I shake my head, my mind screaming to protect Cira even though I know that Elias is right. We stand there, me choking on sobs and Elias holding me as we watch Catcher close in on his sister, and I have to turn my head away. I can't watch my best friend get bitten.

I realize then that Elias is pressing his lips to my temple. "Shhh," he keeps saying, but I can't stop the keening wail that echoes from deep inside me. I press my face into his shoulder, my lips trying to remember a prayer, trying to entreat anything, anybody to save my best friend.

Elias cups his hand over my head, holding me tight against him. "He's got her," he says. His body is tense. I feel his heart beat wildly beneath my cheek.

"He's carrying her out." He tries to sound calm but I can hear the tension in his voice. I turn my head and peek back through the fence and I see Catcher running away from us at an angle, carrying Cira deeper into the Forest.

"Wh—what is he d-doing?" I stammer, grabbing the metal links. I shake the fence, clinks and reverberations radiating out to either side. He's taking Cira away from us, away from the safety.

And then I understand. "The paths," I say, my voice jumping with hope. I turn back to Elias. "He said it before about how you can cut through the Forest to the paths. Maybe he's taking her to another one."

I step away from him, everything in my mind a whirl at once. "We have to try to find them," I say, my hands shaking as I wipe sweat away from my upper lip.

Elias opens his mouth as if to protest and I stare at him. He looks into the Forest where Catcher and Cira are dodging trees. "Grab the packs," he says. "We'll have to run to catch up."

I jump at his words, relieved to have a plan—something to focus on and occupy my thoughts so that I don't think about Cira being in the Forest. Cira with blood on her arms. Cira, who isn't immune to the Mudo. Who's still weak from the blood loss and now infection.

I grab what I can, shoving the full canteens into the packs and throwing what I can't carry at Elias. We run through the empty village to the gate at the other end, opposite where we entered.

Elias shoves it open and starts running down the path, jumping over brambles and dodging fallen tree limbs. My chest is searing but I push myself forward as the full pack sways and bumps against my back. We have to find them. She has to be okay.

As if hearing my thoughts Elias says, "She'll be all right."

I nod because I don't have the strength or the energy for anything else and because I need to believe him. All I can do is force one foot in front of the other and try to stay between the fences as I stare out into the trees, desperate for a glimpse of Catcher or Cira.

We come to a branch in the path and Elias doesn't hesitate before veering right. At some point they should cross this path; they have to. As my feet pound against the ground I can only think: They will make it. They will make it.

Elias begins to pull away from me and I wave for him to go ahead. My legs are burning, my lungs screaming. He turns a corner and then freezes. I slow down, stumbling to a walk. He doesn't draw his knife and so I know that it's not Mudo he sees; it's not danger.

He has to have found Catcher and Cira. I don't want to but I force myself forward, my arms and legs shaking. I can tell from the set of his jaw, from the way he holds his body, that there's something around the bend I don't want to see.

XXXIII

He holds out a hand for me to stop but I don't. I can't. I have to know what happened. I suck in as much air as I can, pressing my fingers to my lips and steeling myself for whatever lies ahead.

Before I can see anything I hear the whimpering and I change my mind. I stop in the middle of the path, one foot hovering above the ground. I don't want to see it. I don't want to face whatever it is Elias is watching, whatever it is that's around the bend.

I realize that this is the way the world works. If I could stop the spin, stop the rotation, I would have done so long ago. I would have stopped it the first moment that Catcher's lips met mine under the moon in the amusement park. I would have held us in that eternity forever.

But of course everything presses forward, even as we dig our feet against the reality of it all. One event tumbles from the next out of our control and we are dragged along, helpless.

That's why I force myself to raise my eyes, to take that step and to face what's happened. Even though I know more clearly than I've known anything else that what I'm about to see will break me.

Catcher sits in the middle of the path. His sister, my best friend, Cira, is laid across his legs. He bends over her, his head against her chest. The sound coming out of his mouth is like the moans of the Mudo. It penetrates me and carries me down into myself so that it's almost impossible to stand.

I look over at Elias, at the way he stands there staring. His face is white, his lips like a ghost. His eyes are wide and his chin trembles. And I realize then that he doesn't think of himself as an outsider—as a stranger. He's one of us. I reach for his hand but I'm too late. He walks down the path to Catcher.

Elias kneels on the other side of Cira. He places a few fingers against her cheek. And then he reaches across her to Catcher and grips his hand. I swallow, barely able to catch my breath as I watch them, my own grief storming all around me.

"Did they . . . ? Is she . . . ?" I can't say it. I take a step forward until I can see her face. See the way she stares into the Forest as if the rest of us aren't here.

Catcher shakes his head no and I sag against the fence with relief until I feel the trace of Mudo fingers along my arm and I pull away.

"But why?" I ask, trying to understand what drove Cira into the Forest. Trying to figure out why she would do something like that. No one answers me. I think about the cuts on her arms. I think about how she'd already tried to give up once before. I wrap my arms around myself, shaking.

I don't know how to fix her. I don't know how to make it better. I don't know what to say or do to help her. Except tell her that we can survive this. That we *will* survive.

And I realize that maybe this is the one thing that will always pull the people of my world together. The more we lose, the more we become the survivors.

▼ ▼ ▼

"Maybe we should go back to Vista," I say softly to Catcher and Elias. Cira sits in the middle of the path staring into the Forest, lost in her own mind. Bandages circle her arms, rusty with dried blood from where her wounds pulled open when she climbed the fence. She hasn't said anything, hasn't explained anything, and my relief that she's okay is starting to simmer into anger and frustration.

The blood infection still rages through her, red streaks radiating up her arms, her skin flush with fever. I'm afraid that if we continue out here in the Forest she'll just get worse. That we'll be too late to do anything about the infection and it'll kill her.

"We can't," Catcher says, looking down at his feet. His voice is despondent, his eyes ringed with deep bruises from pushing too hard and not sleeping enough.

"She's sick, Catcher," I tell him. He grimaces. "I don't just mean from the cuts. I mean . . ." I think about the determination on her face when she climbed the fence this morning. "I just don't know if we can take care of her," I finish weakly.

Birds explode from a bush past the fence, causing us all to wince with their tangle of cries. The Mudo continue to moan.

"The Recruiters are already in the Forest," he says. He's still looking at the ground as if what he's saying isn't a big deal.

I push my fingers against my forehead, tension pulling at the muscles of my shoulders and neck. We're trapped now, no way to go back. I try to keep my breathing steady.

"How far away are they?" Elias asks.

Catcher shakes his head. "They made it to the path the other morning. They're moving pretty fast. But I still thought . . ."

"Yesterday." I can't even put sound behind the word, can only move my lips. The Recruiters have been running through the paths for a day already. I feel sick, my stomach twisting around nothing since we've been slowly running out of food.

"What do we do?" I ask, my voice breaking.

Catcher shrugs. It's as if he's given up the way his sister has and I want to slap him. I've fought too hard for him and for Cira. I've given up everything for them—every chance I could have had for a normal life.

It's not fair for them to stop fighting now. I turn and pace down the path a bit, needing distance. I can't be the only one who stays strong while everyone else gets to fall apart; it's not a role I'm used to or even know how to handle.

Something rustles behind me. I know it's Elias—I've already memorized the sound of his steps on the overgrown earth.

"Gabry," he says softly, the way you'd approach an injured animal. He sets a hand on my shoulder, his touch light, barely even discernible.

I shake my head. Afraid something inside me will explode and I'll either lash out in rage or despair. I want so badly to be like Cira. To collapse on the path and have someone else make the decisions. Someone else fight for me. It doesn't seem fair that I'm not allowed to give up too.

Elias steps closer behind me. I want to lean back against his chest and let him hold me. Let him be the one to keep me standing. But instead I turn to face him. He keeps his hand on my shoulder and now barely anything separates us. Behind him, out of the corner of my eye, I see Catcher still staring at the ground. Cira still lost in her own mind.

Elias's face is a mirror of mine: pain and doubt. He's usually so calm and in control, and seeing him like this makes me wonder what in his life has led him to this moment. His thumb barely traces the edge of my throat, so softly that I think I might only be imagining the touch.

It's supposed to be Catcher standing here with me, not Elias. It's supposed to be Catcher who holds me and comforts me and gives me strength. He's the one I've always known and trusted and dreamed about. But now all these lines are blurred and confused.

I part my lips. I'm about to tell Elias everything about me. That I was born in the Forest. That I've been on these paths and survived and that I hope I can do it again. That somewhere out there is my mother and my past. And somehow, before I even have to say the words, before I utter any of it, I know he'll understand.

"We should keep walking," Catcher says.

It's as if his voice jerks me out of a trance; as if I've been staring at Elias for a hundred years. I shake my head and step away from him. My cheeks begin that slow embarrassed burn and I glance at Catcher, wondering if he notices. But he's silent. His face betrays nothing at all.

▼ ▼ ▼

We trudge down the paths in the thick summer air, choosing which branches to take and which gates to pass through based on the code I figured out in my mother's book of sonnets. Always walking toward the light—following the paths that will lead us to Sonnet XVIII, the lines written in the lantern room of the lighthouse. The afternoon threatens us with thunder, the sky closing in around us, yet it barely rains and our canteens start to run dry. But Catcher doesn't want to leave Cira to forage in the Forest for a stream and with the threat of the Recruiters behind us, we keep walking.

At first I feel uncomfortable being near Cira. Catcher hovers around her, helping her when she can't keep up. She seems to stumble along the path not seeing anything, and I wonder if she really has given up or if it's the blood infection taking over, making her lose touch.

I can't stop wondering how much time she has left. If she'll ever recover.

And then finally the silence between us is too much and I drop back, taking her hand from Catcher's and holding it tight in my own.

"Tell me again how it will be okay," she says, her voice hoarse.

There's so much of her missing, so much of who she used to be—the spark and energy. "It'll be okay," I tell her, hoping she believes my words even if I'm unsure of them.

She stops walking, causing me to stop as well, and smiles. She squeezes my hand and I realize how bony her fingers have become, how narrow her wrists. Tendrils of her hair are loose and limp around her face. Freckles scream against her pale skin.

I glance down the path to where Elias and Catcher keep pushing forward. I tug on her to keep going but she holds me back. "I know the infection's bad," she says. She has to catch her breath as she talks and it hits me again how much effort this whole ordeal's been for her. "I'm not even sure if I'll make it to . . . wherever."

Her eyes are glassy. I swallow and shake my head. I feel the superhero pendant against my chest and I pull the necklace over my head. I step closer to her, reaching around her neck as I fasten the clasp. "You're wrong," I tell her. "Cira, don't—" But she cuts me off by pressing her lips to my cheek, soft and dry.

"I'm dying, Gabry," she says, pulling away. Tears flood her eyes. "I'll never fall in love. I'll never have a family—get to be the kind of mother I always wanted. I'll never know what it feels like to be everything to someone." She smiles softly. "I'll never even kiss a boy. Tell me what it's like?" Her voice is nothing, quieter than a whisper.

I shake my head. I refuse to admit that what she's saying can be true. That she has any reason to worry about whether she'll survive. I don't even want to think about it but she puts her fingers on my wrist and says, "Please," and I see the pleading in her eyes. How desperately she wants to know.

I nod and think back to the night at the amusement park with Catcher. I think about the evening on the beach with Elias. I don't know what to tell her, how to explain the feeling of wanting and yet being so scared it won't happen. That moment when there's no turning back and his lips land on yours. How different it can make you feel. So beautiful and needed and special.

I start walking down the path and she walks next to me, her hand in mine. "It's wonderful," I finally say. "And also a little weird-feeling. I mean, not knowing what to do and how it works." A laugh bubbles up and it feels so refreshing after spending so long thinking about death and infection and the Mudo. "You worry that you're doing something wrong," I tell her. And then I lean closer and whisper, "I couldn't stop wondering what the last thing I'd eaten was." I smile as she giggles.

"I don't want to hear the bad parts," she says with a grin. "I only want you to tell me the good parts."

And so I do. As we wade through the late-day heat I tell her all of it, forgetting that we're in the Forest, that we're being chased and aren't sure of where we're going. Just feeling like friends sharing an everyday afternoon walk.

XXXIV

We're still giggling when I round a bend and see Catcher and Elias standing in front of a gate. Elias's face is pale, his fingers drumming against his leg. I feel my smile falter; Cira's hand goes limp in my own.

"What is it?" I ask them.

"Number eighteen," Elias says. "X-V-I-I-I."

"Oh." I just form the word with my lips. I don't have to pull out the book to know the lines of this poem, the sonnet my mother carved into the lighthouse the day she left. This is the last gate. My heart thrums a little longer as if measuring the beat of the words in my head. As I walk toward the gate, Cira falling in step behind me, I whisper the final line of Shakespeare's eighteenth sonnet: " 'So long lives this, and this gives life to thee.' "

Beyond the gate the path continues, just like all the other paths. The fences on either side, the Forest beyond. The Mudo rising and stumbling toward us.

I walk faster and faster, excitement building inside. My mother could be at the end of this path. And so could my history. So could all the answers. My heart hammers harder, my legs twitch and I break into a jog. Behind me I can hear the others as they follow but I don't bother looking back.

Until I come to another gate. Beyond it I can see the shadows of buildings, the fence opening up as it did for the last village. And suddenly I'm too terrified to take another step. Sweat slides down my cheeks, along my neck and between my shoulders. I'm afraid this village will be like the one before: empty and dead.

Elias comes to a stop behind me. I can hear him trying to catch his breath. I swallow and turn to look at him. Even though we've both been running, his face is pale. He's not looking at me but at the gate. His fingers tremble slightly as he rubs them over his head.

I have this crazy giddy moment when I just want to laugh at us standing here after everything we've been through. Neither one of us willing to take that next step. What would happen if we just stayed here forever, never moving?

And then, as if the Forest is exhaling, pushing me forward, I unsheathe my knife, put my hand on the gate and pull it open.

▼ ▼ ▼

I walk into the village slowly, my head cocked to the side to hear voices or moans—anything to let me know there's someone or something here. I wait for some memory to trigger, for familiarity to wash over me, but it doesn't. In front of me to the left sits the hulking burned shell of a building, charred stone walls toppled, decaying beams jutting out at awkward angles. Well beyond that I can see the outlines of small houses huddled together in the shade of a few tall trees with what looks like platforms strewn through them.

Behind me the Mudo moan against the fences and the wind rustles the leaves in the trees. Crickets chirp and hum in the heat. I walk slowly past an old graveyard, my feet following a well-worn path that's more of a rut in the ground.

Nothing stirs. No one shouts or comes running. The village seems empty and my chest begins to ache with fear that we've hit another dead end. I walk a little farther, wondering if I should call out. I pause by what's left of the charred building. It clearly used to be huge, an old cracked bell lying in the midst of blackened stones and scorched timbers.

My foot slips on a board and a few rocks fall and shuffle, the noise barely anything but enough that I hold my breath. Something stirs off to my left. I turn and crouch, gripping my knife tightly.

A large black dog lying in the sun lifts its head from the grass by one of the gravestones and examines us. I wait for him to bark or growl but he doesn't. Instead he lumbers to his feet, his muzzle sprinkled white with age. He approaches slowly, his tail thumping in a lazy circle, and I hold a hand out to him. He sniffs and pushes his nose against my fingers.

I let out the breath I'd been holding. He clearly knows people, is obviously cared for. That means there must be someone else alive in this village and my heart begins to thunder in my body. The dog yawns as I scritch his ears, his tail beating against my legs.

Just then Catcher and Cira make it to the gate and start walking toward me. Before Catcher can get too close I hear the vibrations of a growl deep inside the dog.

"It's okay, boy," Catcher says, kneeling and holding out a hand.

The dog nudges me away from Catcher, standing between us, the hair on his neck rising as he sniffs the air. I don't understand his change, his instant dislike of Catcher. Suddenly he begins to bark, deep long brays that shatter the stillness of the afternoon. I cringe at the sound and instinctively look around for some place to hide, some place to get away from the dog.

I lose my footing and something shifts in the ruins of the old building, a pebble falling through the debris. I hear voices and my breath catches, my throat suddenly dry. Beside me Elias tenses, pulling out his knife. I see someone moving through the shadows, skirts swishing around her legs as she picks her way through the crumbled mess. She's caught off balance, something large and bulky wrapped in her arms, and she stumbles.

Sunlight breaks through a hole in what used to be the roof and I see her face. I see her white and black hair. The wrinkles around her eyes that remind me of her smile. "Mother," I say, the word gathering from every corner of myself and bursting into hot joy. I feel tears prick my eyes; just seeing her infuses me with the feeling that everything is now going to be okay.

She looks up and her breath catches as she sees me standing at the entrance, the grass waving and bowing around my calves. "Gabrielle." I don't hear her but see the way her lips move, the look of love on her face. I can't help but smile.

She drops the book she's holding and it breaks against a pile of rocks, thin delicate paper exploding into the air, drifting around her like feathers.

And then she's running through the debris and I'm running to her and finally her arms are around me. She still smells like salt and the ocean and the lighthouse. I bury my face against her shoulder as she pulls me tighter. I can hear her heart. It's the feeling of home. Of safety and comfort and love and memories.

She pushes me back, her palms on my cheeks. She stares into my face, searching to see if I'm okay. Her eyes are bright and I feel tears already coursing down my cheeks.

"My baby," she whispers before holding me tight again. It feels so right to be in her arms, as though I'm a kid whose mommy can fix anything.

"I'm so sorry, I shouldn't have—" she starts to say.

"I know," I cut her off. "I'm sorry too. I love you. I've missed you." I've been waiting so long to say those words, to put right the things I told her the night before she left.

I hear her draw a shuddering breath. I can feel the smile breaking across her face and I want to laugh, giddy with relief to be with her again.

Something flutters against my leg and I pull back to look at it. It's a page from the book she'd been carrying, onionskin-thin and yellow. There are faded words typed down the center and then pinched black scrawl in the margins. I squint, trying to decipher what it says, but none of it makes sense to me:

The Sisterhood has gathered. We have been discussing isolation. Cutting the village off from everything. Hoping that in doing so we may be safe from the continued assaults by those searching for a place to survive the Return. What we will ultimately decide will be in God's hands as our survival has ever been in His hands.

Similar pages float everywhere, catching in the grass, sticking to the debris, floating toward the fence. Elias steps forward, thick bunches of paper clutched in his fist where he'd plucked them from where they snagged on the gravestones.

Just then someone else walks out of the ruins of the old building, his head bent over a few dusty bottles. "Mary, I think these might still be okay. The Sisterhood never said anything about—" He looks up as he eases out of the dark of the crumbled walls and into the light. He stops, one hand held over his eyes to block the sun, when he sees me standing there.

His mouth opens and his gaze jumps to my mother's face, confused as to what's going on.

My mother grasps my hand, her smile wide as if she's the happiest woman in the world at this moment. I stare at her, realizing how few times I've seen her so unabashedly happy. Clearly this is someone my mother knows well.

"Harry," my mother says, squeezing my hand tightly. "I'd like you to meet my daughter, Gabry."

He starts to smile, tilting his head to the side a bit, as if he's hearing the trail of a song in the air and trying to place it. He makes his way through the debris toward me and I try to remember if my mother's ever mentioned his name before. If I should know him. I feel awkward standing here, dirty from so many days on the path, thirsty and hungry.

Just then I hear a sharp intake of breath and I turn slightly. Elias stands just behind me. His face is ashen, his mouth open. The papers he's been holding flutter from his fingers.

"Elias, is something wrong?" I ask him.

"Elias?" Harry speaks the name softly, delicately, as if afraid that saying it too loud would break it. He squints and turns back to me. There's a question on his lips. A hint of recognition in his eyes.

"Annah?" he asks, his voice nothing more than a whisper. I know that name. It's Elias's sister's name. The one he's been looking for; the one he joined the Recruiters for. I start to shake my head.

But Harry is not done. "Abigail?"

Everything inside me stops. My heart no longer beats. My lungs no longer breathe. My ears can hear only one thing: the echo of that name on Harry's lips.

I know that name. I know the sound it makes coming from this man. After all these years it comes back to me like a lullaby in a dream.

And then chaos breaks. The dog barks again as Catcher tries to come near. Harry yells a command to him but he just keeps growling, his fur bristled. Cira collapses, retching into the grass. I pull my fingers from my mother's grasp. She tries to reach for me but I step back.

Behind me Elias bolts, sprinting toward the village. My mother reaches for me again but I brush her away. "Help her!" I shout at her, pointing to Cira. "She's hurt and needs your help."

"Gabry . . . ," she starts to say, but I'm already running after Elias, questions burning holes through my memories.

XXXV

I try to call after Elias but I'm running so hard I can barely catch my breath. He sprints toward the cluster of houses, cutting between them as if he somehow knows where he's going, which I don't understand. He takes a hard left and I stumble chasing after him. The sun's high in the sky, beating down hard and every footfall stirs up puffs of dust.

I wait for people to call out to us, to see faces in the windows and doors of the cottages I pass, but there's no one. Weeds spill from doorways and grasses grow from roofs caved in long ago. It's as if the earth is slowly claiming what was once hers.

Ahead of me down a narrow street Elias dashes into one of the buildings and I slow to a jog until I'm standing in the doorway. Inside sunlight filters through broken window shutters, illuminating the dust motes and causing them to glitter. I suck in a breath. It takes a moment for my vision to adjust to the dim interior and when I do I see Elias standing in the middle of a small sparsely furnished room. His back is to me, his arms limp by his sides. He barely moves, only his shoulders rising and falling.

I want to say something but it feels as though this space is somehow sacred. He turns, his eyes skimming over everything in the room: the table under the window, benches arranged around the fireplace, the narrow bed shoved against the far wall.

When he finally turns to me his eyes are wide, his lips parted as if he still feels the same shock I do.

"That man," I say, my voice quiet in the dim light. "How did he seem to know you?"

Elias just stands there and I ease into the shadows, the cool of the darkness soft against my skin. His eyes follow my movement but he doesn't reach out to me, doesn't move at all.

"Why did he think he knew my name?" Hearing the words out loud causes my skin to prickle and I realize that I'm more afraid to hear the answer than I thought I would be. But I have to know. "Why did he call me by your sister's name?"

He takes a step forward and I flinch a little. I don't mean to but I don't understand what's going on and I don't know if I should trust him. If I can even trust myself. He walks to the other side of the room and traces his finger across the table under the window. His touch marks a deep groove in the dust.

I think about the night I first met Elias on the beach. I think about how stunned he looked when he first saw me, how he reached out to touch me as if he knew me. My breath catches as a sudden and absurd thought occurs to me: *Did* he know me?

Everything in the room is so still. It's as if I've walked out of time. Behind me outside I hear nothing, not even the moans of the Mudo.

"Elias," I ask, my voice shaking now. "Do you know me?"

He trails his finger off the table and along the top of a chair and then he stops, his knuckles white as he grips the back of it.

And I break. Tired of his silence. Tired of not knowing if I can trust him. Tired of being so near to him every day and not knowing anything about him. "Tell me what's going on!" I shout, lashing a fist out to my side and banging it against the wall. The sound startles both of us, his eyes snapping up to meet mine.

My knuckles throb but I grit my teeth, refusing to let him know it hurts. I open my mouth to shout again but he cuts in before I have a chance.

"Yes," he says finally. His voice sounds as scared and dazed as I feel. "Yes, I knew who you were."

The room seems to swirl around me. I press my uninjured hand to my forehead and stumble toward the fireplace and fall onto one of the benches.

"Tell me," I say again before I lose the nerve.

He keeps walking slowly around the room as if he needs something to occupy his body while he thinks. "The girl . . ." He clears his throat. "The woman I'm looking for . . . she's not my sister," he says. His voice sounds like water washing over broken rocks.

He stops in front of me, staring at his fingers. "She's yours," he says, finally raising his eyes to meet mine.

"I . . ." My mouth is suddenly dry. I feel a wrenching inside as though I've found the missing piece that holds everything together. Edges of memories blur and fade inside me. I feel as if the room's grown too small, as if I've been buried too deep in the sand and the tide is cresting around my head. I find myself swallowing again and again and again as I try to make sense of it.

I have a sister. So many emotions crash against each other at once that I don't know what to hold on to. What does she look like? What does she sound like? What does she love and hate and care about? Who is she?

One truth struggles to the surface of it all. "You've known," I say. Of course he's known. That's why he's still here. That's why he was always there. At every turn when I was alone he was there. He's known from the beginning while I've known nothing.

Every moment between us has been buried in this lie.

He nods. He looks miserable. He holds himself guarded as if afraid of what I'll do. "She's your twin," he says softly. "When I first saw you on the beach . . ." He pauses, shaking his head. "I thought you were Annah."

I close my eyes, press my face into my hands. How could I not know I had a twin? All these years. How could I have forgotten that? How is any of this possible?

"You knew," I say. "All this time we've been going through the paths, you knew about this village. You knew everything about it." I think of all those times I was afraid we'd made the wrong decision coming into the Forest. All the moments I was so sure we'd die on the path and no one would ever know. Anger begins to throb inside. "You should have told us," I tell him. "We were terrified!"

He holds up his hands, his face pale and eyes wide. "No," he says. "I didn't know. You have to trust me, I didn't."

I snort. Trust? After finding out that from the very beginning he's been keeping everything from me? I cross my arms over my chest and stare at him.

"Look, I knew I was from the Forest. Of course I knew. And I also knew that you were too. But when you didn't recognize me . . . When you told me your name and it wasn't

Abigail . . . I realized you didn't remember. . . ." He presses shaking fingers to the side of his head. "I just wasn't sure you'd want to know. Like maybe you'd forgotten for a reason. I didn't want to mess up your life."

This time I actually do laugh but even to my own ears it sounds desperate. "Mess up my life? Look at it now. I'd say everything's pretty well messed up."

He tightens his lips together in a thin line. "I'm sorry," he says.

And just like that the anger that had been coursing through me is suddenly gone, leaving me feeling weak and defeated. "What happened?" I whisper. Realizing that more than anything else, we're somehow tied together.

He slumps onto the bench across from me, our knees almost touching. "We were neighbors," he says. "This was my house. You and Annah lived across the street. There weren't that many kids our age around to play with—you'd just turned five and I was almost seven." He stares at the floor as if looking into the past and I try to see it all in my mind but there's nothing more than haze.

"The paths were forbidden to us but one day I stole the key to the gate and convinced you two to sneak out and go exploring and we got lost." He stops and looks at me, his eyes hollow, his lips drawn. Words begin to spill from his mouth, urgent words. "You fell and skinned your knee and wanted to go back but I didn't want to. I was afraid I'd get in trouble because you were hurt and I was mad at you because I wanted to keep playing. So I . . ." He swallows again. I can feel the pain and desperation radiating from him and I want to reach out and grab his hand but I don't.

I'm having a hard time catching my breath. A hard time

remembering that this story is about me and not some other girl, some stranger.

"Your sister and I kept going down the path." His eyes flick to meet mine and then bounce away again. Sweat glistens on his temples. "We kept exploring. You asked us to wait for you, not to leave you alone, but I was so . . ." He rubs a hand over his head, almost clawing at his skin. "Angry. I was mad that you'd tripped and wanted to go home and I didn't." He stands up and walks across the room until he's staring down at the empty table.

I can't remember anything of what he's saying. I stare at my knee; there's a scar there. I thought I knew what it was from. I run my fingers over the puckered skin as Elias talks.

"I pulled Annah down the path with me away from you. We left you crying." I can hear the tears in his voice, the misery and pain and guilt. "We got lost. I thought I knew where we were and when it started to get dark I tried to go back for you."

I hurt hearing the words, but not for myself: for him.

"But I couldn't find you." He's barely audible. "You were gone. And then I was too terrified to go back home even if I could find the way. I'd lost you, it was my fault. I was afraid of what your father would say or do. I was afraid of getting in trouble so I ran."

His throat convulses again and again and again. "I took Annah and ran," he says, the words coming out in a hot rush like a confession. "I don't know how long we followed the paths," he tells me. "It was autumn. It rained enough for water. We found berries and flowers and grapes. We found a way out. A gate at the edge of the Forest hidden by a partially caved-in tunnel in the mountains. It was near the Dark City and when people asked questions about us I just told them she was my sister. That we were looking for our parents. I was able to find enough in the empty villages in the Forest to trade so we could pay the rents in the Dark City. But I could never find our way back home and eventually gave up trying."

He turns back to face me. He looks like a different person, his face so twisted with self-loathing that I almost gasp. "It was my fault. All of it. She never knew warmth or her parents or a full stomach because of me."

I'm numb. He rushes toward me and kneels in front of my bench. He takes my hands in his but I can barely feel them. I don't know what to think, what to say or do. I should hate him for lying to me but I'm also sorry for the pain he's clearly suffering.

"I'm sorry," he says, the words a hot rush. I close my eyes, my chest crushed under the weight of this new knowledge. I don't know how to sort it out. He's crying now, tears bright in his eyes and his shoulders jerking. "I didn't tell you because I didn't want you to hate me."

Do I hate him? I wonder. I stare at him, at his misery, and can't decide.

"Please," he begs me. "Please tell me it's okay."

I open my mouth but nothing comes out. All I can think about are paths and scraped knees and promises and sisters. It swirls around and around in my head, the whole of it out of reach. It just feels like a story and I wait for it to feel like truth but it doesn't.

XXXVI

"It's okay," says a voice from behind me and I jump, not realizing anyone else was there. I stumble from the bench and see my mother and Harry in the doorway. She sweeps into the room and grabs me into a hug, holding my head against her shoulder.

The feel of her is so familiar and I close my eyes, falling into her comfort. She stands back, her hands on my cheeks, her thumbs brushing away the falling tears. "My girl," she says softly and I nod. Because she's the only mother I've known.

Over her shoulder I see Elias trembling in the corner, his back straight but his lip caught between his teeth. He stares at Harry, his eyes wide. "What?" he asks in a whisper.

Harry walks over until they're face to face. "You were a child, Elias," he says. "It wasn't your fault."

Elias squeezes his eyes tight as if he can block out what's coming next. "I took them past the gates," he says, his voice small. "I'm the one who left Abigail—Gabry—behind. I'm the one who didn't take Annah back. It's my fault. And now I've lost Annah and the village is dead and it's because of me." His body is shaking as he gasps for breath.

Harry's eyes are bright too as he reaches out and grabs Elias's shoulders. "I'm telling you—none of that is your fault. It's all okay." Elias shakes his head but Harry pulls him into a hug and I can hear the way he cries.

My mother wraps her arm around my shoulders, pulling me tight, and I realize that I never knew how much guilt Elias kept trapped inside. How much he's carried around with him since that day so long ago. What it must have been like when he saw me in the ocean—when he realized that I was still alive.

"What happened to the village?" I finally ask. "Where is everyone—why is it so empty?" I swallow and dig my nails into the skin of my knee, trying to find the courage to push through the question. "What happened to my—our—families?"

My mother sighs, a heavy sound in the stillness of the little house. She walks over to the fireplace. "I don't know how much you know, Elias, or how much you remember from the stories I told you, Gabrielle, but Harry and I were raised in this village."

She looks at Harry as she speaks, as if it's just the two of them in the room sharing the same memory. "When we were around your age . . ." She pauses, her cheeks beginning to burn a little red. Harry's cheeks redden a bit too. I've never seen my mother like this around a man and it makes me feel a little embarrassed, as if I've read her private thoughts. She clears her throat. "None of that really matters. What matters is that the village was breached. The Unconsecrated got in and some of us escaped down the path to get away."

She looks at Elias and me. "You have to understand—we were raised to believe there wasn't anything else in the world but us. We were the last survivors of humanity. We weren't allowed to ever leave the village and when we ran down the paths to get away, it was terrifying."

Harry walks across the room to stand near her and I watch how aware she is of his nearness, how they stand together. I've heard this story before in bits and pieces but I don't remember my mother telling me about Harry or what role he played.

"I . . ." My mother stares at her hands. "I made it to the ocean. Was washed up onshore but I'd left behind Harry and my best friend, Cass, and a little boy named Jacob." She swallows and I'm about to reach out for her when Harry takes her hand.

She looks into his eyes as she says, "I tried to go back. I asked them to send people after you but they thought I was crazy. They thought I'd washed ashore from a shipwreck and had gone insane from the sun and salt water." She pauses. "They wouldn't go after you," she says in a whisper, talking only to Harry now. "They wouldn't let me go either."

Harry squeezes her hand. "It's okay, Mary," he says. They stare at each other just a moment longer and I glance away, feeling uncomfortable.

"We made it back to the village," Harry says, turning to face Elias and me. "They'd been fighting the Unconsecrated, fending them off. The last bastion was the Cathedral—infection had roared inside and they had to set it on fire to kill them. It was the only thing they could do," he adds softly.

"There weren't many of us left then. Not a lot of people survived. I married Cass and we tried but were never able to have our own children. We raised Jacob the best we could. Eventually a few others had kids—you, Elias, were one of them. Jacob eventually married and they had twins. That was you, Abigail." His face washes of color and he clears his throat. "I mean Gabry," he corrects himself, adding, "and your sister, Annah."

Just hearing about it all makes it seem so real. "My mother," I whisper. "What was she like?"

Harry glances at Mary before he continues. "She was born after the breach," Harry says. "I think that's part of what Jacob loved about her, that she was born free of all that went on in those days. It also meant that she didn't understand that part of him, the part of him that grew when he was outside the fences."

I smile, thinking about her. Wondering about her. I sit on the bench and pull my knees to my chest, wrapping my arms around my legs.

Harry pauses again and my mother reaches out and squeezes his hand. He looks into the empty pit of the fireplace. "It isn't easy for a woman to carry twins," he says hesitantly, and my heart begins to beat faster, my head feeling light. "And the Sisterhood—the women who used to run the village—they were the caregivers, the Cathedral our infirmary. When it burned we lost everyone who knew anything about medicine. We lost supplies. A simple pregnancy was difficult enough . . . but the complications with twins . . ."

I close my eyes and lower my face into my arms, knowing what's coming next. Not wanting to hear it.

"She died having you and your sister," he finally says.

All the times I wondered about my mother. When I tried to remember her voice and her smell. When I felt empty and wrong for having forgotten her. It was because I never knew her.

"What happened?" I ask, my voice muffled.

I hear a shuffle as Harry shifts. My mother murmurs something to him. "There weren't enough of us who survived the breach," Harry finally says. "When the three of you disappeared . . ." He takes a deep breath. "Jacob couldn't get over losing the two of you," he says, and I lift my head to look at him, the world blurry through the haze of my tears.

"He rallied some of the other villagers and they went out looking for you." He shrugs and even now I can see the weight of the years on his shoulders. For the first time I realize just how old he and my mother look. Just how much they've been through in their lives. He looks at his fingers linked through my mother's.

"They never came back," he finishes. "Cass and I stayed behind. She said she'd spent enough time in the Forest and just wanted to live out the rest of her life safe behind the fences. Slowly everyone else died and last year Cass passed away in her sleep." His voice cracks when he says this and my mother rests her fingers along the side of his neck. He cranes his head down, brushing his cheek against her touch and she smiles softly.

I think about the two of them alone in this village—the only ones left. Never knowing if there ever was a world beyond the Forest and no longer caring. Being content just the two of them, safe. I think about how close I came to choosing the same life and I realize how much I'd have missed.

"I don't remember any of it," I whisper. Feeling as though I've somehow failed the people who once loved me. Who once stormed into the Forest to find me. "Nothing here is familiar."

"It's okay," my mother says, coming to sit next to me. She pulls my braid off my back, trailing it through her fingers like she's always done when I'm upset. It would be so easy to believe her words. But I can't. I can't let go of the past that easily.

I stand up, needing something but not knowing what. A memory, something to ground myself to this place.

"Which house was mine?" I ask Harry, hoping that somehow it will stir something inside me.

He points. "Across the path, down three doors," he says.

I walk slowly through the room and my mother starts to follow me. I want her to be with me so badly but I feel as though I need to do this alone. "Can I have a moment—just me?" I ask her and she nods, reluctantly.

▾ XXXVII ▾

Once outside I walk a short distance and then stare at the little cabin in front of me. It looks like the others stretching out on either side of it. Empty. Abandoned. Weeds tangle in what used to be a small yard, a vine overtaking half the house and springing from the chimney.

But there's something different, something about it that feels off. As if the windows are set slightly farther apart or the roof is slanted at a different angle. I approach it slowly, the sounds of the afternoon fading away.

Its door is closed, the boards warped and gapped. I push it open and something rises inside me. Not a memory, not a vision, but a feeling. Something familiar. An expectation.

Scattered inside is a table, a few chairs. A bench, a counter. Grass trails against my calves as I walk around the room. I stop in front of a wall. Facing me is an old piece of mirror, framed by delicately carved wood.

I know what I'll see even before I step in front of it. My

reflection will be dull and blurred. Specked with the age of the glass. But there will be two of us in the mirror. As there always have been.

Yet when I open my eyes there's only me staring back. I reach out and touch the surface of the mirror. There's someone else out there with the same face. The same eyes and chin and ears.

A deep ache blooms inside me, radiating out over my skin. There's so much I missed because of Elias. But then I think about my mother. About the ocean and the lighthouse and I wonder how I could ever wish to give that up.

If I could choose the life I would have wanted to lead, which one would I pick?

There's a photo tacked to the wall beside the mirror and I reach out and brush my fingers over it, clearing away a coating of dust. It's an old photograph of silver shiny buildings stretching to the sky and marching into the distance. A bright yellow border dances around the image, the words *New York City* spelled out in big letters. I stare at the photograph, trying to remember it, but I can't.

I look back at my reflection, wondering how I've lost everything. I feel like a stranger, as if it's been years since I last saw my reflection. I look different—my eyes a little more haunted than they were before, my mouth a little tighter. I look like my mother; I look like Mary. Not physically but in the way that we all look when we've faced the reality of our world.

I reach out my hand and touch the mirror. Out there somewhere I have a sister. Excitement and hope prickle over my skin. My reflection smiles at me, possibility gleaming in her eyes.

And then something wavers and shifts in the mirror and I

see someone step into the doorway behind me. I turn my head, embarrassed at being caught staring at myself, and find Catcher watching me.

Self-conscious, I tuck a strand of hair that fell loose from my braid behind my ear. I wait for him to ask me what's going on but instead he just says, "Cira asked me to find you."

"Oh," I say. I'd forgotten about her. About everything except me, really. "Is she okay?" I ask.

He shrugs, looking past me at the mirror. He steps farther inside, walks slowly around the edge of the room. "I found the others just up the road a bit and told them about the Recruiters—at this point, based on when I saw them last, they're probably only a day or two behind us. That guy Harry and your mother are helping to gather supplies. He's the only one in the village, said everyone else either left or died."

I cross my arms over my chest, my skin suddenly clammy. All these houses now useless and abandoned. What would have happened if I'd never been lost in the Forest? If I hadn't skinned my knee and we'd all come back at the end of the day? What would have happened to my family?

"We're leaving tomorrow. The path continues on the other side of the village and you and everyone else will go down that and I'll pull down the fences—flood the village with Mudo so the Recruiters can't get through." His voice is so flat, so impersonal that I flinch.

I turn back around and look at the mirror. Look at what used to be my home. I've only just found it and already I have to leave. I close my eyes, searching for a memory to hold on to. Something to take with me. But nothing comes. Carefully I pull the picture of New York City off the wall and slip it into my pocket.

"Your mother—I mean Mary—is with Cira now trying to do something about the blood infection but she wants to talk to you," he says in that same voice.

"So you know," I say, not even bothering to ask it as a question. He knows that Mary isn't my mother.

He shrugs and walks out of the little cottage. His indifference stings me. He's supposed to be my friend. He's supposed to be someone I can trust—someone I thought I was falling in love with. I rush to catch up with him as he weaves along empty walkways.

"Catcher, wait," I call out to him, but he doesn't even slow down. When I finally reach him I grab his arm, the heat of his skin a searing reminder of his infection. I pull him around until he faces me.

His eyes are ragged and red. I haven't noticed how hollow his cheeks have become and I wonder if he's been eating recently.

"Why didn't you tell me, Gabry?" he asks, and in his words I can hear the despair. He grips my shoulders so desperately that I'm almost afraid of him. "You could have trusted me," he says softly, his voice cracking.

I don't know what to tell him, how to explain how *I* didn't even want to face the idea of who I was before. He moves his hand from my shoulder to my neck, his fingers trailing along the base of my skull, warming me. He leans down until his forehead touches mine and between us is nothing but heat.

"Do you ever think about what might have happened that night if I'd climbed the coaster?" he asks. "How things might have been different?" His thumb slides along my neck. "If only I hadn't been afraid of heights."

I think back to that night. I can see the outline of the

chipped unicorn on the carousel. I can smell the salt in the air, taste it against the back of my throat. I remember how I gave him an excuse to stay behind.

I've thought of that moment so many times. I've replayed that night a million different ways. If I hadn't been so scared; if I'd only waited a heartbeat longer before swinging, none of this would have happened. None of us would be here now.

But I don't tell him this. Instead I say, "My mother used to tell me that sometimes it's worth letting go of those things, worth forgetting."

He smiles just a little, the corner of his mouth curving up.

"You survived, that's what's important. That's what matters." I slip my fingers between his until we're gripping each other.

"I don't know," he says, staring at the place where our bodies touch. "I don't know what the difference between surviving and existing is anymore. What are the Mudo? They exist. I think life has to be about more than that—or else what separates us from them?"

I think of Elias then. Of the night we escaped the town and how he stood by the bridge with the Souler he called Kyra and told me that there was no difference between us and them. I didn't want to believe what he was saying then but now I'm not so sure. It's hard to stand in a forgotten village in the last gasp of survival and wonder if that's all we're doing anymore. Struggling to hold on against a losing battle.

I swallow, thinking about what I wish I'd told Elias then. "What about love?" I ask Catcher softly. "That's something that separates us. That's what life is about."

He pulls his head away from mine and traces the edge of my face with his fingers. His smile is wistful and it scares me because I don't know what he's thinking. I don't know who he is anymore—not the way I used to.

"What happens when you don't have love?" he asks. "What happens when you can't?"

A hollow feeling begins to expand inside me. He sounds the way Cira did the last time I saw her before she cut herself: He sounds like he's giving up. "You have me," I tell him. "You have me and Cira."

He steps back away from me and I hold on to him as long as I can until we're no longer touching. Around us are empty cottages and cabins, weeds and the whirring of crickets as evening begins to pull tight around the village.

"Could you have ever loved me?" he asks. His voice is raw.

My breath catches. "Yes," I whisper, feeling as though I'm losing something by saying the word. I try to remember my dreams from before but I can't anymore. Once I was able to see a future for us so clearly. My life was Catcher; it was being his. I always thought that losing him would be losing that future as well. But now when I close my eyes and try to imagine Catcher and me together I see nothing.

He doesn't ask the question I'm most afraid of: Do I love him now? Because I don't know anymore. My eyes blur with tears and I bite my lip trying to hold them back.

Catcher stares at his hands. "Do you think there's anything left in them after they turn?" he asks.

"I don't know." I think about the Soulers and their Mudo. I wonder if they believe there's something left, something they're preserving. If it really is eternal life. The ultimate resurrection. I used to think the Mudo were nothing but monsters but now I'm not sure.

"I think I'm scared that's what I'll become," he says. "I

think that's what terrifies me the most. That somehow I'll be trapped."

I don't want to think about Catcher like that, don't want to imagine having to kill him one day. I reach out and take his hand in mine again. "I won't let that happen."

He follows the outline of my fingers with his thumb. The silence weaves around us.

"Elias is a good person," Catcher finally says. "He looks at you the same way I used to. The same way I wish I could now."

I can feel my skin turning red, heat crawling up my neck. I want to tell Catcher that Elias is a liar; that all this time he's kept my past from me.

"Elias isn't you," I say instead. "You've known me your whole life. We've always known each other. It's supposed to be us." Why can't Catcher understand this? Why does he keep pulling away from me?

He trails his hand along my jaw, tilting my head back toward his, and I think that maybe this time he'll kiss me. For once it will be like before. "He'll keep you safe," he whispers instead.

"You keep me safe, Catcher," I tell him, needing him to understand. Afraid that if I can't make him see that he's the future I'd always expected, it will never happen. That I don't know what will happen instead.

He shakes his head. "I can't keep anyone safe anymore," he says. "Cira's asking for you because she wants to say good-bye. She's dying, Gabry." And with that he turns and continues down the walkway, leaving me alone in the shattered evening air, trying to force my body to remember to breathe.

▾ XXXVIII ▾

I follow Catcher through the cluster of overgrown cottages to Harry's, which sits apart from everything else, far away from the huddle of the large burned building that hulks at the other end of the village. Harry's house is large and spacious with rambling rooms surrounding a large courtyard. Gardens thrive around the outside, elegantly drawn waterways with waterfalls meandering through beds of flowers and past rows of neatly planted vegetables. The black dog lies in the doorway to a patio, his nose and ears in the sun but the rest of him tucked into shade. He rumbles as Catcher draws near, lifting a lip to bare his teeth.

"He smells the infection," Catcher tells me, pointing to the dog. "His name is Odys. Harry trained him to alert him to the Mudo."

The dog's growling is another reminder of how different Catcher is now and I see on his face how much it bothers him.

Cira sits on a bench surrounded by bright yellow blooms.

She smiles when she sees me but she doesn't bother getting up. The sun is just hovering over the trees, a last gasp of daylight filtering through the leaves of the Forest.

I notice how frail she looks, how thin. Her breathing is shallow, her lips dry and cracked. I sit down next to her and take her hand in mine. It burns hotter than Catcher's skin, the blood infection raging inside her. I clutch at her fingers as tears burn the back of my throat and I smell the sharp sting of herbs from my mother's remedies that are too late to draw out the sickness.

Elias comes into the courtyard with a lantern and a jug of water. I'm instantly aware of his presence, of his every move and breath. He barely glances at me as he offers Cira something to drink and she waves it away. Just as he turns to leave she asks him, "Do you believe what the other Soulers believe?" Her voice is raspy, uneven.

Elias stiffens. He darts a glance at me before asking her, "What do you mean?"

She smiles slightly. "In resurrection. That the Mudo have a second life. A second chance."

Behind Cira I see Catcher hovering in the shadow of a doorway to a darkened room. He stiffens at her question but stays silent. It's hard to see his expression in the gloaming but his eyes are tired.

Cira prods Elias. "The Soulers talked about it. When we were all held together back in Vista. They told us about their beliefs," she says. "They said it was another way of living. That it's a resurrection."

"They're a crazy cult," Catcher says from the darkness.

Cira closes her eyes. I doubt she even knew Catcher was listening. When she opens them again there's a spark in them.

She turns to face him and says, "But look at you, Catcher! You're infected but you're still alive. It's been weeks and you're still here!"

He stays in the shadow, crossing his arms over his chest and scowling. I don't understand what Cira's trying to say, what her point is. All I can think about is how her fingers are hot against my own, every inch of her a burning fire. She pushes from the bench and walks over to her brother, her legs unsteady. "What if it's my only chance?" she asks. "You know as well as I do that I can't go with you tomorrow. I'll never be able to keep up."

"Don't talk like that, Cira," he says.

I glance at Elias. I feel uncomfortable watching this, as if we're intruding, but he's focused on Cira, his head tilted to the side as if he's thinking.

"What if I'm like you, Catcher?" she asks, resting her hand on his shoulder.

And suddenly I understand everything. Why she went into the Forest before. What she's planning to do now. I start to protest, to say anything to stop her but Elias presses his fingers to my arm, keeping me back.

"It's not worth the risk," Catcher tells Cira. Anguish laces his voice; I can feel it in every beat of my heart.

"There *is* no risk, Catcher. Don't you understand that?" Cira's almost shouting now. "I'm going to die. Either here when the Recruiters come or on the path when I can't keep up. The infection isn't getting better. The fever isn't breaking."

I want to close my eyes, to turn my head away. But Elias just slips his hand down my arm until he's grasping mine, his touch giving me strength and comfort.

Catcher's fingers clench the doorsill. "And what happens if

it doesn't work?" he growls at his sister, echoing my own thoughts. "What happens if you turn into one of them?"

She puts her hand over his. "Then you leave me that way."

A sob breaks from him then. "You can't ask me to do that, Cira," he says. My heart aches watching them.

Cira leans her head against his shoulder, their backs to us. It's an image I've seen a thousand times over my life: Cira leaning in to her brother. Her tilting her face up to him trying to make him laugh when she tells a joke, to make him relent when she's gotten into trouble, to get him to give her whatever it is she's asking for.

I know the look on her face without having to see it. And I know how this will end. Tears burn hot and salty against my throat.

"I'm not asking you, Catcher," Cira says so softly I can barely hear her.

I can't stand to listen anymore. I can't face the pain, can't face the truth that my best friend is dying and wants to become Mudo. She can't know if she'll be immune—none of us can know. What if it doesn't work?

I pull my hand from Elias's and run from the courtyard, sprinting blindly through rooms until I burst from the house and into the evening. I race through the shadows, dodging around cottages and cabins. In the distance I see a hill at the edge of the village and I sprint up it until every part of my body screams for me to stop.

I stand looking out over the Forest just as the sun sinks against the treetops. Behind me I hear Elias approaching. I know his smell, the rhythm of his breathing, the sound of his movements.

"You can't let her," I say as he grabs my arm and turns me

around. "You told me yourself that you don't believe what the Soulers say about resurrection. You told me none of it's true." I pound my fists on his chest and he doesn't stop me. "It's just some stupid cult nonsense. You can't let her do that to herself."

"It's not my choice to make, Gabry," he says.

"But she's going to kill herself," I wail at him. "We're supposed to protect people. It's what it means to be human. We're supposed to take care of them. We can't . . ." I choke back the words, trying to control my breathing. "I can't let her do it," I say, letting the hot tears trace down my cheeks. "What if it doesn't work? She'll be gone."

Elias wraps his hands around mine, pulling me to him. He's safe and warm and strong.

"Is this all there is?" I ask him. I'm so tired of this struggle, of trying to survive when it seems like there's no point to it. When everyone I love dies or changes and I'm left alone. "Is this what life is about? Waiting for death? Looking for it? Inviting it in?"

"No," he says, his voice barely a whisper against my cheek. "That's not what life is."

"Then what is it?" I need him to give me a reason to keep fighting. To keep pushing forward even though it's so hard. Even though I'm not sure I can.

"This," he says, and he presses his lips to mine.

▼ ▼ ▼

His kiss is warm. It's more full of life than any moment I've ever experienced. It's heat, it's pressure and need and desire. His fingers tangle in my braid, bringing me closer to him and my hands pull to his back, feeling the flex of his shoulders under my touch. Sparks shatter in my head and I understand in this moment what he means about this being what life is.

If I could stay here forever, just like this, just the two of us entwined in the darkness, I would.

Elias breaks away first and I lean back in to him but he steps away and my lips only brush the heat of the air. At every spot he touched my skin tingles. I raise my fingers to my lips, feeling dazed. Wanting more. For the first time I'm content with who I am; where I am. I don't want to go back in time. I don't want to erase everything that's happened because I don't want to erase this moment.

"You don't know how many times I wanted to call you Abby or Abigail," he says, his voice hoarse with longing. "All the times growing up when I'd look at Annah and think about you."

His words strike together in my head, leaving a trail of chills down my back. A thought occurs to me that makes my chest ache. "Did you . . . do you think about Annah when you look at me?"

His eyes become guarded. "I think about her all the time," he says. "I've spent so many months going from town to town and city to city looking for her."

"Am I just a replacement for her?" I ask. I think about everything he's done for Annah, all the things he's been through, the guilt he feels. I wouldn't blame him for thinking of her when he looks at me. But I need him to understand that I'm not her. I'm never going to replace Annah.

His face goes white and his mouth opens. He's shaking his head but still not saying anything. He looks both terrified and angry but most of all sick to his stomach. I wait for him to tell me that I'm crazy, that I'm wrong. But instead he just turns and walks away, leaving me there in the darkness with the taste of him still on my lips.

▼ ▼ ▼

The moon is only a sliver in the sky, its sharp edges blurred by the watery heat of the summer night as I walk back to the garden where I left Cira. My mind roars, delighting in the memory of Elias's kiss and then twisting when I think that he might just want me because I remind him of someone else.

When I get to the courtyard it's empty and my heart begins to beat staccato. Slowly, I walk over to the bench where Cira last sat. Draped in the middle of it is a small object and I bend over, tracing my finger along the cord of Cira's superhero necklace. I pick it up feeling the weight of Cira's hopes and dreams—her belief that someone out there was greater than us and would save us.

Around me crickets whir and a bullfrog grunts but otherwise I hear nothing but the distant Mudo moans. Something shuffles behind me and I turn, dropping my hand to the knife on my hip.

My mother walks out of one of the rooms bordering the garden. She hesitates before coming closer, just a brief momentary pause, and I know something's wrong.

"What?" I ask her, not ready to bear the weight of something new.

"It's Cira," she says.

I close my eyes and let my shoulders fall. She steps closer and places her hands on my arms. "What?" I ask, my voice barely more than the brush of the breeze over water.

"She went to the Forest. She asked her brother to get her something to eat and when he was gone she snuck away."

"What happened?" I whisper, still a shard of hope left in me that she was right about the possibility of being immune. My mother's hesitation tells me everything.

My legs go weak and my mother helps me sit. She pulls me against her, wrapping her arms around me and holding me tight.

All I can think about is that it's my fault. I ran away—I couldn't face Cira and her pain. If I'd been stronger, if I'd stayed by her side, she wouldn't have been able to sneak out. She wouldn't have been able to make it to the Forest.

I was kissing Elias while Cira was sacrificing herself.

"Catcher went after her," my mother says. "But it's been a while." She strokes my hair, tucks a strand behind my ear. I stare at the flower Cira last touched, the edge of its petals turning brown and dry. I never got to tell her good-bye.

"Why is everything dying?" I ask her. "This village. Cira. The entire world. I don't understand what the point is anymore."

My mother sighs. "I used to daydream about the world," she says softly. Even though I can't see her face, I know she has a faraway look about her. "About all the possibilities that existed past the Forest. I used to dream about the ocean. It was all I wanted to see."

"How did you know that what you wanted was the ocean?" I ask her, my voice thick with tears.

She shrugs. "I don't know. I'd felt it inside, ever since I was a child. Ever since my mother first told me stories about it."

I think about Catcher and Elias. About how I wanted to stay at the lighthouse, safe inside the Barrier. How I still want to remember and forget.

I close my eyes tight. "What if I don't know what I want?"

I ask her, voicing the fear that rages through me. "What if I never know? What if I'm wrong?"

She places a hand on my cheek. "It will be okay," she says.

I hold my breath, waiting for her touch to bring me comfort. And then I realize that that's been my problem all along. Not only wanting comfort and security and safety, but looking to others to find it when I need to find it inside myself.

I've spent every moment I can remember scared: scared of the Forest, scared to break the rules, scared of the world outside the Barrier. Scared of life. I've always looked at everything as black-and-white: alive or dead, safe or savage.

But then how do I explain Catcher, who will always be infected? Elias, who is both a Souler and a Recruiter? My being born in the Forest but growing up beyond? I could have lived my entire life inside the lighthouse but what kind of life would that have been?

I realize that life is risks. It's acknowledging the past but looking forward. It's taking a chance that we will make mistakes but believing that we all deserve to be forgiven.

I wipe the tears from my face and push myself up to look at my mother. I feel as though she's a stranger to me in so many ways. Seeing this village—seeing where she grew up, how she lived—makes me understand even more how little I know about her.

"Are you happy?" I ask her.

"Gabrielle." She takes my hands in hers and smiles a little. "Life is life," she says. She shrugs, looking up at me. "You choose to live it or you do not."

I stare at her, wanting to laugh at the simplicity of what she's saying. But her words sink into me. It's as if I've been waiting for permission to live my life and she's given it to me.

I'm just about to hug my mother, to thank her for saying everything I needed to hear, when Elias comes running into the courtyard. His eyes are wide and he barely catches his breath before panting out: "Catcher came back from the Forest. He says the Recruiters are closer than he thought. They'll be at the village any minute. He's going to start tearing down the fences—we have to go now!"

XXXIX

I jump to my feet, the serenity of the moment with my mother now shattered. Already I hear the moans of the Mudo creeping through the night air. We have to stay ahead of them. I start grabbing supplies, my head spinning as I try to remember what we'll need.

Odys skitters into the courtyard, his hackles raised and his teeth bared. He paces, a low growl rumbling through him, and then he starts to bark. I keep looking over my shoulder into the night, wondering if he sees something that I don't. Hears something I can't. I hold my breath, waiting.

And that's when I see them, swarming around the remains of the Cathedral. They shamble through the darkness toward us.

"Harry," my mother breathes, dashing back into the house.

My eyes widen; Elias curses and grabs my hand. He slings a bag over his shoulder and shoves my little pack into my hands. I let him pull me through the village, dodging shadows and listening for the moans. In the distance I hear men shouting but all I can do is run. Follow Elias as he races toward a gate I didn't see before at the far end of the village.

"My mother!" I scream to him, trying to stop, but he keeps pulling.

"She'll be okay," he yells back, and I stumble but keep following him.

We race through what once must have been fields but are now overgrown: vines twisting around stray stalks of corn that whip at my arms as we pass between them. My eyes blur in the night and all I can do is put one foot in front of the other. Our breaths, the sound of our feet hitting the ground, are muffled as we swipe at the tangle of foliage. It makes me afraid that if the Mudo are behind us—if there was a Breaker—we wouldn't even hear it coming.

I keep looking over my shoulder, waiting. Terrified that the next step could lead me into the arms of slavering Mudo. Hoping to see my mother running behind me. But there's nothing but shadows trailing us as we run along the fence until we find the other gate.

Elias fumbles with the latch, rust making it almost impossible to flip open. My breathing screams in my ears, the night too quiet, too empty until the Mudo out in the Forest sense our presence and rise, shuffling toward us. They slam into the old chain links, moaning as they try to reach for us.

Finally the gate creaks open and we push through, slamming it behind us. We stand there side by side, staring back into the village. Behind us the trees rustle, branches swaying like the sound of waves on the shore. On either side of us Mudo pound against the fences. In front of us, nothing.

Eventually I can see shapes moving in the dark, stumbling and shuddering. The Mudo filling into the cracks, slowly oozing through the open spaces.

It isn't fair to have finally realized where I'm from and then to have to leave it so soon. I have memories lost here that I need to find! This is my past, this is who I am.

I think about the other village we walked through, the burned-out husk of what used to be a thriving world. How many other villages like that are there in the Forest? How many lives played out here never knowing there was something beyond?

Figures run in the distance, too many to be my mother and Harry. I squeeze my fingers around the gate, pressing against it, wishing I could go back and grab them and drag them through to safety.

Finally I see my mother, her skirt flying around her legs as she runs toward us. In her arms she carries what looks like the book from earlier, the pages clutched against her chest. It throws off her gait and she trips, almost falling.

Someone cuts toward her and for a moment I think it must be Harry. I realize too late that it can't be, that the person is too tall, too thin, too fast. There's no way my mother can see him.

"Mother!" I scream.

She looks up at me, the dim light of the moon illuminating her face for an instant. She smiles, the curve of her cheek soft and smooth. In that moment I see her as a girl. I see her as myself. Running from a breached village, not knowing what her future holds. And then the man behind her rams into her, throwing her to the ground. She tries to keep the book in her hands. She falls awkwardly, legs sprawling. And when her back hits the ground the pages explode around her.

I'm through the gate before I even know what I'm doing. My mouth is open even though I don't know what words I scream. It's just pure rage and terror and horror.

The man is a Recruiter, his black shirt rolled up at the sleeves and dusted with red dirt. He stands over my mother, a knife in his hand. She tries to roll from underneath him but he places his feet on either side of her legs, standing on her skirt and trapping her.

Paper floats around them, the thin edges catching and reflecting what little light exists. It makes time seem too slow. As if gravity has let go for just this moment and we could all float away.

I raise my arm, the air feeling thinner and lighter. If I could run faster, if I could run harder, I could get there. I could stop the Recruiter with the knife.

He doesn't even care that I come at him. He doesn't even crouch and prepare for the impact.

Mudo begin to crowd in the periphery of my vision like clouds against the sun. She's too bright, my mother. Too much to stare at directly.

I don't even see the other figure sprinting out of the distance and neither does the Recruiter. One moment he stands above my mother and the next he's floating, entwined with the pages of her book. As if he's of no more substance than they are.

Sound hits me all at once. The moans, the screams, the shouts of men.

Harry reaches for my mother, his face purple with rage and fear. She grasps for the pages but he grabs her and pulls her to him. Odys lunges at the Recruiter on the ground, his teeth bared and back arched. None of them sees me running toward them.

"The Scripture!" she yells as the Recruiter struggles to stand back up and Odys growls even louder.

Harry circles her wrist with his hand. He's stronger than she is. I don't understand what's going on, why she's resisting. My body screams with the desire to grab her and pull her back.

"It's who we are!" she yells again, struggling against Harry. "It's our history!"

"Those stories aren't as important as our lives!" he shouts, dragging her to the fence. I watch as they struggle; then finally together they sprint past me and through the gate, not noticing me in the shadows, Odys at their heels. I look back at the cover of the book on the ground a few yards away from where the Recruiter staggers to his feet. There are still pages stuck inside, remnants of the whole. I glance at the fence, at the Mudo swarming toward us.

And then I hold my breath as I run and slide to the ground. As I get closer I reach out and hook the edge of the book with my fingers, pulling it toward me. The Recruiter lunges, swiping at the air, but he misjudges the distance and misses me.

I vault to my feet and just when I've found my balance something pulls my braid, snapping my head back. I stumble and the book slips from my grip as I fall, my other hand going for the knife on my belt. But I land on top of it, trapping it underneath me.

I hear the moans as I blink the dirt out of my eye. I feel warmth spraying over my face and I turn to see a Mudo woman sinking her teeth into the Recruiter, her mouth a rictus of terror. He screams and swings his arms, pushing her off him.

Mudo are not predators. They don't hunt. They don't kill

and eat. They're not satisfied once they've tasted the blood of one if there are more around.

They want to infect. They need to infect. Which means that if they sense another living, an Uninfected, that becomes their new target. And that new target is about to be me.

The Mudo releases the Recruiter, infection already burning through his body, and turns toward me, blood smeared along her lips and chin.

And that's when I recognize her. That's when I realize that the Mudo is Cira.

Time is nothing. Space irrelevant. I wait for the spark of recognition between us. For the haze of memories to fall over her eyes. Something inside her to say no, to make her hesitate, to shatter the horror of this moment.

There must be something of humanity left inside Cira. How can death erase it all? How can the same body walk, the same brain exist and retain nothing of who it used to be? I want so badly to believe that the Soulers are right, that there's something left behind.

I kick back. Drag myself across the ground. I dig my fingers into the dirt. Anything to get away from her.

She lumbers toward me, reaching out her hands. Hands that used to thread through my hair. Hands that used to trace over my own.

My best friend is really gone. Every part of her, every memory, idea, dream.

Gone. Dead.

Forever.

The tips of her fingers brush my face. So familiar. But cold. I jerk back. I swing at the air. Kick. But I'm off balance. The night swims around me and Cira lurches closer.

And then she stops, her head snapping back. Teeth gleaming in the night, hands clawing.

My heart stumbles, breath catching. I look past and see her braid wrapped around the Recruiter's hand. Blood smears his wrist and arm; his face is warped with pain.

"Go," he says, barely audible over Cira's moans. "Go!" he says louder.

I don't know why he's letting me escape; why he's holding Cira back from me. Maybe he had a younger sister with blond hair like me, maybe he grew up in Vista and I don't remember him. But his reason doesn't matter as I scramble away, dragging the book with me. I don't look over my shoulder as I run to the gate. Don't want to see Cira, don't want to see her turning back to the Recruiter and sinking her teeth into his flesh once more. Don't want to hear the sound of him killing her.

XL

My fingers shake as I push the remnants of the book into my waistband, letting the back of my shirt flutter over it. I slip through the gate and my mother rushes to me, takes my face in her hands and stares into my eyes. As if with a glance she can know if I'm okay, if I'm hurt.

I want to tell her that I'm hurting more than I ever have in my life. That my body's fine but the rest of me is lost. My best friend is gone—a monster.

How can any of us expect anything in the face of so much death, of a world overrun with it?

My mother rubs her thumb down my temple, tucks a strand of hair behind my ear, presses my braid flat against my shoulder. Her hands tremble.

"We should go," Harry says, coming to stand beside her. But my mother just continues to look at me. As if she's trying to tell me everything I need to know to understand this moment. Where to put it in my life.

And then Harry very gently takes my mother's hand in his and brings it to his lips. Her mouth twitches at the edges, the harsh angle of her shoulders relaxing.

She turns to him. "The village," she says. "The breach. I can't make you leave it again," she whispers, raising her hand to his cheek. If I knew the sound of someone breaking this would be it. "Everything it took from us the first time . . ." Her voice quavers. "I don't know if we can survive the path again. Not knowing . . ."

Behind us the moans of the Mudo stretch and swell, interspersed with men shouting. I want to turn away. It's my fault it's come to this. I'm the reason the Recruiters are here—why Harry has to leave everything he's ever known. I swallow back acrid self-hatred, realizing just how wide the ripples of my actions have spread.

"But this time we know there's more out there, Mary," Harry says. He places his hand over hers on his cheek. "Sometimes you have to chase the idea of something more."

She smiles and catches her breath on a laugh.

"We have to go," he whispers. She closes her eyes and nods and I look away.

Elias leads us down the path away from the village and I trail, glancing back only once. Mudo beat at the gate behind us, the hulk of the burned Cathedral's dull blackness against the dark sky, the houses long abandoned.

This village died long before we ever arrived.

▼ ▼ ▼

We push through the dawn, through the thick afternoon heat, into the evening. Shadows blossom under our eyes, our feet trudging and dragging through the dusty red clay. Odys runs ahead and circles back, his nose turned to the air and his tail low. The path twists and forks and every time we choose one direction over another I wonder where Catcher is, if he'll find us, if the Recruiters will bother beating their way through the village after us.

I try not to think of the possibility that they could have captured him. That he could be hurt.

With every step I feel the weight of the book I've hidden in my bag. I think about pulling it out and giving it to my mother but something holds me back. I want it for myself. She said it contains the history of the village and I want to know what that is. Because it's my history as well as hers.

As the light fades and distances blur we're forced to stop. The path becomes rutted with roots and rocks and it's too hard to navigate, our steps becoming too clumsy and dangerous. We find a spot where the path widens between three gates.

With the excuse that I'm trying to create a false trail to throw the Recruiters off in case they follow us, I walk farther down one of the paths until it bends and I'm hidden from the others. I sit on a rock and pull the remnants of my mother's book from my pack.

The cover's worse for the wear, what was once perhaps just a series of cracks now almost dissolving into dust. The pages are yellow and thin, the edges curling in the humid air. They're numbered, the first part of the binding still intact, its pages in order. But it's clear that hundreds more are missing and the handful tucked in loosely are badly out of order.

I tilt the first page until I find the last of the day's struggling light, " 'In the beginning,' " I read aloud, " 'we did not understand the extent of it.' "

My eyes widen. Written in the margins of the book is a

chronicle of the village, a diary of the Return. It's a history of everything. Growing up, we'd been told the history of the Return—about how one country blamed another, every faction having its own theory for where and how the infection started. We'd learned about it spreading rapidly, no one believing at first that such a thing could happen.

Everyone assumed it was some sort of global hoax until it was too late. All it took was one bite—one infection. That person would die and turn Breaker and would rapidly infect others until the critical mass was reached and a horde would form. It was too much, a tidal wave of dead that swept over the world until the survivors retracted and built walls. Until the Protectorate formed—a loose government controlling information, goods, security.

But we'd always learned the Forest was nothing but a wasteland. They fenced it off to try to control the infection—to try to trap the Mudo. But these pages tell of something different. I greedily skim, skipping where the words are illegible and the ink has blurred.

The village was originally part of a larger network, a series of interconnected nodes strategically placed by the government and its armies at the epicenter of the infection. Some villages were heavily supplied and armored, populated with the chosen few: dignitaries, scientists, women and children. They were meant to ensure our survival. Other villages were the remnants of refugee camps given the scraps of what the military didn't need or couldn't use. My mother's village—our village—was the latter, an abandoned field station left staffed by a handful of monastic nurses.

We were always taught that the government created the Forest. That they'd used natural obstacles like canyons, wide rivers and impassable mountains as natural barriers and built fences where necessary. They'd said they were trying to contain the infection—closing off the worst of it and driving into the Forest any Mudo hordes beyond.

But the diary explains that they hid it for another reason too. The hope was that by flooding the Forest with the Mudo and cutting it off they could accomplish one of two mutually exclusive goals. They would either contain the infection before it spread too far or they would create a safe zone in the last place anyone would dare to look: the center of the infection. They knew that if the first goal failed, the world would fall into chaos. Strongholds would fall to bandits.

But no one would think to look for life in what my mother always called the Forest of Hands and Teeth.

For a while the various villages communicated, traded and shared. But then they began to fall. Survivors escaping from the infected villages would stumble down the paths looking for refuge but would usually end up spreading the infection instead. The network began to collapse. One by one the villages in the Forest succumbed to the infection until there was only a handful left.

And that was when my mother's village cut themselves off. The nurses banded together, their faith in God and duty absolute. They closed the gates, declared the paths forbidden and told the people they were the last survivors of the Return. Any evidence otherwise was hidden or destroyed, including any outsider who dared come near the village.

They passed down their faith, calling the Mudo the Unconsecrated—the cursed by God. They built their worldview around their religious beliefs. But they also passed down their medical training and used it to look for cures. To look for answers. But they never found either. Just isolation and existence.

Interspersed in this written narrative are birth and death records; lists of betrothed; the married; those inducted into the Sisterhood and Guardians, the rulers and protectors of the village. Most of the recent history is missing but I flip through the pages until I find the latest entry. There are creases down the middle of it and it appears torn at the edge, as if it was once pulled from the book and folded.

On one side in a neat script is a list of betrothals and I'm about to flip the page over when a name catches my eye. I trace my fingers over the letters: *Mary*. And it lists her as betrothed to Harry. I flip the paper over, looking for a record of their marriage, but there isn't any. Only the last entry:

Gabrielle was the end of us. She breached the fences. Unconsecrated have overrun the village. Infection rages in the Cathedral and we have closed ourselves off in the catacombs. We are the end. We are all that is left. We will search the tunnels for other villages. Other havens. But we despair that this is truly the end.

God's will be done.

In the last gasp of light I shuffle through the remaining pages but there's nothing more. No explanation. I'm left barely able to breathe, finally understanding what it's taken to survive. And how quickly it can all disappear.

I trace my fingers along the ragged edges of the pages, wondering what it must have been like to be part of the Sisterhood when they decided to close themselves off, what desperation they must have felt, when I see something written on the inside of the back cover:

We will always survive. There is always hope.

I smile at the small words, wondering who wrote them and when. Wondering if that's all it takes to survive: hope.

I hear steps on the path behind me and I snap the book shut, reaching for my knife. But when I turn around it's Harry walking toward me. "Your mother was worried," he says softly. He notices the book in my lap but doesn't say anything about it.

I let the knife fall back into the loop on my belt. My cheeks heat at being caught with the book. I hold it out to him. "I didn't mean to hide it from you," I say. "I guess I was hoping that I would learn something about the village and where I'm from. And maybe about my mother. Learn who she was. If I'm anything like her."

Harry smiles and moves to a rock facing mine. He sits on it, stretching his legs out in front of him. I notice his face tighten some as his knees make a popping noise. "Mary has always been a little obsessed with knowing the truth of things," he tells me and I smile, staring at my hands. "I try to tell her that there are just some things we don't get to know in this world, but . . ." He shrugs. We both know how stubborn my mother is.

"What was my mother like when she was my age?" I ask him and when he hesitates I add, "I mean, Mary. What was she like?"

He laughs. "A troublemaker. Headstrong," he says. I can hear the smile in his voice. "There are some stories she should probably tell you, not me. But . . ." He shifts, stares past the Mudo, past the fences. He laughs again, softly.

"Your mother was a terrible singer," he finally says.

I smile. "She was?"

"Oh goodness, yes," Harry says without hesitation. "The Sisters used to ask her not to sing at services. They made her just move her mouth, pretend."

I feel laughter building inside me, bubbles bursting and floating up, making me feel lighter. I realize that it's been too long since I've laughed.

"She'd sing anyway, of course. Sometimes just to see Sister Tabitha scowl."

We're both snorting with laughter now, our breaths short and sweet.

"You could hear her from across the village," he says. He wipes at his eyes, tears glistening. "As she got older, when she was closer to your age, I think she was embarrassed by it. She wouldn't let anyone hear her. But she still loved it. She used to sing as she did the wash by the river." He shakes his head with the memories coming.

"I would sneak up and listen to her sometimes. She just . . ." His voice grows quieter. "She just seemed to be so full of life when she sang like that. So free. Like the fences . . ." He reaches out, traces a finger along the metal links and pulls it back before a Mudo can grab for him. "Like none of it existed."

He places his elbows on his knees and clasps his hands, staring at them as if they hold the answer to some question he seeks. "Does she still sing?"

I shake my head in the darkness, sad to know there's this part of her I've never known about. "No," I tell him. "Not anymore." It's as though my mother's life has been cut in two and we each hold only half of her memories. And I realize that even combined we would never know the whole. She's greater than the sum of what we remember of her. The woman Harry knows and the one I know are just edges of something larger.

I think about Elias and what he knows of my life in the Forest. And of Catcher and what he knows of my life in Vista. But does either of them know the whole of me? Would either of them crawl to the edge of a riverbank to hear me sing off-key just to be near me?

"You were supposed to be married," I prod him, wanting to know more about her. "You were betrothed." I point to the book. "It says it in here."

He laughs but I can no longer see his face and he's silent for a long time. "I thought I loved her," he finally says.

"You didn't?" I ask.

"I didn't . . . I didn't know her. I had an idea of her in my head. I didn't let her be who she needed to be."

"Does that mean you can't love someone if you don't really know who they are?" I ask him. I think about Elias, about the secrets he always seems to be keeping. As if he's afraid to let me know everything about him.

"It means that if you never try to see them for who they are, then you don't love them enough," he says.

I purse my lips shut, trying to figure out the difference.

"What about now?" I ask him, remembering the way he held her hand, the way she pressed her palm to his cheek.

He picks up a stick from the ground and bends it until it almost breaks. Lightning bugs waver around us, tiny stars of exploding light. "I've been selfish in my life," he says. "And goodness knows your mother has been as well. But that's what love is like when it's fresh and new. It's fire and thunder and heat." He rubs a hand over the back of his neck.

"When you're young you have such expectations of each other. So many needs. And when you're older . . ." He shrugs. "You want someone who understands. We've lived different lives. We've loved different people. But I think that there will always be that . . ." He struggles for the right word. "That understanding we share. Of having grown up in the same world, of having lived through the same memories.

"I have always loved Mary," he says. "Even when she was someone else's. When she couldn't love me I loved her. I'd like to think that maybe if things had been different before, if I'd had a chance to grow up with her, to prove myself . . . but I know it would never have worked. It took everything else, it took her leaving and me going back to the village. Sometimes things aren't meant to be the first time around," he says. "Sometimes you're lucky if they're ever meant to be.

"There's something to be said for feeling like we've known each other forever." He clears his throat and I wonder if he's embarrassed to be sharing so much. To be so open and exposed.

"Your mother . . ." He pauses again. "I think she was afraid to love sometimes. I think it scared her. She was the type to like things that were concrete, like the ocean. Something you could point to and know what it was. I think that's why she always struggled with God. And I think that's why she also struggled with love. She couldn't touch it. She couldn't hold on to it and make sure it never changed."

He stands, his knees popping again. The moans of the Mudo overlie his words, like a melody humming. "You don't have to be that way, Gabrielle," he says, starting back down the path toward our little camp. "Sometimes it's those things you can't touch that you need to hold on to the most."

XLI

That night I dream of gleaming towers and pure white streets. Of sounds and smells. Everything spins around me as I stand in the middle. Lights flicker, people pass but I stand firm. Facing me, only feet away, is another girl. She's tall with blond hair and green eyes. She stares at me through the chaos.

As if together we are the pivot around which the world turns. As if we are the balance to it all.

The sun rises and sets. The world around us crumbles. The people disappear, the sound fades. Plants push through the roads, vines twist up the buildings. And still we stare at each other.

Until the sun sets and this time doesn't rise again. And the moon becomes a hollow shell. The air is cold and sharp like ice. The plants wither and die. The buildings have long disintegrated and it's just the girl and me in the darkness.

She's my sister. My twin. I can see it in her. Feel it in me.

She was always there and will always be there. I reach out my hand to touch her, to hold her but somehow I can't bridge this space between us. I struggle harder, pounding against the impossible invisible, knowing that more than anything else I need her and she needs me and that somehow I have to find a way to get to her.

I wake up to the sound of moans. To the thrashing of the Mudo against the fences, so close on either side of the path. My chest aches from the dream, from the feeling that something's missing and I have to take several deep breaths to calm my frantic heart. I feel warmth in my hand and I turn my head to the side to see Elias asleep next to me. He's curled around me, his breaths puffs of mist in the dewy morning.

His hair is thicker, longer than when I first saw him. Three faded red lines trace down his cheek, a reminder of when we met and I fought him in the ocean. How easily such traces of our past are erased. His face is slack in sleep, his lips slightly parted.

He takes a deep breath, his body shifts and tenses and his eyes open. We're inches apart. He smiles. He reaches out and pushes a strand of hair from my cheek, rests his hand against my neck.

I want to savor this moment, to hold it close like a memory. But then a darkness begins to creep around the edges of my bliss. I think about how I was kissing Elias when I was supposed to be with Cira. How if I'd been there maybe I could have talked her out of trying to infect herself.

I sit up, rubbing my sleep-puffed eyes with my fists, the ache of her being gone still too fresh and new. I push to my feet, grab a canteen and start walking down the path, needing some time to myself to think.

Elias stands behind me. "Gabrielle, wait," he calls out after me.

I don't even bother to turn back. "No," I tell him, waving my hand at him to stay behind.

My thoughts are a storm as I tread down the path, not caring where I go so long as it's away from Elias and my mother and Harry. Cira's necklace rests heavy on my chest and I suddenly feel trapped, pinned in. As though the fences are too close, the sky too low. My muscles bunch and tense, painfully tight, and I shake my arms trying to let go.

I stumble over a rock, throwing myself off balance. I let myself fall to my knees and roll onto my back, my canteen flying. I'm not hurt but even so I just lie there staring up into the watery gray dawn. I don't move. I try not to think. I ignore everything around me.

Pink streaks into the sky mingling with a hue of purple when I hear the steps. At first I think it must be Elias coming after me and then I realize that they're coming from the wrong direction. Dread fills my stomach. I reach for my knife but it's not there, left behind with the others where I slept.

I roll slowly to my stomach and press my body against the ground, pushing myself to my feet as silently as possible. The steps are uneven. My first thought is that it's Mudo trailing us from the village but then I realize that there are no moans. My body breaks out in sweat as I wonder if the Recruiters were able to get through the village. If they've already found us.

I grab a rock in each hand and crouch, waiting. I see the shadow before the person and I hold my breath. The figure walks around the bend in the path.

"Catcher!" I yelp, relieved to see his familiar face, to know that he's okay.

He stops and stands there staring at me. His eyes take a moment to adjust. "Gabry," he says, his face breaking into a smile.

I scramble toward him but before I get close enough to touch him he wavers on his feet. There's something wrong. I reach for him but he holds out his hand, pushing me away.

"Catcher, what's going—" I start to say. But then I notice the scrapes along his arms speckled with blood.

My eyes go wide, fear starting to tingle somewhere deep inside. I take another step toward him but he says, "Don't," and I stop.

He bows his head, the muscles along his jaw clenching and releasing.

"Go back to the others, Gabrielle." His voice is hoarse.

"No," I tell him, my chest fluttering anxiously. "Not until you tell me what's going on." I clench my fists, dig my nails into my palms. I wish I hadn't dropped the rocks. What if the infection is taking over him? What if he's starting to turn? What if the blood isn't his but someone else's?

He shakes his head and stumbles again.

I rush to him, trying to help him stand. He tries to physically push me away but he's too weak. "Gabry, please," he says. "Don't."

I take his arm in mine just as he falls to one knee. There are more gouges along his back, his shirt ripped.

"What happened?" I ask, trying to keep the worry out of my voice. I bend over his shoulder, trying to get a better look but he pushes me away again, this time causing me to stumble backward.

"Catcher, you're hurt," I tell him. I can't understand why he keeps pushing me away. "What happened?"

He looks at me, the pain a haze around the edges of his

eyes. "I know," he says softly. "Running through the Forest—brambles," he mutters. "Branches." He blinks a few times as if he's having a difficult time focusing. Sweat drips down his cheeks and neck. He looks gaunt, his wrists too thin.

"Have you been eating? Drinking?" I ask him. He shakes his head. "Catcher," I say, my voice a mix of desperation and exasperation. "You have to take care of yourself," I whisper. "Let me clean these cuts."

I don't know what will happen to him if he loses too much blood—when they die the Infected always turn, and I can only assume the same thing will happen to Catcher—that if he dies he'll Return. I have no idea how long he's been starving himself but he looks weak and dizzy. Just like Cira when I found her in the Council House. I press my lips together, realizing just how dangerous Catcher could be right now.

"No," he whispers. "I'm infected, Gabrielle," he says. "Don't you understand? I won't let you risk touching my blood. I won't risk infecting you."

I narrow my eyes. "But you don't know if that would even do anything," I tell him. "Plenty of people have been infected and bled on other people and nothing's happened." I think about the boy in the amphitheater who sacrificed himself to the Soulers. How he was bleeding and the Souler woman still touched him.

"That's different," he says. "I'm different. Unless I can know for sure I won't infect you I don't want to take that risk. I can't be the one to hurt you." His eyes go wide and roll back in his head slightly as he loses his balance and throws his arms out to catch himself.

I jump forward, grabbing him. He pushes me back, his

hands on my shoulders. "Please," he says. "Please. I can't take it if something happens to you."

I stretch out my fingers for his face but my arms aren't long enough. I can't reach him.

"I'm going to take care of you, Catcher." The fear in my voice burns into anger. "You should know that by now. I'm not giving up on you."

He closes his eyes, his breathing shallow, and I wonder if I should call out to the others for help. Or for a weapon.

Finally he nods and I peel his shirt away from his body. I have to clench my teeth as the smell of blood hits the air. I tense, waiting for the Mudo on either side of the fence to react. Waiting for their moans to pitch higher, their scrambling to intensify. But nothing happens. Another reminder of how different Catcher is.

How he can pass as one of them.

I grab the canteen and dribble a few drops of water onto a scrap from my skirt and dab at his wounds. Then I hold the water to his lips and watch his throat as he drinks.

"It's the best I can do for now," I tell him, wishing I could do more. Not just for the cuts on his back but for the pain I can see in his eyes. The guilt and self-loathing. "You have to promise me you'll eat and sleep. Stop pushing yourself so hard. Stop punishing yourself."

He reaches out and touches my cheek, the pad of his thumb skimming the path of the tears I didn't even realize I was crying. We stare at each other, all the eroding possibilities flickering between us.

And then he pushes himself to his feet, wobbling just a bit but already looking stronger. I hold out a hand, press it to his chest to steady him. I suck in my breath as the heat of him invades my flesh. The familiarity of how hot his skin is, how his touch scorches. I can't resist curling my fingers against him.

He leans closer and my body mimics his until the barest of nothing separates us. The fire of him spreads through me. I raise my other hand to his chest and move it down and around to his side, feeling the ridges of his ribs. His muscles twitch under my touch.

"Gabry." His voice is low, a warning. I know he wants me to be the strong one; the one to step away and leave him behind. But I've never been the strong one.

I press myself closer to him. Wanting to remember what it was like before. That moment—the instant—before everything changed.

He raises his fingers to my lips. He traces them slowly. I reach out my tongue, touching his thumb. He groans surrender low in his throat and reaches his hand to the back of my neck, grabbing me and pulling.

But then he stops just as his mouth almost reaches mine. He breathes through clenched teeth, panting with effort. We stand that way, so close to a kiss but the distance impossible. He whimpers but doesn't come any closer. "Gabrielle," he says, this time my name a plea.

I close my eyes at the sound of it, at the feel of his anguish. I push my hand up his chest and along his throat and then I tilt his chin up, pressing my lips along his jaw. I want to prove to him that he's alive. That he's not a monster. That he's still who he's always been.

He catches his breath again and again as I touch my mouth to his skin. It burns against my lips, the heat between us almost unbearable.

He trails his own finger down my back, along the edge of my shoulder blade, trailing a line under my arm and along my chest.

I close my eyes and press myself against him. "Catcher," I whisper. Our hearts beat against each other, the blood rushing through our veins. I feel light and dizzy, as if the world's spinning fast enough that it can change time—take us back to the before.

Back before the Forest and Elias and my mother and Daniel and the Recruiters and Cira. Just one memory—one reminder—of what could have been.

Suddenly his arms wrap around me, pulling me tight, his mouth at my throat, at the edge of my shirt, along my collarbone, at my ear.

And then his lips almost close over mine but he stops. I lean in, trying to erase the space between us but it's as if there's too thick a wall of air between us. I can almost feel the outline of his lips; I can just barely feel their heat. But I can't touch them.

A wail begins to build inside me. We're so close. We're almost there. Just this once I want to kiss him the way we did before. Please, why can't he understand this? That if our lips can just touch, if we can just replay that moment, that maybe we can close the gap between then and now. That we can take it all back.

In that moment we are almost Catcher and Gabrielle, standing at the base of the coaster at the amusement park. There's no infection. There was no change. I want to cry with the want and the need of it all, just beyond my reach.

But then he pushes me away, snapping the possibility of the moment. He gasps for air as he stumbles backward. I feel the need, the overpowering desire begin to break through me. His face is awash with horror and shame. He raises his hand to his mouth, pushes his fingers to his lips. Lips that my mouth never touched. His other hand he holds out as if to ward me off. He's shaking his head, tears already falling from his eyes, already burning down my face.

"No," he says as if he can take it all back.

"Catcher," I say. I step toward him, desperate. "It's okay." Please, I just need him to be who he used to be. Because that means I get to go back to being who I used to be as well.

"No!" he screams. I wince at the sound of it. At the meaning of it. The finality. Birds explode from a bush in the Forest and he stares at them as they twist into the air. "It's not okay," he yells at me. "It will never be okay!"

He lunges toward me and a spike of fear digs into my spine. He's never been violent with me. He's never raised his voice and I feel little and small and nothing in the face of it.

He grabs the front of my shirt and pulls me against him, his face hovering over mine. I cringe, no longer sure of what he will or won't do.

"Don't ever touch me again, Gabrielle," he growls. The intensity in his eyes terrifies me. He shakes me and then pushes me back and I fall to the ground, dazed. He stands over me, hands clenched into fists at his sides.

I throw an arm in front of me and cringe, his rage so palpable that I'm afraid he might lash out. He's like a horrifying monster, nothing like the person I know. "Catcher, don't!" I cry out, hoping that my voice will break through whatever's happening to him.

XLII

Catcher stops. His face drains of color. He takes a step back, his eyes dazed as if he's just woken up. His mouth opens and closes. "Gabry," he breathes. He shakes his head, the moment of vulnerability gone. His eyes go flat, empty. The muscles along his neck tremble as he swallows again and again.

"You have to go tell the others," he finally says, his voice soft. Everything from before—the rage and pain—gone. "The Recruiters are coming closer. They'll make it through the village." And then he turns and runs down the path, pushing against the fence for support when he stumbles.

I sit on the ground feeling ashamed and alone and stupid and miserable. It tunnels inside me, spreading darkness like a cloud over the ocean. I want to drown in the feeling, curl up in it and let it pull me away. To wallow in the absolute emptiness. To know that I can't be drained anymore, that I can't be hurt. Because there's nothing left.

It's not that Catcher can't be with me. It's that he doesn't *want* to be with me. He used to make me feel like the most amazing person in the world and now he makes me feel like the worst. Like I'm not worth anything at all.

Sobs suffocate me until I press my arm over my mouth and bite into my flesh, trying to hold it all in. But I can't and I strain at the hurt of it all.

I can't go back to being who I was before. To wanting what I wanted before. It will never be the same. Catcher will never be better. He'll always be infected. Cira will always be Mudo. I will never know my birth mother. Elias will always be elusive. Even my mother now has Harry.

This stupid world keeps spinning and there's nothing I can do. And so I sit in the middle of the path and sob while the Mudo push against the fences moaning at me.

▾ ▾ ▾

"Catcher says the Recruiters are still following us," I say as I approach the others. Harry and my mother stand in the middle of the path talking, my mother's hand resting on Odys's head. He leans against her leg with his tongue lolling. "So we should keep moving," I add. I don't tell them anything else about our encounter but Elias tilts his head and narrows his gaze at my red and puffy eyes.

He kneels on the ground sorting through supplies and I walk past him, leaning down and grabbing my pack. He starts to reach a hand toward me but I sling the bag over my shoulder and evade his grasp. I don't want him to see me like this: hurt and raw.

"Gabry?" my mother asks, her voice filled with concern. But I just shake my head and keep going, needing to be alone inside myself. I don't bother to wait for them to follow me. The morning sky breaks overcast, the wind rustling the leaves in the trees. It doesn't take long before the rain starts, turning the path to mud and causing the rocks to become slippery.

I welcome the drudgery of it, the pinprick stings of raindrops on my face. It seeps through my clothes, trickles down my back like sweat. I wish it would wash me away. During the heavier spots of rain the Mudo wander away from the fences, their senses dulled by the water-laden air. I breathe a sigh of relief, not caring about the mud and the slosh of it so long as I get a reprieve from the endless moans.

During the morning Elias tries to offer small kindnesses and I rebuff them all. He holds out his canteen when I reach for mine and I ignore it. When I stumble over a fallen branch in the middle of the path he holds out his hand to steady me and I don't thank him. I can't look at him or anyone else. I just focus on my feet, on moving forward. I try not to let the waves of desolation from this morning pull me under.

The path begins to steepen as we near mountains and we slip in the mud as we climb our way up, always looking over our shoulders wondering how far behind the Recruiters are. How soon until they'll catch up. Odys presses tight against my mother's legs, his head hunched and coat dripping.

We reach the top of the mountain only to find another, the path splitting and breaking and us pushing farther and farther. The dull afternoon turns dark early, the rain pounding harder and making it even more difficult to navigate. We slide down the hill and start climbing again. Gradually the rain slows and clears, the clouds drifting apart to show stars. With the rain stopped, around us the Mudo moan and wander back to the fences. Thick rivulets of water trickle down the path.

The tenth time I trip over roots hidden by the dark and fall on my hands and knees in the mud, I don't get up. Elias reaches to help me and I swat his hand away.

"Gabry," he says. "Are you okay? Are you hurt?"

I shake my head, damp hair clinging to my cheeks. I'm exhausted. Emotionally and physically.

He reaches for me again. "We have to keep moving."

"Why?" I demand, so tired of caring.

"The Recruiters, they're still back there and—"

"So what?" I'm still staring at the ground, at my fingers clinging to the muck. I want to give up. "Let them find us and take us. We can't just keep running, following this path forever. We don't know where it goes. We don't even know if this path leads anywhere at all."

Elias starts to say something but then I hear him shift away. And I realize that a small part of me wanted him to demand that I push harder. Hoped that he'd give me a reason to keep going. I wonder numbly if he's stopped caring about me as well. If today both men who meant something to me have decided I'm not worth it.

Elias and Harry continue up the path a bit and my mother kneels next to me. "Come on, Gabrielle," she says softly. "Elias is right, we should keep moving forward." She places a hand over mine. "Trust me, we'll be okay. We'll find a way out of this."

I turn to look at her. "I'm not like you," I tell her. "I can't just keep going not knowing. I can't just take it on faith like you did."

She opens her mouth to protest but I cut her off. I need her to know this about me. I need her to stop thinking of me as something I'm not. I'm tired of her thinking the best of me when I've done nothing to deserve it. "No," I tell her. "You've always been like that. You've always known what you wanted."

I take a deep breath. "And I haven't," I finish weakly. I feel the tears pushing behind my eyes and I let them drip down my face, fall from my nose and chin. "I don't know anything," I tell her. "I used to know and then it all changed and you left me and I couldn't figure it out."

I turn away, squeezing my eyes closed. "I wish I were like that," I whisper. "I wish I could be like you."

She pulls me to her and I resist until she pulls harder and I fall into her lap, her arms tight around me. "I never knew," she says, her lips moving against my temple. "I never knew what I wanted. I was always terrified." I feel her body shudder as she draws in a shaky breath. "I was always confused and my mother was gone too and I didn't know what to do without her."

"Then why did you leave me?" I ask. "If you knew what it was like why did you leave?" I pull my legs to my body, curling into a tight ball.

She's silent for a long time. Around us water drips from branches and slides down leaves. On the other side of the fence Mudo slip through the night, their moans heavy. "Because I'm not perfect, Gabrielle," she finally says. "I make mistakes too. I made the mistake of leaving my friends behind in the Forest. I made the mistake of being selfish. I should have gone back for them earlier. I should have fought harder to find out where you came from." She shrugs and I realize that I'm holding my breath.

"You don't have to try to be perfect, Gabrielle. And you need to stop thinking that I can't make mistakes either. It's exhausting to have everyone around you expecting you to be perfect. And it's not fair that you put that pressure on yourself." She reaches out and grabs my head in her hands. "You're human, Gabry. We're both just human. Nothing more. But also nothing less."

I nod, letting her words sink in. It's as if she's somehow given me permission to forgive myself, let go of my mistakes and fears. It's a terrifying thought—I've held on to them for so long that it feels like a part of who I am.

She smiles, the lines around her eyes crinkling. "Sometimes it's the mistakes that turn out to be the best parts of life," she says. "If I hadn't made mistakes I would have stayed in the village when I was your age, I would have married Harry. I would have never found the ocean or traveled."

"Was it worth it?" I ask. "Was it worth leaving to find the ocean? Wouldn't you have been happy if you'd stayed in the village? If you'd had your mother and been with Harry?"

"Oh honey," she says, her voice sounding desperate. "I can't compare the lives I could have lived. One would have been comfort and security. But the other . . ." She sighs. "It was the most love and the most pain and the most wonder I could have ever known."

"But nothing changed in the end," I protest, twisting until I can see her face. "You're still here in the Forest. You're still with Harry. It's as if everything else—the ocean and me—never happened."

She smiles. "I used to think the ocean would be this untouched place," she says, a note of regret in her voice. "Where there wouldn't be death or Unconsecrated. And then when I got there and saw the dead on the beach . . ."

She lifts one shoulder. "I realized that I had to accept the world the way it was. I realized that I had to move on."

"Did you?" I ask.

She's quiet a moment, thinking. "I don't know. Eventually I did. Sometimes I still think back to that feeling, seeing the ocean spread out before me that first time. Knowing it was real and that I'd believed and it was true.

"It changed everything, Gabrielle. Who I am changed. Who Harry is. If we had been together from the beginning . . . it would be different. I don't need Harry to complete me anymore, I just need him to be with me."

I turn my head until I can see the stars through a gap in the clouds, not sure I understand the difference.

"You can't give up, Gabrielle," she says, her voice softer than the air. "Not on any of it. The path, your friends." She pauses. "Your family."

I pull away from her, wrapping my arms around my legs and squeezing them against me. "You mean Annah," I say.

She leans forward. "I mean me," she says. "I'm not a perfect person, Gabry. I've made mistakes and I'll keep making them. Just like you'll make mistakes. And so will Harry and Elias and Catcher."

I stare at my fingers, twisting them around each other, pushing at my nails and watching them turn white. I think about Elias and how he still blames himself for losing me. How he blames himself for losing Annah. How he seems so afraid of messing up with me again. And how I've been afraid to really let myself go with him. Terrified of making the wrong decision.

My mother places her palm flat against mine. "It's never been a perfect world. It's never going to be. It's going to be hard and scary and, if you're lucky, wonderful and awe-inspiring. But you have to push through the bad parts to get to the good."

"What if there aren't good parts?" I ask her, the tears creeping back up my throat. "What if I've already lived the good parts and there's nothing left?"

She laughs, throaty and deep. "Trust me when I tell you that there is plenty left," she says. "You just have to take the risk sometimes in order to find them. Step outside what's comfortable and safe."

I swallow, feeling my pulse flutter at the possibility of her words. "What if I'm too scared?"

She looks at me for a long time. "I grew up hemmed in by fences. Everything we learned and knew was restricted. The Sisterhood knew there was a world outside our village but made us believe we were the last ones. They regimented every part of our lives—convincing us that to believe anything different from what they taught was to endanger our very existence."

She tucks a strand of hair behind her ear. She's never told me any of this before. She's told me stories about growing up in the Forest but never what it was like to be raised in it. I feel as though I'm catching a secret glimpse of her, not as my mother but as a girl who was once my age. Who faced the same fears that I do.

"I wanted you to have a different life, Gabrielle," she says. "I felt danger every day, terror and fear, and I wanted you to grow up knowing nothing but safety and security. I thought that raising you in the lighthouse, where you could see past the Barrier—see that there was a world out there—would make you want more. And maybe I was wrong. Maybe I just taught you to be scared of anything that wasn't safe.

"Maybe we'll always live in a world of fences," she says, waving her hand at the chain links on either side of the path. "But they're to keep the Unconsecrated out. Not to keep you in."

I let her words roll through my head and nod. And we sit together for a while listening to the Mudo thrash against the fences and the water drip through the night and then finally she stands and pulls me to my feet and we push on up the path toward morning.

XLIII

It's the middle of the next day when we first catch a glimpse of how close the Recruiters are behind us. We've pushed ourselves up another peak and look back to see them weaving down the mountain across the valley.

By the time the evening edges around us we can sometimes hear them. Their shouts threading through the air, mingling with the sound of the Mudo.

There's been no sight of Catcher since he left me the morning before. I'm worried that he's hurt worse than I thought and isn't taking care of himself. That he might be out in the Forest alone and dying. I dig my nails into my palms trying to drive my thoughts away from him but I can't.

"Maybe we should split up," Harry suggests as darkness presses in and we're forced to slow down. He looks down the mountain where we can see a line of torches marching steadily along the valley. Odys leans against his leg, a soft whine escaping him as if he can smell our fear.

"No," my mother says, and we keep walking, exhaustion in every step.

Elias takes the lead and my mother and Harry trail behind us a ways. I feel awkward around Elias, as if suddenly I don't know what to say to him. As if I've ever known what to say to him. He glances back at me as he walks and when he hears me stumble he's always there with a strong hand offered. He steadies me but then turns back to the path. I feel awful for having pushed him away so many times before and I wonder if I've messed things up beyond repair. But then I remember all the times he's pushed me away as well and I purse my lips and keep walking.

And then one time he doesn't turn away. He stands facing me, his fingers still cupping my elbow. His touch tingles up my arm. "Gabry," he says. I can barely see him in the night, I can just feel him, feel the heat outline of his body, the blurry edges of where his skin fades to darkness. He leans closer. I can feel him struggling for words and I hold my breath, waiting.

But he just shakes his head and backs away from me, his grip sliding slowly from my arm. I want to call him back. To tell him not to go. He stands still for a moment, just staring at me. "I'm sorry," he says. "I shouldn't have. . . ."

I don't move. I don't breathe. I just wait. And hope.

Something changes in his face; the hesitancy slips away. He strides over to me and wraps a hand at the back of my neck. I gasp. His face is inches from mine. "I'm not Catcher," he says. His fingers press into my skin. "I'm never going to know you like he does. I wasn't there all those years. I'm never going to know the you before all this as well as he does."

His thumb traces behind my ear and my chest flutters at the touch. "But you're not the same either. You're not the same girl you were before and he's not the same boy. We've all changed. Everything in our world has changed. It's never going to be the same again."

He hesitates. My entire body tingles with anticipation. "I'm sorry I left you in the woods when we were kids," he says. "I'm sorry I wasn't there all those years. I'm sorry I missed growing up with you and that I made you miss growing up with your family. I was supposed to take care of you and I didn't. I failed. But I'm here now. I know who you are *now*. I know who you've become. You're not Annah. You're not even Abigail—you're Gabrielle."

All I can think about is what my mother said the night before about how none of us is perfect. How we all make mistakes. And how sometimes those mistakes make our life richer. I'd have never seen the ocean if I'd never been lost in the Forest as a child. I'd have never grown up with my mother or known Cira and Catcher. I'm who I am today because of Elias.

He presses on, the heat of his breath on my face. "And you're the one I want," he whispers. As he talks his lips skim over my own.

Before I can say anything, before I can even react, he pushes his hand into my hair. "I know that to you everything has changed for the worse over the last weeks. But for me . . ." He pauses, rests his forehead into the curve of my neck. "Before you my life was nothing but wandering and solitude and death. Now with you there's possibility."

He pulls back until we're looking into each other's eyes. "I'm falling in love with you, Gabrielle. Not with the person you used to be, but *you*." He touches the center of my chest, his palm spreading flat against me. His words explode inside me, touching fire along my veins and spiraling into my heart. I can't help but lean in to him, feeling the weight of his touch.

"We spend so much time worrying about the Unconsecrated and the fences and wondering about the before time," he says, his voice soft and urgent, full of excitement. "We never build anything new. We just watch everything old crumble around us."

His eyes are so light in the darkness, so bright that I feel as if I'm enveloped in the blaze of the lighthouse. I nod because I do understand what he's saying; I've felt it too.

"I want more than that," he whispers. He leans toward me and I hold my breath.

I feel something building and growing inside me. A desire to be something, do something great. The possibility that I *could* be someone better than I am.

"We can be so much more," he adds, his mouth against mine.

It's as if everything shifts around me, the pieces that didn't fit together finally twisting until they match. The terror that had been clouding and suffocating me begins to filter away, dissipating in the night. "I want something more too," I whisper. "I want more than looking back and wishing for what was or what could have been. Who I was or could have been. I want . . ." I lick my lips, tasting him. "I want you."

He smiles against my mouth. He kisses me in the darkness and I wrap my arms around him. I feel his desire to keep me safe, the curl of muscles along his shoulders, the way his hand presses against my back. But I also feel my own strength, my own determination. I finally feel as if I've found myself.

He steps away from me, his grin glowing in the night, and I can't help but laugh because I know that my smile is as big as his. He starts walking down the path backward, his eyes shining as he looks at me, energy pulsing between us.

And suddenly I no longer care about that first kiss with Catcher. Suddenly everything is all about here and now with Elias and me and what we can be together.

I used to think that I would give anything to go back to that moment in the park. To save Catcher. To save us all. But now I'm not so sure.

"Gabry," Elias says. He holds a hand out to me and I smile, anticipating the feel of his skin against mine. He walks away as I draw closer, laughing and smiling and teasing, waiting for me to chase him. And then he takes another step and is gone.

I stand there staring at nothing, not understanding how he suddenly disappeared. Then I hear the scream. I lunge forward, into the space his body just occupied. There's nothing, my toes curling over emptiness. I almost slip into it before I'm able to fall backward and away.

"Elias!" I shriek. I crawl forward. My hands shake and then my fingers feel the end of the path where it suddenly drops away. Sound blurs, roaring one loud rush through my ears. The air tastes wrong, of salt and rot. I push my head out and look down, feeling the ground crumble away underneath me.

I swallow. "Elias!" My voice shakes and panic stretches around me. Closing me in, pulling me tight. The rushing grows too loud—I can't hear anything. Not my own shouting, not my own heart, nothing.

I reach my hand out, terrified, feeling into the empty air. Grasping for him as if he could be just beyond my reach. I lean out farther into the void. "Elias!"

A hand grabs my ankle. Yanks me back. I scream and kick, the panic consuming me. Until I feel his heat, the sear of

Catcher's skin. His breathing comes in ragged gulps, his face white in the night. I try to roll away from him but he holds my legs pinned to the ground. "Don't move," he says.

I nod, my heart pounding. Wondering where he came from; how and why he's here. If he's been watching us this whole time, listening. He crawls out next to me until he can push his torso into the blackness. "Elias!" he calls out.

I sit up, scrambling back from the edge of the path. "You have to get him, Catcher. He has to be okay. You have to make sure he's okay," I beg. All I can see is Elias's face just before he fell. If I'd reached out for him. If I'd said something. Anything. I squeeze my eyes closed, trying to force away the thought.

The same words roll repeatedly through my head: Elias is gone, Elias is gone, Elias is gone.

I grind my jaw, feeling the pain in my teeth. Elias is gone. He said he loved me and now he is gone.

And then I hear something. It's not even a sound but I know it's there. The same way you feel the buzz of a gnat before it bites in the evening. I scrabble back to the edge. "Elias!" I screech as Catcher throws out an arm to hold me back.

I dig my fingers into the ground and hold my breath. I wait. I hear him.

"Elias," I call out again. "Elias, are you okay? Where are you? What happened?"

His voice is strained when he shouts back, "I'm caught on something. I can't see anything."

I choke on relief, swallowing back the desire to sob. "Are you okay?"

He hesitates. In the silence all I can hear are the moans of the Mudo on the other side of the fence bordering the path. "Elias!" I call out again in a panic, afraid that he's fallen farther or passed out.

“I’m here, Gabry,” he says. He sounds weaker now. And I don’t know why he won’t tell me if he’s okay.

I turn to Catcher and grab his shirt. “You have to get him,” I say, desperate. I know what I’m asking him to do. I know I’m asking him to risk himself for someone else who loves me. For the man I’ve chosen over him. “Please, Catcher, please, you have to help me get him.”

XLIV

Catcher doesn't hesitate. He just nods and vaults the fence beside the path, running into the woods. I look around, searching the ground with my hands, trying to find something useful. Something that will help pull Elias up. But there's nothing. On either side of me the fence just ends, the path falling away to emptiness.

Catcher returns with what little dry wood and leaves he could find. Harry and my mother finally catch up and they help him arrange it, trying desperately to start a small fire for light. Odys circles around them, trying to herd Catcher toward the fences until he finally comes to sit by me, whining and nudging my hand with his cold nose.

I lie at the edge of the path, my head over the nothingness. Wind blows my hair over my lips and around my neck. "Elias, can you hear me?" I ask him. I strain, hearing him grunt. Behind me I hear muttering as they try to strike the fire, try to coax it to life. But everything is soggy from the rain.

"Elias, you have to hold on," I tell him. "Please, just listen to me. You have to hold on for me. Please, for me. I'm sorry." I should have pulled him to me. I should have grabbed him and kissed him again. He wouldn't have fallen otherwise.

I close my eyes and wish for the sun. All these times I've asked the earth to spin slower—to take me back—and now I will it toward dawn.

In the darkness below sounds begin to churn, something I didn't hear until now. It's as though a river is rushing at the bottom of the cliff. It fades and blends with the echo of the Mudo moans around us and causes Odys to skitter and pace. I can't hear Elias anymore and my blood burns with panic.

It's almost morning, I can taste it in the tang of the air, hear it in the stirring of birds in the trees. Any moment the day will break, giving us the light we need.

"We have to hurry," I shout over my shoulder. I turn to the fire and see Catcher puffing at the embers. Already the sky is starting to blink awake. I strain to see Elias but still see nothing, only the blurry edge of the rocky cliff and the faint outline of my hands as I reach into the emptiness.

Catcher finally wraps two branches with a spare shirt from my mother's bag and lights them in the fire. He carries one to the edge of the path and hands the other to Harry, who follows him.

I watch as Catcher lowers the flame into the semidarkness, sweeping it over the cliff. I catch my breath when I finally see Elias at the edge of the light. "I can get down to him," I say, pulling my legs around to the emptiness. But Catcher holds me back.

Already the sky's a glow surrounding the horizon. It oozes

over the mountain across the valley from us, slowly filling it with light.

I look at Catcher, ready to tell him to let me go, but something in his face stops me. The fire jumps and trembles as he reaches for Harry's torch with a shaking hand. He holds both torches out over the void and then he lets them go.

The flames look like broken birds as they flutter down. And just before they extinguish we can all see the movement. The flick of an arm, the edge of a jaw.

None of us moves, none of us breathes or says a word. Just below where Elias lies caught by a fragment of fence, Mudo reach for him, their fingers scraping the earth of the cliff for him. I don't know how many there are but right now they still can't get to him.

"Elias, don't move," I say, knowing my voice doesn't have enough force to reach him. I see blood leaking through his shirt, trailing down his arm and dripping into the frenzied Mudo below him.

Without taking my eyes off Elias, as if my gaze can keep him safe, I grip Catcher's arm, my fingertips biting into his skin. "You have to help him," I say.

The world continues to spin us toward day, the light growing stronger as Catcher eases over the edge of the cliff. Already I can see more of our surroundings, see that the edge of the mountain's washed away. Uprooted trees are twisted with what's left of the fence that bordered the path, all of it strewn down the side of the mountain.

Elias lies against one of these sections of fence caught between two brittle-looking young trees about twenty feet down from where we are. Below him the Mudo struggle toward him, their fingers raw and bloody from trying to climb up the rocky dirt. I hold my breath, hoping the mountain's too steep for the Mudo to reach him.

Catcher starts to make his way toward Elias, holding on to roots and bushes, when his feet slip out from underneath him. I press my hand to my mouth, wanting to call out for Catcher to be careful. Wanting to beg Elias to say something to let me know he's okay. But as the sky lightens I can tell even from here that his face is white, his lips pressed together in pain and his leg cocked at an unnatural angle.

At that moment all I want in the world is for Elias to be okay. Rocks slide under Catcher's feet, bouncing down the hill, a few striking the Mudo before falling into the darkness of the valley. Catcher slips again, stumbling down a few feet before he's able to stop himself by grabbing on to a sapling.

I close my eyes. I can't watch. I know that my heart will stop completely if something happens to Catcher or Elias. I hear more rocks and dirt tumble down the hill; I hear Odys whining and Harry whispering what sounds like a prayer.

But all I do is think about Elias, remember the touch of his lips on mine, focus on the sound of his voice when he told me he wanted to be with me. Feel in every part of myself how much I care for him—how much I desperately need him to be okay.

Finally I hear my mother sigh with relief and I open my eyes. Elias lies on the ground, Catcher standing over him panting and sweating from the effort of pulling him back up the cliff. All I can do is stare at Elias, afraid to move closer. At his leg, which doesn't look right. Which is broken and twisted. At his face, which is ashen and washed with pain.

My mother pulls off his shirt, which is now stained with blood, and hands it to Catcher to hold against a wide gash in

Elias's side. Harry rummages through the packs for water and extra clothes to tear up for bandages. My mother runs to the dying fire and grabs two unused sticks. She lays them next to Elias's leg, her face grim. She places one hand at the ankle and the other at the knee. She takes a deep breath and then I hear the snap. I see Elias's eyes open wide, his body buck and stretch.

The Mudo push against the fence, smelling the blood, needing it. Their moans mingle with the echoes drifting over the cliff, surrounding us, making it difficult to think.

"Is he going to be okay?" I ask quietly, trying to stay out of the way while my mother works on his injuries.

No one looks up at me. No one answers. Elias pants loudly, grunting with pain.

I think about the cuts on Cira's arms. How living on the path in the Forest caused the blood infection that would have killed her. That could kill Elias as well if he hasn't already lost too much blood. I swallow again and again, trying to stop my mind from thinking such thoughts. Trying to concentrate on the here and now and not worry about what's next. Because I don't know what can be next for us. Not with his leg the way it is. Not with the Recruiters so close behind us.

I stare down at where Elias's blood drips onto the ground. I want to dig it up and somehow force it back inside him. Anything to make this situation better.

"Come here and hold this," my mother says, calling me over and pointing at Catcher. I kneel next to her. "Press here, hard." She places my hands over the shirt. I nod, feeling the material already damp with Elias's warm blood. She pulls Catcher down the path toward Harry and they speak in lowered voices. Even though I can't hear them I understand what's going on by the way they stand and move.

They're trying to figure out what to do. There's no way Elias can walk.

I'm left with Elias. Left feeling him bleed against me. Left with the sound of the Mudo pulsating at the fences. I wipe my cheek on my shoulder, tears and sweat and pain. Odys lies next to me, his heat pushing along my leg as if to give me comfort.

I stare at Elias's face, twisted and flushed. I take his hand in my own. I lean closer to him. "Elias?" I murmur. I don't want to believe this is happening. Even if we constructed something to carry him on I'm pretty sure he couldn't keep going. He's too hurt. He wouldn't make it.

I don't even know if we'll be able to go any farther anyway, now that the path's been washed away.

He cracks open one eye, the lightness of it swallowing me. Every part of him is contracted in pain, every muscle rigid. "You have to go," he says, barely opening his mouth. "The Recruiters."

I shake my head, my shoulders hunching as I try to catch my breath. My tears blur everything but I don't want him to see. I want to be strong for him; I need him to have hope. "We'll be okay," I say.

"Tell them to make you go," he says. He pushes my shoulder. My hands slip from the bandage on his side. "Catcher!" Elias yells out.

Catcher runs over. I shake my head and struggle with Elias. "Stop," I tell him. He's using up too much energy, he could be hurting himself worse.

"Take her," Elias says. His eyes are wide, his voice urgent. "You have to make her go. The Recruiters will use her to control you. You can't let them get either of you."

Catcher looks at me but I'm staring at Elias, my hands pressed back against his side. I'm not going to let him push me away. Not the way Catcher did. I refuse to let him give up on me. "I'm not going anywhere," I tell him.

Elias turns to Catcher. "I'm a Recruiter. Leave me here. They'll take care of me. They have to. It's part of the oath."

"You're not one of them anymore," I cry. Despair boils inside me and I twist it into anger so that I don't drown. Because he's right. He can't keep going with us and he needs help.

Elias is grabbing Catcher's arm now. "They'll have to take me back to Vista, it will buy you time."

"The path ends," I tell him. "We can't go any farther."

"It has to keep going," he says. "Annah and I escaped through the mountains. You can find a way," he says. "You have to."

"We're not leaving you here." I clench my jaw, desperate to somehow make this right. "We're not leaving you out here alone. What if you're wrong? What if they try to use you to get to Catcher?"

"It's better than you," he says softly.

XLV

A shadow falls across me, across Elias's face. "We'll stay with him," Harry says, his voice soft. My mother crouches, puts a hand on my shoulder.

I shake my head, helplessness pooling inside me. "No," I say, my voice cracking. "I'm not going. I'm not leaving him." I lean over Elias again. "I'm not leaving you," I whimper. "I'm going with you."

"I can't walk, Gabrielle," Elias argues. "I can't go with you. You don't know what they'll do to you to get to Catcher. I do! You have to get away from here." His breath is hot on my face.

I know he's right. I know I have to leave him. But I just want more time before we're forced apart.

"Catcher," Elias says, turning his head to look at him. "You take care of her."

Catcher nods.

I close my eyes. I can't get my bearings. Everything's happening too fast.

Elias wraps my hand in his. "Find Annah," he says softly.

I bite my lower lip, afraid of screaming out the misery I feel inside. "I don't want to leave you," I tell him. "What if we don't make it out of the Forest?"

"You will," he says, cupping my cheek with his palm. "The paths always lead out eventually. Trust me."

"There was supposed to be more," I tell him, pressing my mouth against his. I can taste his pain and despair mingling with my own. "I'm not ready. I can't do it alone. I'm too scared."

He smiles. "You're the girl who swam through the ocean."

"But I had you there with me."

"You're the girl who survived this Forest alone," he says.

"That was different," I whisper. "I didn't know enough to be frightened."

"Do you remember when I told you there was no difference between us and the Mudo?"

I nod.

"It's because they survive," he says.

"But they don't love. They don't remember." I can feel the hopelessness swallowing me.

He presses his lips to my jaw, to the corner of my mouth, to my ear. "I promise I'll find you again," he whispers. "I promise you I'll remember you. And I promise I'll love you."

I kiss him one last time. This time it doesn't matter that Catcher and Harry and my mother are watching. Nothing matters but Elias. I want to push my love and hope into him, to heal him with it. To have everything he said before be true, as if wanting something enough will make it happen.

Because I want Elias. More than anything else I want to be with him now and forever. Nothing can change that.

I press my face into his neck, feeling him, smelling him,

tasting his skin. And then I pull away from him, wondering if it's impossible to hope we'll find each other.

"You have to go," Harry says. "The Recruiters aren't that far behind us anymore. I can already hear their shouts through the trees." He hugs me and hands me a pack, his fingers lingering on my shoulder.

I turn to face my mother, who stands next to him. Odys sits at her feet and presses his muzzle against my hand. I scratch his ears, unable to believe that I have to leave her again.

"What am I supposed to do?" I ask, my voice small and scared.

She places her hands on my cheeks. I think of all the moments in my life that we've stood alone together, just the two of us against the world. Of how much of our life that we've shared. And yet I feel as though this divide has opened between us, a gulf showing me just how much of her I didn't know.

I always thought of her as my mother and not a woman who used to be a girl like me.

"You stay safe," she finally says. "You love. You survive. You laugh and cry and struggle and sometimes you fail and sometimes you succeed. You push." She smiles, her voice watery. "And you always remember that your mother loves you."

I place my hand over hers. "Will you be okay?" I ask her, afraid that I might not see her again. Worried that I should have taken better care of her somehow. "What if you get in trouble for leaving? For going beyond the fences?"

She sweeps her thumb over my cheek, smudging away my tears. "It will be okay, Gabrielle. Don't worry about me—it's my job to worry about you, not the other way around. I finally get to show Harry the ocean," she says. "I'll take care of Elias. We'll find you again. I'm not letting go of my baby girl that easily."

My heart breaks at her words, at the hope and finality of

them. We stare at each other, neither one of us wanting to be the one to turn away. The one to leave. "I have something for you," I say, trying to delay the inevitable. I reach into my pack and trace my hand along the broken binding of the book she dropped while fleeing from the village. I pull it out, the edges of paper crumbled and cracked, and give it to her.

She gasps, placing a hand over her mouth as her eyes widen with surprise.

"I wasn't able to save it all," I tell her. "But I was able to pick up some of the pages."

When she reaches for it her hands are trembling. She holds it, brushing her fingers over the faded words stamped on the cover. "This is everything from the Return," she says. "It's the history of the village. Of everyone I knew."

"I know," I whisper. "I read some of it. I just . . ." I look down at it. "I needed to know."

She looks up at me. "Thank you," she whispers.

In the distance I hear the Recruiters shouting, getting closer. The sun's breaking over the mountain across the valley, urging us forward.

Catcher stands by the cliff where Elias fell, Odys growling whenever he tries to get closer to us. "I think only this top part's been washed away. I can see where the path starts up again," he says. "Partway down the mountain. I think we can make it."

I turn back to Elias, his eyes squeezed shut tight against the pain, sweat on his forehead. I reach down and brush my fingers over his lips, along his jaw, and he looks up at me with a soft smile.

He touches my chin with his finger, tilting my head until I'm forced to look at him. "I found you once before," he says. "I promise I'll find you again. When you get out of the Forest go to the Dark City." He reaches around his neck and pulls out the leather cord with the metal disk bearing the Recruiters' seal on it. For the first time I notice tiny numbers etched on the other side. He drapes it over my head, where it twists against the superhero necklace Cira gave me.

"I'm a citizen, that should get you entrance," he says. "I promise you I'll find you."

I begin to shake my head. The world's too big—it's too easy to get lost. But he presses his hand against my cheek. "I'm not letting you go, Gabry," he says. "I'm not leaving you. I'll go back to Vista, I'll do what it takes to recover and then I'm coming for you. I promise. Just wait for me in the Dark City."

Elias grabs my fingers before I can stand up. "I love you, Gabrielle," he says, his face fierce. "I won't lose you again." In his eyes I see everything—the promise of us. And in that moment I believe it.

Then Catcher's there beside me. He's pulling me to my feet but I fight with him until I'm back by Elias's side, my mouth against his ear. I want to tell him that I can't bear to leave him but I don't know how. Instead I can only say "I love you" and watch as he closes his eyes, a smile touching his lips.

"Go," he says.

And I nod and back away from him until I feel Catcher standing next to me. I try to hold back the sob that bubbles in my chest.

"He'll be okay," Catcher murmurs to me. And I want to tell him that I know but I can't.

The morning's still struggling; the sky is beginning to burn bright along the edges but is still not able to dissipate the mist hovering in the valley below. We can barely see enough to make out the remnants of the path partway down the cliff from where we are. It looks as though some huge giant walked by and swiped his hand along the side of the mountain, digging out the earth, uprooting trees, flattening bushes, slinging mud and twisting fences.

"I think the path's still intact down there," Catcher says, and I nod because I don't know what else to do. Mudo are beginning to gather below us, stumbling over roots, slipping along loose stones, tumbling down the steepest parts and falling into the darkness.

I look back at Elias lying on the ground, my mother kneeling next to him. He lets his head fall to the side, his eyes cracked open. His face is white, his muscles tight with pain. I want to run back to him, slip my hand into his and take whatever punishment comes by his side.

"Go," he mouths.

Trying to swallow the burning in my chest, I turn, ease over the edge of the cliff and start skidding down the side of the mountain.

Catcher goes in front of me, testing the strength of branches to hold on to, pointing out roots where I can wedge my feet. Even so I slip more than climb, the dirt loose and rocks constantly shifting whenever I think I have solid footing.

Every time I try to glance up behind me I fall, my elbows scraping against the ground, brambles tangling around my legs. Soon both Catcher and I are panting with the effort and even though the sun hasn't fully risen we're both coated with sweat.

"You can do it, Gabry," he keeps telling me every time I stumble. And I don't respond, just stay focused on grabbing anything to keep me from falling.

Where the slope's steepest he slides down first, catching me when I tumble after him. We make it to a thin ledge and I glance up at the cliff edge about sixty feet above, seeing my mother standing there with her hands on her hips. Her face is tight with worry and she looks over her shoulder every few heartbeats. I wonder how close the Recruiters are. If we'll be able to get enough of a head start to escape them.

There's enough light now that the leaves on the trees glisten and shimmer, the sun's rays streaking through the sky above. Not too far below us the path resumes, the fences intact, twisting through trees and curving to the right down the mountain and eventually running into what looks like the remnants of a road.

But between us and the path the mountain flattens out for a short distance into a thin strip of land with Mudo scattered over it, all of them reaching for me.

My heart races as I clench my hand around a thin tree trunk, using it to keep me steady. Catcher stares down, the tips of the Mudo's fingers just barely brushing along the ledge beneath us. I kick their hands away from me but Catcher jumps down into the midst of them. I have to press my face into my arm to stifle my scream, still not used to how easy it is for him to walk among the dead.

Bodies tumble where he lands and then he's on his feet, arms swinging. He grabs the Mudo wherever he can and shoves them down the mountain. They don't even notice him, their focus so intent on me, their hands reaching for me.

Catcher grunts as he knocks the Mudo aside, their bodies flung off into the valley like broken dolls. Legs tangle around arms, torsos shuddering where they strike tree trunks, the moans weaving through it all. He doesn't stop, just keeps pulling and throwing and pushing until there aren't any Mudo left between me and the fences.

When he's done he stands there, shoulders heaving, hands half clenched, staring up at me. In that brief moment I see that there's nothing left of him that I used to know. There's nothing of the boy I grew up with.

▾ XLVI ▾

I stand on my ledge and look at him, the ferocity of his expression, the pain written across his body. The sun keeps seeping down the mountain, its rays illuminating him, making his hair glow like pure light. And then he holds out a hand and I catch a glimpse of the old Catcher, the one still buried inside. The one that will never fully be him again.

"You could get away, you know," I tell him. "Just slide the rest of the way down the mountain and walk into the Mudo. They'd never find you."

"No" is all he says. I stare at him a long moment but he doesn't add anything else and so I take his offered hand, his skin slick with sweat, and let him help me down.

We keep scrambling, our barely controlled fall caught by the fences twisted over the opening to the path. We're just climbing into the safety of the other side when I hear shouting above. I look over my shoulder and see my mother on the edge of the cliff waving her arms in the air, her mouth moving.

Just then a Recruiter runs up behind her and grabs her

arms. My body goes tight seeing them struggle so close to the edge. He's trying to pull her back but she's still shouting to me. She frees one hand and points down into the valley as if trying to tell us something but before I can understand the Recruiter grabs her again.

Like slow motion I see a blur of black roar from her side: Odys. He tangles in the Recruiter's legs, tripping him, and then before I even realize what's happening the man falls over the edge. His body tumbles right at us, his arms reaching out to stop himself, smacking against a tree as he falls past.

My mother freezes, staring, and then her eyes meet mine across the distance.

"Run," Catcher says, tugging on my arm. "We have to run!" Already more Recruiters are beginning to slide down the mountain after us and Catcher's dragging me away until I can no longer see them or my mother. We race down the steep path, more like falling than running. Branches slap at my arms and face and roots trip me and I struggle to follow Catcher as he tears through the woods.

It's still the dusk of early morning here underneath the tree canopy and it's hard to judge distance. My toe catches a rock and I hit the ground rolling. Catcher doubles back just as I'm pushing myself to my feet, a long scratch snaking down the back of my arm, blood dripping warm on my fingertips.

He's just holding out a hand to help me up when he hesitates. He cocks his head to the side as if listening for something in the distance. I glance over my shoulder, wondering if he hears the Recruiters behind me. But then the sound of something else tickles my ears.

Like a river. Or a waterfall.

Catcher walks down the path slowly, each step hesitant. I follow him.

We eventually run into a dead end against a tall wall made with dusty red bricks. It reaches into the distance to either side of us, bordering the winding arc of the road I glimpsed earlier on the other side.

We have no option but to climb it if we want to keep pressing forward.

I hold my breath as I slip my fingers along the bricks, searching for the weak spots and handholds. It's difficult to find places to wedge my toes but eventually I struggle to the top, throwing a leg over so that I'm straddling the wall.

The sound of water's stronger up here, the rush and roar of it. Catcher finally climbs next to me, both our hands gripping the edge of the wall just like the first night we crossed the Barrier.

The wide road running along the other side of the wall is nothing like the old stories I'd heard growing up of gloriously long highways with bright shiny cars. Instead, scattered along this road are rusted heaps of old twisted metal that seem like extinct creatures dozing in the sun. Only now most of them are beginning to shake with Mudo inside beating against the glass, trying to escape and get to me.

The road curves languorously to a wide bridge that stretches over a valley, joining up with another road bordered by an identical high brick wall on the other side. The bridge is huge, at least six cars wide, and lists sharply to the left, the other end of it appearing to crumble into only a narrow strip of concrete. Bordering either side runs a chain-link fence that's curved at the top as if to keep people from jumping, except now it serves to keep a swarm of Mudo trapped on the bridge.

They start shambling toward us, sensing me, and I'm acutely aware of the cut on my arm. Of the blood trailing along my wrist. Crumbled against the edge of the bridge rests an old overturned yellow bus. Other cars tangle around it, creating a barrier of twisted metal that for now keeps the Mudo from escaping the bridge and reaching us.

But they're piling up behind it like water trapped by a dam. They push and shove and start to crawl over one another, building a pulsing mound of bodies. Soon they'll crest over the top and flood the road, trapping us even more.

"You can go back," Catcher says to me as we both stare openmouthed at the obstacles we face. "We can try to overpower the Recruiters. Or I can just hand myself over. Tell them they don't need to take any of the rest of you." His voice is even, emotionless and I ease my hand between us until I'm gripping his fingers.

He looks over at me. His face appears drawn and tight, dark circles under his eyes. "I don't know how we can make it, Gabry," he says, so softly it's like breathing.

Behind us I hear shouting. I hear the crash of the Recruiters through the trees. It won't be long until they catch up. Mudo pry themselves from broken cars, shuffle and shift on the road, finding their way through the crushed and twisted mess.

I start to walk along the top of the wall toward the bridge. To my left the mountain drops sharply down into the valley; to my right is the road and then nothingness on the other side. Our only hope is to keep pushing forward. I stare at the fence along the bridge. On the side closest to us it stops halfway across, broken where it's fallen away. But on the far side it looks as though it stretches across the entire valley.

"Gabry," Catcher says, my name like a warning. I turn and

look at him crouching on the wall, his knuckles white where he grips it. His face glistens with sweat.

"We can make it," I tell him. My heart flutters in my chest, making it hard for me to catch my breath.

He shakes his head. "There are too many Mudo," he says.

"There's a ledge," I tell him. "Along the side of the bridge where the fence attaches. I can walk along it."

"There are Mudo on the bridge, Gabry—there's no way to keep them off you."

Sweat trickles down my back, making my shirt stick to me. "Not if I climb on the other side of the fence," I tell him. "Put it between us. It will keep them from me."

Catcher scoots a little closer, still clutching the sides of the wall. He looks where I'm pointing and his face blanches. "That ledge isn't even a foot wide," he says. "It's a hundred-foot drop!"

"I'll hold on to the fence," I argue.

"If you put your fingers through those links the Mudo will bite you."

I squat so that I'm face to face with him. "That's why you have to walk along the bridge on the other side and press against the fence where I hold it. You have to keep them from me." I try to hide the terror in my voice. I try to sound confident and convincing but inside I'm petrified.

He drops his head between his shoulders. "I can't, Gabry. I can't watch you do that. The height."

I think about the last time we were face to face on top of a tall wall, remembering what he told me. How scared he was and how he did everything to comfort me. "I know you're scared," I say. "But we have to do this. It's the only way we're going to be able to get away. We can do this."

And then before he can talk me out of it I take a deep

breath and jump down from the wall, landing on the road with a soft thud. Energy swirls with the fear thrumming through me. The feeling that I can do this. That I have to do this.

I pull the knife from my hip, the grip and weight of it familiar. I try not to think of Elias, of the night he handed it to me. The way he looked at me as if he knew me. As if he expected me to know him.

The Mudo start to stumble toward me, the sound of them filling my ears. Some of them pull themselves from under cars; others claw around the twisted metal. All of them moaning, all of them reaching for me.

And then I feel the familiar compression of air as Catcher lands next to me, his weapon drawn.

Behind us the Recruiters approach the wall. Their shouts echo through the trees. That's when I start running.

As we get closer to the bridge it becomes harder and harder to move quickly. I slip between two cars and hear a shuffle, a creak. A hand wraps around my arm. I scream and jump back but another hand tangles in my hair. I can feel their moans along my skin, smell their death. I'm afraid I won't be able to escape and I fight as hard as I can, trying to yank away, but I can't get free. They're trapped inside the cars, reaching through windows and doors for me.

I let my legs buckle and the weight of my body pulls free of the Mudo. I roll back from them. And then Catcher's there, shoving them away. He tries to throw them off the side of the road and down into the valley but more begin to stir in the old vehicles, their hibernation ended by the scent of human flesh. We keep running, dodging cars where we can, crawling over them where we can't. With each step I dread the feeling of teeth sinking into my skin.

Finally we close on the bus blocking the entrance to the bridge and I scramble toward it. My hands are slick with sweat as I try to grasp the sun-warmed metal and manage to hook my fingers over the edge of a broken window, tiny pebbles of glass sinking into my flesh and drawing hot blood. I don't care about the pain, only about escaping.

Just as I pull myself up I feel a whisper of a touch on my knuckles and I yank my hand back, slipping but still able to keep my purchase against the rust-pocked metal.

They huddle on the seats inside, standing on the window frames. Children, no more than five or six years old, all wearing identical blue sweaters. The boys wear brown pants, the girls matching skirts with socks pulled to their knees. One girl has two pigtails springing from the sides of her head. Another boy still wears his glasses.

They stare at me, their tiny fingers clutching at the air, wanting something—needing it—and knowing that I'm the one who can provide it. And when they moan it sounds like whining, like a toddler crying.

I can't breathe. I've seen Mudo children before but they were bloated bodies on the beach. They were rare and they never looked like this. They never looked real and almost normal. Almost alive.

And then blood drips from the cuts on my hand. It falls through the air and lands on a boy's cheek, right at the edge of his mouth. A streak of red against his pale white skin.

I see his nostrils flare the instant his senses ignite. And then his eyes go wide and his mouth opens, lips pulled back from his teeth. His moans are harsh and demanding as he claws at the air.

XLVII

Just then Catcher clambers up the bus after me. On the ground to either side of us the Mudo are writhing, pushing, piling up on each other, moments away from washing over us. One crests above the others, just making it onto the back of the bus, when an arrow strikes its head.

I look back over my shoulder to see the Recruiters running along the top of the wall toward us, crossbows drawn. They shoot at the Mudo, trying to clear a path to us but also keeping us safe, and it occurs to me suddenly that we're useless to them dead.

The bus is crushed against the far wall of the bridge, shoved against the fence. I slide my knife back into the scabbard on my hip and rub my hands along my shirt, trying to dry off the blood and sweat. I'm just reaching for the ledge when Catcher puts a hand on my shoulder.

"Are you sure?" he asks. He can't keep the worry from his eyes and I know he thinks this won't work.

"Yes," I tell him because I have to believe we can make it. I have to believe there's a chance. Behind us one of the Recruiters is running across the road toward us, determination fierce in his eyes. As I step out onto the ledge and thread my fingers through the fence Catcher tugs two of the children from the bus and tosses them toward the Recruiter.

The man drops to one knee and lines up his crossbow. Just as he's taking a shot more Mudo crest over the bus like water breaking a dam and they flood toward him. The Recruiters shout and let loose with their bolts. But I stay focused on the ledge and take a deep breath, telling myself to be strong. To believe in myself.

Facing me, Catcher steps into the mass of Mudo on the bridge, his body pressed against the fence. The ledge I'm standing on is barely wide enough for me to find purchase with my toes and I grip the metal links, feeling the heat of Catcher's chest on my fingers.

"Don't look down," he tells me, but it's too late. The mountain drops away beneath me, the valley below still swathed in morning mist, the sound of water thundering and echoing around us.

Mudo lunge for me, pounding the fence, trying to pry Catcher's protection away from me. It would take only an instant, one moment of him tripping or falling back and they'd get to me, their teeth sharp against my fingertips. I swallow and feel my legs begin to shake.

"Keep your eyes on me, Gabry," Catcher says, and I nod and raise my head, staring at him. "Are you ready?" he asks.

I nod again. And then slowly we begin to inch along the side of the bridge, Catcher staying in front of me, the Mudo pushing and pulling and moaning around him. I take a step, shift my hands on the fence and Catcher mimics my position, always keeping the dead teeth from my flesh.

I focus on each tiny movement. Each placement of my toes. Each curl of my fingers around the rusty metal. I feel the fence undulate under my touch, the Mudo rattling it.

And I concentrate on Catcher's eyes. The way he presses his hands over mine to keep them safe. The knowledge that he'll do anything to protect me.

Behind us the Recruiters scream and shout as they try to fight the Mudo, unwilling to give up and battling their way down the road.

"Did you know there are all these old towns and cities in the Forest?" Catcher asks me.

Sweat weaves down my neck and along my shoulders. Blood still trickles from the gash on my arm, dripping from my elbow into the void below. As we get farther out over the valley the wind streams around us, pushing my hair into my face. "What?" I ask him, the metal of the fence biting into my fingers. My toes are beginning to cramp from gripping the tiny strip of concrete.

We keep stepping, keep moving. And he keeps trying to distract me from everything but him. Not worrying about the fact that a few inches of concrete and an old flimsy metal fence are all that's preventing me from falling hundreds of feet.

"Out in the Forest," he says. "I came across one when I was doubling back one night to see if the Recruiters were following us. Not one of the fenced-in villages but a whole city that just died."

I swallow and nod. I glance down and my foot slips, a hunk of the bridge dislodging and spiraling down. Catcher thrusts his fingers through the fence, trying to grab my wrists. I lock my hands on his, my entire body shaking.

"Don't look down, Gabry," Catcher murmurs to me. "We're almost there." But that's a lie. We're barely halfway across. The Mudo swarm around him, jostling him, but he keeps his grip firm. Everywhere around him is death. Every space is filled with their moans.

We keep stepping to the side, my feet sliding along the narrow strip of concrete, Catcher shifting along the fence, me trying not to think about the emptiness below.

"The thing about these cities," Catcher continues, his eyes locked on mine, "is that it's like nothing's changed. No one's scavenged them because they're overrun with Mudo. But because there aren't any living people around, all the Mudo are downed. Just . . . lying there. Silent."

I remember Elias telling me about the afternoon he spent in the old airplane monument. About the silence of falling snow. And I keep sliding along the bridge, Catcher's hands over mine every time I shift my grip.

Just over halfway across a pile of cars are wedged against the fence, keeping it clear of Mudo. Catcher begins to scramble over them and then stops.

"What's going on?" I ask. The wind's stronger here, whipping moans around my body. Catcher's sweating, rivulets rolling down his temples and along his jaw.

Mudo begin to pile against the wreck, trying to reach me but held back by the mangled metal. Catcher stares at the road on the other side.

"What is it?" I ask.

He licks his lips, his voice trembling when he answers. "There's a gap in the bridge," he says.

I look along the length of the fence but don't see a break anywhere. "What are you talking about?"

"The road's broken away," he says. "The Mudo are slipping through. Falling."

I glance down and see bodies raining from the bridge,

reaching for me even as they fall. "Then we just have to make it past and they can't follow us," I say. "Then we won't have to worry about them getting to me."

He says nothing and I wish I could reach my fingers through the fence and grab him. He won't look at me. "Catcher?"

"There's a whole section of the bridge fallen away, Gabry. I can't get across."

When he looks back at me his face is ashen. I slide along the fence until I'm past the cars. Then I see what he's talking about. There's nothing, just a gap, the concrete crumbling, rusty metal rods twisting around themselves. Beyond the gap is where the bridge lists to the side. The only thing spanning the distance is the narrow ledge where I'm standing. If it were to crumble, the entire section would collapse into the valley.

"There's a ledge on your side too," I tell him. More Mudo drop through the gap, their moans dimming as they fall away. "You can make it across—just hold on to the fence like I am."

He looks at me and shakes his head. "I can't."

"Listen to me, Catcher." He's still shaking his head, staring at the gap and the drop below. "Look at me." He turns to me, his face even whiter, his eyes wide.

"I can't do this, Gabrielle. I can't," he whispers.

I feel a ripple along the fence and look back to see a Recruiter trying to follow us. Except instead of gripping the fence with his fingers the way I am, he's using two metal hooks crudely fashioned from the scraps left from the cars.

My toes are cramping, my calves screaming. "You don't have a choice," I tell Catcher. "Neither of us does. We can't stay here. We can't go back." I hesitate before adding in a softer voice, "Come on, Catcher."

His hands tremble as he starts to slide off the car toward the fence. The muscles along his jaw tighten.

"You can do this," I murmur to him as he reaches for me. He threads his fingers through the metal links and I place my hands over his. He looks me in the eye and I can see that he's having trouble focusing.

"It's me, Catcher," I tell him. "Just look at me."

He nods and I feel the way his breath quakes as it brushes against my cheeks. He steps onto the ledge and then we're standing facing each other, our hands grasped through the fence.

Slowly I slide a foot to the side and he does the same. But when I start to reach for a new handhold his eyes go wide and his gaze drops. He starts to choke, panic bolting through him.

"Just one more step, Catcher. We can do this together," I tell him, trying to keep my voice calm. But he's already shaking his head, already trembling so badly that he's having trouble keeping his toes on the narrow ledge. One of his feet slips and his mouth opens but no sound comes out. He's dangling, the other foot losing purchase.

I struggle not to scream, seeing him hanging like that, his fingers desperately clinging to the fence.

My legs are already cramping, but I squat until my face is right in front of his. "Catcher," I whisper. "Look at me, Catcher."

I feel heartbeats shudder through me. I feel his pulse under my fingers. He cracks one eye open but his gaze dances around.

"Catcher," I whisper again and he finally looks at me. "I can't do this without you," I tell him. Tears blur my vision, softening the edges of his face. "I need you. I know you're terrified. I'm terrified. But you have to do this. You have to hold on."

"Why?" he asks, and I can tell he's not just asking why I need him but why we're here. Why all of this has happened to us. Why we're bothering to keep pushing.

I think about my sister and how I have to find her. I think about Elias and how I have to do what it takes to see him again. I think about how I promised him that we can build something together. I think about my mother and what she told me life is all about: We either choose to live it or we don't.

"Close your eyes," I tell Catcher. He sucks in a breath and looks down into the mist and whimpers. "Remember the night we crossed the Barrier? Remember how you told me to trust you? Now you have to trust me. Close your eyes."

Slowly he lets his eyelids flutter shut and I feel his fingers tighten even more under mine.

"You know where the ledge is—raise your left foot until you're on it," I tell him, and he does until we're both standing.

"Now slide your left foot along the ledge—follow my fingers." I guide our hands along the links. His lips part and his forehead creases in concentration. I want to laugh at how familiar the expression is but I focus on keeping my voice calm and soothing. Slowly we ease farther down the bridge.

The Recruiter is able to move faster, coming closer and closer, but I say nothing to Catcher, just keep murmuring to take the next step, to worry only about the next step.

But then the Recruiter stops. He stares at me along the length of the fence. And he looks down. I can feel his body shudder, the way it causes the fence to undulate. I know I shouldn't. I know that looking down will only terrify me even more but I can't help it.

The morning sun's burned away the mist so the valley below is now clear. The scope of what I see drowns out every other sense: There's no river, no water. Instead, hundreds of feet below the bridge the ground shifts and writhes. At first I think maybe it's a field of some sort but then individual colors begin to pull apart.

And all at once I understand what it is. Like a river flooding its banks, the entire valley is full of Mudo. The sound is not that of a raging waterfall but the pounding of two hundred million feet. The moans of a hundred million mouths. They pour through the valley, more people than I have ever seen. More people than I ever thought could have existed in one world. And they sense me, reach for me but are trapped by the mountains.

I dig my fingers against the fence. Dizzy and hot, I press my face against my shoulder. I feel as though everything inside me has fallen away and left the shell of my body here to stare at the vision.

They're endless, stretching beyond the horizon and spreading around me like forever. They heave and moan, frothing over each other, cresting and falling. The pure depth and vastness of it all beyond comprehension, my eyes unable to focus on any individual. Instead I'm drowned in their need. They ripple and swell, the bodies of the Mudo, like the ocean. Like the dead-tossed waves.

XLVIII

Catcher feels me stop and opens his eyes. "What's wrong?" he asks, panic laced around the words. I shake my head, not knowing what I can say. Not knowing how to explain it to him.

"Don't look down, Catcher," I whisper. "Please don't."

But of course he does, he can hear it in my voice. He gasps. "A horde," he murmurs, the word already echoing in my head. We both learned about them in school and just as with the Breakers we never paid much attention, only talking about it as a way to scare the younger children and incite nightmares.

It's overwhelming to look at them all, each spot of color a person who once was. To understand that they've just been lying here, downed in a sort of hibernation, waiting for the scent of a living human to awaken them. To realize that if such a huge mass of Mudo approached a city or town there would be no defense. That this is what the Recruiters have been fighting against outside the Forest.

And that someone like Catcher—an Immune who could walk among them—could direct them. Could control them.

The wind slips down the mountain, brushing over my skin, along my sweat-soaked neck. A drop of blood slithers along my arm, pooling on my elbow and then falls through the air.

"We have to keep going," I whisper. The Recruiter's still frozen in place behind us on the fence, staring at the horde. Back on the road the rest of them keep fighting the Mudo, taking them down one by one. Soon enough they'll be able to chase after us again.

I continue talking Catcher step by step across the gap but in my head a thousand thoughts roar as I try to find a way to stop them from following us, to keep us safe. And I keep coming to the same conclusion: the only way to cross the gap is the fence; the only way to stop the Recruiters is to find a way to break it.

When we finally reach the other side of the gap, Catcher almost kneels to kiss the crumbling concrete. On this end of the bridge there are cars piled against the fence, so the Mudo can't reach me. But already I can feel how the bridge tilts at a steep angle, making it harder for me to keep my toes gripping the ledge. The metal of the chain links bites harder into my fingers as I'm forced to bear more and more of my weight with my hands.

Behind me the Recruiter is almost to the gap, the hooks he's using to grab the fence making it easier for him to move along the ledge. "We're not going to hurt you," he calls out to me. "You'll be safe with us, I promise."

I shake my head and wedge my toes into the links, trying to hold on. With each step Catcher takes, I feel a small rumble through my legs, the bridge shuddering under his new weight. Suddenly my grip feels even more precarious.

"Catcher," I wheeze, my arms screaming with the effort. "The cars." I take another breath. "On the other side of the bridge." Sweat drips into my eyes, blurring everything. "See if you can roll them against these other ones." I shift my hands. "The bridge is unstable—we have to throw off the weight and if we pile enough up maybe they'll break the fence."

His eyes widen. "Are you kidding me? The fence is the only thing keeping you on this bridge."

I nod my head and wipe my face against my shoulder. "I know," I tell him. "But, it's the only way. I'll keep going. But you have to break it."

He jumps onto the car closest to me and rests his fingers on my own. "It's too much of a risk," he says. "We can just keep going, try to put distance between us."

I taste salt, not knowing if it's tears or sweat. "I can't let them get you, Catcher. I can't spend the rest of my life watching them use you. Knowing that it's because of me."

"Gabry," he says again, my name a plea. But I just shake my head.

"I'll be okay. I can make it," I tell him, trying to sound convincing. I start moving away, slipping my fingers out from underneath his.

Behind us the Recruiters keep making progress, starting to run for us. I struggle along the fence, the sharp tilt of the bridge making it harder and harder to hold on. I close my eyes and try not to think about the horde. Try not to think about how destroying the bridge erases the only link between me and Elias. Between me and my mother. Hoping that Elias was right and there will be another path out of the Forest. A way to find the Dark City.

Behind me I hear the screech of metal as Catcher pries open the door to a car. I hear a horrific scraping sound as the car grinds across the bridge and then the fence shudders as the car collides with it and I try not to scream. Already I feel the concrete under my toes moving and straining; the bridge groans with the sudden shift of weight.

The Recruiter grunts and I look up to see him lose his footing. He's frantic as he dangles, trying to crawl back up onto the narrow ledge. But he can't. The only things keeping him from falling are the hooks, and even from here I see his hands weakening.

"Please," I hear him utter. His eyes bounce everywhere: the sky, the Mudo, the other Recruiters on the bridge, me. In that instant he isn't a Recruiter—a monster—he's just like Elias and Cira and the others. Just someone who left his family and maybe his friends to serve and find a better life.

Then I hear a loud screech as another car crumples against the others. The fence bulges under the weight of them. The bridge lists at an even sharper angle. And the Recruiter lets go, his black shirt fluttering around him. Even as he falls through nothingness, his arms scramble for something to grab, some way to save himself.

His eyes lock on mine. I see the terror. The realization of what's to come. I bury my head in my shoulder but I know when he hits the ground—I can tell from the crescendo of moans, the horde's voices growing louder, a tidal wave of noise and need.

I'm almost to the end of the bridge when I hear a loud crack and the whip sound of metal tearing. The fence pulls tight under my fingers and then seems to disintegrate. I shuffle as fast as I can along the ledge and scramble for the road just as an enormous rumbling tears through me.

Catcher's running as behind him everything dissolves at once. A high-pitched squeal turns to screeches as cars shift and pile up on top of each other. What's left of the bridge tilts farther and farther to the side at an impossible angle and then starts to crumble in on itself.

A huge section tears free and crashes down into the valley, the sound so loud it's like thunder breaking in my head. Catcher reaches me and shoves me on top of the brick wall bordering the road and we stand there panting, feeling the reverberations along the ground.

A few Recruiters stand at the edge where the bridge now ends, staring at us across the massive gap. It's as if we're holding our breath as we face each other over the horde. One of the Recruiters, a large man with a red slash of fabric over his chest, points toward Catcher and me—whether in a salute, a farewell or a vow to find us, I don't know. But I do know that there's no way for them to follow us and for now we're safe.

Eventually they turn and start making their way back, the man with the red the last to leave.

I trace the line of the path up the mountain until I see the cliff where Elias fell, see the rest of the Recruiters clustered like black beetles. But I can also see my mother and Harry standing apart from them, holding each other, the small form of Odys sitting by their side.

And then I see another figure next to them, leaning on them for support: Elias. He raises a hand toward me and I raise my hand like an echo. A promise that I'll do whatever it takes to be with him. To find Annah and wait for him in the Dark City.

"We made it," I tell Catcher, still in shock. Still amazed that we were able to survive crossing the bridge over the horde.

"Where?" he asks.

I turn to him, feeling myself try to smile. "Here," I say. "Alive." It feels strange to stand here on the wall, to not be running. A few Mudo struggle against cars dotted along the road, try to shamble toward me. But for this moment we're safe.

Catcher starts to smile as well. "What's next?"

I stare at where the bridge has dissolved. There's no way for us to ever go back. "We keep going," I tell him. "We find a way out, make our way to the Dark City, look for Annah and wait for Elias."

He nods, still grinning, and when we've caught our breath and our legs have stopped shaking we meander along the top of the wall along the road until we find the path again. As on the other side of the valley, the two fences dead-end against the wall, the safe space in between leading up into the mountains and away from everything we've known before.

Catcher climbs down first and holds his hand up to me. I pause for a moment, thinking about another wall and another time. Thinking about how afraid I felt that night and how I pushed myself forward anyway. I reach up and touch Cira's superhero and Elias's metal disk resting against my heart. And then I jump down from the wall and start up the path toward the Dark City.

EPILOGUE

Catcher and I spend the afternoon walking in easy silence, the rumbling of the horde falling away behind us. We're both exhausted and finally reach the summit as the sun falls into the trees. I wonder for a moment if we'll see the lighthouse or the glint of the sun's reflection off the ocean in the distance but I know we're too far away for that, too deep in the Forest.

As darkness settles around us a thousand memories race through my mind: I'm a child climbing the stairs to the top of the lighthouse and my mother is teaching me to light the lamp. . . . She's holding me against her during a storm. . . . She's teaching me how to pound bread dough, how to name the stars.

But the one that freezes in my head, that stops the spinning, is of her standing at the edge of the ocean, her toes digging into the sand as she stares at the horizon.

That's who my mother will always be to me. Fierce against

the edge of the world. I push my feet into the dirt of the mountain, listening to the trees sway overhead like waves against the shore. That's who I am now as well, I realize.

I stare out into the darkness. Somewhere out there, somewhere back down the path, is my village. Beyond that is Vista, the lighthouse that will continue to turn, and the waves and the coaster, and beyond that is the Dark City.

There is a world eking out a living at the edge. Clinging on to more than survival. They love and believe and question and hope.

I press my hands into the grass around me, feeling the blades tickle my palms and fingers. Elias was right. Survival is not enough. There has to be more.

There was more for my mother. She pushed past the edges. She tempted the ocean. She wandered the coast. She kept the lantern in the lighthouse burning for anyone else out there to see and find.

I tilt my head back and watch the stars shimmer in the night. I hold my breath and wait and then I see it, the dot of a satellite humming through them all. I hold up my hand and follow it with my finger. Wanting to touch the before time. I wonder if somewhere across the valley Elias is doing the same, touching the same memory and thinking of me.

I close my eyes and think about the feel of him next to me, the way he traces his thumb over my knuckles when he holds my hand. The way my name sounds on his lips. The promise we made to find each other. The belief that we'll be together again—that this can't keep us apart. Not anymore.

I understand now that we'll never live life as it was before the Return. We'll never recapture that time. The satellites will fall from the sky, the ruins will crumble to the earth and eventually the roller coaster will collapse. We'll all die and the Mudo will continue to hunger.

It's the nature of our world.

Maybe, though, it's time we learned that we don't have to live within the boundaries we set up. Maybe we have to learn to push those barriers. To reclaim some of what was lost. And to build a new world.

ACKNOWLEDGMENTS

I'm so incredibly grateful for the people who've cheered me on, offered thoughts, advice, research, and generally just stuck with me over the past year during the writing of this book. I'm overwhelmed by your generosity and love, and "thank you" never seems like an adequate phrase to express how deeply I appreciate all of you, including all the readers out there.

Jim McCarthy is more than I could have ever asked for in an agent, and I feel lucky every day to be working with him. Krista Marino, my editor, shows endless patience and brilliance at every stage—she's downright amazing. Kelly Galvin, my publicist, works tirelessly and yet always has time to spend an afternoon catching up and sharing secrets. I've loved continuing to work with the fantastic team at Delacorte Press over the past year and am constantly overcome by their enthusiasm and dedication. Many thanks to Beverly Horowitz for her support, to Jocelyn Lange and the subsidiary rights department for introducing Mary and Gabry to so many countries, to Vikki Sheatsley for the beautiful design, to Jonathan Barkat, whose photograph was the inspiration for the coaster by the sea, and to Colleen Fellingham and Barbara Perris for their attention to detail. To the many sales associates I've been lucky to meet online or in person: Lauren Gromlowicz, Tim Mooney, Dandy Conway, Deanna Meyerhoff and Cristin Stickles. Also a big thanks to Jessica Shoffel, Kimberly Langus, Rebecca Platkin and Becky Green.

During the writing of this book I've been lucky to meet some very amazing writers who've grown into amazing friends. Thanks to the 2009 Debutantes, Gothic Girls, Team Castle and especially my "Writing Group": Saundra Mitchell (who was willing to read and critique at any hour), Sarah MacLean, Heidi Kling, Aprilynne Pike, Sarah Rees Brennan, RJ Anderson and Sarah Cross. Thanks also to Diana Peterfreund, a truly fantastic friend and critique partner, Justine Larbalestier and Holly Black for giving me the chance to expand this world and my voice, and Ally Carter for one particular phone call in which she gave me the most perfect advice.

Without Kris Finlon, I'd still be trying to figure out critical details of the plot. Thanks also to: Shea Mucci for giving me insight into the effects of a forest fire, Dennis and the crew at 300 East for sharing all the celebrations and excitement, Darren Cassese and Kymm for the author photos, and Madeira James for the gorgeous online presence.

I never know how to adequately thank my family because their love and support can never be summed up easily. Their enthusiasm for my writing is without bounds and constantly thrills, amazes and humbles me. Thanks to Bobby and Doug Kidd for letting me borrow their romance; to my father, Tony Ryan, for car rides when he helped me work through plot details and for always supporting my imagination; to my sisters, Jenny Sell and Chris Warnick, for being early readers (and for not being able to put the manuscript down while cooking dinner)—I tear up thinking about how lucky I am to be your baby sister. Also thanks to the Davis family for supporting and loving me as if I'd always been one of their own (and for accepting a daughter-in-law who brings zombies to the family). Finally, as always, to John Parke Davis. Stephen King once said that every author writes for one reader. JP is that reader.

ABOUT THE AUTHOR

Born and raised in Greenville, South Carolina, Carrie Ryan is a graduate of Williams College and Duke University School of Law. She now lives and writes in Charlotte, North Carolina. *The Dead-Tossed Waves* is her second book for young readers. Look for *The Forest of Hands and Teeth,* the companion title, available from Delacorte Press.

To learn more about Carrie Ryan, please visit her at www.carrieryan.com.

Turn the page for a special preview of the companion to

THE FOREST OF HANDS AND TEETH

and

THE DEAD-TOSSED WAVES

▾ I ▾

This city used to be something once. I've seen pictures of the way it gleamed—sun so bright off windows it could burn your eyes. At night lights shouted from steel like catcalls, while all day white-gloved men rushed to open doors for women who tottered about on skyscraper heels.

I wonder sometimes what happened to those women when the Return hit—how they were able to run, to survive, with such absurd contraptions strapped to their feet. How different the world must have been before—safe and carefree.

The city's nothing like that anymore. Now bare beams scrape the sky like splintered finger bones. Half the high-rises have fallen, and scavengers pilfered the intricately scrolled ironwork long ago. There's not much of anything left, just the fear that seeps foglike through the streets.

Fear of the Recruiters. Fear of the Unconsecrated. Fear of tomorrow.

Even so, this city's been my home. Other than the village I

lived in as a child, this is the only world I've known. It's sharp-cornered and raw, but it's a refuge for those with a will to survive. You pay your rent, you follow the rules and you do what it takes to keep living.

Which is why I find myself on the Neverlands side of the Palisade wall that cordons off and protects the Dark City as the last dregs of evening slide across the sky. This is where Elias would go when he was desperate for money, desperate to trade so we could pay our rent and stay in our tiny flat for another year. It's where anything can be found, and it's where, after the blade of my only knife broke this afternoon, I've come for help.

Clutching the replacement blade tightly, I've started to cross over one of the air bridges strung between two buildings when I hear a deep rumbling cough. It's approaching dusk and storm clouds hover over the river, causing the light to drip a dull green. I shuffle faster toward the next roof, determined to get back to my flat in the Dark City before night falls, but as soon as my foot lands on the rickety bridge a voice calls out, "Wouldn't do that if I were you."

I freeze, the frayed rope railing in one hand. I've been alone long enough to have learned to look out for myself, yet something about the warning makes me hesitate. Just as I start to take another step the voice says, "Look down," and I do.

The alley a dozen stories below is dark and choked with shadows, but even so I see something moving. A moan floats up, echoing softly between the buildings as it rises. The setting sun breaks through a narrow gap in the clouds and the light streams down the alley, glinting briefly off what look like eyes and a cracked row of teeth.

As my eyes adjust I begin to make out dozens of clawing fingers reaching for me amid a pile of broken bodies that should have died from their fall but didn't. Or maybe they did die and infection has brought them back as plague rats. I shiver, disgust rolling through me.

Carefully, I inch back onto the roof, noticing that the wooden boards I was just about to step onto are rotten. One step more and I'd have been down on that heap as well.

"You're the first one to listen to me and not take a dive," the voice says, and I spin, pulling my new knife between us. A woman sits tucked between two crumbling stone chimneys. In her hand she clutches a charred wooden pipe that feebly chokes out smoke.

I glance around the roof, expecting some sort of trap. The woman gestures toward my knife. "Don't bother," she says. "Just me up here."

She puts the pipe back in her mouth, the end of it burning a bright red, and in that instant I get a clear look at her face. Thick dark lines painted around her eyes are smudged by tears or sweat or both. Then the ember fades, drawing her back into shadow.

But not before I see the raw circle around her wrist, festering with infection. The flesh edging the wound puffs and oozes, and I recognize it as a bite. I pull my knife back up between us, refusing to let it shake.

I'm usually pretty good at avoiding a fight with the Unconsecrated. No matter how careful you are, there's always the risk that something will go wrong and they'll get their teeth into you somehow.

The woman shrugs and inhales. The light makes her skin glow again, and I watch how her hand shakes. Cracks etch through the powder she used to make her old skin appear blushing and fresh—it looks like a fractured mirror instead.

I think of my own face, the scars overlaying the left side of my body like a thick spiderweb. Her cracks can be washed away. Mine can't.

It's easy to see that she's close to the end—when the infection will kill her. I glance down again at the pile of bodies below, their feeble moans filtering into the night. She'll be one of them soon. If she's lucky someone will take care of her before she turns. If she isn't . . .

I swallow.

With a sickening heaviness in my stomach I realize I'm the one who's going to have to kill her. It makes me feel off balance, and I take a few steps away from the edge of the building, suddenly unsettled by such height.

The last of the evening light slides down my body, a final brush of heat, before disappearing for what will be yet another night of forever. The woman's eyes aren't on my knife; instead they focus on my face.

She inhales but her chest barely moves. She considers me a moment, staring at my scars. "There are men who like 'em like you—messed up," she says, nodding. Her gaze slips past me, back down the island, toward the ruins of the bigger buildings of the Dark City in the distance.

No they don't, I think.

She exhales a wavering line of smoke. "But more 'n likely, they're the ones that want to do the messing." She pushes a thumb into the corner of her mouth, as if tidying up a lip stain that she's no longer wearing. The gesture a habit of so many years that has become useless.

I should say something. I should be comforting or consoling or helpful. This woman's infected and she's facing the final moments of her life and I realize how utterly useless I am faced with the enormity of what's going on. Instead I clear my throat. How in the world could I know what would give this woman comfort?

I look back across the roof I came from. It would be easy for me to just retrace my steps—leave her for someone else to deal with. But that seems unnecessarily cruel. After all, I'm alone in the city like she is. Maybe if I were in her position, I'd want someone to listen to me at the end.

She picks at the edges of the bite, pressing against the angry red infection lines streaking up her arm. "You got a man?" she asks. "You in love?" She sounds nervous, like she's uncomfortable. Like she understands what I'm going to do and she's just extending her time a bit.

The question takes me aback. I try to say yes and no at the same time and instead it just comes out as a grunt. "I have a . . ." I stumble over the word, then mouth "brother." It's the lie Elias and I have told everyone to make our living together in the Dark City simpler. We've said it for so long it feels like truth. "He joined the Recruiters."

"When?" Her eyebrows pinch together.

The question has weight to it—if he joined up before the Rebellion it means he wanted to change the world into something better. If he joined up after it means he's a masochist who gets high on the power of controlling people with no hope.

"Three years ago." I've rarely had to say it out loud. To acknowledge how long he's been gone. Before, I could just go from day to day, tomorrow to tomorrow to tomorrow, without having to bundle them all together in heaps to represent weeks and months and years.

The woman laughs, her wet mouth open and lip curled in

where she's missing a few teeth on the left side. She doesn't even have to say how absurd the hope in my voice sounds. We both know the survival rates of Recruiters who joined before the Rebellion: one in seven. Only that one ever makes it home after his two-year term is up, and Elias should have been back a long time ago.

Anger darts through me. Maybe that's what she wants. To make it easy for me to thrust the knife into her chest. To make me want to feel the jolt of the blade grazing over her ribs and the squelching heat of her blood. I take a step toward her, narrowing my eyes. She's as good as Unconsecrated, and I've put them away before.

She just slips the stem of the pipe through the gap in her teeth and inhales, burning a red glow between us. "Oh, honey," she finally says, but it's not judgment I hear, it's pity.

It unsettles me, and I turn to the side so she can't see the expression on my face. Even so, her gaze traces over my scars again, one by one. She tilts her head as if trying to piece them together into some sort of pattern.

"Oh, honey," she says again, and I know it's for the misery of this moment.

"You been waiting for him all this time?" she asks. The concern in her voice sounds like the way a mother would talk to a daughter, and this opens up a fresh ache inside me. I nod.

"The city's dying," she says. Her voice is calm and gentle. Soothing. "You should leave. Find a new life." She drags the thin strap of her shirt up over her shoulder but it just slides down her arm again.

I shrug. "This is my home," I tell her. I know I sound defensive.

There's silence between us for a bit. Not real silence—that doesn't exist—but as quiet as it gets in the Neverlands with the moans drifting from the alley and the sound of someone yelling the next block over.

"I had a man once that I stuck around for," the woman says. She pokes a toe through the tip of her worn shoes and I wait for her to tell me more, but instead she just contemplates her foot awhile and then shrugs.

"Some men have a strange idea of what love is." She pushes a strand of greasy hair back behind her ear and I see bruises dotting her neck.

What she doesn't understand about me and Elias is that I promised him I'd wait for him to come back, and leaving would mean he's dead. I know there's nothing else that could keep him from coming home to me. The evening he left he said he'd find me again, and I believe him.

But a dark thought seeps into my mind, one that's been curling around the edges of my consciousness for months: Elias left my sister alone in the Forest of Hands and Teeth when we were kids. Why should I ever think that he wouldn't leave me?

The woman stands and I whirl to face her, pulling the knife back between us, ready to end it. She doesn't come closer or threaten me in any way. She just flips her pipe over and knocks it against one of the chimneys, spirals of embers twirling and fading around her legs and feet.

"Did you ever think about what you really wanted your life to be like? Like when you were a little girl?" She moves toward the edge of the roof. The darkness seems to stretch forever.

I think about the village where I was born. Where I had a sister and a father and a community of people who loved and took care of me.

That. That's what I want my life to be like. Not this city. Not these scars. Not this loneliness. I remember the moment in the Forest when my sister fell and scratched her knee and how bright the blood looked. How desperately the dead clawed at the fences while Elias and I walked away from her.

But I tell this woman none of those things. Instead I shake my head. "No."

Her face falls a little as if she was expecting a different answer. "Ever wonder what you'd do if you knew you were going to die?"

"We're all going to die eventually," I tell her.

She smiles, more like a wince. "I mean if you knew when," she clarifies. "If you only had a few days." She inhales sharply and adds, "A few moments."

I shake my head. It's a lie, but I don't want this woman to know me any better than she already does. Being here for her death—that's already more intimacy than I've shared with anyone in years. I don't want to like this woman—I don't want to care about her—because then this moment and the one that's coming next will hurt too much.

I refuse to have feelings about someone when I know they're going to leave me. I feel sorry that I can't offer this woman something different, but I have to protect myself more than I have to protect her.

Her eyes begin to glisten and her shoulders shift as she pretends to laugh. "Oh well," she says, waving her dirty pipe in the air as if it could clear this world away. "Oh well," she says again, barely a whisper.

She begins to shake. I've seen it before, the infection taking a firmer grasp, burrowing in deep for the kill. Any minute now she'll collapse, her body giving out and dying. And then she'll Return, clawing for my flesh.

I move toward her, knife tight in my grip, but she jerks her head, waves me off with a fling of her arm. She's standing on the ledge of the roof. Below us the plague rats moan.

"I just . . . ," she says, raising a hand to her head, patting her hair into place. She presses her lips tight, her nostrils quivering as she takes a deep breath. "I just wanted someone to remember," she says then. "I just wanted to be beautiful to someone, just for a little while."

And before I can ask "Remember what?" or "Remember who?" she tips forward and jumps. The rushing air pulls her hair from her face, and her body twists like a ribbon caught in a breeze for a moment before she tumbles into the darkness.

She doesn't even scream.

I don't have to run toward the ledge to know what happens to her. I hear the thump of her body hitting the concrete below. The sound of her bones breaking, of her skull shattering.

I drop the knife and press my face into my hands, dig my fingers into my forehead, as if that will hold me together. I shouldn't have been the person here at her death. I don't even know the woman's name or who to tell that she's gone.

And suddenly I realize just how closely her situation echoes my own. How no one would know or care if the same thing happened to me. How unlikely it is that any of the few neighbors remaining in my corner of the Dark City could even recall my name, much less notice if I went missing one day.

I've never felt so alone in my life. Sure, I've spent the last three years on my own, but I've always focused on surviving and waiting for Elias. This woman's done something to me, though. She's made me recognize a kind of gap inside, and now I don't know if I'll ever figure out how to close or fill it.

▼ ▼ ▼